All in Scarlet Uniform

ALSO BY ADRIAN GOLDSWORTHY
FROM CLIPPER LARGE PRINT

True Soldier Gentlemen
Beat the Drums Slowly
Send Me Safely Back Again

All in Scarlet Uniform

Adrian Goldsworthy

W F HOWES LTD

This large print edition published in 2013 by
W F Howes Ltd
Unit 4, Rearsby Business Park, Gaddesby Lane,
Rearsby, Leicester LE7 4YH

1 3 5 7 9 10 8 6 4 2

First published in the United Kingdom in 2013
by Weidenfeld & Nicolson

A CIP catalogue record for this book is available
from the British Library

ISBN 978 1 47124 707 1

Typeset by Palimpsest Book Production Limited,
Falkirk, Stirlingshire
Printed and bound by
www.printondemand-worldwide.com of Peterborough, England

Mixed Sources
Product group from well-managed
forests, and other controlled sources
www.fsc.org Cert no. TT-COC-002641
© 1996 Forest Stewardship Council
FSC

PEFC Certified
This product is
from sustainably
managed forests
and controlled
sources
www.pefc.org
PEFC
PEFC/16-33-418

This book is made entirely of chain-of-custody materials

With thanks to Gareth Glover, whose labours in the archives keep providing so much great material for these stories

A bold fusilier came marching back through
    Rochester
Off for the wars in a far country,
And he sang as he marched
Through the crowded streets of Rochester,
'Who'll be a soldier with Wellington and me?'

    Who'll be a soldier? Who'll be a soldier?
    Who'll be a soldier with Wellington and me?
    And he sang as he marched
    Through the crowded streets of Rochester,
    'Who'll be a soldier with Wellington and me?'

The King he has ordered new troops onto the
    continent,
To strike a last blow at the enemy.
And if you would be a soldier,
All in scarlet uniform,
Take the King's shilling with Wellington and me.

    Take the King's shilling! Take the King's
        shilling!
    Take the King's shilling with Wellington and me.
    And he sang as he marched
    Through the crowded streets of Rochester,

'Take the King's shilling with Wellington
    and me.'

'Not I,' said the butcher, 'Nor I,' said the baker
Most of the rest with them did agree
To be paid with the powder and
The rattle of the cannonball
Wages for soldiers for Wellington and me.

Wages for soldiers! Wages for soldiers!
Wages for soldiers for Wellington and me
To be paid with the powder and
The rattle of the cannonball
Wages for soldiers for Wellington and me.

'Now I,' said the young man, 'have oft endured
    the parish queue
There is no wages or employment for me
Salvation or danger
That'll be my destiny
To be a soldier for Wellington and me!'

To be a soldier! To be a soldier!
To be a soldier for Wellington and me!
Salvation or danger
That'll be my destiny
To be a soldier for Wellington and me!

Now twenty recruits came marching back through
    Rochester

Off to the wars in a far country
And they sang as they marched
Through the crowded streets of Rochester,

> *'Who'll be a soldier with Wellington and me?'*
> *Who'll be a soldier? Who'll be a soldier?*
> *Who'll be a soldier with Wellington and me?*
> *And he sang as he marched*
> *Through the crowded streets of Rochester,*
> *'Who'll be a soldier with Wellington and me?'*

• • •

This is one version of a song dating back at least to the beginning of the eighteenth century, when the words were 'Malboro and me'. It was sung to a traditional Scottish tune called 'Oh Bonnie Wood O' Craigielee' and is now better known as 'Waltzing Matilda'.

CHAPTER 1

Pringle clasped his hands tightly behind his back and tried hard not to shiver. He did not want to die on this bleak October morning, but he was a captain in His Britannic Majesty King George's 106th Regiment of Foot, and as an officer he must never show agitation or the faintest hint of fear. Often the show of courage was more important than any order he could give, for confidence was almost as rapidly contagious as fear, and it did not matter if it was an act.

Over a year ago Billy Pringle had helped throw the French out of Portugal, then been chased through the mountains on that grim march to Corunna. This summer he had come through the carnage at Talavera when they had fought the French to a standstill. There always seemed to be more French, and they never gave in easily. He took a musket ball at Talavera, which slashed a cut across his belly, but in spite of a bout of fever he had pulled through and all that was left was a pale scar. So many had fallen or been forever maimed on those two days in July that he counted himself lucky to have got away with little more than a scratch.

The slightest shift in the Frenchman's aim and he would not be standing in this field beside the river and wondering whether he would live to see the sun set. The thought was chilling, and it felt as if his very flesh was shrinking in a desperate effort to make him small and safe.

It was damned cold, while the persistent drizzle speckled the lenses of his glasses and made his shirt cling tightly to his body. With an effort, Billy Pringle stood up straight and kept from shivering, maintaining the act. He knew it mattered. Now that he had seen war in all its confusion, horror and brutal simplicity he understood that the pretence was important. Men watched each other, and most of all the men watched their officers. The veterans knew that it was all a sham. Officers and men alike pretended unconcern and somehow became brave, so that otherwise sane men did what seemed insane and battles were won. It also meant that 'sane' men would choose to face death, acting a part to impress others or themselves. It was almost a shame that the death and mutilation were so dreadfully real.

'Major Tilney is concerned about the weather,' said Captain Truscott, who had returned from consulting with a Light Dragoon officer, and now jerked Pringle from the thoughts that kept his mind away from the grim reality of this place. 'His principal does not wish an unfair advantage, and is willing to postpone the affair.'

Truscott was nervous, although only a close

2

friend like Pringle would have spotted the signs. His fellow captain was a precise man, as punctilious in his duties as in his private affairs. His left sleeve, empty since he had lost an arm at Vimeiro, offered the readiest of reminders that this was no act. Every few minutes Truscott unconsciously reached up and rubbed the buttons on its cuff. The rest of the time his right hand kept clenching and uncurling. Captain Truscott did not care for this business, but was determined to perform his role as second properly. Thin-faced and always inclined to frown, the injury had left him drawn. Yet now Billy recognised a deeper concern in his friend's features.

'Tell him . . .' Pringle's voice cracked so he paused for a moment, took a long breath, coughed, and then continued steadily. 'That is to say, thank him for his concern, but please assure him that there is no inconvenience. I can see well enough without my spectacles, should the rain become worse.' Pringle was tempted to add that he had marched and fought through rain, sleet and snow last winter, while Tilney and his fellow light dragoon were snug in England, before deciding that there had been enough insults. More importantly, Truscott would not approve of such levity, and so once again Pringle acted a part and made himself speak with appropriate gravity.

'You are sure?' Again the simple fact that the question was asked betrayed Truscott's doubts about the whole business.

'Certain,' said Pringle, his voice steady.

Truscott looked at him for a moment and then gave the slightest of nods. Without any more words, he turned and marched over to speak to Major Tilney.

'You're a bloody fool, Billy,' said Hanley, who remained beside him.

'Thank you, I am obliged for such a kind sentiment.'

This time Pringle could not help grinning, in spite of the solemnity of the occasion. Truscott would not approve, but Hanley cared little for convention. A man who had seen his dreams of becoming a great artist shattered, Lieutenant Hanley was forced to join the army because he had had no other choice. He cared little for convention and seemed baffled by most ideas of honour, but he had fought beside Pringle and gradually adapted to life in the regiment. More recently he had shown a talent for intrigue and gathering information about the enemy, and Billy suspected that his friend was more naturally spy than soldier.

'Delay matters,' urged Lieutenant Hanley, tugging his heavy boat-cloak more tightly around his neck. 'That way Williams can sort out this mess himself.' Like all the others in the little field the lieutenant was dressed in civilian clothes, but he was the only one who nevertheless did not obviously look like a soldier. Hanley was a handsome man, his skin tanned by the years spent in Spain before the war.

He was a shade taller than Pringle, and more than a year of campaigning left him looking fit and strong, but he was still generally dishevelled and inclined to slouch.

Pringle shook his head. 'Too late for that. A blow was struck.'

'Yes, by you, in fact!' Hanley's smile faded when he saw his friend's hard look.

The last days were a confused blur of searching for an errant girl and then a light dragoon officer. It was little more than a month since his detachment had returned to England from Portugal, and Pringle's initial euphoria at coming home had rapidly faded. He was alive, but found peaceful England duller than his dreams. Billy Pringle began drinking once again, as heavily as ever he had done before the regiment went off to war. The responsibilities and shortages of campaigning had made it easier to be sober. Pringle chafed at idleness, far more than the others, and so the sudden flight of their friend Williams' sister gave him a purpose and he had embraced it like a lover. Williams, Truscott, Hanley and Pringle had all gone hunting for the girl.

The trail proved easy to follow, and led them separately towards Cheltenham, but it was Pringle who arrived first, spoke to her, and decided to act. He should probably have waited, and might have done so if he had not felt so alive for the first time in weeks. Billy took Miss Williams with him and realised that he was drinking far less, although with hindsight it was probably still more than was wise in the circumstances. Lieutenant Garland of the 14th Light Dragoons was hardly in a better state when Pringle confronted him. Billy thought that he spoke calmly and with courtesy, but suddenly Garland was yelling and then damned Pringle as a liar. The light dragoon was flailing his arms in agitation, and when Billy thought that the man was aiming a blow his instincts took over, only the blocked swing turned into a punch which rocked the smaller dragoon back on his heels. Major Tilney and several other cavalrymen were all there to witness it. A gentleman could not simply strike another without consequences, but nor could he call another man a liar, and so it was Pringle who challenged in defence of his honour. Truscott arrived later that evening, and he had negotiated the business by meeting Tilney several times during the next day. No apology was forthcoming and the whole thing rapidly assumed an inevitability.

'It is my affair now.' Pringle managed a thin smile. 'Or would you have me meekly submit to a caning at the hands of that schoolboy?'

Garland was not yet nineteen, his cheeks shaded with wispy hair as he desperately sought to emulate the luxuriant side-whiskers of older light dragoons like the major. The lad clearly idolised Tilney, and Pringle suspected the latter had played a prominent role both in insisting on the duel and in the original affair. The two cavalrymen had met Kitty

Williams and her older sister Anne at Bath, where the girls were acting as companions to the elderly Mrs Waters. Pringle only knew a little of what had followed from Anne's modest account. Flirtation led to an understanding, and repeated excuses for clandestine meetings where Kitty was unaccompanied, and after the sisters' departure there was secret correspondence, aided by Mrs Waters – that 'silly, wicked woman', the girls' mother had said sharply. Then just a week ago Kitty Williams had sneaked away from her home and vanished, leaving a note to say that she was going to seek true happiness and would soon have splendid news. By the time Pringle found her that dream had died, for she was red-eyed from long weeping and almost at the end of her meagre funds. As he coaxed the story from the girl, Billy guessed that Anne's suspicion was right, and that there was a deeper reason why Kitty Williams feared to remain a spinster.

'It would not do,' said Pringle after a long pause. 'Besides which, Bills would kill the little cuss.'

Hanley frowned. 'No great loss to anyone, I suspect. And yet do you not plan to do just that in a moment?'

'I might.' Pringle spoke slowly as if mulling the matter over, but in his heart he was sure. 'But I will more likely merely nick him or miss altogether. With Williams it would be a certainty. Bills is a bad man when it comes to fighting.'

Hamish Williams was taller than both Hanley and Pringle, who were themselves big men. His

7

mother was a widow, the family lacking funds and influence, and so, when her son determined to be a soldier, he had joined the 106th as a volunteer, carrying a musket in the ranks. A gentleman volunteer lived with the officers and served with the soldiers, waiting to perform some act of valour sufficient to win him a commission. Williams managed this feat in Portugal in '08, survived unscathed and then later won promotion to lieutenant.

Pringle had seen Williams fight, and heard tell of other deeds he had not witnessed. Shy, awkward in society and pious, Hamish Williams was an unlikely friend, but had become a very close one to the other three. Billy had two older brothers, and was fond of them both, but since they had followed their father and grandfather and gone to sea at a young age he could not claim to know them as well as he knew his friends in the 106th. His own poor eyesight had kept him out of the Navy, and after Oxford even his already disappointed father had to admit that Billy was unsuited to the Church. Pringle decided to become a soldier, and now he found it hard to imagine another life.

He felt that he was a more than decent officer, and after four battles and twice as many skirmishes he was experienced and considered himself to be capable. Even so, he had to admit that Williams had taken to battle more naturally than any of them, and indeed seemed almost at home in the

8

chaos. Williams was a very good officer, but he also killed readily and with considerable fluency, and Pringle was beginning to understand how rare a thing this was. Billy doubted that he had ever taken any man's life, although it was hard to be sure. More than a few times he had fired his pistol into the chaos and smoke and perhaps one of the balls had struck a mortal blow, but more probably it had not and he preferred to believe this. Williams fought with a skilful savagery that was almost chilling.

'Then let him slaughter Garland,' suggested Hanley.

'And how would that help Miss Williams?'

'Avenge the slur on her good name by righteous punishment.' Hanley's disdain for honour was obvious. 'I can remember you helping me to lie like an Irish horse-trader when we needed to stop Bills from meeting Redman.'

Pringle chuckled at the memory. 'Dear God, that seems like an age ago.'

'It would not offend me to be called a liar.'

'Well, my dear friend, with all due respect, you are a liar,' said Pringle.

'Yes, and a damned good one. So what has prompted such a change on your part?' asked Hanley, who expected the world to be open to reason.

'Ask me after it is over.'

'You may not be here to ask!' Hanley was studying his friend closely and his face changed, suggesting sudden enlightenment. 'Oh,' he said after a moment, 'there is something else. Do I take it that Miss Williams is in pressing need of a husband?' Hanley's natural cynicism matched Pringle's view of human nature, but in this case he had a particular sympathy for he was the child of an illicit liaison. Neither of his parents had wanted anything to do with their bastard, although to be fair his late father had provided an allowance, and so he had been raised as best she could by his grandmother. For all his disdain for convention, Hanley felt the stigma deeply, and had no great wish to have it inflicted on another child. 'In that case, try not to kill him too much!'

'Gentlemen, you may take post!' Truscott's voice carried across the clearing.

'Good luck, Billy,' whispered Hanley as his friend strode towards the tent peg marking his position. Earlier on Truscott had paced out the distance and the elegant Tilney had driven the pegs into the damp earth, and then looked at the traces of mud on his gloves in evident distaste.

Two subalterns of the light dragoons stood at the edge of the field, chatting away in voices that were nervously loud, until the major glared at them. With them was a civilian doctor, a hunched, ill-favoured fellow with the red face and prominent veins of a hard drinker. Otherwise secrecy was preserved and no one else had come to watch the encounter.

Pringle stood behind the peg. The seconds had

agreed on an exchange of at least two shots at a distance of twenty paces before apologies could be offered, since if the argument was easier to resolve then it should already have occurred. The range was at the upper end of convention, and suggested that neither Tilney nor Truscott wanted to make a fatal wound too likely. Principals were not allowed any say on such matters. Nor was Pringle permitted to reject the right to take the first shot. It had been agreed, and that was an end to it. Garland had given first offence and so should be the first to stand fire. Major Tilney was the first to insist on this point. Billy Pringle was not sure whether this marked him as a slight or extremely close friend to the young lieutenant.

Tilney was also willing to permit Truscott to seek assistance when unable to perform his duties. Hanley moved to his side as the captain selected a pistol from each of the two identical cases of matched pairs. Then the lieutenant took these and loaded them in turn, while Major Tilney charged the other pistols for his principal. Neither man did the other the gross discourtesy of watching him as he went about this task.

Pringle and Garland waited at their marks. The rain slackened, although both men were already thoroughly wet, their hair flattened on to their heads. Garland stared boldly at his opponent, and, not to be outdone, Billy met his gaze. Neither man showed any sign of animosity, and Pringle wondered whether the light dragoon was genuinely without malice or simply dull-witted. Billy envied the cavalryman his silk shirt, and wondered whether it was warmer than his. Fragments of silk were easier for a surgeon to pick out of a wound than the threads of cotton. He knew that his father and brothers, like a lot of RN officers, always tried to wear a silk shirt and stockings with their uniform on a day of battle. Soldiers less often had the time for such careful preparations, or the capacity to carry so full a wardrobe on campaign – excepting the Guards, of course, for the 'Gentlemen's sons' always had plenty of servants and pack animals to shield them from the worst rigours of campaigning.

Pringle let his mind wander rather than think about the coming ordeal. Then he noticed Garland start slightly when Tilney brought him the loaded pistols, and it was pleasing to see a trace of anxiety in his opponent. For a moment Pringle almost felt sorry for the boy. He could not blame him too much for wanting to tumble Kitty Williams. The three Williams sisters were pretty, with fine golden hair just like their older brother, and Kitty was a bold flirt of seventeen summers with the shape of the very ripest young Venus. Pringle doubted the seduction had been entirely one-sided, and part of him thought that bedding the little minx would be a damned sight more pleasant a use of his own time than this challenge, but that would not stop him from putting a ball in the randy little dragoon. Williams was a friend, and on brief acquaintance he had developed a great esteem for Anne, a taller, somewhat serious girl closer to her brother in character, and more Juno than Venus in shape. It was not just a question of desire. Billy was inclined to desire any half-decent woman he saw. There were feelings for the eldest Miss Williams that he had not yet had proper chance to understand. That prompted the absurd thought that it would make it all the more unfortunate if he got himself killed this morning, but it was too late to change anything.

'A matter of honour,' he said softly, and permitted himself a wry smile.

'I beg your pardon?' asked Hanley, who had brought the pistols.

'Nothing of importance,' said Pringle.

'I believe you will need these.' Hanley spoke almost casually, and Billy wondered whether he too was becoming tense. He took the first of the pistols in his left hand, holding it by the middle of the barrel with the muzzle pointing behind him and away from Garland. He glanced down to see that it was already drawn back to full cock, shifted his grip to grasp it properly and then held it down against his leg.

'Stop!' A feminine voice broke the tense silence. Pringle turned to see a dishevelled and pale-faced Miss Williams emerge from the grove of trees behind them. There was mud spattered liberally on her dress and several tears in its hem, while her bonnet was so wet that it had partly collapsed on one side. The promise that Kitty would stay in her room at the Cock Horse had evidently lasted less than a hour, and she must have lost her way, for the path to this quiet spot was hard to follow.

'Madam, you have no place here!' The only time Billy had ever heard Truscott shout so loud was when he had ordered the battalion forward at Talavera – a captain in command because all the senior officers had fallen. 'Hanley, see to the lady and keep her out of the way.'

Major Tilney looked angry. Pringle thought that Garland was confused, and the boy's cheeks flushed in spite of the cold. Hanley gave him the other pistol with even less ceremony and lurched off towards the girl. After more than a year in the army he still seemed incapable of standing straight.

'Come, sir, we must proceed,' ordered Tilney.

'In a moment, sir; I shall not be rushed,' Truscott replied, smarting at his tone. 'Mr Hanley, kindly keep Miss Williams back.'

The girl was breathless, unable to do more than stammer incoherently. Hanley took her gently by the shoulders and urged her back to the top of a grassy bank.

'It is too late to change anything,' he said firmly, and the sadness in his voice moved her more than its force.

'But he might die,' the girl said feebly. It was unclear who 'he' was.

'Gentlemen, make ready,' called Truscott. Pringle turned so that his right shoulder pointed towards Garland, who matched the movement. It offered

14

the smallest target to an adversary, although Billy Pringle could not help thinking that his greater height and broad stomach made him a far better mark than the slim light dragoon.

'Now that you are ready, Major Tilney will give the orders to fire,' said Truscott.

Miss Williams stood close beside Hanley, his arm round her shoulder. She was breathing heavily and he knew that this was no longer mere fatigue.

'I cannot watch,' she gasped, but when he glanced down her eyes were open and as excited as they were fearful.

'Gentlemen.' Hanley would not have thought that someone could shout and drawl at the same time, and yet somehow Tilney managed it. 'I shall call your name in turn, and give you leave to fire. You will then present and as promptly fire. Do you understand?'

Pringle nodded. Garland said nothing and made no gesture.

'Do you understand, Mr Garland?' asked Tilney.

'I understand,' said the lieutenant, his voice higher than normal.

'Good, then we shall begin.' He paused, standing at attention and in silence. Miss Williams reached up with both hands and pressed Hanley's fingers tightly as they rested on her shoulder.

'Mr Pringle,' Tilney ordered, 'you may give fire.'

Billy raised his arm, the pistol feeling suddenly heavy, and levelled it at Garland, whose eyes were closed. A gentleman did not pause to aim and so

15

without hesitation Pringle squeezed the trigger so that the hammer slammed down and the flint sparked.

Nothing happened. Either the powder had shaken out or the earlier drizzle had left it too damp to flare.

'Bugger,' hissed Billy Pringle to himself, and he could not help wishing that the meticulous Truscott had been capable of loading instead of the well-meaning but militarily casual Hanley. Still, the cause did not truly matter any more, as a misfire counted as a shot.

'Dear Lord, he is safe,' whispered Miss Williams, making her sympathies clear. Hanley wondered whether the girl realised that duelling was illegal, and that if either man died all present could be charged with murder. Yet his friends, who in other circumstances he held to be prudent and sensible, most certainly knew this and were still doing this damned silly thing – as was he, although at least he did not have to be happy about it.

'Mr Garland,' called Tilney without hesitation, 'you may give fire.'

The light dragoon seemed surprised to have survived the shot and perhaps did not fully understand what had happened. It was known for men to forgo a shot when their opponent misfired, but there was no sign that the thought had entered Garland's head. He raised his pistol and fired. The report was muffled by the wind, which instantly whipped away the dirty smoke.

Billy Pringle felt something flick through his thick brown hair. He dropped his discharged pistol on to the grass and reached up with his hand. His hair was damp, but only from the rain.

'Is there blood, sir?' demanded the major. The surgeon seemed finally to wake up, his creased red face alert as he went forward, his legs swishing through the long grass.

Pringle held up his hand, fingers stretched wide. 'No blood,' he said.

'There is no wound,' said the doctor after a close inspection. Pringle could smell the gin on the man's breath and wished that he had some. It seemed unfair that the offence could be given after a good few drinks, while the encounter must be fought by the sober.

'Mr Pringle, prepare yourself,' called Tilney as the surgeon retreated. Pringle switched the loaded pistol to his right hand and again held it down against his leg.

He noticed that the watching dragoon subalterns had turned to look behind them. A tall horseman was riding hard through the meadow beside the stream. The wind had dropped, and Pringle caught the dull pounding of heavy hoofbeats. It was a big piebald horse with heavy features and thick legs, and its rider was an officer, his cocked hat covered in oilskin and his cloak blowing behind him to reveal a scarlet jacket.

'It's Ham,' said Miss Williams in a loud tone of genuine surprise. Pringle had not become used to

17

the nickname the sisters used for their brother, but had already recognised that it was Lieutenant Williams in the flesh.

'Damn it, sir, I will brook no more impediments or interruptions.' Tilney sounded outraged. 'Go about your business, sir, and leave us in peace.'

'Forgive the intrusion,' said Williams. 'I am here merely as a friend, and as a witness.'

'Well, sir, be damned to you if that proves your funeral as well as ours,' snapped Tilney. 'Now dismount and call no more attention to yourself. You must not distract the principals. I do not know how the infantry conduct affairs of honour, but in the cavalry we insist on proper decorum.' Pringle saw Williams bridle, and Truscott also stiffened noticeably, but both men evidently decided that one duel was enough for the day and made no issue of the remark.

The elegant light dragoon major waited impatiently as Williams dismounted, hitched his reins around a fence and then walked over to join his sister and Hanley.

'Mr Pringle, I say again, prepare yourself.' Tilney waited, fingers drumming impatiently against the tail of his coat.

'Mr Pringle, you may fire.'

Pringle levelled his piece and again pulled the trigger. Again the flint sparked, but the main charge failed to ignite. His muttered oath was longer this time, and he turned to glare at Hanley.

'Mr Garland, you may fire.'

18

The discharge seemed louder this time, carried to them by a sudden hard gust of wind, and Hanley felt the girl flinch at the noise and flame. The ball went nowhere near Pringle, although whether this was intention, the wind or mere poor aim it was impossible to say.

'Gentlemen, you have withstood two fires,' called Truscott. 'It would be fitting to end this affair with apologies.' He looked at Garland, who had given first offence and so must be first to relent.

'No apology.'

Pringle was surprised, although after two misfires it would be reasonable enough for the man to see himself as safe. For his part, he was ready to make public apology for the blow, but it seemed that he would not have the opportunity.

Williams, his sister and Hanley watched Truscott and Tilney consult each other.

'How did you get here?' asked Hanley quietly.

'Long story,' Williams said, and then Truscott called Hanley to join him. The principals were to exchange one more shot, and so he was required to load. Pringle would have preferred the more capable and martial Williams to do the job, but it was a concession for Hanley to be involved and Major Tilney was by now in no mood to extend a further courtesy.

'Take care to load this well,' was as close as Truscott came to direct criticism, but Billy Pringle raised one eyebrow quizzically when Hanley passed him the pistol.

'Gentlemen, prepare yourselves.' The two men were already in place and in the proper stance, and so Tilney paused only briefly before he continued.

'Mr Pringle, you may fire.'

Billy Pringle raised his arm until it was straight and pulled the trigger. There was the familiar snap and spark, and then he almost jumped when the main charge went off and the pistol jerked back with the discharge.

Lieutenant Garland dropped like a shot rabbit.

Kitty cried out and buried her head against her brother's chest.

'Well, I'm damned,' said Billy Pringle.

CHAPTER 2

It was not a bad wound. The surgeon quickly proclaimed as much and, although Pringle had grave doubts about the man's skill, in this case he was obviously right. The ball had nicked Garland's right arm just above the elbow, and then cut a furrow across his body. A rib was probably broken, but the bullet had not gone in and if bound up and kept clean the injury would heal quickly.

There was a lot of blood, very bright against the whiteness of his shirt, and this looked worse than it was. Pringle could hear Miss Williams sobbing and the scarcely sympathetic noises her brother made to calm the girl.

It was not usual for the defeated party to summon his opponent, but after a few minutes Major Tilney had beckoned to him. Garland sat up, supported by the two dragoon subalterns, and hissed in pain as the surgeon pulled the bandage tightly around him. Relief was flooding over Pringle, for whatever the consequences of this day at least there was now no chance of facing the gallows. In truth most juries were reluctant to convict, and witnesses – especially military witnesses – managed to forget all that they had seen if the affair was a properly conducted matter of honour, so that it was rare for anyone to be punished. Yet it did happen, and the Army Act expressly forbade duelling. It was hard to know how much sympathy they would receive from the new colonel of the 106th.

Then Pringle forgot these thoughts of the future – a future he now confidently possessed – and suddenly wondered whether his adversary felt well and bitter enough to insist on taking his third shot. Billy stopped in mid-stride, the thought chilling, for he was suddenly certain that this time he would die. The Talavera wound began to itch, and it started to rain again, steadily this time, drops spattering loudly on his already soaked shirt and misting his lenses.

Pringle took a deep breath and with a great effort walked the last few yards.

'I trust you are not badly injured?' he asked, for courtesies, however absurd, were important. Apart from that, he could think of nothing else to say.

'A trifling wound,' said Garland, doing his best to appear brave, and Pringle respected him for the effort, and then the man grinned, and Billy began to warm to the lad. 'I hope you will not take that as an insult to your skill with a pistol.'

'I believe we have had sufficient insults,' said Pringle, smiling in turn.

'I could not apologise,' continued Garland, and

then paused because the surgeon was tying off the bandage, and so stood between the seated man and Pringle.

The doctor finished and stood up. 'We must get you properly cleaned up and then to bed,' he said.

'In a moment, my dear Dr Stubbs, in a moment. Would you leave us please? You too,' he said, turning his head to the two subalterns. 'I believe that I can stand.' Garland winced a little as they helped him up, and then clearly felt embarrassed by this show of discomfort and stood up straight, his face impassive. 'Perhaps your second should be present?' he suggested to Pringle.

Truscott was summoned, and only then did the wounded lieutenant continue.

'As I said, I could not apologise, for I believed what I said, and as I understand it, an explanation rather than an apology may only be offered after three shots. Is that not correct, Frederick?'

Major Tilney nodded. 'Quite correct, Robert.'

Pringle knew that it was common practice in some cavalry regiments for officers to use each other's Christian names except when on duty.

'An arrangement might have been made if the circumstances were known,' said Truscott.

'Thank you, Frederick, I was confident that I was right.' Garland ignored Truscott as he looked at his superior officer with something akin to worship. Tilney was of no more than average height and had a round face with somewhat heavy

23

features, but in every other respect he was the epitome of the elegant and dashing light caval-ryman. It was obvious that the major was fully aware of his poise, for his manner exuded an immense sense of his own superiority.

'I was no doubt mistaken to accuse you of lying, Captain Pringle.'

Pringle bowed.

'But I feel you were mistaken,' Garland continued. There was the hint of an accent in his speech, although Billy could not quite place it. Somewhere from the north-east – perhaps Durham or Newcastle? Father in trade, probably, and no doubt highly successfully, so that he was able to send his son away to school and then buy him a commission in a fashionable and expensive regi-ment. That would explain the longing for the major's approval. Tilney was the son and heir of a general, albeit one who had bought his promo-tions to colonel and then become a general through living long enough for his turn to come. As far as Pringle knew, old General Tilney had never once seen action – not that that mattered for a man's place in society.

'I love Miss Williams, and have esteemed her most highly since our first introduction at Bath – for which I once again owe you thanks, Frederick.'

Tilney gave the slightest of nods. Pringle saw little trace of marked affection on his part, and sensed more tolerant amusement – much like a man watching puppies at play. He could not help feeling that the major was making sport of them all. He had not known that Tilney had introduced them, and wondered once again whether that was the limit of the major's interest and involvement.

'My adoration is both fervent and fixed,' said Garland, and the choice of words made Pringle believe that here was someone else acting a part. 'And yet I had not believed my suit to be successful.' He glanced at Tilney. 'My feelings are unchanged, but I do not believe that there was anything resembling an understanding between myself and Miss Williams – much as I might wish for one. There was most certainly no promise.

'And so, when you came and insisted that I honour my obligation to the lady, there was no obligation. It took me quite by surprise, and the impression of compulsion made me angry.' Garland gave a half-smile. 'Since I left school, I have never permitted anyone to compel me to do anything.'

Pringle had heard similar sentiments from many fellow officers, and if he was honest took the same pride in his own freedom to act. It was all a little absurd, given that every day they obeyed orders as part of their duties.

'I will not be compelled, sir – I simply will not.' The accent was stronger now. 'I shall marry Miss Williams with the greatest joy in the world if she now accepts my offer, but I could never be made to do anything, even so desirable a thing as that.'

Billy Pringle did not know what to say. He wondered whether this was how Hanley felt most of the time, as if peering through a misty window at folk who were foreign in almost every way, their behaviour following rules that were as absurd as they were strict.

'I am happy to hear it,' said Truscott, once he realised that his friend was not about to speak.

Pringle rallied himself at last. 'As am I,' he managed. He was not sure whether he wanted to roar with laughter at the ridiculousness of the whole thing or shoot Garland again for risking their lives and careers for so small a point of conduct and pride.

Miss Williams and her brother were summoned, the girl demure now, her face cast down and full of worry. Garland asked for a moment for them to be alone, and all save Kitty withdrew a discreet distance so that they could not hear what was said. Pringle was the only one to notice the glance of intense hatred – and also, he was sure, disappointment – that the girl shot at Tilney as he passed. Hanley and the two subalterns joined them as they watched.

Then Kitty yelped like the schoolgirl she still really was and flung her arms around the wounded Garland, making him wince with pain.

'Will his family permit the alliance?' Williams

asked Tilney, for Truscott had explained the lieutenant's resolution.

'His parents are indulgent,' drawled the light dragoon officer with a barely perceptible hint of disapproval, 'and he is a younger son. No doubt there will be an allowance – perhaps not a large one, although I dare say enough for modest tastes. You would be a better judge of whether or not that meets the lady's expectations.'

Pringle pressed Williams on the arm, for he knew the man was insulted and feared a new quarrel and perhaps even the shattering of this happy resolution. 'I believe Lieutenant Garland wishes to speak to you.' Williams' father had died in an accident at work when the children were all young, and once he became an adult he assumed the role of guardian to his sisters.

The big man strode forward, bidding his sister to go with Hanley and Truscott back to the inn. Williams was almost as concerned as Truscott to behave properly – perhaps more concerned, for his origins left him sensitive to any hint that his gentility was not recognised by others.

'I had not been aware that it was you who introduced the couple, Major Tilney,' said Pringle in as innocent a tone as he could manage. Billy was glad to have his jacket and long coat back on.

'It was of little moment. I was introduced to the lady by a friend at the Assembly Rooms. Garland was a cornet in my troop in the Twelfth, and followed me when I exchanged into the Fourteenth.

He had few connections in Bath, and it seemed reasonable for me to make some introductions. Miss Williams has a charming appearance, and as the opportunity arose I made them known to each other.' The tone suggested that both were of no real account in society and so well matched. 'Garland is a willing enough fellow, but apt to overreach himself.'

'I am glad that he overreached his aim, at least,' said Pringle, surprised that the major was telling him so much. He strongly suspected that Miss Williams had originally set her cap at Tilney himself, and wondered how long – and how well – they had known each other before Garland appeared. Tilney spoke of both the young people in a way that indicated absolute unconcern for their welfare.

'Poor Robert had even presumed to pay attentions to my own sister,' Tilney went on, 'and so the transfer of his affections to Miss Williams came as a considerable relief to us. Can you imagine it – the fellow's father digs coal!' The two light dragoon subalterns sniggered appreciatively.

'Not in person, one would imagine.'

'Oh, of course, but that scarcely makes it any better. Such dirt does not easily rub away.'

Pringle felt that the major's sneers were aimed mainly at his fellow dragoons. He must appear a good fellow for condescending to befriend young Garland, without ever diminishing his own superiority. It was sad to think of the lieutenant trailing eagerly behind a man who constantly reminded the world of the junior officer's lack of breeding.

Thank God I'm not in the cavalry, thought Pringle, and was relieved to see Williams helping Garland walk over to join them. Matters were concluded, and arrangements made, and so finally they could get in out of the rain. Pringle longed to be warm and dry, and to eat the hearty break-fast he had been unable to face before they left. He would also be glad to see the back of Tilney, whose sneering manner was already tiresome.

'A charming young lady,' he heard the major say softly as the light dragoons and the doctor took Garland away, 'and I do enjoy charming young ladies.'

'Bastard,' muttered Pringle, and then felt guilty and was glad Hanley had left, for he knew his friend disliked the word. He would lay ten to one that Tilney had seduced Miss Williams and then passed her on to Garland for his own convenience and amusement. Eight to one the major and not the lieutenant was the father. If that was the case then best to hope that Garland did not realise – or less plausibly that he did not care. Pringle was not inclined to worry too much one way or the other about Kitty Williams, but the contentment of her brother and older sister mattered to him a good deal. He had risked life and career for them – and because he struggled to cope with the dullness of being away from the war.

Williams approached, holding out his hand.

'Billy,' he said, 'I do not know how I can thank you, or apologise for subjecting you to this when it should have been my job.'

There was no point explaining his fears to Williams. Perhaps he was wrong, and had simply grown too untrusting of his fellow men.

'Don't mention it, old boy,' he said, and smiled. Sometimes it was simply easier to act a part.

CHAPTER 3

'Soldiers, Daddy, look, soldiers!' cried a small boy perched on a man's shoulders. The father was stocky, his clothes threadbare, and although he was still young there were flecks of grey in his black hair. He neither looked nor answered his son, and instead pointedly turned away, so that the lad now saw Williams and his little face erupted into even greater ecstasy. 'A soldier! A soldier! Look, he's got a sword!'

Williams smiled at the boy and ignored the father's sour glance. A few days in charge of a recruiting party had soon accustomed him to the hostile expressions provoked by the sight of a soldier. The army was for the desperate, and he had been sent around the mill towns precisely because business was bad and workers were being laid off. The 106th was ordered to recruit itself up to full strength and its new commander, Lieutenant Colonel FitzWilliam, was determined to find the best material. They needed to act quickly. The regiments in Portugal and throughout the empire always needed men. Worse still, one of the biggest expeditions ever seen had gone earlier in the year to Holland. Most of those corps had not yet returned, and from all Williams had heard, many of the men never would. Fever had ravaged the army, taking the lives of thousands and leaving as many more unlikely to recover. Its new commander wanted the 106th to take the pick of the bunch before the whole country was thronged with recruiters.

'Hello, soldier,' said the boy.

'Hello, young man,' Williams replied, and this at least prompted a grateful smile from the father. The man had quick, intelligent eyes, and hands that were soft underneath some recent blisters. Williams guessed he was educated, perhaps a clerk, but had recently been forced to take any work he could get to feed his family. An older woman appeared beside the man.

'A soldier, Gran,' said the child, pointing in case she failed to notice Williams. Then doubt creased the small forehead. 'He should have a horse.'

'I'm sorry, sir,' apologised the woman, whose face was heavily lined with care.

'It is fine.'

'But he should have a horse,' the boy continued, with utter conviction. 'He's a soldier.'

'He is in his stable being fed,' said Williams.

'Good.' That appeared to resolve the mystery, and further conversation became impossible when on the far side of the square the drummer from Williams' party plunged into a series of flamboyant tattoos, the sound echoing off the houses and for a moment checking the busy hubbub of market day. The boy was carried off into the mass, his father accompanied by his grandmother. The child was obviously delighted with the sights and sounds and began waving his hands as if he had sticks and his father's head was a drum.

Williams made his way through the crowd towards the redcoats, and could not help sighing at the thought that he had possessed a horse for a few brief weeks in the summer. The mare was an Andalusian, fast, elegant and well mannered even with an inexperienced rider like Williams. It was a gift given after Talavera as a reward for saving the life of the Spanish commander, and from the very beginning the subaltern had known that it was too fine and delicate an animal for a mere subaltern in the line to feed and maintain. Williams had no funds beyond his pay, and was unable to afford proper feed to keep the mare in condition, let alone a groom to care for her. He had sold the horse when he reached Lisbon, and received the princely sum of two hundred guineas from a newly arrived major general. The price was fair, perhaps even a little low, and it was more money than he had ever had – almost than he had ever dreamed to have. When they reached England and finally received eight months of back pay in one lump sum, for a while Williams felt himself to be rich.

It did not last, and his funds were now much diminished. There were bills to pay, for all the usual deductions had steadily accumulated, and it seemed that more than half of his wages vanished in the twinkling of an eye and the scratching of a pen in an account book. Then there were presents for his mother and sisters, and since then the drain of hunting for the errant Kitty, and of taking her up to Scotland with Garland, where the two were wed in that strange ceremony over the anvil. Both Garland and Tilney were due to join their regiment in Lord Wellington's army, and so there was no time for the banns to be called.

Williams had gone to represent the family, and although brief acquaintance convinced him that Garland was sincere and to be trusted, it was proper for him to be there. Kitty had done better than she deserved, winning a decent and well-off husband at the end of her silly and dangerous adventure. The impression of her great good fortune was reinforced when they visited Mr and Mrs Garland on their way back south. An initially tepid welcome quickly became very warm, for the parents clearly doted on all of their children and were delighted to see their son happy. Kitty flattered them with enough obvious sincerity to win them over. She had always been personable, and had a social confidence that Williams himself utterly lacked. For the moment she would live in Bristol with his mother and sisters, until 'her hero returned from the wars'. The willingness not to be a burden on her husband's parents had very much helped to win over Mr Garland, who seemed a good deal shrewder than either his wife or younger son.

The young couple remained with the Garlands for a few days when Williams hurried to rejoin the battalion. Yet once her husband took her to Bristol on his way to Plymouth, Kitty would need the support of his family. Williams could already see his funds draining away, for even if Garland helped there were bound to be greater expenses.

'Now come, all my brave lads, and enlist today in the finest regiment in the whole army!' The drummer had finished and Lance Sergeant Dobson's voice carried across the square. 'The One Hundred and Sixth are taking just a few, high-spirited young men – those whose hearts beat high to tread the path to glory!'

Williams moved to the side, waiting to play his own part.

'We are the Hundred and Sixth and we are the youngest corps to serve the King. To our enemies we are a terror, and them Frenchies shake at the knees when they see us.' He paused a moment for effect. 'Almost as much as the village maidens' hearts flutter at the sight of a fine young buck in the red facings of the Hundred and Sixth!' Williams could not see Dobson through the crowd, but knew that he would now direct a wink and gesture towards the comeliest woman in sight. 'Aye, miss, you know what I mean!' There was laughter, as well as a few squeals of shock.

'Look at me,' said Dobson. 'Almost an old man,

and yet here I am with a new young wife just this year. Beautiful she is, and almost straight out of the nursery.'

That was generous, and hid a tragedy. Dobson's wife of many years, and the mother of his three children, had died in an accident during the retreat to Corunna. The new Mrs Dobson was widowed a week later. In the army way, they had remarried soon afterwards. Dobson must have been past forty, his gaunt face creased and tanned by a succession of tough campaigns. For all his years, he was as hard as the teak his skin resembled. Annie Dobson was scarcely a child, being twenty-seven, and her looks, though pleasant enough, were far from beauty, not least because she seldom smiled in company. Dobson's wife was prim and very proper, and Williams had to admit that she had done her husband a world of good. In the past he had been frequently promoted and inevitably broken to the ranks for drinking. The death of one wife, and the arrival of a new one, had changed him, and the old veteran had been sober ever since. Williams hoped it would last.

'It's all because of these red facings and the bright red cross on the Colours of our regiment. We're the youngest corps, and you all know that young men are the bravest and most vigorous.' Williams imagined the prettiest woman again being singled out. 'Only the best for the fair, for a beauteous maid can take her pick, can't she, miss?' More laughter, and louder, but less convinced squeaks of outrage.

'That's the One Hundred and Sixth! Always ready and always steady! The French know it and so do the lasses!' Williams smiled as there was more laughter from the crowd. The motto was one devised by Lieutenant Colonel Moss, who had fallen in Portugal. Williams had once admired the man, but now understood that he was dangerously unwise and had led the battalion into a tight spot at Roliça, costing many more lives apart from his own. Moss had been ambitious, and ever eager to promote the regiment. Only he had ever used the slogan during his lifetime. Then, months later, it had reappeared as a joke, used more often to speak of women than of the French. Williams suspected that before he joined the army he would have found it vulgar, and yet now it made him laugh. He had marched and fought with the regiment for more than a year. The redcoats were often crude in speech and actions, unbecoming in appearance and had a capacity to drink themselves senseless and behave like beasts that far surpassed even that of his fellow officers. Williams still admired them and trusted them with an affection close to love.

'We're the boys who saved the day at Vimeiro – who kept them Frenchies at bay when led by that great hero Sir John Moore, even though they outnumbered us ten to one! But then, who here doesn't know that one English lad is a match for ten Frenchies!' Williams might have believed that once. Now he knew that the French were as brave as anyone, and some of the finest soldiers in the world. In truth the wars were going Bonaparte's way. Austria had surrendered after renewing the struggle earlier in the year, and Spain was on her knees. Britain was running out of allies once again, and there were probably at least ten French soldiers for each redcoat.

'Talavera, my boys, have you heard that glorious name?' Williams had to admit that Dobson was good at this game, working the crowd. He idly wondered whether the veteran remembered listening to similar patter on the day he first joined the army. 'Ah, I see you have. It made our bold commander a lord, and twisted the nose of Bonaparte's brother, so that he ran off with his tail between his legs and a British boot kicking his arse!

'We were there, lads, of course we were, showing the way and standing tall amid shot and shell until the Frogs gave in.'

Williams remembered the French bombardment. Most of the battalion was in England, but three companies had been stranded in Spain and he and Dobson and the others found themselves fighting in a unit cobbled together from other detachments. They had not always stood tall, for orders had come to lie down in the long grass. Men had still died, smashed into bloody fragments by cannonballs, and when the French infantry came the redcoats had stood up to face them. Williams had never before seen so bitter a fight.

Dobson and Hanley had fallen, fragments of a howitzer shell striking both men in the legs, and they were lucky to escape being burned alive by the grass fires that raged after the fighting was done. Many were not so fortunate, and Williams wished that he could forget the screams of wounded men being roasted to death. No one could tell whether they were British, French or Spanish.

'Glory, and the path of honour! That's what I'm offering to any lucky lad chosen to join the One Hundred and Sixth under Colonel FitzWilliam, the son of a lord and as brave and generous a gentleman as you could hope to meet.'

Williams had not yet met his new commander, who had been away during his two brief visits to the battalion since they returned from Portugal. Major MacAndrews had led the 106th after Moss fell. The Scotsman was old for his rank, and had captained the Grenadier Company when Williams first joined. MacAndrews had proved himself a superb battalion commander, but he was not a rich man. FitzWilliam purchased command of the 106th and so the major was once again a subordinate. If it was not especially fair, it was simply the way of the army. In the summer Williams had found himself leading a company at Talavera. It would no doubt be years before he became a captain and won the right to do so. Even in his brief moment of wealth he had owned nothing like the £1,500 needed to buy a captaincy.

'If that isn't enough, then I'll tell you about the

rewards. Each man gets a uniform as smart as it is easy to clean.' Dobson and the other two members of the recruiting party were resplendent in new red jackets and trousers, the buttons gleaming and belts whitened with pipe-clay. The spearhead on his half-pike was polished like a mirror, and a knot of tall red feathers was tucked into the cockade on the front of his shako and towered over the normal white plume of a grenadier, chosen from the biggest men in the battalion. The resplendent martial perfection of the recruiting party was the product of special issues of equipment and many hours of labour. On campaign clothes were faded, torn and patched, if not replaced altogether.

'And apart from good bread, meat and other vittles, every man gets his tot every day. Now isn't that better than starving through a hard winter?' That is what the army promised. What it delivered was a different matter.

'And think of this. Every day – every single day – the newest young hero receives a bright silver shilling.' Williams knew that a man was lucky to carry away one shilling a week after the deductions were made for food, equipment and laundry. That was assuming the pay was not months in arrears.

'That's wages, isn't it, my lads,' said Dobson. Williams had worked his way nearer the front of the crowd now and saw the mixture of expressions, the young men excited by the prospect, while the older ones scorned it as a pauper's wage.

'But best of all, when the King gives you the first shilling he adds in a great prize, a bounty no less, to show how much he values the brave fellows who serve him. Here I have a golden guinea.' Dobson held it aloft. The coin was as highly polished as his buttons. Sadly the sun was hidden behind clouds today and the guinea failed to gleam. 'Twenty-one shillings, no less. Look at it, lads.' Dobson held it out on the flat of his palm to show two likely youngsters standing in front of him. Both looked like farm boys and one was barely five feet tall so would have to enlist as a boy at lower pay, but this was not the time for such detail. 'Look at it, don't it gleam beautifully?

'One golden guinea, but that's not all our King wants to give you. "Dob, old son," he says to me, "I want the most dashing in my special Hundred and Sixth, and I'll not have them treated a mite less well than the young heroes they are." True as I stand before you, that's what he said.' Most of the audience laughed, although one of the farm lads stared in fresh awe at a man who knew the King.

A drum stood on the ground, and Dobson now flicked the coin so that it gently bounced on its skin and spun for a moment before falling. 'So it isn't just one golden guinea for the lucky few.' Some recruiters liked to count the coins out one by one, but Dobson reckoned the jingle of coins was more inspiring and so took a purse and emptied it out. Even in the dull light, the gold

41

glittered in the imagination of many who watched them tinkle down. 'Fifteen bright golden guineas!'

Williams politely pressed through the crowd as they had arranged.

'That's just when you join. Clever and brave fellows will soon find themselves promoted to corporal or sergeant, and earning twice as much. Why, they may go further.' Dobson pretended to notice Williams for the first time. 'Look at that fine officer over there. A year ago he was my rear rank man, and stood behind me firing his musket at the French.' That was true enough, although a gentleman volunteer was a very different thing to a private in the ranks. Only the ablest and luckiest private soldier made the leap to commissioned rank, but they were few indeed. 'Now he's as fine and rich a gentleman as any you could meet.' Dobson dropped his voice to a stage whisper. 'Won't talk to the likes of me any more!'

Williams paid no attention, and tried to guess which young woman Dobson had earlier singled out. There were a couple of likely candidates, but when one turned towards him he saw the pleasant, plumpish face of a girl of no more than sixteen, ginger hair peeping out from under her bonnet, and knew that this was the one. The officer raised his hat courteously.

'Would you excuse me, dear lady?' he said, gesturing to show that he wished to pass. Whenever possible Dobson picked redheads, knowing that his officer was desperately in love with Major MacAndrews' red-haired daughter. Miss MacAndrews was currently with her mother in Scotland, and Williams had neither seen nor had word from her since coming back to Britain. When he had gone with his sister and Garland north of the border it had been very hard not to keep going and seek them out in Aberdeen.

The plump girl blushed, then giggled a little as she curtsied, stepping back to permit the officer to pass. Williams kept going, raising his hat each time he needed to get past anyone. His small part in the performance was limited, and the rest could be left to Dobson, Corporal Murphy and the drummer. They would soon invite those 'wishing to apply' to join them at the Black Lion and there regale them with tales and drinks and convince as many as possible to join. So far Dobson was sticking to small beer, but Williams worried that the task of a recruiting sergeant risked a relapse into his old ways. At least Murphy could drink like a fish and still tell plenty of grand yarns of adventure and loot.

It was unpleasant to have to stretch the truth to convince men to join. At least Williams could be sure that his men would not follow some of the worst practices – getting a man drunk and then slipping the King's shilling into his pocket, swearing blind the next morning that he had volunteered. There were stories of other sergeants hiding a shilling in a man's mug, so that he took the coin that way. As he left the square he saw some other recent posters stuck to a wall. One was for the 7th Hussars – the Old Saucy Seventh, as it proclaimed – and in a matter-of-fact tone declared that since '. . . the regiment is mounted on Blood Horses, and being lately returned from SPAIN, and the Horses Young, the Men will not be allowed to HUNT during the next Season, more than once a week'. Williams supposed that the statement was true in its own absurd way, for he had never heard of private soldiers or NCOs in any cavalry regiment ever riding to hounds. He shook his head and walked on.

Before dusk Dobson and Murphy brought him eleven volunteers. Williams found a local doctor well practised in such matters and paid him to give them a cursory inspection. Two were rejected – the first because he could barely see, while the other failed to make the minimum height even with folded paper packed into his shoes. The rest were sworn in by the magistrate. The pair of farm boys were among them, and there were half a dozen who gave their occupation as mill worker. Their desperation was nothing compared to the ninth man, the father whose son had chatted to Williams so happily earlier in the day. His name was James Raynor, and when the whole party marched out of town the next morning his face was hopeless, certain of never seeing his boy again. Williams hoped that he was wrong.

'Well done, Dob,' Williams said to the lance sergeant as they marched off the next morning.

'The colonel should be pleased. At this rate his battalion should be back to full establishment.'

'Aye.' Dobson sniffed. 'Hunger is always the best recruiting sergeant of all.' The veteran stated the facts, his tone free from judgement. He seemed to think for a while, and then looked at the young lieutenant. 'Not sure it's quite "his" battalion yet, though.'

'I do not follow.' Williams had found it well worth listening to the veteran's opinions.

'The colonel is still a stranger. Hasn't been with us in any of the actions.' Dobson had seen plenty of service in other regiments, but Portugal had been the first campaign for the 106th. Since then it had seen plenty of hard knocks. 'Reckon he's a smart enough man to want to make us his own.'

Williams was intrigued. 'How?' he asked.

'Best way would be to send off some of the characters who have been with the battalion all the way. Old Mac, of course.' Dobson grinned. 'Sorry, sir, I mean Major MacAndrews. Then probably Mr Pringle.' He winked at Williams. 'You too, Pug, begging your pardon.'

'I am only a lieutenant.'

'You know how to fight. So do the others.'

Williams was still unsure. 'Then won't he want us? If he is smart.' It was best to speak frankly to Dobson, at least in private. The man knew the army and how it worked.

'Oh aye, he will when the time comes. Up till then he will want to take the battalion by the scruff of the neck and stamp his mark on it. Easier to do that when some of the big characters are off. So I reckon it won't be long before there are some temporary postings. That's if he is as smart as he looks.'

They marched on in silence for a while, Murphy and the drummer leading the recruits some distance ahead of them. Williams thought about Dobson's idea. He did not want to go away so soon, now that there was a chance of seeing Miss MacAndrews again. Part of him wanted to dismiss the veteran's suspicion. Unfortunately it made a good deal of sense. After a while another thought came to him.

'How about you, Dob? If he really wants the characters out of the way.'

The grin was even bigger now. 'Depends how smart he really is.'

Williams knew there was more than one way to take that, but decided not to press the issue. The sun came from behind the clouds and he had to squint as they marched on. It was not strong, but there was still a hint of warmth and that was good to feel on the skin.

'I think he is smart,' Williams said after a while, and half hoped that he was wrong.

CHAPTER 4

'Here's to Christmas at home!' said Williams, raising a glass of Hanley's champagne. A series of wins at cards had left his friend in funds and inclined to celebrate. Williams loathed almost all alcohol, but the discovery that he quite liked champagne was fairly recent. The toast was one they had repeated often enough on their way back from Talavera, when all of them were weary and Pringle and Hanley both recovering from wounds. Now it rang rather hollow.

'Well,' said Hanley thoughtfully, 'perhaps Spain is more home to me now than England.' Orders had arrived detaching him from the battalion and sending him back to the war.

'You were most welcome to stay with my family,' said Williams.

'Yes, and the invitation is most kind.' Privately Hanley was relieved. He and Pringle had visited Bristol and met Williams' family – as it turned out, in time for his sister to run off. Mrs Williams was severe at the best of times, and he doubted Christmas would be any too jolly. Now that the newly married Mrs Garland was there, no doubt

47

lording it over her sisters, the idea of another visit had little appeal.

'Do you know any more about your orders?' asked Truscott.

'Nothing has been said, although I am to go to London before I leave.' Hanley mused for a moment. These were his closest friends, and the urge to tell them fought against a growing habit of secrecy. 'Do you remember Baynes?'

Truscott thought for a moment, but Williams at once looked up sharply.

'Oh yes, that portly civilian who was with Wellington's staff at Talavera,' said Truscott. 'Some political wallah or other. Is he involved?'

Williams knew Baynes to be considerably more than that, and so guessed that there might be a certain delicacy involved in Hanley's role. 'Good luck, William,' he said, and then thought it better to change the subject. 'I wonder when the battalion will follow you?'

'You've been listening to rumours again, young Bills,' said Truscott.

'The battalion is once again reunited, and with all the recruiting parties out, we may soon be back to something like full strength. Is it not reasonable to suppose that such a rare thing will before long be sent abroad?' Only the absence of the three companies driven back to Portugal had prevented the 106th from being sent on the expedition to Antwerp earlier in the year, since almost every other unit that had come back from Corunna had joined the new expedition. 'By all accounts the corps coming back from Holland are in no state to be sent abroad again.'

Truscott shook his head sadly. 'That sounds as if it was a ghastly business, and little more than a waste for no good end. However, simply because the regiment is in prime condition does not mean that we will go back to Wellesley's army.'

'MacAndrews is going,' said Hanley.

'True,' Truscott conceded, 'but on detached duty of some sort.'

'It is a training mission to aid the Spanish,' Williams explained. He had not shared Dobson's suspicion with the others.

'Well, God knows they need all the help they can get in that regard,' said Truscott, remembering the night before Talavera when thousands of raw Spanish conscripts panicked and fled at the sound of their own volley. 'Good luck to him, though, as I doubt it will be an easy task.' In the last year British and Spanish armies had not cooperated well, leaving considerable bitterness on both sides. 'Still, I have not heard the details of his orders.'

'He is to take a number of officers and good sergeants,' said Williams. 'A third will come from the battalion and the rest from other corps. The colonel asked if I wanted to volunteer for the duty.' Lieutenant Colonel FitzWilliam had arrived that morning and seen Williams in the afternoon. He was friendly, full of praise for the lieutenant's record and the fine conduct of Williams and the other men from the 106th who had fought at Talavera.

'I presume from your talk of Christmas at home that you did not accept?' Hanley grinned. 'That's a shame. It would have been nice to have company on the voyage.'

'Sorry. The colonel gave me the day to consider it, but I would prefer to wait and go back with the whole battalion.'

'You surprise me,' said Hanley.

'Ah, I believe I may have an explanation,' said Truscott. 'Am I correct in assuming that the major's family is remaining here?'

Williams nodded. His friends knew of his feelings for Miss MacAndrews, but even so it was difficult to speak of them. 'It has been a long time,' he said. 'Perhaps too long, and it may be that my hopes are in vain.' The lieutenant seemed ready to plunge into gloom. They had all heard the stories of other suitors for Miss MacAndrews. It was even said that the new colonel was much taken with the major's daughter.

'Another glass, gentlemen?' suggested Hanley, wondering whether FitzWilliam wanted to send a rival off to Spain to clear the field. As he rose to fetch the bottle he patted Williams on the shoulder. 'Good luck, Bills.'

'Well, I fear that we have strayed from the point in hand,' Truscott continued. 'The battalion will no doubt be sent off some time next year, but there is no assurance that it will go back to

Wellington's army. Have you not heard the stories of this planned expedition to the East Indies?'

'Yes, and when I came through the depot a month ago, the mess was full of talk of us training to be light infantry,' said Williams.

Truscott shrugged. 'It has happened to other corps. And in the main they have chosen battalions with good numbers of active young recruits, much like us.'

'Perhaps, but here we are a month later, and it seems that no one is speaking of it any longer even as a possibility.'

'True enough.' Truscott accepted his refilled glass from Hanley and took a generous sip. 'I did hear tell that they could not provide sufficient muskets of the light infantry pattern.'

Williams drank more carefully, eager to make the champagne last, as his friends were always quick to refill an empty glass and he rarely cared for more than two. 'Portugal or Spain still appear most likely.'

'If the new ministry still wants to fight there,' said Truscott cynically. Yet another government had fallen after the debacle of the expedition to Antwerp, this time in such acrimony that two former ministers had fought a duel.

'They must fight there,' said Hanley quickly. He had lived in Madrid for several years before the French came and had seen what their soldiers had done to protesting crowds. He loved Spain, and in spite of a still lingering admiration for France's revolution and for Bonaparte, he wanted the country to throw out the invader.

'They certainly should,' Williams added with less passion, but considerable assurance.

Truscott carefully wiped up some spilled champagne with his one hand. His friends knew he liked to be left to do such things himself rather than be helped. 'You may both be right, but that does not mean that they will. Napoleon is free again to lead all his armies into Spain. If he does that, then I do not see that there is the strength to resist him. Only a year ago Moore declared that Portugal could not be defended. Spain is crumbling, if it has not already crumbled. Much as I admire Major MacAndrews, it is hard to see his efforts making any difference.'

They finished the bottle in gloomy silence.

Pringle arrived that evening, leading in more new recruits. The battalion paraded the next morning, and then was busy with drills and inspections until lunchtime. That afternoon Lieutenant Colonel FitzWilliam invited him to his rooms for a private chat.

The colonel was of average height, but Pringle only noticed this when he stood close to him. FitzWilliam was the son of an earl and his upbringing, combined with his years in the Foot Guards, produced a confidence and poise that magnified his presence. It looked as if he had been poured into his uniform, the coat suggesting a broadness of shoulder and slimness of waist that stopped just short of caricature and gave an impression of height. FitzWilliam's face was very round, an effect deliberately reduced by his full side whiskers, a little darker in shade than the hair on his head. By no means a handsome man, the colonel had presence, helped by the lively spark in his brown eyes and the smile that spoke of a ready wit. His welcome was warm, and full of praise for the battalion's record and Pringle's own conduct.

'I saw the One Hundred and Sixth marching out from behind the hill at Vimeiro, and then again when they tumbled back that French column,' said the colonel. 'Was on Burrard's staff in those days, so did not have a chance to do more than watch.' He modestly waved down Pringle's instinctive praising of staff work. 'Well, the next time we get a chance to have a go at the French I shall be with you.'

'Do you know when that might be, sir?' asked Pringle, who already felt comfortable talking to his commander.

'Not before next year, I suspect. Probably in the spring or summer.' FitzWilliam gave a disarming smile. 'And before you ask me, no, nothing is certain as yet. Perhaps Portugal, perhaps the Mediterranean or further afield. I fear Horse Guards have yet to inform a mere lieutenant colonel!

'Still, that is for the future. When the time comes I shall rest easily knowing that you have my Grenadier Company.'

'You are too kind, sir, too kind.'

'My dear fellow, I am merely stating the truth,' said FitzWilliam with obvious sincerity. 'The battalion has been well led, or it would not have distinguished itself so highly in Portugal and Spain. I was not present to witness Moore's campaign, but have already listened to those who were. However, I should be indebted to hear from you of Talavera.'

The colonel listened avidly to Pringle as he described the last campaign. Throughout he smiled encouragingly, only interrupting to ask questions that were always pertinent. Pringle began to realise that there was a sharp and clinical mind behind the suave exterior. FitzWilliam gave every impression of being a serious soldier, and Pringle responded by speaking in greater detail, giving his own opinions and the reasons for them.

'Tell me more of the Spanish,' said the colonel as Pringle reached the end of the campaign.

'I have seen something of them, although in truth Hanley and Williams have seen far more. They were at Medellín.'

'A grim day.' It was one of many defeats suffered by Spanish armies. 'I shall most certainly seek their views, but I should also greatly value your own.' FitzWilliam launched into a series of questions, about Spanish officers and their backgrounds, the quality of their NCOs – 'We all know they are the fellows who matter the most' – of drills and tactics, their commissariat and its limitations, the generals and the government supporting them. Billy answered as best he could. It reminded him of Oxford, and he felt that he was being guided towards some conclusion.

'So, from all that you have seen, do you believe that we can win the war with our allies in their current state?'

'No,' said Pringle, surprising himself with the speed of his answer and the firmness of his conviction. 'With Austria gone and the rest of Europe humbled, Bonaparte can lead three hundred thousand bayonets into Spain. Only in the most favourable conditions can the Spanish withstand the French in the field. We can beat them, but cannot match such numbers.'

'And so the answer?'

Pringle fought against the urge to say that Britain should leave a doomed cause. He did not want to believe that, and felt that he did not even though it was hard to come up with reasoned arguments against the proposition. 'Time,' he said, testing the idea in his mind as he spoke. 'The French will want to win quickly, but may find that harder than they think. If they have not shown skill, the Spanish are certainly determined. Many of the defeats have come from rushing too hastily against the enemy, pitting raw soldiers against hardened battalions. In time the Spaniards will make better soldiers.'

'And then the numbers become more balanced.' FitzWilliam smiled. 'Have you heard about the reorganisation of the Portuguese army?'

'A little,' said Pringle, sensing that he understood the colonel's line of reasoning, but was still unsure of its implications for him. 'General Beresford has taken a staff of English officers and is retraining their regiments.'

'Quite so. It is said that he is doing wonders. Once the Portuguese are ready, they will at least double the size of Wellington's army. The Marquess Wellesley' – that was Wellington's older brother, currently serving as envoy to Spain's Central Junta – 'has suggested a similar endeavour with the Spanish. It is a much more delicate matter, and for the moment kept to a small scale.

'Perhaps you have already heard that our own Major MacAndrews is to be sent to Spain to establish a small training camp. The purpose is to take sergeants and corporals from the Spanish army and train them in drill, outpost duties and fighting in open order – the Spanish have few skirmishers, and that places them at a grave disadvantage against the French voltigeurs.'

Billy Pringle thought that he at last discerned the colonel's purpose, and so the conclusion did not take him wholly by surprise.

Colonel FitzWilliam looked at him steadily. 'MacAndrews is to take with him a party from this regiment as part of his command. I feel that you would be highly suited to this duty. It needs experienced men, otherwise there is little reason for the Spanish to pay any attention. Even so this is largely a gesture, but if Spanish generals begin to see that better non-commissioned officers make for better regiments, then they may permit an expansion of the idea.'

Pringle was unsure what to say. On the one hand, the frustrations of recent weeks made the prospect of returning to Spain attractive. He liked and respected MacAndrews, although he doubted whether the scheme was practical. The Spanish had their own ways of doing things, and seemed unlikely to relish instruction by foreigners.

'I confess to a degree of reluctance to leave the regiment,' he said after a pause, feeling that this did not yet commit him to a decision.

FitzWilliam seemed delighted. 'That sentiment does you the greatest credit. However, it need not be for long. I will want my best officers with us when we take the field next year, indeed I shall. The whole business should not take much more than six months. MacAndrews and any others may rejoin us in good time.'

Pringle was sceptical, and perhaps FitzWilliam sensed his doubts.

'It would do no harm to have experience of detached duties. In two years you will be eligible for your majority, will you not?' The colonel had obviously checked the records. He was correct, although without the funds to purchase it was unlikely that Pringle would be promoted so soon. 'On another matter, an absence from the country may prove prudent.'

'Sir?'

'This business of calling out Garland. An over-officious JP was inclined to investigate the matter. Thankfully word reached a cousin of mine who let me know, and together we were able to persuade the fellow not to make an issue of it.'

'I am most grateful, and regret putting you to the trouble.'

FitzWilliam brushed aside the thanks and the regret. 'These meetings are always unfortunate, but sometimes cannot be avoided – especially when a lady's honour is at the root of the business. From what I understand your motives were good, and it is a pity that the wretched fellow did not act more sensibly and avoid the matter in the first place. Still, it is no doubt too much to expect a cavalryman to be anything less than a fool.' The colonel chuckled to himself. 'Halfwits to a man, in my experience. It is to be hoped his new bride is clever, or we must worry for any children.' Pringle was unsure from the colonel's expression whether the last comment was meant to be barbed and to imply calculation on the part of Williams' sister. If so, then the man was more shrewd than he had hitherto realised. Billy Pringle knew that he was being outmanoeuvred.

'However,' FitzWilliam continued, 'it is a particular shame that you were the challenger. I do not want my officers to win a reputation for seeking out duels. A posting to Spain is not a reproof, indeed it is not. You are ideal for the job in hand and it will be of advantage to you in the future, but it will do no harm to get you away from the battalion and the country for a short while. It is not an order, of course.'

'Of course not, sir,' said Pringle, 'and of course I shall be happy to go in the circumstances.'

'Splendid, absolutely splendid,' said the colonel, and offered him a cigar.

CHAPTER 5

Williams turned the corner and almost bumped into Mrs MacAndrews.

'Be careful, you clumsy ox!' The lady spoke loudly and with a flash of temper so that her words were almost shouted. 'Mind where you tread,' she added more calmly, and then broke into a smile. Esther MacAndrews was tall, dark-haired and remained an exceedingly handsome woman although well past her fortieth year. She had terrified Williams and most of the other subalterns from their first meeting, and even though in his case deep affection had long since surpassed the terror, it did not remove it altogether. He recoiled, stammering apologies.

'Why, it is Mr Williams. I had quite forgot that you were back with the regiment, or otherwise I would have expected to be run down!' Williams coloured, much to her satisfaction. Esther MacAndrews stepped back. 'I wonder if you remember Jane?' she asked maliciously, for she was fond of the lieutenant and knew of his regard for her daughter.

Williams had last seen Miss MacAndrews on

board another ship when the fleet sailed from Corunna. Before that he had rescued her when she was left behind during the army's retreat, and together they had escaped through the mountains, alone for a while and then with an ever growing group of stragglers. Williams and this ragtag band had held a bridge against a French column before they rejoined the army. He had seen the girl in snow and rain, weary and filthy with travel, had watched her and the soldiers' wives doing their best to comfort wounded, sick and dying men, her dress stained with their blood and pus. He had also seen her naked, drenched by the cold river, and had held her close to keep her warm so that she did not die. There was another time – an all-too-brief moment – when he had held her in his arms and felt her lips pressed against his. That was a better memory than their last conversation, when she angrily rejected his proposal of marriage. Ever since then he had picked over the encounter in his mind, trying to understand where he had gone wrong and find the source of her rage.

'Good day, Miss MacAndrews,' he said, raising his hat, and then, remembering his manners, turned back to the mother. 'Good day, Mrs MacAndrews, my sincere apologies. I really was not looking where I was going . . .'

'No, you were not,' said Esther. 'You are almost as clumsy as my husband.' As usual when amused or angered, her Carolina accent became more pronounced. Aware that his attention had shifted, she went on with exaggerated seriousness. 'He has been known to trample everything in his path, crushing flowers, dogs and maidens too beneath his clumping feet.'

Williams looked confused, and for the first time he saw that Miss MacAndrews was also taken aback and appeared to be struggling for words. He knew that he was staring and that this was rude. Jane was beautiful in a way that struck him almost physically, whether she was in elegant finery at a ball or tramping through the mountains in a torn and dirtied dress, or pulled from the water like a half-drowned rat. Today she wore a white muslin dress with a pale blue pelisse over it to keep out the cold, and although much shorter than her mother she carried off the high waist of current fashion through the excellence of her figure and movements. As usual, a few curls of red hair peeked from beneath her bonnet, this tiny hint of imperfection only adding to her startling good looks. Her skin was fair, her eyes a rich blue-grey, and then she flashed those neat white teeth and gave him that wide, generous smile.

'Good day, Mr Williams,' Miss MacAndrews said, bobbing down in a slight curtsy.

They stared at each other for a while.

'Well, isn't this nice,' said Esther, realising that the conversation needed some assistance. 'Now, Mr Williams, you must tell Dobson to come and visit his grandson, now that we have returned from Scotland. He is a fine, healthy lad and is growing by the day.' During the retreat to Corunna Dobson's pregnant daughter Jenny had fled from the army and fallen in with Williams and Jane. They – well, if Williams were honest, he must admit chiefly Jane – had helped her give birth to a son, and then cared for the child when the mother fled again, abandoning the unwanted baby. Jane had grown very fond of young Jacob, and at the end of the retreat her mother was equally entranced. The decision already made before he was consulted, Major MacAndrews had gracefully offered to raise the boy.

'I am most delighted to hear that, and shall certainly tell Lance Sergeant Dobson at the first opportunity.'

'Lance sergeant? Ah yes, I was glad to hear of his promotion. That will please his wife, and the major always says he is the most wonderful fellow as long as he is sober.' Since joining her husband last year, Esther MacAndrews had come to know the life of the battalion very well, taking a particular interest in the followers.

'Yes, he is an excellent soldier.' Williams paused, raising his hat once again to the mother. 'Now, ma'am, with your permission.' He turned to Jane. 'Miss MacAndrews, I wondered whether you might do me the honour of accompanying me on a short walk?'

'Certainly,' said Mrs MacAndrews, speaking with such firmness that she answered both the question addressed to her and the one to her daughter as well. 'I need to make sure that young Jacob has been washed and fed, and then sort out our things after the return from Scotland.' She darted a mischievous look at Williams, and then spoke to her daughter. 'Do not be too long, Jane. I expect that Colonel FitzWilliam will want to pay his respects now that we are back. Good day to you, Mr Williams, I am most pleased to see you again.'

Williams led the girl along the path beside the river. They stopped several times to greet groups of officers and others promenading with their wives. At first they said little. He asked about her health, the recent trip to Scotland to visit her father's sister and the baby's welfare. The answers, save to the questions about the latter, were brief in the extreme and interspersed with formal comments on the growing inclemency of the weather. Each time they met someone it was almost a relief, saving them from so stilted and awkward a conversation. In company with others, the pair of them spoke naturally. When they walked on, both immediately became ill at ease once again. Williams had never known the girl to act in this way. In the past, it had only ever been he who was shy and clumsy when they met. It was not as if they did not know each other well. Cut off for more than two weeks during the winter's campaign, they had seen each other's true nature and spoken of things that neither had ever talked about with anyone else. He had longed so much to see her for some ten months, imagining reunions, but never anything like this.

Suddenly it all seemed so absurd, and Williams threw his head back and laughed out loud.

'I do not understand,' said Jane, peering up at him and frowning. She looked so earnest that Williams found himself unable to stop laughing, prompting a flash of anger. 'Mr Williams, have you quite lost your wits!' Miss MacAndrews stared at him, and then began to chuckle herself. 'I really do not understand,' she said again.

Gaining control of himself, Williams at last found a voice. 'I do beg your pardon, but I believe that is the very first time that I have ever had the advantage of you in conversation,' he said.

'Guffawing like a donkey scarcely counts as conversation in most circles.'

'Well, you know me to struggle in society. But please do forgive me. I have waited so long to see you again, and then have proved dreadful company.'

Jane smiled. 'It is well mannered, if insincere, of you to take all the blame when it should be shared evenly. It is very good to see you.' He thrilled at that. 'We were so worried when your ship vanished in the storm and did not arrive in England.'

Williams would have preferred another pronoun, but the sentiment was so obviously genuine that he was able to take pleasure in that. 'It was a ghastly time. We nearly sank and . . .' He hesitated briefly. 'I was so afraid that something had happened and that I had lost you. It was not until the end of March that Major Wickham told me that you were safe, and I do not think that I have ever before known such relief. I had been so afraid that for a moment I almost liked that blackguard.' A thought struck him, and he became awkward again. 'I am sorry, I had no wish to insult your friend.'

'Mr Wickham is no friend of mine.' There was a hard edge in the girl's voice. Williams guessed that Wickham had done his best to seduce Jane, and was pleased to hear such hostility.

'That I am glad to hear.'

'But let us leave so unpleasant a subject. Tell me something of your adventures.' The coldness stayed in her voice, and Williams guessed at the cause. During the last months someone who was with him in Spain had written letters back to friends in the regiment at home. Apart from other news, there was much about him, with wild stories of amorous misadventures. Williams was painted as an unrelenting and unsuccessful pursuer of women, as a ridiculous Lothario chasing a Spanish aristocrat, a Portuguese courtesan and even some of the soldiers' wives. Major Wickham had laughingly told them of some of these stories, courtesy of his wife. Williams was not sure whether Lydia Wickham was the recipient of the letters. An inveterate gossip, she may simply have been the keenest to spread such tales.

'The fighting was hard,' he began slowly, 'but somehow I doubt that is your chief interest. Miss

MacAndrews, I am aware that a good deal has been said about me. I had hoped that you were the one person who did not need my assurance that there is no truth in any of it.'

She stared at him, her eyes large and vivid, and it was a while before she spoke. 'Well, I would not have minded if there was just a little truth in the stories. Not much, you understand, but just a very small amount.'

'You still hanker for a Jones, I fancy, a hero imperfect in just the right ways.'

Jane's lips parted in a grin. 'Well, there is something to be said for a Welsh name.'

'For that sentiment I am grateful, and though it may not be in all the right ways, I can boast of many imperfections.' The mood was now so much easier, almost as if they had not been apart for so long, but there was one difficult subject he had to broach. 'Your mother spoke of Lieutenant Colonel FitzWilliam being likely to pay his compliments.'

'Now it is your turn to doubt,' said Jane sharply, 'but then I suppose I cannot with justice resent that. The colonel is a fine and kind man. I believe that he likes me and has displayed signs of that partiality. There is no more to it than that, as yet.'

It was not quite full reassurance, but was at least encouraging. 'He seems a good man,' said Williams, who always tried to be fair. Silence returned for a good five minutes as they walked to the end of the path and turned around to return.

'Where do we stand, Mr Williams?' It was Jane

who broke the silence at last, and the suddenness of the question shocked him. 'And if you tell me that we stand on the riverbank, then I shall do my best to fling you into it, small though I am!'

'Where we stand is that I asked you to marry me and you refused.'

'A precise, if somewhat blunt answer.'

There seemed to be no more. Jane's eyes were dancing with amusement. 'My feelings are unchanged,' he went on. 'I love you, and that is all there is to it.'

'Blunt now becomes positively brutal. This must be how the French feel when facing you!'

Williams struggled for balance, a sense so familiar from encounters with Miss MacAndrews. 'How would you like things to stand?' he asked, and saw from her face that this was the right response.

'Perhaps as if we were meeting for the first time, so that we may begin afresh. Please, let things not be rushed, but let us see how we both feel. Such fervent admiration as yours is a little uncomfortable for a lady to receive. It is bound to make her wonder whether you truly love her, or merely the idea she represents. Now, I do not wish to offend or doubt for a moment your sincerity, which I know to be genuine. It is simply that there is plenty of time and I am still young. It is hard to know my own mind, but the one thing of which I am sure is that I do not wish to be rushed into anything. But I am fond of you, Hamish, very fond indeed.'

His heart leapt. If these were not the words he wanted to hear, it was still the warmest she had ever been, and that combined with the sweetness of her voice meant that he did not mind the use of his unfortunate Christian name.

Williams took her hand and pressed it gently. 'As you wish,' he said.

'I am glad,' she said, 'but it is getting late and we must hurry.'

They walked on in silence, comfortable this time, and when Miss MacAndrews slipped her arm through his he felt that he might burst with sheer excitement. Yet there was one more thing to say, and he feared that it would spoil this new-found harmony.

'It seems that fate conspires to give plenty of time,' he said as lightly as he could.

'I do not understand,' said Jane, and Williams felt her arm stiffen.

'Your father leaves for Spain soon, and I am to go with him.' Their arms now seemed more entangled than gloriously intertwined.

'Those who go are volunteers, as I understand it.' Miss MacAndrews' eyes were angry.

'Pringle was most strongly urged by the colonel, and since his only offence was committed on behalf of my family, I could not in all honour permit him to go on his own.'

'Honour,' she said harshly. 'He is a grown man and scarcely alone. You speak of honour and yet choose to leave.'

Williams reeled, and almost before he knew it found himself quoting. '"I could not love thee, Dear, so much, loved I not honour more."' Jane was fond of verse, and in the past had delighted in exchanges of quotes, but as he spoke he suspected Lovelace had been an unwise choice.

Her arm slid free and she took a pace away from him. Her face was red, and she was breathing deeply, chest rising and falling in a manner that made his throat dry.

'Then take your honour, sir, and may it be a comfort to you!' She recovered herself a little, and then spoke more levelly. 'Good day to you, Mr Williams. Thank you for your company, but I must hurry away.' She turned and strode off.

Williams wondered what to do. They were on a path running through the meadow by the river and two hundred yards from the street leading into town. He could scarcely follow her without feeling absurd, and it would doubtless be uncomfortable – as well as ill mannered – to walk beside her, and rude to pass her. Then inspiration came to him, and he hurried to catch up.

'Miss MacAndrews,' he called politely. 'Please forgive me, but there is one more thing.'

To her credit Jane turned, her anger barely concealed. 'I am late, Mr Williams, and have no time.' She stopped and he reached her.

'It is just this.' He smiled, but failed to thaw her mood. 'Back in the winter when I did not know if I would live or whether your ship had perished in the storm, I made myself a solemn promise.'

'Indeed,' she said, her face doubtful.

'Indeed,' Williams replied. His right hand shot around the girl's waist and his left took her shoulder, pulling her towards him, lifting her face to his. Jane gasped. Then Williams kissed her.

Jane staggered when he let her go. She was shocked and confused – and that was something he had rarely seen before – and in her agitation she panted for breath. Williams fought the urge to take her in his arms again.

'How dare you!' Miss MacAndrews said at last, because she could think of no better retort. As suddenly as he had lunged, her right hand flicked up and slapped him hard on the cheek. She turned and pattered away as fast as she could, not looking back.

Williams went in the other direction, even though that meant taking the long way back. He kept smiling to himself, feeling that this was the first time he had ever come away from one of their arguments feeling that he had the advantage. It was a small triumph, and he fervently hoped that it would not cost him too dearly.

Nine days later, Williams stood with Pringle, looking back at the shore as their ship worked its way out into the channel. He had not seen Miss MacAndrews again, and did not know whether the fondness she had admitted was now for ever

71

spent. Her father leaned on the rail a little further along, and his manner was no different towards him, but that might mean anything or nothing.

They were leaving Britain again, and to Williams it seemed barely the blink of an eye since they had returned. It had all started so well, as he posted home, arriving on a Sunday to be told his mother was in church, and he had marched down in his best uniform and simply sat beside her without saying anything, joining in the hymn even though it was the last verse. He remembered vividly her surprise, and the look of pride and relief she had given him, and then, when they had returned to the house, she had embraced him. Mrs Williams was not given to displays of affection, and he could not remember her ever acting like this before. By the next day she was back to her usual distant self.

The only emotion she had shown after that was anger at Kitty's folly, only a little mollified by the news of her marriage. Williams and Pringle had stayed a night with his family on their way to Plymouth, and his mother's manner towards the new Mrs Garland remained frigid. Williams had quietly given his mother a good deal of his funds, feeling that his other two prudent sisters ought not to be less rewarded than Kitty. That sparked a thought.

'You and Anne enjoyed a good deal of conversation,' he said to Pringle.

'Your eldest sister is a very fine woman.'

Williams nodded. 'Yes, she is, and it is only a shame that others do not share her sense.' He took a deep breath and spoke quietly, for he did not want anyone else to hear. 'I am sorry, Billy, so sorry, that my family have caused all this.'

Pringle waved his hand airily. 'No matter.' He looked at his friend and grinned. 'To be honest I was finding the predictability of life more than a little dull. In many ways I shall be glad to be active again.'

The ship came out into the channel and was immediately hit by the swell, the deck lurching under them. 'Oh, dear God,' moaned Pringle. His face had lost all colour save for a faint hint of green. Williams was a poor sailor, but it still amazed him that Pringle, who came from a naval family, succumbed to seasickness so instantly.

Williams watched his friend stagger across the deck, heading for the companionway and the thin solace of his cot.

'I really am very sorry, Billy,' he whispered to himself.

CHAPTER 6

They did not see Fort La Concepción until they were almost on top of it. All of them were weary, having marched a long way through the winter's cold. The snow had stopped, but their breath steamed as they walked across the thin blanket of white that covered the rolling fields. They had crossed from Portugal into Spain several miles further back without noticing any great change. Those who had served here before knew that, while the land looked the same on both sides of the border, the people were startlingly different in speech and customs for so small a distance. Yet on this bleak day the two nationalities had something in common, for neither Portuguese nor Spanish villagers were fool enough to be abroad. The night before they had heard howling, and more than once today had seen the tracks of wolves in the snow.

The snow also made it harder to see the square fort, but only a little harder, for the engineer who first laid it down half a century ago had been a master of his trade. It lay on the top of the highest ground, but was so artfully blended into the landscape that it was almost invisible from any distance.

'In its way, quite beautiful,' said MacAndrews admiringly, and leaned down to pat the neck of his horse.

Pringle shaded his eyes as he stared at the low ramparts and then pointed. 'Looks like smoke, Colonel.'

The Scotsman followed his gaze. 'I do believe you are right. Well, a fire and hot food will be most welcome.' He thought for a moment and then grinned happily. 'You know, I am still not used to being called that,' he said. MacAndrews held the local rank of lieutenant colonel as commander of the mission to the Spanish army. Local rank was temporary, tied to a place and lasting only as long as the specific duties that warranted it. It meant no change to his actual rank or seniority within the battalion, and so he had not bothered to alter the insignia on his epaulettes. Still, it was nice to have both the title and the pay, even if it was just for a short while. 'Well, let us take a look at our new home,' he said. 'Will you bring up the rear, Billy?'

'Sir.' Pringle turned his mule and walked the beast back along the column. A few of the other officers rode mounts of one sort or another. Most walked alongside the men, although all save Williams had most of their baggage stowed on the donkeys that followed, urged along by a pair of Portuguese boys hired in Lisbon. The former volunteer still carried a pack as full or heavier than those of the ordinary soldiers.

Altogether there were eight officers, thirty-seven non-commissioned officers and two drummers in MacAndrews' little force. They were a long way from Wellington's main army or any large Spanish force, but as far as anyone knew the nearest French outposts were a good forty miles away and not likely to come closer any time soon.

Pringle came to the end of the little column and nodded to Williams.

'Christmas at Fort Conception,' he said, pronouncing it the English way. It was 24 December, and just a year ago they had been much further into Spain under Sir John Moore.

'Well, they do say home is where a man hangs his hat!' Williams stamped his feet for warmth, letting the rear rank go on and the boys pass him with the donkeys. 'Soon be warm, Raynor,' he said, as the man went by, riding on Williams' own mule. The new recruit was skilled with pen and account books, and had only lost his job through drunkenness. Williams had encouraged MacAndrews to take him along as they would need someone to act as clerk, and that meant that within months of joining, Raynor was an acting corporal, able to send more money home each month to help his mother care for his son. His wife was dead, and from what Dobson had said it had been that loss more than anything else that turned Raynor to drink. The veteran had promised to do his best to keep the man in line. Dobson and Murphy – both now made up to sergeant – were with the party, and as Williams glanced at them, hunched against the cold, their greatcoats stained with mud, he could not help thinking back to their immaculate turnout when serving in the recruiting party. Their wives were in England with the regiment, for no followers were permitted to accompany the detachment.

'I suppose conception is an apt enough name for the season,' mused Pringle, but when he saw that his friend was baffled he explained. 'I presume it comes from the immaculate conception.'

Williams shook his head. 'I cannot quite get used to the Iberian tendency to give martial things such sacred names. Wouldn't something like Fort Defiance be rather more inspiring?'

'Today, I believe I would settle for Fort Plum Pudding!'

'Ah yes, the gallant defence of Plum Pudding. It'll go down in the annals of history without a doubt.'

'Thank God we kept the holly flying,' said Pringle happily.

The column came to the big square blockhouse, where a Spanish sentry shivering in the shadow of the gate directed them towards the fort itself. The sunken road took them through the fortified stables.

Closer to the fort, Williams tried to imagine attacking the place. In the old days castles had

had high walls, so that the defenders could throw, drop or pour things down on the attackers. High walls were usually thin and certainly easy to see, and once cannon were perfected they were desperately vulnerable. It was an easy thing to knock them down, their own rubble tumbling down to provide attackers with a ramp leading into the place.

Modern walls were made to be very thick, but their main defence was that they were low. As the column trudged along the approach road, Williams could see that there was a smooth earth bank – a glacis – ahead of the main walls, so that only the very top of the rampart itself was visible. That made it hard for gunners to hit the wall, for most shot would bury itself in the glacis or be deflected up to fly harmlessly over the rampart. The deceptively gentle slope had another advantage, and even though he was expecting it, Williams was amazed at how deep the ditch was when they crossed the little bridge spanning it. One of the great bastions shaped like a spearhead jutted towards them as they reached the ramparts themselves. Gunners loved to fire at a long straight wall, for the balls would smash it quickly, and so engineers planned forts so that everything was at an angle and it was hard to strike directly at the stonework.

MacAndrews and his men turned to the right, going along the covered way – a road sheltered by the glacis so that the defenders could move around the outer perimeter and be safe from enemy fire.

No good engineer permitted a straight approach to the main gate, and so they had to pass another footbridge and go through a demilune – a smaller outwork shaped like a bastion, but standing free of the main wall. Finally they came on to the main arched bridge leading to the big gate, the Spanish coat of arms carved on the low tower above it. Everything was made from the same well-cut blocks of pale grey granite.

'A bitch of a place to attack,' said Captain Reynolds of the 51st Foot, looking up at the rampart and then along the wide ditch. 'Although at least it's not flooded.' Reynolds was one of the officers posted to MacAndrews from other units. Williams judged him to be a vulgar fellow, but in this case could not challenge his verdict. In the chaos of an attack it would be hard for men to find their way through this maze of ditches and false walls before they could place ladders up against the main ramparts. Those ladders would have to be long, and so awkward to carry, other-wise they would not be high enough to reach from the bottom of the ditch to the top of the wall. All the time the defenders would be firing at them, for the bastions and ramparts were angled so that the fields of fire from the cannon mounted on them interlocked. There were no safe places for the attackers. The glacis and covered way offered protection from the outside, but no shelter at all from the defenders' fire. The square fort with its corner bastions, demilunes and angled ditches and banks looked in plan like a purely technical exercise in geometry, but all the science served a grim and very practical purpose. Fort La Concepción was designed to kill.

Williams shuddered for a moment, and hoped that everyone would assume it was simply the cold. He pictured in his mind's eye the confused attackers being mown down by storms of canister and musket shot. It had never before fully registered that all the terminology of this calculating and coldly logical form of warfare was in French. It rather suggested that the enemy were very good at it.

MacAndrews was greeted warmly by the bespectacled Captain Morillo of the Princesa Regiment, his Spanish counterpart. After the briefest of welcomes, he led them into the esplanade, the sunken square inside the fort itself. It was surrounded by rooms set into the backs of the ramparts, and on the north-west side the grand governor's quarters where they would live and work. Morillo ushered them inside, where warm stew was waiting. He had two lieutenants to assist him, half a dozen experienced sergeants from his own regiment, and fifteen more men to act as sentries and perform other fatigues.

Before he went in, Williams walked up one of the ramps leading on to the main walls. These were wide enough to mount heavy guns, the granite backed by tightly packed earth faced with more stone. They were also empty. There were no cannon in the fort, and the bastion on the north corner was a tumbled ruin. Fort La Concepción, the perfect and beautiful example of the engineer's trade, was broken.

'The French did it,' said a voice, and when Williams turned he was surprised to see Morillo. He stiffened to attention.

'Back in June of '08 when they held Portugal. The garrison was too small to fight and sneaked away before the French got here.' Morillo's English was slow, but precise, with just a hint of an accent. 'Then they decided they could not hold it, so they blew up the bastion, stripped the place of guns and took them back to Almeida.'

'We marched to Almeida when they surrendered,' said Williams. 'The locals were none too keen on letting them go.' After Vimeiro, the British had signed a treaty letting the French evacuate Portugal and carry away all their plunder.

'Cannot say I blame them. So you have been here before?'

'Not directly. We came to Almeida last autumn.' The fortified town lay five miles away, guarding the road into Portugal. On the Spanish side, the town of Ciudad Rodrigo protected against invasion going in the other direction. 'After that we marched into Spain and joined Sir John Moore.'

'So you have seen some service, then.'

Williams nodded.

'And your commander, is he experienced?'

Williams was surprised that the Spaniard had

81

not been told about his counterpart, and was uncomfortable discussing his superior. However, there could be no harm in speaking the truth. 'I believe he is the finest officer it has been my honour to serve under.'

Morillo stared at him, as if judging his sincerity. 'He seems old.'

'Promotion rarely comes swiftly to a man without wealth or powerful friends.'

The Spaniard rubbed his chin. 'Yes, well, it is no different in our army.'

Williams looked at him more closely, and realised that he was older than he had first thought. Morillo's size and manner, as well as his glasses, reminded him a good deal of Pringle, and he had assumed that they were also of an age. Now he could see flecks of grey in Morillo's hair and lines around his mouth and eyes. Williams guessed he was closer to forty than thirty.

'It is hard to rise far for a man who is not an hidalgo,' explained the Spaniard. 'I was five years a sergeant. I would guess that is why they set me to be a drillmaster now.' His face was grim. His hand moved from his chin to his brow, and he rubbed a scar just visible under his cocked hat.

'Yet if I am not mistaken, you have also seen a good deal of service. Am I not right in recollecting you from Medellín?' Morillo started at the name. 'I watched as you and your grenadiers charged the French battery.'

'A bloody day,' the Spaniard said, shaking his

head. Soon after that charge the flanks of the Spanish army had collapsed, and then regiment after regiment of French cavalry had swept on to the plain and slaughtered half the army. Morillo was staring at Williams closely, and then tried to snap his fingers, but the sound was muted because of his gloves. 'And you were there with Cuesta's staff afterwards. Ah, you are that Englishman!' Williams and Dobson had saved General Cuesta's life, and then later, as they fled with his staff, Morillo and his grenadiers had appeared, still formed amid all the chaos, and escorted the party to safety.

Morillo held out his hand.

'Lieutenant Williams, One Hundred and Sixth Foot,' said Hamish as they shook hands.

'Well, perhaps this will do some good after all. That is, if it is not too late.' Morillo sighed. 'Come, let us get back into the warmth.'

MacAndrews gave the men an easy Christmas Day. It was scarcely a feast, but the redcoats produced bottles of brandy in that mysterious way Williams had come to expect even if he could not understand it, and together with the wine brought by the Spanish, most of the officers and men alike felt worse for wear the next day. Colonel MacAndrews and Captain Morillo both looked as fresh as their brightly polished buttons and showed no mercy to the sore heads of their followers. The two senior officers had spent much of Christmas Day shut in their office as they discussed and planned. On 26 December the men were set to fatigues, clearing more of the barracks ready for the expected students and making the fort more like an active garrison. Williams was sent on a patrol with Dobson and Murphy and two Spanish sergeants to get a feel for the area. Williams had not drunk at all, and Dobson had resolutely kept to a single tot, in spite of repeated assurances from his comrades that Mrs Dobson would understand given the season. Murphy had drunk like a fish, but as ever seemed none the worse. The British and Spanish NCOs eyed each other warily at first, but after two hours of marching, and exchanges in the few words they possessed of each other's language, they began to get along well.

MacAndrews and Morillo met every day for a long session, refining their plans, for both were earnest in their desire to make the training mission a success in spite of all the difficulties they faced. Language was a big problem. Neither of Morillo's officers spoke any English, and only a few of the sergeants knew some words. Williams and Pringle knew a little Spanish, but were more comfortable in Portuguese, and only Reynolds was moderately fluent. Several on both sides spoke French, and so conversations became an odd mixture of different tongues and fervent gestures.

MacAndrews convinced Morillo that they should teach a simplified form of the British army's drill, with Dundas' manual for formed manoeuvres and other publications for skirmishing and outpost duties. Spanish regulations had changed too much in recent years to be standard in all of their armies, or even regiments, and also did not cover some matters well. In addition, the British system was most familiar to his own staff. However, Morillo was adamant that the orders must be given in Spanish. That was the only way that the men could be sent back to their regiments in a position to pass on their training.

'We do not wish to join the English army,' he said.

'The Portuguese are retraining with British officers mixed with their own and using English drills and orders,' MacAndrews pointed out.

'We are not Portuguese,' came the reply, and that was an end to the matter.

Together they translated all the commands, and then spent the next two weeks practising with their own men, forming them into groups and drilling them in small mixed squads for as long as the light lasted during these short winter days. The Spanish learned the drills, and the British learned the words of command. There were mistakes, angry exchanges and moments of pure farce. Williams' orders once resulted in half the parade facing in the opposite direction to the other men. Laughter helped to ease the difficult moments, while MacAndrews' and Morillo's enthusiasm and determination were alike infectious.

The first group of NCOs arrived for training. There were twenty of them, drawn from regiments in the Marquis de la Romana's Army of the Right, and led by a young lieutenant. None of the men had muskets, and so MacAndrews had to ride to Almeida and persuade the governor, a Colonel Cox who was in the Portuguese service, to provide him with a wagon-load of the weapons. Until these arrived, the firelocks of MacAndrews' and Morillo's men were shared out for each drill.

On the last day of January a larger party of almost one hundred men came from the Army of Estremadura. A one-armed sergeant led them, and he was the only man with any experience. The rest were boys, conscripted into the army barely a month before. Some looked as young as fourteen, and none had received any training or equipment. They wore their own clothes, and many shivered in the cold because they had no greatcoats or other protection against the driving rain.

'Do they take me for their quartermaster?' MacAndrews angrily asked Morillo when they were alone.

'They know the English have plenty of money,' he said simply, and then shrugged. 'And they do not trust you.'

'How about you?' said the Scotsman with a twinkle in his eye, for he had come to like and rely on his colleague.

Morillo smiled. 'I'm thinking about it.'

'Well, we must change our plans and begin with

the fundamentals of drill. Now, how shall we divide them up, and who shall we put in charge?'

It meant more trips to Cox to beg for supplies. The recruits each received a grey greatcoat, which the Portuguese in Almeida managed to find in a forgotten storeroom. They were faded and musty, and must have been intended for taller men than the Portuguese, which might explain why they had not been issued. On most of the recruits the hems went down past their ankles or even brushed the ground, but they were warm. MacAndrews gave Corporal Raynor plenty of work, writing out clear copies of his own spidery drafts, bombarding Wellington's headquarters and the political authorities in Lisbon and Seville with requests for stores, supplies and money to buy locally what he needed.

'I told you,' joked Morillo. 'We Spanish all know that the English are rich.'

'Well, I'm a Scot, and I've been poor all my life!'

They did their best with what was available, and slowly help came in, but MacAndrews sometimes felt that he was abandoned and forgotten, of as much use and interest as this slighted frontier fort.

Then, as winter came to an end, the war caught up with them.

CHAPTER 7

Hanley looked at the gangs of workers piling the spoil from the ditch into a rampart and wondered whether this was yet another sign of defeat. The heights of Torres Vedras on the approaches to Lisbon were a hive of busy activity as fortifications were prepared. It was the beginning of March, and he greatly feared that the year 1810 would see the end of the war.

'I presume these are intended to cover an embarkation, should it become necessary.'

'You are the soldier, William. You tell me.' Baynes always pretended complete ignorance of all military matters. He was a stocky man, with an immense belly barely enclosed behind the straining buttons of his waistcoat. His neck was thick, his face jowly, and even the slightest effort made sweat pour down his red cheeks, making him dab at them with a once brightly coloured handkerchief. As always, Hanley found himself thinking of the portly, gout-ridden and usually either jovial or bellicose characters of stout Englishmen drawn by cartoonists – a John Bull sprung to life.

On first meeting him, it was easy to mistake

Mr Ezekiel Baynes for a simple man of business. Some might even think him stupid, but only a true fool would go on believing this for any time. As a trader in wines and spirits, Baynes, Hanley suspected, had been cunning and successful. Openly merely a man assisting government representatives with his local knowledge and connections, he was in fact one of the most important collectors and inter-preters of information and intelligence regarding the enemy, advising generals and ministers alike. Hanley knew from experience that Baynes was very clever, coldly calculating, suspicious by nature and utterly ruthless. He controlled a network of spies and informers, manipulating them as skilfully as a puppeteer pulled the strings on his marionettes, and with barely more affection for them beyond their usefulness.

'Things are not going well for our cause,' said Hanley, looking into the man's pale grey eyes and knowing that it was impossible to read them.

'No, they are not. A precise man might perhaps quibble at the presumption that we have a single cause. Possibly that is true if by "we" you mean purely His Majesty's Government, although due emphasis on the "possibly" would be prudent even in this case. If it is extended to our noble allies in Spain and Portugal, then the word is stretched considerably. Yet if stripped to mean no more than a general desire to expel the French from their countries, perhaps it will stand. For the majority at least.' He appeared to think for a moment, but

Hanley now doubted that such pauses were anything other than deliberate. 'There are some who welcome French rule, and with every defeat there will be more and more who decide that such a policy is wisest.'

'Has it become so bad?'

'It is still in the balance, but there have been too many lost battles.'

'They need a general who knows how to win,' said Colonel Murray, having jogged up to the top of the rocky outcrop to join the other two. Murray was Lord Wellington's Quartermaster General, helping the British commander to run his army from day to day, turning his plans and decisions into action. He also supervised the gathering of intelligence, and so worked closely with Baynes. A slim, dapper Scotsman, Murray was every inch the soldier, and he and the merchant worked well together. 'Damn,' he cursed, as his boots slipped on the wet grass and he had to press one gloved hand to the ground to stop himself from falling.

'Mistakes happen in war,' said Baynes with a smile.

'Damn again,' muttered Murray, whose grey trousers were now stained with mud on the knees. 'Aye, mistakes happen, but if fools are in charge they happen a damned sight more often. Ocaña was a bloody shambles.'

'Some of that was the Junta,' said Baynes. 'After so many defeats they were screaming at the generals to attack.' He turned to Hanley. 'Politicians are prone to blaming the army when it fails to make their imprudent schemes work. And then they expect the army to give them a miracle to clear the mess up.'

'Well, they got their grand attacks, and lost more than twenty thousand men to no purpose,' Murray added brutally. 'What's left of the armies are a wreck.' He gave a grim laugh. 'That's what comes of letting politicians give the orders.'

'Those politicians have paid a high price,' said Baynes, 'at least by their standards. Let us hope that the new Regency Council proves more competent, for Spain has paid an even higher price.'

In January Marshal Soult had taken a big French army south into Andalusia and overrun it in weeks. Granada had fallen, as had Seville, which had served as the capital of free Spain since Madrid was lost. 'Hardly anyone fought them,' the merchant explained, 'and city after city simply opened their gates. In some places crowds were cheering for King Joseph.' Napoleon had placed his older brother on the throne of Spain.

'Cadiz is secure?' asked Hanley, who had been watching the French near Badajoz since arriving back in the country.

'It is, and that is some comfort,' said Murray. 'General Stewart and his regiments have been permitted by the Spanish to reinforce the garrison.' That was something, for in the past the authorities had feared the creation of a new Gibraltar, making them reluctant to accept the presence of British troops. 'It will be a very tough nut for the French to crack, and even then something they will not be able to do quickly.'

'And no bad thing to find more appropriate employment for General Stewart.' Baynes' face was wooden, apart from his eyes, which danced with mirth. Stewart had for a while been in overall charge of gathering intelligence. It had proved an unsuitable role for a man happier leading bold – perhaps over-bold – cavalry charges.

Murray ignored the comment, although Hanley was aware that he had a similar opinion of the general. 'Cadiz is secure and we must be grateful for that, but we should not let ourselves get carried away. Almost all of Spain is under French rule.'

'The guerrillas and partisans would dispute that,' said Baynes.

'And we must be glad of that,' Murray responded, 'and help them as much as we can, but in the end the French will complete the conquest of each area. The same is true of the surviving strongholds.

'Napoleon is probably coming soon. He is already sending tens of thousands more soldiers to reinforce his armies here. The guerrillas nibble away at them, but they cannot stop the French from going where they will. It really is just a matter of time.'

Murray's assessment was as true as it was bleak, and yet Hanley felt his tone suggested more than simply resignation or stubborn defiance. Past experience told him that the pair wanted him to work things out rather than simply be told. That meant that there must be some hope, although he found it hard to see it. To give himself time, he decided to ask a question. 'Is the Emperor coming back to Spain?'

'So he says,' Murray replied. 'There has been a lot of talk in the Paris papers about him coming to hurl the leopards into the sea.' Hanley looked puzzled, prompting the colonel to explain. 'Haven't you heard him call us that before? It's from the leopard on the royal coat of arms. Never had a clue why he should think it insulting, but there you are.'

'For the moment Boney is busy,' said Baynes, taking over the conversation again. 'He is negotiating to marry an Austrian princess after divorcing Josephine.'

Murray sniggered. 'That should keep him busy. A nice young bride to warm his bed.'

'It may also help to keep the peace in Europe for years,' Baynes added grimly. 'His peace, that is, although the past experience of the royal houses suggests that a mere marriage alliance will not hold them back when it becomes inconvenient.'

'Yes, perhaps, but no one will fight Boney at the moment after so many victories. So if the laddie has any sense – and he's no fool, plump young princess or not – then he should come here and finish off what he has started by conquering Spain and Portugal.'

Hanley could still not see any cause for hope. 'So the war is lost.'

Murray winked at him. 'Not yet.'

'I find it hard to see how we can win,' said Hanley.

'For the moment it may be a question of not losing.' Baynes was smiling, but Hanley felt there was less confidence in his eyes than he saw in Murray. 'Time can be on our side as well, as long as we can gain enough of it. In time we can grow stronger, and in a lot of time the Spanish can perhaps rebuild their armies.'

Murray produced a map, and laid it out on the boulder in front of them. 'Help me hold this down,' he said, and so Hanley picked up some stones to use as weights.

Baynes took over as the two soldiers made the map secure. 'Portugal is the key to it all, and Lisbon is the key to Portugal. If we lose that then we lose the country and probably the war. The Portuguese army is getting the training and funds that the Spanish lack. You soldiers would judge better, but from all I hear the regiments are shaping up nicely. With them, Wellington can double his strength.'

'Aye, but we'll still be outnumbered when Boney comes.' Murray gestured at the map. 'Now, there are three ways he can come with a proper army and heavy guns. There's the central route that

Junot took back in '07, but we can probably discount that one. The land there is barren, the roads scarcely worthy of the name even by Portuguese standards, and the area so heavily plundered that an army would starve. That leaves two choices – north or south. Everyone has known that for centuries and so there are fortresses guarding the roads. In the south we have Elvas in Portugal and Badajoz over in Spain. It's none too healthy down there – you remember all those men lost to fever when we camped there after Talavera?' The other two men nodded. 'But it is certainly perfectly practical as a route.

'The other option is the northern road, guarded by Almeida on this side of the border and Ciudad Rodrigo on the Spanish side, and that is probably the weakest of all the fortresses. I am inclined to think it the more likely of the two routes, and so does Wellington, but it is far from certain. It will be easier for new forces coming from Spain to reach there quickest. However, the French are keeping us guessing, demonstrating against both. Reynier is not too far from Badajoz, while Marshal Ney watches Ciudad Rodrigo. Last month Ney marched from Salamanca and closed on the city, demanding surrender. The governor told him politely to go to hell, and after a couple of days he sloped off.'

'I believe Herrasti to be a good man,' said Baynes.

'Let us hope so.' Hanley caught the doubt in Murray's voice. 'He did not have much to fear.

Ney had no heavy guns and not enough food to mount a siege. We hear tell that he is using his artillery caissons to carry food rather than ammunition because he is so short of wagons.

'The greater part of the army is concentrating to the north, ready to meet the French if they come that way. Wellington is leaving "Daddy" Hill to watch the southern road.' Hanley remembered the kindly and capable General Hill from Talavera and wondered whether Major Wickham was still on the general's staff. 'If they do come that way then the rest of the army can quickly shift to reinforce him.'

'We want you in the north, William,' said Baynes. 'It will be important to know as much as we can about what the French are doing. There should be plenty of signs betraying their intentions if we are keen enough to spot them.'

Murray took over again. 'When they invade they will need food for a big army, carts to move it and a train of very heavy ordnance to batter their way into any fortress blocking their path. Try as they might, they cannot readily hide such preparations.

'Time is more important than almost anything else. We need time to be ready for them, and then we need to slow them down. A big army consumes supplies at a prodigious rate. The more we can slow them, then the greater their problems will become and all the while we will grow stronger.'

'Will that make enough difference?' Hanley asked. 'The odds still appear too great to beat.'

'God help us, another croaker,' said Murray, rolling his eyes.

'I do not understand.'

Baynes offered enlightenment. 'Lord Wellington is plagued by officers, many of them senior, writing home and proclaiming that Portugal cannot be saved and that the war is already as good as lost. Such letters and opinions readily make their way into the newspapers, those sources of so much wisdom.'

Colonel Murray glared at the heavy irony. 'A lot will depend on our allies,' he said. 'The Portuguese are sound.'

'At least if some of their leaders stop trying to engineer succession rights to the Spanish throne for Ferdinand VII's Portuguese wife.' Baynes' voice dripped with sarcasm. 'And strangely enough, not all are so convinced that it is worth obeying the British and sacrificing so much on behalf of an ally who may simply sail away if things turn bad and leave them both ruined and subject again to the French.'

'Britain cannot afford to lose this army,' said Murray defensively. 'But I suspect that she also cannot afford to lose this war and leave all of Europe under Boney's thumb. So we must avoid that, and that means holding on here. The Spanish can help, if the guerrillas tell us all they see and make life difficult for the French, and if Ciudad Rodrigo puts up a decent fight.'

Baynes smiled. 'Herrasti pledged to fight to the last drop of blood.'

'Words are one thing,' said Murray, 'actions another. If talk was all it took, then every last Frenchman would long since be dead or chased back across the Pyrenees.' He looked meaningfully at the merchant.

'There is a particular reason for sending you, my dear William. In Andalusia there were too many defections to King Joseph. More than a few previously staunch supporters of Ferdinand VII suddenly changed sides. Several now have high offices in Joseph Bonaparte's regime. Others are simply considerably richer than they were. It is in part a sign of the way the wind is blowing, but the French have some good men at work ahead of their advancing armies.'

'Velarde,' said Hanley.

'Possibly. We have received no definite news of him since the summer.'

Luiz Velarde was one of the artistic circle Hanley had known in Madrid before the war. He had risen quickly in the patriot forces, and seemed to be working gathering information for their benefit, sometimes with another of the young artists, José-María Espinosa. The latter had accepted service with King Joseph, but sold secrets to the British and Spanish alike. At Talavera, Velarde had helped with a deception plan, but a pretended defection to the French now seemed real. Since he had gone, Espinosa and most of the network of sources had died at the gallows or in front of firing squads.

'It may be that he is dead,' Baynes continued. 'If not, then it would be a happy outcome if we can arrange to make that the case.'

'I am no assassin,' said Hanley, remembering the last conversation he had had with the merchant before he had left for England last year.

'My dear boy, of course not, but as you told me some time ago, you are a soldier, and killing the enemy is part of the job.'

For a moment it looked as if Murray would say something, but in the end he must have decided against it.

'You will go to Ciudad Rodrigo,' Baynes continued. 'When you report, send first to Brigadier General Craufurd who commands our Light Brigade forming the outposts of the army. Colonel Murray and I will sometimes be visiting his staff, but even when not, he has orders to pass on all your communication to Lord Wellington's headquarters.'

'Now, I think that is all of my part in this, for the moment.' Murray looked at Baynes, and the merchant gave a gracious wave of his arm. 'Good. Now, I must find Colonel Fletcher and ask a few more questions. Good day to you both, and good luck to you, Hanley.' Murray shook his hand firmly.

Baynes watched him go. 'Oh dear, I fear my talk of assassins offended him. It often surprises me how coy some soldiers are when it comes to talk of killing.'

'Not killing, but murder.'

'A distinction that often escapes me, I fear,' said Baynes with deliberately exaggerated innocence. 'I have little doubt that Velarde will exert the utmost efforts to kill you.'

'You now sound certain that he is there.'

'Do I?' Baynes dabbed at his cheeks with his disreputable handkerchief. 'Well, perhaps I am, or perhaps I am simply getting nervous. So much is at stake that the least thing may tip the balance.' Hanley had rarely seen the merchant looking so committed. Or so worried. Then the moment passed, and Baynes' red cheeks seemed to glow with happiness. 'Oh, I do have some pleasant news, for it is more than likely that you will run across some old friends from your regiment up in that area.'

'The training mission to the Spanish,' Hanley began.

'Is not far from Ciudad Rodrigo,' said Baynes, cutting in. 'I believe your friends Pringle and Williams are there, as well as that splendid rogue Corporal Dobson.'

'It is Sergeant Dobson now.'

'Of course, my mistake.'

Hanley caught a flicker of amusement and was sure Baynes was playing a game, once again pretending ignorance. 'Is this your doing?' he asked, and did not for a moment expect an honest answer.

'My dear boy, I am merely a humble adviser and a simple civilian. How could I possibly play a role in the orders given to soldiers? However, it is certainly a happy chance, and they may be of help to you. You cannot tell me that Dobson is not a skilled killer.' Baynes smiled, looking like an innocent child except for his eyes. 'Or your Mr Williams, for that matter.'

CHAPTER 8

Williams tried to rub some life back into his hands and was grateful for the shelter provided by the officers' tent, even if the flaps were tied back and let the wind in. There was the heavy drumming of raindrops on the canvas as yet another downpour started, and in less than a minute individual beats were lost in a constant onslaught. The storms did not last long, but were bitter when they came, and his greatcoat was so wet that he had allowed Dobson to take it into the chapel and dry it by one of the fires lit by the greenjackets of the 95th.

'Foul night,' he said, to make conversation with the three subalterns in the tent, and as true Englishmen they considered the matter and then solemnly assented. Dolosa, one of Morillo's officers from the Princesa Regiment, nodded politely, while following little of the conversation.

'Been foul days and nights ever since we came up here,' said the bespectacled Lieutenant Mercer. The three battalions of the Light Brigade had arrived at the end of January and, supported by Hanoverian Hussars of the King's German Legion, they formed the advance posts of the British army. Since then it had rained almost every day.

'Still better than "Dough Boy hill".' That was Simmons, a small, very keen youngster who was undoubtedly on his first campaign.

'True enough. We had almost one hundred men in the company when we landed, part of one of the finest brigades ever to leave England.'

'Yes, I remember seeing you arrive at Talavera,' said Williams. The Light Brigade had force-marched very hard, but still missed the battle itself.

'You were there, Mr Williams?' asked Simmons.

'In Mackenzie's Division.' Williams felt the mood warming towards him. 'Captain Pringle was wounded near the end of the battle.' Pringle had a patrol of Spanish soldiers camped and forming its own outpost a mile and a half further down the River Agueda. Now that the British outposts were ahead of Fort La Concepción and the French had come closer, MacAndrews was extending the training to give more direct experience. In turn, parties of thirty new recruits were sent out on route marches and patrols, with some of the experienced Spanish NCOs and British leaders in charge of them. The French were enough of a presence to help give a sense of purpose to what they were teaching, and care was taken not to expose the training parties too much. This was the furthest forward they had been.

'Well, in just over half a year since then we have lost more than forty men – and none to the French,'

Mercer added. 'Fever and flux in the main. And so, yes, Mr Simmons, rain or not, it is certainly a good deal healthier up here in the north.

'And rain or not, it is time to do the rounds. Perhaps you will be kind enough to show our guests something of the position?' The young officer nodded eagerly in response. 'I'll not take you down to the pickets themselves, though, Mr Williams,' Mercer continued. 'Unfamiliar voices and more people than they expect on a dark night is a recipe for a mistake.'

Williams understood the caution. At least the rain had stopped, and he was just thinking that it should not be too uncomfortable stepping out into the night without his greatcoat when Dobson appeared, bringing it with him. The sergeant and a Spanish corporal named Gomez joined them as the enthusiastic Simmons showed them the position.

'This is the company's alarm post,' he said, tapping the side of a big boulder some fifty yards short of the crest of the ridge. The cloud had cleared for the moment and a bright moon revealed the rugged landscape at the top of the bluff. Simmons led them up. There was just a gleam in the valley below to suggest the line of the river. 'We have to report every day on the height of the water. At the moment all the rain means that it is almost at flood. Hence the advance of the infantry so far, because most of the fords are too deep to use. If it were dry, we would be further back and only the cavalry so far forward.'

Williams did his best to explain to Lieutenant Dolosa. His Spanish was improving, and the Spaniard now had a smattering of English, but these were complicated matters. Gomez understood English quite well, and that was the reason they had chosen to bring him.

'Where are your sentries?' asked Williams.

'Two men on the bridge itself, and then a sergeant's picket of a dozen men some fifty yards further back up the slope. The path winds tightly on both sides as it climbs up the valley. The rest of the company are where you saw them in the chapel, with half always kept awake, and then three companies back in the village of Barba del Puerco.'

'Beard of a pig,' said Williams.

'I beg your pardon, Mr Williams?'

'I think that is what the name means – pig's beard,' he replied, and sought confirmation from Dolosa. The Spaniard nodded and then shrugged, unwilling to speculate on the whims of the local farmers.

Simmons chuckled. 'Funny thing to call a place. They are thirty minutes from us.'

'And the French?'

'Are on the opposite side of the valley. You can see their picket in the daytime. Generally they behave, although they do tend to take pot shots at us now and again. Haven't hit a thing, though, as the range is absurdly long for a common musket.' The 95th carried rifles, and in the past Williams had noticed their disdain for more old-fashioned weapons. 'Most days they call across that they will see us tonight and slit our throats, but as yet they haven't stirred.' Simmons grinned, his teeth gleaming in the moonlight. 'I nipped across there just after dark and could not see any sign of anyone.'

Williams could not help smiling. The lad was not boasting, although obviously proud of his boldness. He was also impressed by the young officer's precise knowledge of numbers and distances, and said as much when he returned to the tent.

'Standing orders for the brigade,' explained Mercer, who had returned from his rounds. 'All courtesy of the general, God rot his black soul.' Simmons and Lieutenant Coane were taking a turn sleeping inside the chapel, and he had sent the rest of his party to join them in resting.

The hostility of many officers in the Light Brigade to their commander was something Williams had already encountered. In fact, Mercer's attitude seemed mild compared to some.

'Are you sure that I should not present my compliments to Captain O'Hare?' asked Williams, wishing to change the subject. Pringle had sent him to inform the British picket of their presence, but by the time they had missed their path in the darkness it was late and the captain had retired for the night. At least Billy had told him not to return until daylight.

'No need, old boy,' said Mercer. 'The captain

was feeling unwell and it is best not to disturb him.'

It was rather odd, but from the lieutenant's expression Williams guessed that this was not an unusual occurrence. The subject was obviously a delicate one, and for a while they lapsed into silence.

Then a shot split the night air.

Jean-Baptiste Dalmas had learned how to be patient. It was a skill that had eluded him when he was a schoolmaster and the slowness of his pupils had frustrated and angered him. Most of them tried their best, and he could still picture the strain of concentration on many of their simple faces as they struggled with Latin or geometry alike.

That was ten years and many lifetimes ago. His exemption from conscription was removed when a local beauty began to favour him instead of the major's son, and six months later he had fought at Marengo and become a sergeant. After Austerlitz he was commissioned, and by the time the Polish campaign was over and he had charged at Eylau and Friedland, he was a captain. Dalmas liked being a soldier and knew that he was a good one. The problems were so much simpler, and direct action brought clear results. Much more satisfying than trying to beat knowledge into young minds. Thankfully he had found many enemies to be as unimaginative as his former pupils.

Dalmas had spent the day watching the bridge and the British soldiers guarding it. There had been little to see, as he lay concealed behind a nest of boulders on the French side of the valley. He watched as sentries were posted, saw them relieved and visited by their officers doing the rounds, and then had watched with amusement when a lone Englishman had crept across the bridge and crawled about on the French bank. It was entertaining tracing the man's steady progress. The fellow came close at one point, but Dalmas knew that someone who did not move was hard to see and so waited, half holding his breath, until the dark shape of the Englishman moved on. It was all about patience, but at the end of the day the French captain felt that he had the measure of this enemy. They seemed capable soldiers, and Dalmas had fought the British before and knew that they could fight hard and so should not be underestimated. These men wore green uniforms, which meant that they were light infantrymen armed with rifles. Such weapons were accurate, but slow to load, and men who killed from a long distance were often reluctant to let the enemy come close.

Satisfied at last, Dalmas crawled back from his little nest, feeling pains in his limbs as the blood started to flow again. He was cold and stiff, his long coat drenched from the earlier rain, but he had learned all that he could about the enemy position and knew that the plan could work. He reached the road and followed it as it twisted and turned up the steep side of the valley.

The first company of infantry was already sitting on its packs just behind the ridge and the others were coming up to join them. A group of officers in long cloaks stood beside the resting men. Dalmas went up to them and saluted.

'Ah, Dalmas,' said Général de Brigade Ferey. 'Not in your helmet today!'

Captain Dalmas belonged to the 1st Regiment of Cuirassiers, although he had lately heard that the detachment in Spain was to be combined with others to form a new regiment, the 13th. Perhaps he would return to them one day, but for more than a year he had served as an additional ADC on the staff of Marshal Ney. Disdaining the fripperies of flamboyant uniforms so popular with most staff officers, Dalmas made a point of wearing his steel helmet with its black horsehair crest and his heavy cuirass. It was a mark that he was a serious soldier, and perhaps a conceit, for only a determined man would keep such uncomfortable gear when he did not have to wear it. Tonight he wore instead a soldier's bonnet, and had plain trousers and simple hessian boots rather than the knee-high boots of his regiment.

'Didn't want to rust, General,' he said cheerfully. Ferey was not yet forty, and had a fine record as a fighting general. Dalmas liked the man, trusted his judgement and hoped to rise as far himself.

The Emperor was generous when it came to rewarding success.

'So, what have you seen?' Ferey had offered to send one of his own aides with Dalmas, but the latter had refused and had a good enough reputation to be given his way.

'A pair of sentries at the bridge. Then a dozen men a short way back. All are their green riflemen. Does not look like more than a company here, and the rest are back beyond the top of the crest.'

'Shouldn't be too much of a problem, then.' The general drew his sword, and swished the blade impatiently so that it hissed in the night air. 'What is the approach like?'

'The road is easy to follow, but winds a lot and is steep. The river flows high and fast and is very noisy. That should cover the sound until they get close. The bridge is narrow and long, and turns sharply to the right as you approach from our side, and less so on the far bank.'

'Barricaded?'

'No.'

'Well, that's very kind of them.' The general turned to one of his own aides. 'Get them up and ready. The first two companies go in unloaded, but have the captains check that the men have dry cartridges in their pouches.' Ferey did not want an accidental shot to warn the British. Dalmas was inclined to agree with him, although it meant that they would be unable to fire if they ran into opposition. Perhaps for the best. If men could fire, then they were more inclined to stop and shoot rather than keep advancing, and the trick tonight would be to press on whatever happened and overwhelm the outnumbered defenders.

'Permission to go with them, sir,' asked Dalmas.

'Denied,' replied the general instantly and with some force. 'Old red-faced Ney wants you back in one piece,' he added more quietly. 'I have a good man to take them in. Better an officer they know rather than a stranger.'

No doubt the general had some favourite to reward, Dalmas thought sourly. The attack should work. The whole brigade had moved to a village several miles away, and so they had slept in the dry and not had far to come. Six elite companies, the grenadiers and voltigeurs supposed to be the pick of their regiments, were in the lead, with the main force of the brigade moved close enough to support if necessary. If they could surprise the enemy, and then go in hard and fast, they should be able to storm the position and kill or capture all of the British. Dalmas had seen no sign that the greenjackets were expecting them.

'Have you fought the rosbifs before?' asked the general.

'They are tough – stubborn like the Russians, but more flexible.' It was the British who had given Dalmas his only defeat when he was in command, and he knew that a man needed to win a lot more victories to make the Emperor forget any failure. Over a year ago, when the redcoats were fleeing to Corunna, Dalmas had been sent to take another bridge and open a way behind the enemy. It nearly worked, but a redcoat officer named Williams in charge of a ragged force of men from many regiments had somehow ended up in his way and then repulsed his attacks. Since then Dalmas had constantly played over his decisions in his mind. There were mistakes and he would learn from them, but so much of it had been luck. It was not so much his pride that irked him. A soldier needed to be proud, but Dalmas felt himself to be a clever man, in control of his emotions, and he resented far more the stain of failure which had interrupted his previously rapid rise. The former schoolteacher wanted to make his name and his fortune while there were still wars to fight and glory to be won.

General Ferey left him and walked across to where the two companies stood in rank.

'Lads, we are going over that hill and then over a bridge and up the other side!' he announced. With the noise of the wind he had no need to worry about the sound carrying to the enemy. 'There's a half-company of fancy fellows in green waiting on the other side. They think they are clever because they have rifles and can shoot further than us, but it's night, and they couldn't see a donkey's arse at thirty paces, let alone shoot it.' Dalmas saw the men in the front rank grinning. They all wore long greatcoats and had their white cross-belts over them. On their shoulders were epaulettes of the elite companies – red for the grenadiers and green and yellow for the voltigeurs, although in the dark he could see little more than their shapes and the dull gleam of their white cross-belts. No one had bothered to fit plumes to their shakos, although one of the leading grenadier companies wore tall bearskin caps instead, making each man look bigger.

'You all know how it's done,' continued General Ferey. 'Yes, I can see you, Dubois, hiding there in the rear rank. This'll be a picnic compared to Austerlitz. Take that ridge on the other side and there is a gold piece in it for every man.' He paused for a moment. 'And double rations of food and wine!' They were all smiling at that and nodding, but had sense enough not to cheer.

'One last thing. These fellows are English so they are no match for Frenchmen. But they're not like the Spanish and are proper soldiers – just not very good ones! Kill any bastard who fights you, but let them surrender and treat the wounded with respect.

'That's all I have to say and all you need to know. So go and do it!'

As the column marched up the hill, Ferey walked back to Dalmas and his staff. 'We go with the supports, but everyone stays this side of the bridge until it's over,' he said firmly. 'Too many officers over the other side will only confuse things, and we need to keep it simple.' The two assaulting companies marched on, and the general and his staff joined the second column formed from the remaining four companies. 'We go halfway down the slope and then watch.' He appeared to have a thought. 'In fact, Dalmas and Legrand, hurry on up there and watch from as close to the bridge as you can.'

Dalmas liked the general, and was happy to be given this task. Legrand was as bulky as his name suggested, and moved clumsily across the rocky slope, but at least the constant roar of the river would drown that out. Dalmas could see the darker shade of the leading grenadiers moving along the road beneath them, but could not hear them. The same ought to be true of the sentries. He hurried on, letting the general's aide cope as best he could, and was soon lying face down on a big outcrop. He drew his glass and focused the lens on the far side of the river. A movement caught his eye, and he knew that it was one of the British sentries. Dalmas shifted the telescope and again spotted movement, this time just above the parapet on the bridge itself. He sensed that the officer in charge was doing just what he would do, detaching a sergeant and six or seven good men to stalk the sentries. Dalmas flicked back to the enemy bank, and struggled for a moment to spot the guards. Then darker shadows moved quickly and surrounded them.

He was looking in just the right spot when a red gout of flame erupted from the black night as a weapon was fired, and in that instant he thought he saw a man slumping to the ground and another being wrestled by three men.

'Damn,' said Dalmas, just as Legrand stumbled down beside him. For the moment it was hard for him to see anything apart from the bright flame only slowly fading from his eyes. The night seemed blacker than before, and he knew that it would take a few minutes to adapt again.

A volley of half a dozen shots ripped out from further up the British slope.

'Stand to! Stand to!' shouted Lieutenant Mercer, as men began to bundle out of the little chapel. Half the reserve was always to be awake and dressed, and these men were first while the others hastily pulled on jackets and belts, for they had slept with trousers and boots on.

Williams was impressed by how quickly the greenjackets stood to arms. Mercer was already forming them into a line two deep at the alarm post, and other men were running up.

'Coane!' Mercer called. 'Be so good as to fetch the captain.'

Dobson was suddenly beside Williams, and handed him his musket, before unslinging his own. 'It's loaded, sir,' he said. Williams had forgotten giving it to him. Corporal Gomez was beside him, his own firelock held ready.

'The lieutenant has gone to Mr Pringle,' said the Spaniard in his clear but heavily accented English.

There was no point in saying anything to that,

and perhaps Dolosa was right, although whether he could find his way to the picket in the dark was another matter. Williams took the two NCOs and joined the riflemen.

'We are with you, Mercer,' he said, and got a nod in response.

There had been scattered shots while they formed and then after a minute or so there came an intense rattle of musketry. Then it went quiet.

'Come on, boys,' said Mercer, and took them forward.

'Don't shoot, don't shoot!' cried an English voice, and a man appeared over the crest.

'Don't fire, lads,' called the lieutenant.

'The bridge is taken, Sergeant Betts fallen and they are pouring across like demons,' gasped the soldier, but then he fell in with the rest and followed them back over the crest and down the slope. A few more survivors came towards them, two of them dragging the unconscious sergeant, whose jaw was shattered by a musket ball.

'There they are!' shouted a voice. Williams could not tell who it was, but then he spotted the darker shapes moving up the slope towards them. The moon appeared again, and he could see figures, their white belts catching the light.

'Just a bit further, boys,' shouted Mercer. The French were swarming across a more open patch where the path widened for a short distance. 'Halt. Present!' The line of three dozen or so greenjackets stopped and brought their rifles up to their shoulders. Williams was on the left, with Dobson next to him and Gomez as the sergeant's rear rank man. Their muskets were much longer than the stubby rifles.

Suddenly, two men further to their right fired, great gouts of flame stabbing into the night, and then shots erupted all down the two ranks of greenjackets. Williams had forgotten the 95th's practice of letting the men fire in their own time rather than to order.

'Fire!' he yelled, but Dobson must already have reacted for his musket flamed beside Williams as he shouted the word. Gomez fired a fraction of a second later and then the officer pulled the trigger of his own firelock and felt the charge go off and the musket slam back against his shoulder.

Then there was silence – a quiet that seemed unnatural after the rippling volley – and all that he could hear was the men unbuttoning cartridge boxes, the slight snap as they bit off the ball, and then the scraping of ramrods.

'Well done, lads,' called Mercer. 'Pour it into them.'

French drums began to beat, the drummers hammering out the unrelenting rhythm of the charge, urging the men on. The moon had gone behind the clouds again, and it was hard to see the enemy clearly, but Williams did not think they were coming closer.

The French fired, some fifty or so muskets shattering the darkness with flame and noise, and

Williams could hear balls snapping through the air a foot or so above his head. More enemy grenadiers fired, and he could tell that the small group of riflemen was heavily outnumbered. He remembered Simmons telling him that the main supports were half an hour away and tried to work out how many minutes had passed since the alarm had been given. It was so hard to tell once the firing started, but he doubted that much time had gone by. If the French made a determined charge, he was not sure that the small picket could hold them.

His musket loaded, Williams fired down the slope.

'Get moving, you damned fools, get moving!' Dalmas shouted, and then pushed himself up and ran forward. The attack was stalling and someone needed to get the men moving again. Some would die as they closed, but that was inevitable, and more might well die to little purpose if they simply stopped and fired.

'You're not going!' called General Ferey, who grabbed him by the arm. Dalmas had not seen him and his staff standing at the head of one of the reserve companies. 'It is not your business.'

They all looked up the far side of the valley and could see the flashes of muskets. The general made a decision.

He tapped an officer on the shoulder. 'LeRoque,' he said, 'take your company up there and try to work around their flanks. Go!'

The officer doubled forward, the rattle of the company's equipment and the pounding of their feet lost in the roar of the river below. The men were voltigeurs, the skirmishers of a battalion, and supposed to be chosen from cunning, agile men, and perhaps they would be able to outflank the British, but Dalmas wished the general had ordered them straight up the road. That would be a risk, as there was a chance that they would stop and start firing like the men already there, but if well led they might just as easily get the whole line going forward again.

There was more firing from up the slope, and Dalmas thought that their soldiers were edging slowly towards the English, but wished that he was up there and able to do something. Then he wished that they were fighting anywhere other than near a damned bridge again, but he was not a superstitious man, and quickly dismissed the thought.

'Get forward,' he muttered under his breath, 'get forward.'

CHAPTER 9

Williams knelt behind a broad rock, and now that the moon was out again and he could see better, he tried to take careful aim. Dobson was sitting with his back to the stone, loading his musket, and Gomez crouched down beside him ready to fire. Without orders the British had shaken out of formation and sought cover on the craggy, boulder-strewn slope. The French were doing the same, and although the two sides were little more than ten or fifteen yards apart, he guessed that so far they had done each other little harm.

He aimed at the silhouetted head of a French officer who was making flamboyant gestures, trying to urge his men on. The drums were still beating, but the enemy had not charged. A few Frenchmen crawled forward to find whatever cover they could in the more open patch, but so far their officers had failed to get their men to make a rush.

Confident of his aim, Williams closed his eyes for a moment before he pulled the trigger, but that only partly shielded him from the dazzling flame of his own shot. He blinked a few times, but when he could see properly again, the French officer was still there, and it looked as if the man was beating one of his own soldiers with the flat of his sword. Williams slid back behind the rock and began to reload. He saw Mercer and Simmons scurrying along behind the skirmish line, and when he had finished charging his musket, he scampered over to join them.

'Well done, lads,' Mercer kept calling out, 'we're holding them!' The moonlight glinted off his glasses and he gave a broad smile as Williams came up. 'Not as hot work as Talavera, I suspect,' he said cheerfully. 'But our brave fellows fight like Britons.'

A bullet smashed through the right lens of his glasses, punched through the eye behind and drove deep into the lieutenant's brain. Mercer's head snapped back, and then his whole body slumped down. Simmons looked stunned, staring at the friend who had been so lively a moment ago and an instant later was dead.

'The devils!' shouted out a young private who was crouched in a low hollow next to them and had just finished reloading. 'They have shot Mr Mercer!' The boy sprang to his feet and waved his rifle high in the air. 'You rogues,' he screamed at the French, and it struck Williams that men said such strange things in battle.

'Come on, boys, avenge the death of Mr Mercer!' The private ran forward into the clearing, and Williams wondered for a moment whether the whole skirmish line would follow him.

'Stop, you daft sod!' shouted a voice, and no one else moved.

The young soldier ran forward, going in a straight line, and balls flicked up the grass or pinged off rocks as he passed, but nothing touched him. He ran down the slope, vaulted over a voltigeur who lay on the ground reloading and just stared up open mouthed at the mad Englishman.

Williams could see the French officer he had fired at gesturing to his men to shoot the lone greenjacket down, and then the rifleman was just a few yards away and the lad swung his rifle up to his shoulder. The flame seemed almost to touch the officer, whose head shattered into a spray of blood and bone that in the darkness looked like a brief wild smear.

Both sides seemed stunned, but only for an instant, and then a dozen French muskets flamed and the young private's body jerked and shuddered as the balls struck home at so short a range.

'Silly bugger,' said a voice as the man dropped.

'Brave bugger,' said another rifleman.

'Dead bugger,' said a third.

Williams patted Simmons on the shoulder. 'Your company, Mr Simmons.'

The young second lieutenant blinked, gulped and absent-mindedly wiped some of Mercer's blood off his own cheek just as if it were rainwater. 'Of course,' he said. 'Would you be good enough to watch the left flank for me?'

'Keep firing, boys,' shouted Simmons, his voice

high-pitched but steady, and it was better that they heard someone they knew.

Williams passed his musket to Gomez, who was now reloading and handing the charged firelocks to Dobson. He drew his sword, and paced up and down behind the skirmish line. He saw movement on the far right of the French line and guessed that they were trying to get around behind him.

The officer ran back to the end of the line. He saw a private from the 95th, staring in shock at a comrade stretched on the ground, and when he got closer he could see that part of the man's skull had been ripped open. The fallen soldier groaned softly, but nothing could be done to help him.

'Come with me,' he told the other man, and then, after he had passed another four or five greenjackets, he took another pair from the line. 'Follow me!'

Williams led them to a big outcrop just beyond Dobson and Gomez. 'The French are trying to get around us.' He pointed at the shapes of men slipping between the boulders ahead of them. Amid the noise of shots, they could catch shouted orders and encouragement, and the constant drums.

'Wait until they get closer, and you can see a clear mark.'

The French came on quicker than he expected, their white belts bright.

'Fire!' called Williams out of habit, but in spite of their training the greenjackets responded and five shots spat out in a little volley that dropped two of the leading voltigeurs. The rest fell back and took cover, and in a moment they too were firing, balls striking the rocks the British were using as cover.

'Sergeant Dobson, you are in charge,' said Williams, who was thankful that the three men from the 95th were privates and that the old veteran was senior. 'Keep them back. I need to see Mr Simmons and make sure they are not trying anything on our right.'

Williams jogged away. A rifleman was crawling back from the skirmish line, but he could not stop to help and pressed on. Another man lay dead, and Williams was afraid that the French numbers were beginning to tell.

'Who the devil are you!' demanded a thickset man, with a pistol in one hand and his curved sabre in the other. 'And where the hell is Mercer?'

'Mercer is dead, and Simmons in charge.' Williams could smell brandy on the man's breath and guessed that this must be Captain O'Hare. 'I'm Williams of the One Hundred and Sixth.'

'Never heard of him,' came the gruff reply. 'How is the boy doing?'

'He is doing well,' said Williams, and the pair started moving over towards the right flank. Simmons was there, taking men from the line to stop the French working around the British position. As they began firing at the enemy, the young second lieutenant reported as best he could amid the noise. Williams told them what was happening on the left.

'Good lad, Simmons!' said O'Hare. The man may still have been a little drunk, but as far as Williams could see it would not prevent him from doing his job here. 'You too, whoever the blazes you are. Back to the other end of the line, while Simmons stays here.'

'Right, my bonny boys!' O'Hare's Irish accent grew even stronger. 'There's no parcel of bloody Frogs going to walk over Peter O'Hare!'

Williams ran back to the far end of the line. It had gone dark again, and he stumbled once on a fallen backpack, but pressed himself up again and ran on.

'We will never retire!' shouted the Irish captain, his voice loud but calm, as if he were stating an obvious fact. 'Here we stand. They shall not pass, but over my body!'

'Ol' Pete's in a right fit,' laughed a corporal as he passed.

When he reached Dobson, Gomez was just passing the veteran a loaded firelock. One rifleman sat behind the boulders, gently rocking back and forth as he clutched an arm that looked to be broken.

'Sent the other two lads further up the slope to stop the *crapauds* getting around us,' said Dobson, and then he pulled the trigger.

'Well done, Dob,' said Williams, and went to look for the pair of greenjackets.

'*En avant! En avant!*' The shouts were loud and close. Williams could see the two privates crouched behind a thorn bush, and then spotted three voltigeurs coming from the side towards them.

'Ware right! French infantry!' he called, and wished that there had been time to learn the men's names. The men turned, saw the new threat. One fired, and the noise was strange – louder than usual and followed by a weird hissing – but one Frenchman was down, groaning horribly. The other two came on, and the rifleman dropped his weapon and fled. His comrade fired a moment later, and Williams was close enough to see a Frenchman's forehead blossom into dark blood as the man pitched back, but the third voltigeur was coming on, his bayonet reaching towards the greenjacket.

Williams flung his right arm out in a wild slash and his sword managed to knock the man's musket aside. The rifleman reacted quickly, flicking his rifle around in his hands and jabbing at the Frenchman with the heavy, brass-capped butt. The voltigeur dodged, but that gave Williams time to recover, and he was just about to cut down when his foot slipped and the blow became a carve that sliced into the man's nose and across his cheek.

The Frenchman spat an insult mixed with a spray of blood at him, and twisted his musket and

126

bayonet round to thrust at the officer. Williams grabbed the barrel of the voltigeur's musket, feeling the heat through his glove, for the man had obviously been firing, and then the private from the 95th slammed the butt of his rifle into the Frenchman's face, knocking him out.

'Thanks,' said Williams as he tried to get his breath back. He looked around, but no more Frenchmen were coming from that direction and he presumed these were a few bold spirits who had worked their way behind the British.

The private who had fled reappeared, looking sheepish. 'Needed a new rifle,' he said by way of explanation, and Williams noticed that the man he had shot was impaled through the chest with a slim rod of metal. 'Shot my ramrod as well as the ball.'

A bugle sounded, the notes clearer than the drums and carrying over the shots and shouts. Williams looked up and saw a line of men spilling over the crest.

'It's the supports, Billy Boy,' said the man to his friend who had fired off his ramrod. 'It's the colonel.'

'Up, lads!' O'Hare shouted. 'Stand up. Now we'll show these rogues a thing or two.'

Williams signalled to the two riflemen to rejoin the main line and then sped back to Dobson and Gomez.

'Fix swords!' This was a very deep voice, carrying strongly down the slope. The rifle used by the 95th was short, and to help it match the reach of muskets its bayonet was very long, the brass hilt shaped like a sword. Williams listened to the scrapes and clicks as the blades were clipped on to muzzles.

'Might as well help them, Dob,' he said. Gomez grinned wickedly as he slid his own bayonet on to the muzzle of the musket. 'We'll go to the left, and make sure none of the French get missed in the dark.'

'Charge!' The same loud voice echoed along the side of the valley, and a cheer went up, as well over a hundred greenjackets ran as fast as they could down the rocky hillside.

Muskets flamed ahead of them. Williams saw a rifleman drop, but there was no check, and the weight of their packs made it harder for the men charging downhill to stop than to keep going.

Dobson loped along beside him, but Gomez was streaking ahead. Williams watched as the Spaniard jumped on to the top of the boulder and then kicked the Frenchman crouching behind it in the face, before jumping down and thrusting with his bayonet.

There were fewer shots now, and instead screams and grunts somehow audible over the noise of the torrent. They caught up with Gomez, who was busy rifling the pockets of the voltigeur he had killed. No more French were to be seen, but there was still fighting further down the slope, and Williams was about to lead them down when he looked at Dobson and realised that his belt showed just as brightly as the white belts of the French.

'You two stay here,' he said. 'That is an order, Sergeant Dobson,' he added when the veteran looked inclined to respond. 'Too easy for the Ninety-fifth to see those belts of yours and think you are Frenchies.'

Williams made his way cautiously down towards the bridge. The French were in full retreat, but isolated men still fought on. He passed a rifleman tending to a wounded comrade, and then headed towards the same loud voice that had ordered the charge. The owner proved to be a giant of a man, bigger even than Williams himself, and he strode down the hill with his men, calling out encouragement. It struck Williams that the 95th were a good deal more vocal in battle than regiments of the line, but perhaps that was all part of their new style of warfare.

He had to use his hand to support himself as he scrambled over a bigger outcrop, and then he dropped into a little dell and saw an officer grappling with a pair of French grenadiers. Williams started forward, sword ready, but before he got there, a broad-shouldered greenjacket shot out from the side and ran one of the grenadiers through, so that several inches of his sword bayonet came out of the man's back. He dropped rifle and bayonet as the Frenchman slumped down, screaming in agony, and together the private and the officer beat the other grenadier to the ground with their fists.

Williams pressed on, and after a moment's searching once again found the very big officer, who seemed to be in charge and so presumably was the battalion commander. As he watched, the man flicked his right arm forward in a peculiar way that did not seem to make sense as a gesture. Then he dropped, and Williams wondered whether he had been hit, even though he had not seen the flash of a musket or heard a shot. He ran on, and as he got nearer, the man stood upright again, and this time Williams was close enough to see a stone in his great fist, before the man flung it down the slope at the enemy.

'Take that, you French blackguards,' he boomed out cheerfully, before bending down to find another missile, which followed the others. 'Well, enough fun,' he added as he saw Williams approaching. 'Ninety-fifth, rally on me!'

Williams saluted. 'Lieutenant Williams, sir.'

'Pleasure to meet you. Didn't realise anyone had stopped by for our little soirée, but you are most welcome. How many are you?'

'Three, sir.'

'But each worth a dozen, I am sure,' said Lieutenant Colonel Beckwith, and then he turned and looked about him. 'Where are you, Phipps?' A bugler stepped forward. 'Good fellow. Now sound the recall.

'Quite a night,' said Beckwith. 'No one expects

riflemen to stand up to line troops, but we are something different.'

'The men charged as boldly as any line regiment, sir,' said Williams, and meant it.

'Kind of you to say so,' said the colonel, obviously delighted. 'Now am I correct in thinking you are with the Spanish outpost on our right?'

'Yes, sir.'

'Good. I sent a company that way in case they were under attack, and brought the other two up here.'

Williams wondered whether the company had gone to cover the ford in support or because the 95th were afraid to trust their flank to Spanish soldiers.

The riflemen began to rally, and Beckwith was soon giving orders for a strong detachment to watch the bridge.

Stewart, the adjutant and the man Williams had seen tussling with two grenadiers, arrived and reported. 'Twenty-three casualties altogether, sir. Poor Mercer killed, along with seven men killed and fifteen wounded. Against that, at least two French officers dead with a dozen of their men. Perhaps half as many wounded and one or two prisoners. Reckon they must have carried the rest of the injured away.'

Williams felt the adjutant was being optimistic. It was often surprising how a fierce fight might still produce only a few casualties. Not that that was much solace to the ones who were hit.

'Looks as if half of them were drunk, they came on so wildly.'

Perhaps, thought Williams, once again deciding that it was better to say nothing, but maybe the French were simply brave.

A prisoner was brought to the colonel. In the attack those few Frenchmen he had seen looked like hardened veterans, but this captive was a mere boy, shivering more with terror than cold. To Williams' amazement he still carried a musket, held low in both hands. Beckwith spotted the same thing.

'Best to take that off him,' he said in a rumbling whisper. The private escorting him reached for the weapon, and the prisoner let go with his right hand before the soldier had grabbed it. The musket's butt fell heavily, butt striking the ground so hard that the flint snapped down, setting off the powder in the pan and then the main charge, and sending the ball punching through Beckwith's shako.

For a moment they all simply stared in stunned surprise, the Frenchman in abject horror. Then the private reacted and brought his rifle up, pulling the hammer back with a click and pointing straight at the prisoner's head. 'Ye damned murderer,' he said in a thick Yorkshire accent.

'Stop!' ordered Beckwith, with a composure Williams found particularly impressive. 'No harm done, except perhaps to my hatter's heart. Let the poor fellow alone. I dare say the boy has a mother. Just knock that thing from his hand to prevent

132

him doing any more mischief with it, and then kick him on the bum and send him to the rear.'

'Aye, sir,' said the rifleman happily.

'Well, it looks like all the excitement is over,' said Beckwith as they left. Then he guffawed with laughter. 'Now that would have been a damned silly way to die,' he added, pulling off his shako and sticking his finger through the holes in each side.

An hour before dawn a bedraggled Pringle arrived at the chapel used by the outpost. With him were only Sergeant Murphy and two Spanish NCOs.

'Dolosa arrived some time after all the shooting started. Said that the Ninety-fifth were under attack and that we must withdraw, because we had only raw recruits with no more than ten rounds a man.' Pringle paused, hungrily devouring a bowl of stew brought by one of the greenjackets. 'I suppose he was right in a way, but I said that I wasn't going and that I did not think he should either. He went anyway, although I'm pleased to say these two fellows chose to stick with me. But it did mean that when the Ninety-fifth arrived, my outpost consisted of myself and three men. Just as well the ford was too deep to cross,' he added glumly.

'Where are they now?' asked Williams.

'Goodness only knows. Still stumbling about the hills, I expect, making a damned poor show of themselves, and scarcely presenting a ringing endorsement of our tuition.' Pringle spooned up the rest of the stew with great satisfaction.

'There was tea around as well,' Williams said mischievously, knowing that Billy hated the stuff, but faced constant pressure from his soldier servant to change his mind.

'Well, that is one relief. At least there is no Jenkins lurking about, mug in hand, and waiting to pounce. Less pleasant is the prospect that we now have to go and find our soldiers.'

Williams forced himself to get to his feet. He was tired, and in the last thirty minutes had struggled to keep his eyes open.

Pringle noticed his expression. 'I know, I know,' he said, 'but it must be done. That's unless you can arrange for the French to attack again and give us an excuse to stay.'

'We could send an invitation.'

'Or we could just do our job.' Pringle looked even wearier, having had a difficult march to get there while it was still dark. 'Cannot say that it is my idea of fun either, but there you are. So come along, young Bills, and let us find our wandering schoolboys!'

'That may not prove so difficult.' Williams pointed back towards the crest, where a forlorn figure in an ill-fitting greatcoat was threading his way among the rocks.

'Hmm, bit late, but at least that one went in the right direction.' Billy Pringle sighed.

A couple more of the recruits now appeared

from behind the chapel, and walked towards some French prisoners – one of them the young lad who had almost shot Beckwith – with looks of hatred on their faces.

Pringle decided to solve the matter in the most practical way open to any officer. 'Sergeants!' he called.

CHAPTER 10

anley loved Salamanca, and part of him wanted to follow the priest as he returned to his college after handing over the package of letters. Instead, the British officer took out his glass and focused on the distant towers. It would be pleasant to walk across the Roman bridge into the city, but even more useful to talk to some of his sources directly, instead of simply reading reports. There were always more questions, and someone's expression helped when judging their reliability. Yet Salamanca was the main base of Marshal Ney's 6th Corps, and it was simply not yet worth the risk. Nor was there enough time to linger, for he needed to hurry if he was to make his next meeting. Closing the telescope, he hauled himself back into the saddle, and then prodded the mare in the flanks to set her trotting back between the scattered trees and brush.

His guide was waiting, back where the trees were denser, and the officer's smile prompted the usual curt nod as its sole acknowledgement. Benito had lost an arm last year, and so his ability to fight with El Charro's band had gone, but Hanley had quickly come to trust his knowledge of the country. He suspected that this was the legacy of long years as a thief and smuggler before the war. It was hard to tell the man's age, for although his thin remnant of hair was white and his skin looked like old parchment, he was strong. Even one-handed, Hanley reckoned that the man would make a nasty enemy.

They rode for three hours through the steady rain, and in truth Hanley was disinclined to speak, more concerned with keeping his boat-cloak tightly drawn around his neck. Sometimes they stopped at farms to eat, but on this damp April day Benito grunted that there was no one he trusted near by, and so they tethered their horses outside a small shrine next to a ruined cattle pen and sat to eat. Hanley had some ham to add to the loaf provided by the guide, and he watched in fascination as Benito one-handedly flicked open his knife, and then, gripping the meat between his knees, carved it into thin slices.

'*Bueno,*' he said a little later, after eating the simple meal with every sign of satisfaction.

The pair rode on for another four hours, and still the rain fell, but only once did they see any signs of a French patrol, and then in the distance. It was hard to be sure with the steady rain misting the air, but Hanley thought that they were dragoons, and Benito led him away quickly. Patrols were the real danger, because otherwise they gave a wide berth to all the French posts. Ney's corps was spread thinly, and from captured letters Hanley knew that the French were having problems gathering food and fodder.

By nightfall they had reached a small band of guerrillas led by a captain who still wore the faded yellow jacket of one of the regular cavalry regiments. He had barely twenty men, a couple of them deserters from the foreign regiments in French service, and so contented himself with watching the enemy, only attacking isolated stragglers or making night-time visits to the houses of those who proclaimed loyalty to Joseph Bonaparte.

'Junot is laying siege to Astorga,' said the captain, after Hanley had shared some wine with him. They were in a farmhouse high up in the hills, and had sentries posted along the only two paths to come this way. Hanley was not sure whether the farmer was an old friend or too scared to refuse the band of partisans. 'He moved at the end of March. The city is holding, but for how long . . .' The Spanish officer shrugged.

He was hearing the same news from all his sources, and was sure now that it was true. Ney remained dispersed around Salamanca, and General Junot's 8th Corps had gone north to attack the fortified city of Astorga. It was almost the last important stronghold in that area, and when it fell – there was no one capable of marching to the city's relief and so it was not a matter of if, but when – the French would dominate yet more of Spain.

138

'Sieges are usually costly,' said Hanley. 'Think of Saragossa.' During the early stages of the war, the Aragonese city of Saragossa had tested the French sorely, the defenders not giving up when their walls were breached, but fighting street to street and house to house. It was said that at one stage the French and Spanish battled for days inside the cathedral. The first siege failed, but the French came back, and although their losses were dreadful, in the end they took the place.

'Astorga is not Saragossa,' said the captain. 'Its walls are old and there are not many defenders.'

'A month?' asked Hanley.

'Maybe three weeks,' said the Spaniard, and Hanley could see the deep gloom in the man's eyes. He was seeing the same mood wherever he went, for everyone could see that the French were winning. Men like this were not giving up, but were unable to see any real hope, and so they fought on without it because they loved their country and hated to be trampled by the invaders.

Time was important. Hanley still did not quite understand why Murray and Baynes had hammered home that point, for as far as he could see it would take years and not months to make a difference. Yet if they were right the French did not seem to realise it. Even a few weeks of delay while one of the corps marked down to invade Portugal was sent off to the north meant that it was a little longer before that invasion could start.

The French did not seem to be in a hurry. Napoleon had not yet come, but a copy of *Le Moniteur* reported his marriage to Princess Marie Louise of Austria, so perhaps he would soon leave for Spain. For it was certain that the French were preparing, and as Hanley searched through the letters brought by the priest he saw plenty of signs of this. Ney was gathering reserves of supplies at Salamanca, and had ordered the construction of dozens of big new ovens. That meant he planned to turn stocks of grain into bread or hard-tack biscuit for use when the campaign actually started. The French marshal was still short of transport wagons and the beasts to pull them. Hanley's sources had also managed to steal several orders for local commanders to buy any they could find and send them back to the corps. Hanley smiled. It was always a sign that the French were desperate for something when they spoke of paying, for when things were easy to find they simply took what they wanted. That only made farmers and merchants careful to hide as much as they could, so in harder times coin was used to coax them.

Money featured heavily in the documents and reports. The Emperor had ordered his armies in Spain to fund themselves locally, and no doubt that was easier to say in Paris than to make a reality in the field. Hanley read of bickering between the marshals and generals, each trying to keep the resources from the region he controlled for personal use. In some cases that use was very personal indeed, as men plundered the country and kept the money for themselves. One of his best sources had sent a bundle of letters describing the row between Ney and General Loison after the latter arrested eleven women from the town of Benevente and demanded a huge ransom from their families for their release.

'I wouldn't pay,' said the captain gruffly when Hanley told him about it. 'There are always more women.'

It was a woman who provided the best of Hanley's reports – or rather a lady. The world knew her as La Doña Margarita Madrigal de las Altas Torres, the widowed daughter-in-law of the head of one of the greatest families of Old Castile, and as a heroine of the siege of Saragossa. Hanley knew that her heroism was as real as her identity was false. The real lady had died of fever as she returned from the New World, and so her maid had taken her place and used her mistress's wealth and position to fight the French. La Doña Margarita – even Hanley still thought of her naturally by that name – received reports from people all over the country, paying where necessary, and passing it on to the Allied armies. Last year she had travelled widely, her family connections securing her passes from both sides, but that was when she had pretended to be pregnant with the heir to the title. The baby was 'born' near Christmas, and for the last months she had remained in one of the family's houses in Salamanca. Hanley did not know where the boy came from, but presumably it was an orphan or a child whose parents were willing to part with him.

Hanley wondered whether the secret would remain a secret for very long. For the moment, the lady was busily gathering every piece of information she could. There was a lot about the arrival of several companies of engineers. The officers and men were there, but at the moment their equipment and supplies were still at Burgos some three hundred miles away. General Ruty headed the engineers, and one letter forwarded by La Doña Margarita explained that he had had to convince the paymaster of 6th Corps to advance him 200,000 francs to feed his soldiers and purchase tools for them.

The detail about the engineers was exceptionally good, and La Doña Margarita explained that much came from a new source, the mistress of a major on Ruty's staff. The woman called herself Molly, claimed to be English and was certainly a foreigner of some sort, and expected to be well paid. La Doña Margarita had given the woman what she wanted, and Hanley believed that she had done the right thing. When the invasion came the French would rely on their engineers to besiege the fortresses in their path, so keeping a close eye on Ruty and his men was well worth the expense.

Hanley's mind wandered to think more about La Doña Margarita herself. She was a tall, dark-eyed and dark-skinned young woman, with a round face and very long black hair. He admired her both as an agent and a woman, and that was one of the reasons it was so tempting to sneak into Salamanca and meet her again. Another was the mistress of the engineer officer, but that was for more practical concerns. If the girl really was British, and both willing and able to win the confidence of French officers, then she could prove extremely useful. Hanley also had an idea about her, and although he knew that the odds were long he was more and more convinced that it would prove true. During the retreat to Corunna, Dobson's daughter Jenny had fled from the army and her newborn baby. After Medellín, Hanley had been captured, and before his escape he had a fleeting glimpse of Jenny working with a party of whores to entertain French officers. Her hair was dyed, and La Doña Margarita said in her letter that the major's mistress had fair hair. Jenny was determined and very ambitious, and if it was she then Hanley was all the more convinced that she could be useful. He would like to find out, but he knew that there was more to it than that. La Doña Margarita and Jenny Dobson alike stirred feelings he had not felt since he had ceased to love Mapi, the young dancer he had kept during his years in Madrid. She was out there somewhere, another source spying on the French, but Hanley

143

was still not sure whether he had the courage to face her. A visit to Salamanca held far more appeal.

Yet it was not to be for some time, and before dawn he and Benito set out, heading back towards Ciudad Rodrigo. The morning was quiet, and for once the sun shone and the rain clouds stayed away. At noon, Benito left Hanley outside and rode into a village not far from the main road. He came back with news that a big French foraging party was sweeping the country ahead of them. They went to the north and rode hard across a stretch of hills too open to provide any real concealment. The ground was wet, so there were not the usual clouds of dust to mark the passage of bodies of troops, and that meant that the French infantry were only a mile away when they came over the brow of a rise and saw them coming towards them.

Hanley and Benito drove their tired mounts as fast as they could, riding in a wide arc off to the north again. Isolated riders were a suspicious sight in this country, and for a few minutes two mounted French officers gave chase, but when they failed to gain on the fugitives they returned to the safety of the column. It was unwise for one or two Frenchmen to stray too far, for that risked capture or assassination, and after more than two years of war in Spain every one of Napoleon's soldiers had heard the stories of torture and mutilation.

The cavalry were usually more determined, and when late in the afternoon Benito jerked his head behind them and said '*Mira!*' Hanley's heart sank when he spotted the hussars. There were ten of them, all in the drab grey uniforms of the 3ième Hussars of Ney's corps, and they came on steadily, no more than half a mile away.

Hanley doubted that the French were acting on anything more than suspicion. In the past he had bluffed his way past French patrols, but today he wore his red coat and knew that he could not pass as a civilian.

'Come on,' he said to his guide, and they urged their horses into a canter. The hussars kept pace but did not gain. Hanley and Benito were well mounted, but the animals were tired, and perhaps the French were fresher. After forty minutes the grey-uniformed hussars were barely any further behind them and the two men could feel their horses slowing. Hanley's mare almost tripped several times and that was a sure sign that she was becoming exhausted.

A quarter of an hour later and the French had gained a little ground, but at this rate they would not catch up with them before darkness had fallen. Yet the French kept coming, and that could only mean that they did not need to reach their prey, and were confident of driving them into the arms of someone ahead of them.

'Which way?' asked Hanley, knowing that Benito was more likely to get them out of this situation. The Spaniard nodded forcibly ahead of them, and the British officer felt that the best thing was to trust his guide. If the French caught them then the Spaniard would be hanged or shot. Hanley would be a prisoner, and that would no doubt be dull, but unless he resisted it was unlikely that they would kill him. Grimly he wondered whether he would get to see Salamanca sooner than he thought.

The French light cavalry crept ever closer, and then one of them fired a carbine at a range that was still absurdly long and Hanley realised that they must be signalling. His mare was foamed in sweat and stumbled so badly that he almost lost his seat. He patted her neck and urged her on.

There were shouts from their left and another group of grey hussars appeared from behind the ruin of a stone barn. These men were barely five hundred yards away, and when Hanley looked he saw that they wore round fur caps rather than shakos, and that made them members of the elite company of the regiment.

Benito took them to the right, but not as sharply as Hanley expected, and he wondered whether his guide was trying to avoid the patrol behind them. A glance in that direction showed that these were now a little closer, but the men in black fur caps were much nearer and surely the greater threat as they spurred their horses into a gallop.

Hanley whipped his mare mercilessly, and from somewhere she found enough strength to break into a canter as they went up the slope of the rise to their right. The men from the elite company were closing, and when he looked back over his shoulder, he could see that they had already halved the distance. Several had stubby carbines in their hands, but were sensible enough not to waste the shots firing at a running target from the back of a bouncing horse.

Benito was a smaller man, and his little pony was beginning to outstrip the mare bearing the weight of the big Englishman. Then Hanley saw a horseman ride out on to the top of the hill ahead of them and he knew that the game was up. The man wore a drab brown coat, but his helmet was unmistakably the high brass helmet with horsehair crest worn by the French dragoons. Two more riders appeared a moment later, both carrying lances, and while one wore a wide-topped French shako the other had the square hat of a Polish lancer. Hanley was too tired to wonder why a patrol should be so mixed, but that really did not matter because they were boxed in and had nowhere left to go.

'French!' he called, as Benito headed straight towards the three riders on the ridge, and Hanley could not believe that the man had not seen the new danger. He wondered about trying to cut away to the left, but knew that he would not make it and so in blind faith or resignation he kept after his guide.

A long line of horsemen appeared on the height, and some wore wide-brimmed hats and others seemed to have every headgear known to the armies fighting in Spain. More than half had lances, but the rest carried bulky infantry muskets, and these now aimed them and fired, the noise and smoke making several of their ponies and horses shy.

'El Charro!' cried Benito – the closest Hanley had ever heard him come to enthusiasm – and then he saw the man himself, waving in greeting.

CHAPTER 11

Julián Sánchez García was these days formally Don Julián, a brigadier in the Spanish army, but when men spoke of him it was almost always as 'El Charro', for the nicknames sported by the guerrilla leaders made them seem more than mere men. Hanley guessed that he was in his late thirties, but with his big moustache and bushy whiskers it was hard to tell his age more clearly. Brigadier or not, Don Julián had the hard face and hands of a man who had served as a sergeant in the army and then worked his own land for long years before the war. He was as tough and unforgiving as the earth of Old Castile. It was said that the French had slaughtered his family, and when Hanley looked into those cold eyes he could believe it. He hated the French with a passion, but it seemed that he would not kill any of them today.

'No point,' he said. The hussars had retired at the sight of the guerrillas, but had not gone far and now formed in a single line and watched them. 'Surprise has gone, and I don't want to lose anyone for no good reason.' He winked at Hanley. 'If I hadn't come out to save you and the worthless carcass of this old bandit, then it might have been worth an attack. Probably should not have bothered, but there it is. If we charge now they'll just pull back, and somewhere out there is another squadron or two.'

The guerrilla leaders who survived were cautious men, fighting when there was least risk and keeping at a safe distance the rest of the time. Don Julián had only some of his men here today, and none would think any less of him for running away. These men planned to be alive on the day they chased away the last Frenchman.

Hanley had met Don Julián in Ciudad Rodrigo, but this was the first time he had ridden with his band, and seen his men close up. Nearly all wore some items of uniform, but blue French infantry jackets mingled with the green of chasseurs and dragoons, and the whites, yellows, light and dark blues and myriad other colours of Spain. There were battered cocked hats, shakos of every nation – one man even had a Highlander's bonnet – as well as an array of helmets and sombreros and civilian tricorne hats. Some of the French helmets were dented, and a few coats stained with the blood of their previous owner. Their weapons were as varied, with rapiers, a few antiquated broadswords and the straight swords or curved sabres of every type of cavalry regiment. Others simply carried wicked-looking knives to back up their lances. Most had some sort of firearm, even if it was just an old horse pistol or blunderbuss. It was hard not to think of Falstaff's ragged regiment, for the men would almost have been a parody of soldiers if it were not for their capable manner. El Charro's men did not move in ranks or formations and looked like banditti, but as they went, there were scouts on all sides and the men looked ready to kill or escape without the need for any order.

They pulled back without leaving a rearguard.

'They won't believe it isn't a trap,' said Don Julián complacently, and as they rode he and Hanley exchanged news.

The French were getting more active. 'It's not yet the big attack,' said the guerrilla leader, 'but their foraging expeditions are getting bigger and each time they go further. There are more troops near the border facing the British outposts. You know about Astorga?'

'Junot has attacked the city.'

'Yes, and there is talk of a threat to Badajoz.'

'Lord Wellington still thinks the main attack will come here,' said Hanley.

'So do I, and I think it will not be long once Astorga falls. You were not here two weeks ago when a French brigade came nosing around outside Ciudad Rodrigo. A lot of those whoresons of hussars who were chasing you, and a couple of battalions of infantry.' At times the farmer and the sergeant were close beneath the surface. *A charro* was a nickname for a man from Salamanca, but sometimes it was slang for a roughneck or peasant.

'They came and had a look, surprised a picket and took some prisoners, and then strolled off again. Must have been looking at the defences and sniffing out the town's strength.

'Will your Lord Wellington fight for Ciudad Rodrigo?' The question was abrupt.

'I am only a lieutenant.'

'You're a man, aren't you? Then tell me what your gut tells you.'

'Perhaps, at least if the circumstances are right,' Hanley said after a while, and then grinned. 'He won't want to lose anyone for no good reason.'

Don Julián Sánchez García was silent for a while. 'He has sense, that one,' he said finally, 'but I wonder if he is a killer.'

Late that night they rode into Ciudad Rodrigo, and the next morning Hanley found that the town's governor wanted to know the answer to much the same question.

Lieutenant General Don Andrés Pérez de Herrasti was short, like El Charro, but unlike the guerrilla leader in almost every other way. He was twice Don Julián's age and had the mild expression of a schoolteacher or village priest. His white hair was worn long and neatly tied back in the fashion of the last century, and his manners were those of an impeccable Castilian gentleman. This was merely one meeting of many held since he took command, but that did not prevent him from donning his full uniform, the deep blue coat heavy with gold decoration on the high collar, cuffs and turnbacks, and his heavily plumed hat carefully brushed.

'It must always look as if I have not the slightest doubt of holding this city until the end of the world,' he said to Hanley. 'And so I put on a show and hope that the people believe me, just like we must put on a show for the French. This place is old, just like me, and if the fire is still in the blood neither of us can claim the same strength in our flesh and bones as once we had. We must pretend, and do our best, and hope in the end for help.

'Your general writes to tell me that he shall do everything in his power to support us.' Herrasti did not ask the question, but merely watched Hanley closely. The British officer could not tell whether or not he was satisfied, but after a few moments he moved on and listened as they went through what they had learned.

'So the French are coming. When?'

El Charro spread his hands. 'By the summer. It is hard to see why they should wait any longer.'

'Any news of their siege train?' asked the general.

'Nothing new,' said Hanley. 'The order to gather some fifty heavy cannon and mortars at Burgos was issued earlier in the year, so we must assume that they are being prepared.'

'Hmm, they probably don't need all fifty for this old place,' said Herrasti, 'although it is nice to be respected. Now my problem is not guns so much as gunners. Out of my five thousand men barely a quarter are regular soldiers. The volunteers are keen, but it takes time to teach them simply how to march and load a musket. Artillerymen need much fuller instruction. I have the cadets of the Artillery School, but apart from a few of their instructors, they are just boys and none have ever fired at the enemy. It will be very hard to smash the French batteries before they can shatter our walls. I have sent to La Romana and Del Parque for more gunners, but so far . . .' The general trailed off, resigned to the unwillingness of the nearest Spanish commanders to reinforce him. For a moment he looked even older than his years.

'No matter. So when the battering train is ready, they will come. Will anything else delay them?'

'Astorga?' suggested Don Julián in a flat tone.

'If it lasts the month we shall be lucky,' said Herrasti dismissively.

'It keeps Junot away.'

'Ney has almost twenty thousand veterans,' the governor said firmly. 'He does not need Junot.'

Hanley was sure that the 6th Corps was smaller than that, but thought it better not to argue the point. 'Wellington could concentrate more men than that and be here in less than a week. You are not on your own, sir. Ney cannot risk attacking on his own and being overwhelmed. He barely stayed a few days before you chased him away back in February.'

'So for the moment the British frighten the French enough to keep them at bay. At least until they gather more soldiers.'

154

'Lord Wellington may be able to bring other divisions up from the south,' said Hanley, but in the end he knew that the French should be able to muster so many men that the British could not hope to face them in the rolling plains around Ciudad Rodrigo. They wanted the Spanish town to delay the French, so that the defences of Portugal had time to become stronger.

The governor was understandably disinclined to see his garrison as merely a difficult stepping stone on the French path to Lisbon. 'He must come, I tell you, he must.'

As Hanley rode out of the gate and over the Roman bridge spanning the Agueda he could understand the Spanish reluctance to place their faith in the British. The road to Almeida took him close to Fort La Concepción and he was sorely tempted to ride over and visit his friends, but he resisted the urge and pressed on over the border to the big Portuguese fortress with its high cathedral. That evening he met with the governor, Colonel Cox, in a room overlooking the ramparts. Several of his Portuguese staff were present, as was Brigadier General Craufurd and his ADC, Shaw Kennedy. There was little sign of great enthusiasm or trust for their Spanish allies, and especially General Herrasti.

'The man is a fool and a rogue.' Cox's already ruddy cheeks seemed to glow with passion. 'Damned fellow isn't fit to command a corporal's guard, let alone a fortress. Wellington has tried to get him replaced, but as usual the dons do nothing. We're the only ones bothering to keep an eye on the French, eh, Hanley? Doubt he had a clue what they were up to until you told him.'

'Will he fight?' asked Brigadier General Craufurd. He was quite short and slimly built, and when he had removed his hat and dripping cloak after coming into the room, Hanley saw that his hair was grey. He was forty-six, older than Wellington and most of the other senior officers, and this was the biggest command he had ever received in a career marked by disappointment. Baynes had explained that Wellington had asked for him, and given him this plum of a prime brigade in close contact with the enemy because Craufurd was a scientific soldier, a man who had thought about and studied outpost duties for many years. The brigadier's expression was certainly highly focused and spoke of a great force of character, but Hanley could not quite make up his mind whether it also hinted at real intelligence. Craufurd dominated a room of bigger men, and not simply by his rank. His hair must once have been as black as a raven, and even now repeated shaving left his chin heavily shadowed. It helped to create a sense of brooding presence, of immense strength and temper just waiting to explode.

Hanley could not tell the brigadier's attitude to Herrasti, but felt that it was worth supporting the Spaniards. 'He stood against Ney back in February.'

'No more than a feint.' Cox was dismissive, and

unwilling to be contradicted by a lieutenant. 'When the French come properly he'll fold at first sight. They're all the same. It won't be the Spaniards who save Spain, because they haven't the stomach for it. Look at that affair at Barba del Puerco last month. The only Spaniards near by ran off into the night, and then turned up when it was all over to go looting.' Cox's Portuguese staff grinned at this uncharitable assessment of their neighbours.

There seemed little point in arguing, and so Hanley said nothing until he was asked to give his report.

'Well, they are not hurrying,' was Craufurd's assessment after asking several more detailed questions. 'This may give us a splendid opportunity to strike first and give Ney a drubbing.' Hanley was amazed that anyone should talk of the British attacking, but the brigadier said no more and instead summarised the reports gained from his own pickets and patrols. 'The French are pushing a little more boldly, but as yet nothing serious.

'The Agueda is lower than it was, and so we have pulled back the infantry so that there is time to react. On 6 April they probed as far as San Felices el Chico, so the KGL and the Ninety-fifth turned out to meet them. The French were foraging, and after stripping the place they pulled back.

'It confirms all our reports that they are struggling to feed themselves. I also suspect that their boldness is intended to conceal their vulnerability. However, as it is, we can still communicate freely

157

with Ciudad Rodrigo, and there should be no difficulty sending them another powder convoy.'

'Hope it is not throwing good money after bad,' muttered Cox, 'but at least the blackguard will have no excuse not to fight when the time comes.'

'We must keep the road to Ciudad Rodrigo open as long as possible. It will let us send aid, and perhaps do more. On top of that, it helps to make life difficult for the French and that is a worthy end in itself. Are the guerrillas active, Hanley?'

'Yes, as much as they can be. Don Julián Sánchez has something like two hundred men. His is the biggest band and the best organised.'

'Fine. Thank you for your efforts, Hanley. I want you to go with a patrol from the KGL hussars tomorrow and see what people are saying to the north.'

'Sir.' Hanley had hoped for a rest, but had not been optimistic.

'Now, Colonel, perhaps you could treat us all to that fine dinner you promised!' The brigadier spoke lightly, but although he struggled to be jovial he did not quite manage it and it came across as brusque. If Cox was offended he did not show it, perhaps used by now to Craufurd's manner. Hanley was pleased to be included in the invitation and spent a pleasant few hours chatting to Shaw Kennedy, a serious and capable young man who appeared devoted to his chief.

'He had to surrender his brigade at Buenos Aires,' he whispered after the wine had flowed.

158

'That's a dreadful thing for anyone, and especially for a proud man who knew how the thing should be done.' A harsh expression came into his face. 'Whitelocke ought to have been shot.' Hanley had heard such comments before. General Whitelocke had botched the whole expedition to South America. He had been court-martialled, and although condemned he suffered no more punishment than the ruin of his career.

After Cox and the brigadier had retired, the ADC proposed one last toast. 'Here's to grey hairs, and damnation to white locks!' The Portuguese staff officers looked baffled, and Hanley wondered how much of General Craufurd's simmering anger came from the shame and frustration of this earlier defeat. He hoped that it would not prejudice him against the Spanish, or make him too eager to clear his name, but there was little he could do in either case.

A little later, Hanley sat in the small room allocated to him and wrote a ciphered letter to Baynes to be enclosed with the reports and captured documents. It gave his own impressions of the mood of allies and enemies alike.

The French are waiting. As yet there is no sign of our old acquaintance or other royal agents. This seems unlikely to change until the main invasion is imminent.

CHAPTER 12

Temporary Lieutenant Colonel MacAndrews was still angry, prompting another savage assault with his riding crop against the top of the parapet. Already punished, this time the shaft of the whip snapped, and several inches at the tip flicked around loosely for a moment before hanging limply down. The Scotsman stared sadly at the ruined whip, his anger deflating.

'There is nothing I can do,' explained Captain Morillo.

The Scotsman knew that was true, and over the last weeks he had come to like and respect his Spanish colleague. 'Damn it, but they were starting to learn their trade properly.'

'They were also better outfitted than half the soldiers in the army.'

By the end of March, the Scotsman had managed to beg and borrow boots, grey uniform jackets and trousers, and some old shakos and belts to equip the recruits sent by the Army of Estremadura. Properly accoutred and given weeks of drill, the raw country lads had started to look a little like soldiers. Then a Spanish colonel had arrived late one night, praised their work and dined cheerfully with MacAndrews, Morillo and the senior officers. The next morning the man was just as jovial when he marched the recruits away to serve with General La Carrera's division, who were stationed on the flank of Craufurd's British. A few days later another hundred new conscripts appeared, without a musket, jacket or belt to their name. Soon other small parties arrived, some of them men from the guerrilla bands.

'They really do think that I am their damned quartermaster, don't they?' MacAndrews snapped angrily at his colleague. He gently flicked his whip, watching the tip spin wildly for a moment, and then sighed. 'I was actually beginning to feel proud of them,' he said wistfully, and without any open signal the two officers resumed their walk around the ramparts of the fort.

'I cannot be too hard on men who panic at night,' MacAndrews added after a dozen paces, thinking back to the flight of Pringle's detachment at Barba del Puerco. 'Especially when they are raw and are not set a good example.'

Morillo had already apologised for the conduct of Lieutenant Dolosa. 'He was once a very brave man,' he said, 'but I fear he has seen too many defeats and too many friends killed as they stood alongside him.'

MacAndrews grunted, and but for his temper would have been more sympathetic, for he had seen men lose their nerve before. Sometimes they recovered, but others seemed broken for life. No one could really be sure how long his own store of courage would last.

'There, but for the Grace of God . . .' the Scotsman muttered, and could not help wondering about a couple of the redcoated officers sent to him. From the ramparts they could see the different parties training in the courtyard or outside the fort. Captain Reynolds looked positively bored as he watched a dozen of the Spanish NCOs practising skirmishing. Beside him a young lieutenant fidgeted, barely able to keep still, and then visibly jumped when the first man fired off a blank charge. It was always the way with detached services. Commanding officers usually sent either their best men, eager for advancement and to learn new things, or the ones they did not care to have serving with their battalion. Yet all in all he felt his team were good, and as the weeks passed they had begun to make real progress. The Spanish NCOs were shaping up very nicely, and although it had not been the purpose of his mission to train raw recruits, the Scotsman was doing it to the best of his ability.

In the courtyard below them, a Spanish corporal barked at his men to hurry as they filed into the armoury to collect their muskets. In the last week MacAndrews and Morillo had changed the routine of the fort, so that the recruits were issued with muskets only when they drilled and had to turn them in again at the end of the day. It was impossible to do the same with uniforms, and even with firelocks and bayonets the system was not infallible. Most of the guerrillas slipped away at the first opportunity, taking with them a new musket, cartridges and clothes. Some recruits, their heads filled with tales of heroic ambushes, full bellies and pockets, and no discipline, went with them.

'Two more of the rogues vanished last night,' said MacAndrews wearily.

'*Viva Fernando y vamos robando*!' Morillo repeated the old joke, and when MacAndrews looked puzzled the Spaniard offered an explanation. '"Long live Ferdinand VII and let's go robbing!" They have all heard the stories of the brave *guerrilleros* – and heard about the armies slaughtered by the French dragoons. Which would you choose?'

'We could increase the guard,' said the Scotsman doubtfully.

Morillo looked at him, but said nothing, for they had had this conversation before and the conclusion was bound to be the same.

'I know, I know,' MacAndrews said apologetically, 'the men are working hard enough as it is and there is no sense in wearing them out. The recruits must do duty as sentries and we cannot afford reliable men to watch them at all times.' He shook his head, for neither man could think of a better way of doing things. 'Nor is it good for young soldiers to know that they are not trusted.'

They came to the ramp leading down into the fort, and MacAndrews paused for a moment and turned to face his colleague. 'Sometimes I wonder whether we serve any useful purpose.' There was only so much that he and Morillo could do, and it fell far short of the original idea for this mission. 'No doubt that devil of a colonel will return as soon as we have knocked this new company into some sort of shape.'

'At least we are not doing any harm,' the Spaniard said with a wry smile. There was sadness in his eyes, and MacAndrews tried to imagine the sorrow of a proud man whose country was occupied by a stronger, perhaps overwhelming, enemy. For an instant he wondered whether to make a joke about the English holding Scotland, but doubted his colleague was in the mood for so frivolous a comparison.

'Aye,' he said, drawing the little word out as only a Highlander could.

The sound of shouted orders came from beyond the walls, followed by a spattering of shots as Reynolds' men went through their exercises. 'The non-commissioned officers are coming on with their open-order drill,' said Morillo with genuine satisfaction. So far the Army of the Right appeared to have forgotten the batch of NCOs, or perhaps someone somewhere was content to let them undergo more thorough training.

'They are all good men,' conceded MacAndrews, 'eager, and quick to learn, but there are so few of them.' He set off abruptly, for once catching Morillo by surprise, and the Spanish officer had to jog for a few paces to catch up.

They passed a young sentry, face rigid with concentration, and the boy presented arms with quivering intensity and a reasonable approximation of the correct movements. MacAndrews raised his broken crop in acknowledgement.

'They are all learning,' he said when they were out of earshot. 'At least we can draw some satisfaction from that.'

Morillo smiled. 'Yes, although I fear we cannot assume too much of the credit. They are far more eager not to look bad in front of the Portuguese that to impress us,' he said. In the last month Colonel Cox had sent a detachment of his infantry to stand guard at the old fort. 'Probably done more than we have to make the fellows want to learn and do well.'

Hoof beats echoed from the tunnel behind the main gate as two officers rode in, resplendent in their tall Tarleton helmets and heavily braided blue coats.

'Morning, Ross,' MacAndrews called out, once again raising his crop so that the broken end flapped wildly for a moment and made one of the horses step to the side, its neck arching away. The rider whispered softly to the beast, and with the gentlest touch of his heels and a firm grasp on the reins steadied him.

'Good morning, Colonel,' Ross replied when the horse was calm. Captain Ross and his six guns of the Royal Horse Artillery were another recent arrival and were now using the fort as their headquarters. The 'Chestnut Troop' – named after their matched teams – looked superb and showed every mark of efficiency. In the RHA not only were the gun limbers drawn by six horses apiece, but all of the gun crews also rode, so that they were fast and highly manoeuvrable. 'I bring good tidings of great joy.'

The artillery officer handed his reins to the other rider and swung nimbly down before he spoke again. 'Tomorrow, sir, I shall have a section of guns at your full disposal. General Craufurd gives his enthusiastic consent, and so my pieces are at your service, ready to smite whomsoever stands in your path.'

Ross was a bright, eager man, and MacAndrews felt his glum mood recede. 'That is excellent, most excellent.' The Scotsman had asked for the loan of a single six-pounder to add some excitement to a field day involving all of his little command. Although the troop was based in the fort and kept many of its carts and wagons there, its guns were usually out serving with Brigadier Craufurd's outpost and support line. MacAndrews had made gentle enquiries before sending in a formal request, and had not been too hopeful of securing the use of a single gun. Now it seemed that he would have two cannon at his disposal.

'It will be good for the men to hear guns fired,' Morillo said, for he and MacAndrews had come up with the idea together. 'There is a danger that the noise of battle overwhelms young soldiers, so it is better if they are prepared.'

Captain Ross grinned. 'I am firmly convinced that cannon fire is an essential part of any education. Unimpeachable sources assure me that these days the masters at Eton regularly shoot at their pupils. They do the same at Harrow, it is said, and no doubt it will spread in time to the universities. Sadly the aim of the Fellows is likely to be poor, otherwise they might do the nation a great service.'

It looked as if the gunner had more to say, but he was interrupted by the arrival of a lieutenant wearing a red-brown uniform and the high-fronted Portuguese shako.

'Beg to report, sir, but the colonel sends word to say that the drill is about to begin.'

Craufurd's command had recently been reinforced by the arrival of the 1st and 2nd Regiments of Portuguese *caçadores*, expanding his brigade into a division. These light infantry battalions were frequently in or near the fort, and MacAndrews had gladly accepted an invitation to watch them at their drills.

'Thank you, Lieutenant . . .?'

'Matthews, sir.' The Portuguese Regency Council had appointed the British Marshal Beresford to reorganise their army, weakened by years of neglect, and then wrecked by the French invasion. It was almost a question of starting from scratch and forming an entirely new army. Beresford brought with him a large number of British officers, each given a step in rank as a reward for transferring to the Portuguese service for the duration of the war. Some were commissioned from capable sergeants, and the Scotsman wondered whether Matthews was such a man, as he looked to be about thirty.

Matthews proved garrulous, full of enthusiasm for his new regiment and its soldiers, and MacAndrews soon decided that he was not a former sergeant. Such men were often capable, but tended to lack confidence when speaking with men who might once have commanded them. More likely Matthews was simply an elderly ensign, lacking either money or influence, who had seized this opportunity for late advancement. Silently, the Scotsman wished him luck.

As they followed him out of the fort, Matthews chattered away, mostly telling MacAndrews what he already knew. It was still interesting, since in essence the reorganisation of Portugal's army had provided the inspiration for his own mission – distant though that purpose now seemed to be. Then for the next hour MacAndrews watched the Portuguese form from column to line and back again, deploy as skirmishers and advance or withdraw with supports in place.

First impressions were good. The men were well accoutred and neat about their persons, while weapons and equipment were obviously in good order. The care needed to keep a firelock clean was something his staff struggled to convey to their raw recruits. Teaching such a basic thing was far from the original purpose of his mission, and MacAndrews tried to stop himself brooding on the evident impossibility of doing what he was supposed to do. He could not help envying the Portuguese their long months of training, plentiful resources and the active support of higher authorities.

'We follow English drills, of course, and in future the word of command will also be in English,' Matthews explained. 'As *caçadores* – the Englishman mauled the pronunciation of the word – we are modelled on the Ninety-fifth, and follow the system developed under Sir John Moore at Shorncliffe.'

MacAndrews scanned the ranks of the battalion. Apart from the shape of shakos, and the colour of the uniforms, the Portuguese resembled the green jackets of the 95th. Yet when he looked closer, he saw that all carried the standard long-barrelled musket. 'I do not see any rifles,' he said enquiringly.

'None have yet been issued, although we do live in hope,' Matthews explained. 'Nevertheless we stress practice firing at a target, and officers are encouraged to take part . . .'

After a while Lieutenant Matthews' commentary flowed past MacAndrews and made little impression. He was much more interested in what his own eyes told him. Yes, the Portuguese were promising, he decided, but as the drills went on he began to spot more than a few moments of confusion or clumsiness. Some of the British officers shouted too much, and he suspected many as yet spoke Portuguese only poorly and tried to make up for this by yelling at their men. Similarly, a good few of the Portuguese officers had little English. Marshal Beresford carefully alternated the nationalities at all levels, so that a Portuguese battalion commander had a British second-in-command and vice versa. It seemed fair, and as far as he could tell there was no serious friction between the two nationalities.

As they walked back at the end of proceedings, MacAndrews did not have to ask Morillo to know that a similar arrangement would be impossible with the Spanish. The captain also pointed to other changes.

'Being paid regularly and fed most likely makes as big a difference as any training.'

'Eventually, anyway,' MacAndrews said. All in all he was unsure that the new regiments were ready. Clearly Brigadier General Craufurd and others had similar concerns, for a week later Marshal Beresford sent his Quartermaster General to inspect them. Colonel D'Urban was an intelligent young light cavalryman who cheerfully greeted Williams and explained to MacAndrews how the young officer had helped save General Cuesta at Medellín. He was even more delighted to meet Morillo again.

'I remember your grenadiers charging the French guns.'

'With you riding alongside us, as I recall, Colonel,' said the Spanish captain.

'Oh, I was only an observer.' On the next day D'Urban was again an observer, watching both of the Portuguese light infantry regiments marching, performing manoeuvres and acting as skirmishers. His slim, handsome face betrayed no emotion, but in the privacy of his rooms, MacAndrews was able to draw more from him.

'They are not ready – especially the Second Regiment. Oh, there is plenty of promise, but they need more time and training. I cannot think why they were chosen, other than perhaps the logical mind of someone on the staff who must send the battalions out in numerical order.

'You know the importance of the first engagement for young soldiers, MacAndrews?'

The Scotsman nodded. 'Yes, for good or ill they tend to carry the spirit of it through the rest of the campaign.'

'Indeed, and so we must make sure that they acquit themselves well. Training is one thing, and they do need more of it, but even the best drills cannot give them that confidence in success that comes from facing the enemy and beating him. The French are still the bogeymen who have enslaved Europe. Our young fellows hate them and want to defend their country. Some of them know that we have beaten the French at Vimeiro and elsewhere, but they haven't, not yet, and until they do the belief will not be there that they can. The few who served at Oporto and Talavera last year scarcely fired a shot. A wise precaution, but it means that the army as a whole is unblooded. The doubts remain. Worse still, our own countrymen are all too inclined to express similar doubts in a manner that is not tactful.'

MacAndrews nodded again. As a Scot he firmly believed that the English disdain for foreigners was all too often loud and obvious, and this view was only confirmed that night in the mess. Thankfully D'Urban had hurried away and refused their hospitality.

'Training is all very well,' said Captain Reynolds of the 51st, emphasising his frank opinion with darting gestures of his cheroot, 'but in the end it comes down to pluck and bottom.'

MacAndrews felt that was an uninspiring view for a man forming part of a training mission, but there were clearly others who shared the sentiment, for there were murmurs of approval. Reynolds shot an unkind glance at Lieutenant Dolosa, the only Spaniard visiting with them this evening.

Reynolds was a heavy drinker, and this tended to make him more than usually free and forthright in his opinions. 'But in the end we all know that it won't make a blind bit of difference, even if these chasseurs do put up a decent fight.' Few of the British officers coped well with pronouncing the word *caçadores*, and so most preferred to use the French name instead. Foreign corps in the British army were often named chasseurs.

'Not the sort of bottoms I'd like to see at the

moment,' commented a distinctly merry RHA subaltern who was their guest. 'I could do with my own twenty-four hours in Lisbon!' He had unruly ginger hair and a face almost wholly covered in freckles.

Pringle could see that Dolosa was struggling to understand the English and the allusion. 'Lord Wellington has restricted leave in Lisbon for those near the city to no more than twenty-four hours,' he explained.

'Yes, says that's enough time for anyone to be in bed with the same woman!' the gunner chortled, and was soon choking on his wine, spraying liquid in all directions. Dolosa looked disgusted. MacAndrews had heard the story and doubted its truth – or at least, the truth of the explanation.

Reynolds seemed to resent the change of subject. 'Portugal cannot be defended,' he announced in an unnaturally loud voice. MacAndrews was pleased to see Williams politely ask Dolosa to accompany him on his rounds, ostensibly to deal with any problems of language. From his expression, Billy Pringle looked as if he wanted to go with them.

'Cannot be defended,' repeated the captain. 'Sir John Moore said that more than a year ago and he was the finest officer this country has ever produced.' MacAndrews noted the easy assumption that wherever an Englishman was, Britain remained 'this' country.

Williams cast a look over his shoulder, but could

not easily stop and stay in the room. He left, although clearly with regret, for there were fewer more ardent champions of Moore's name, even if he was equally full of praise for Wellington.

'Moore was a great man and a hero,' said Pringle. 'Yet he fell more than a year ago, and it is not reasonable to suppose that he could have possessed knowledge of the future.'

MacAndrews was pleased. He had wanted to make the same point, but disliked a mess where the colonel dominated talk and so he preferred to listen wherever possible.

'The land has not changed, nor the character of the people.' Reynolds' voice was slurring.

'Who gives a damn about the character, just give me my twenty-four hours and I'll be satisfied!' the horse gunner chipped in again.

'At the moment you look barely up for ten minutes,' laughed another subaltern.

'You tell me what has changed!' Reynolds demanded loudly, his glowing face leaning forward across the table towards Pringle. MacAndrews had to admit that most changes had not been for the better. His first war had been against the American rebels – or patriots, or these days noble heroes – and he knew what it was like to taste the bitterness of defeat. There was something of that air now, everyone waiting for the unstoppable invasion. At least there was no danger of a French fleet brushing aside the Royal Navy and making a new Yorktown. The redcoats would be able to escape, and he had heard a rumour that the newly trained Portuguese would go with them, perhaps to England or to join the royal family in Brazil.

'Lord Wellington knows how to fight, and he seems confident.' Pringle spoke quietly. MacAndrews had noticed that the bespectacled captain drank far less now that they were busy and back in Spain. Lately he had been finding every excuse to lead marches or go on his own to some of the villages near by. It did not interfere with his duties, and knowing the man well, MacAndrews could not help wondering whether Billy was getting his own twenty-four hours somewhere. That reminded him of something, and he remembered an overdue conversation that he must have with another of his officers.

'Wellesley's just a glory hunter.' Reynolds almost shouted the words, and only with an effort calmed himself. 'Five thousand men sacrificed last year just to win a title!' Sir Arthur Wellesley became Viscount Wellington after the victory at Talavera. The Whig press had said as much and worse in the months that followed, and claimed the Tory government pretended the battle was a victory merely to save its own tottering reputation.

'You were not there, sir,' said Pringle levelly.

MacAndrews was marginally more Whig than Tory, but held all politicians in equal contempt for the mess they had made of the American business and of almost everything else in his lifetime.

Politics was always a dangerous subject in the mess, and now was leading to even more serious disagreements.

'What is your meaning, sir?' said Reynolds, trying hard to focus on Pringle.

'Gentlemen,' interrupted MacAndrews, 'let us have no party here. I am confident that you will all do your duty well, and leave the great matters to those His Majesty appoints. Now raise your glasses.' He nodded to the subaltern serving as president.

'Gentlemen, the King!'

'The King, God bless him,' they chorused.

'And damnation to Bonaparte,' added MacAndrews with a grin.

Half an hour later he found Williams standing up on the western rampart. The lieutenant had completed his rounds, and Dolosa must have retired, but MacAndrews knew that Williams had a habit of standing alone on the walls after his duties were done. It was raining again, but so finely that they scarcely noticed.

'Just like home,' said MacAndrews as he came alongside, waving down the lieutenant's instinctive stiffening to attention.

'Wales is often like this,' said Williams after a long moment, 'and Bristol not much better.'

'Have you had letters from your family in the last package?'

'Yes, I am pleased to say my sister Anne is a reliable correspondent. Indeed, she even writes now occasionally to Pringle. She and my whole family are very grateful to him.'

MacAndrews did not want to talk about the duel, but certain pleasantries could not be avoided. 'Your other sister, Mrs Garland, is well, I trust?'

'Oh yes. The child is expected in May.' Williams' tone was innocent, and MacAndrews thought it better not to pry. The news that his sister was with child had reached them soon after they arrived at the fort, the post taking time to catch up with them. As far as he could tell Williams seemed delighted.

Now seemed as good a moment as any, although he wished he had not become involved. 'Mr Williams,' he began, 'I must speak to you for a moment not as your commanding officer, but as Jane's father.'

Williams' face registered surprise, and then obvious fear, and MacAndrews suspected that the man was terrified of being forbidden to have any more to do with Jane. It was difficult not to laugh, but he knew the lieutenant to be a serious man devoted to honour and proper behaviour. If I tell him to cease all contact with her he probably would, thought Alastair MacAndrews. Either that, or elope with her.

'Her mother writes to me asking that I ask you a question.'

'My intentions are entirely honourable,' began Williams nervously, 'and I make no presumption of favour or . . .'

MacAndrews cut him off. 'I do not doubt any of those things, but that is not the point. The point is . . .' Now he hesitated, and wished that Esther was here to do her own dirty work. 'That is to say, my wife asks . . . Just what in hell's name did you do to Jane back in England?'

The shock returned, closely followed by panic, and Williams' eyes suggested desperate fears of stories about him, until he saw the softness of MacAndrews' smile.

'I . . . that is . . .' he stammered.

'I am not accusing you of anything improper. Jane was agitated before I left, and her mother writes to say that she has remained in a similar mood as the months have passed. Apparently she talks about you often.' He smiled. 'I fear not all is complimentary.'

Williams' face fell, and MacAndrews wondered whether he had ever been as naive as this man, and sadly felt that he probably had.

'Jane is a wilful girl,' said her father. 'Contrary at times. And trying to force her to do anything is perhaps the best way to prevent her from doing it.' He patted Williams on the shoulder. 'You might consider writing to her.'

Despair was replaced by puzzled hope. 'You would not mind, sir?' said Williams, and MacAndrews wondered whether the title was given as father or colonel.

'I am not so stern a parent as to forbid my child all contact with the wider world.' He kept his expression serious. 'And I should add permission to write a few letters falls considerably short of a formal blessing.' MacAndrews was finding it harder and harder to keep his face impassive, if only to maintain his authority.

'No, sir. Of course not, sir. I am honoured. Thank you, most profoundly.'

'In the greater scheme of things, what I think will have very little bearing on what Jane decides. For all our bluster, I strongly suspect that is the fate of fathers and husbands alike – indeed, of all men. But perhaps I should say that my blessing would be withheld from any suitor who was not a captain at the very least.'

Williams still appeared to be brimming with hope, and MacAndrews wondered whether he was listening.

'Goodnight to you, Mr Williams,' he said, pulling the collar of his coat up as he wandered down the ramp. When he was almost there a great whoop echoed across the promenade. MacAndrews calmed a young sentry who looked around nervously at the sudden noise, and stopped the man from reaching back to draw his bayonet.

The Scotsman waited until he was in his room and then began to laugh. Part of him felt sorry for the fellow, for he liked the young man a good deal, and suspected that the path to winning his daughter's heart would not be an easy one. However, at least his next letter to Esther would be simpler to write, now that this duty was

179

performed. Writing to his wife was at once sweet and painful, bringing her even closer to his thoughts, and yet all the while reminding him that she was far away.

Alastair MacAndrews missed her, and could not even console himself with the belief that he was achieving any worthwhile thing by being in Spain in the first place. He longed to be with his family again, but in the meantime, he must simply struggle on to do his best, write regular letters and feel the surge of excitement whenever replies arrived. Opening a pouch kept inside his battered travelling canteen, the Scotsman fished out a bundle of old letters and began to sort them, just as he had done so many thousand times before. In some cases the paper was almost brown with age, stiff and liable to crack unless handled with great care. Jane's earliest letters were in pencil, now so faded that it would have been a struggle to make out the words if he had not known them so well. In contrast Esther had always attacked each page in bold, confident strokes of ink, but thought so quickly that she was inclined to miss out words as she wrote. MacAndrews felt his grin broadening as he read one from more than a decade ago. 'I am', it said, and both then and now he had known this somewhat biblical statement to mean 'I am well'.

He laid the letter down on the pile, saving that pleasure for the lonely hours after he had finished writing to her. There would be no need to say that he found his present duty frustrating, or that he feared a failure which might hinder rather than help his already dim prospects for getting a battalion of his own. Esther would know already, and the thought of her washed over him and brought contentment. As he began to write, MacAndrews knew that he was the most fortunate of men.

CHAPTER 13

The water flowed noisily through the wide bed of stones, and Hanley's mare did not like the look of the narrow bridge. It was no more than a raised stone causeway, without side walls, and the horse stopped, and then tried to back away, before mingled curses, encouragement and flicks of his whip took the animal across. The German hussar escorting him walked his own gelding over the narrow bridge with nonchalant ease.

They pressed on into the bigger, eastern part of Fuentes de Oñoro, threading their way through the maze-like streets. The buildings were stone and most were single-storey, but near the churchyard there was a taller house, with a balcony above the grand doorway.

Hanley was surprised to see Pringle emerge from that very door, but immediately called out in greeting.

'Well, hello yourself,' his friend replied after a moment. 'Just passing through?'

'On my way to Celorico.'

'Moving in exalted circles again, I gather.' Billy

grinned. At the end of April the French had moved much closer to Ciudad Rodrigo, and in response Lord Wellington had shifted three of his divisions and moved his headquarters to Celorico to be nearer the border. 'Is the game about to start?'

'Soon.'

'Thought so,' said Billy. 'They have started repairing the fortifications at Conception.'

'They?'

'Well, Colonel Cox tried to get Spanish labourers, but neither pleas nor coin got him anywhere, and so he has sent the Ninth Portuguese regiment to do the work. The place is a lot more crowded than when you last visited.' Hanley had managed to call on his friends twice in the last months. 'Makes training difficult, if it wasn't hard enough in the first place.'

'So why are you off wandering?' Hanley was genuinely curious, for there was a slightly sheepish air to his friend.

'Been begging as usual. We are short of cartridges and powder in general. You know MacAndrews, he likes to have the men firing at targets.' Pringle, Hanley and Williams had all served in the Grenadier Company when the Scotsman was its captain, and knew his fondness for making drills as realistic as possible. 'I rather believe I have lost count of the number of occasions when I have given thanks for the old man's diligence, so I am sure you'll agree that it is a worthy aim. I tried Cox at Almeida, but I think he is fed up with our constant requests,

183

and none too keen on all things Spanish on top of that. So I have been down to the Third Division.'

'Any joy?'

Pringle shook his head. 'Might have been better to send Bills, as one Welshman to another!' Major General Picton was the new commander of the Third Division and had a reputation for his fiery Celtic temper. 'The general didn't exactly mince his words,' Pringle added ruefully.

'An unsuccessful trip, then?'

'Looks like it.' Pringle reached up, lifted his glasses a little and began to massage his eyelids with his fingers. A door creaked on a hinge that sorely needed oiling and someone appeared on the balcony of the house. It was a young woman – very young, for Hanley guessed she was barely sixteen – and there was a broad smile on her round face. The girl was pretty, with long dark hair, full lips and eager eyes. Her dress was a pale pink, and that was unusual in the country areas, as was its plunging neckline. There was still a good deal of the plumpness of a child about her figure. Still smiling, she reached down with one hand and then noticed the two horsemen and drew it back.

'You must be tired,' said Hanley, and then paused deliberately before adding, 'after so long a ride.'

'What? Oh yes, of course. Sore bums all round,' Pringle replied cheerfully, and then sensed that they were not alone. He looked back over his shoulder at the balcony and gave a little smile. The girl had plucked up a mantilla, and now draped it demurely to cover her chest and shoulders. Her expression was more formal, but she could not hide the excitement in her eyes. 'This is Josepha,' he said stiffly.

'Your servant, ma'am.' Hanley bowed as far as was possible on horseback. 'Been improving your Spanish?' he asked his friend.

'I am a serious soldier.'

'You almost sound like Bills! Good luck with your endeavours, but I fear we must hurry on.' He urged his horse straight into a canter, and it took the hussar a moment to match him, but the soldier could guess why the officer was grinning from ear to ear.

At the next village Hanley stopped to water their horses and speak to the priest, who sometimes had news. In this case it merely confirmed what he had already heard, but did allow one question.

'Who owns the big house in Fuentes de Oñoro?'

'Ah, that is Don Fernando Martín. He owns a lot of land and several houses.' The old priest cocked his head to one side, trying to understand the reason for the question. 'He is ardent for Fernando VII. One of his sons was killed last year by the French and he hates them bitterly. His daughter is betrothed to Don Julián Sánchez.'

'Does he have more than one daughter?'

'Just one, little Josepha.'

As Hanley and the hussar rode on, he wondered

whether his friend was aware that he was playing with fire.

'Boney isn't coming,' said Colonel Murray as the meeting began.

Hanley made no reply.

'I take it from your ecstatic reaction that you were already aware of this – and I had so hoped to dazzle my audience with my godlike knowledge. Pity.'

Baynes took over, his voice dripping with irony. 'The Emperor has decided that he cannot leave France and pressing affairs of state – and no doubt the eager pressing of his little Austrian princess.'

'Good luck to him,' said Murray, 'and let us hope good luck to us as well.'

'It speaks of immense complacency, and we must all hope that he is mistaken.'

'Are you ready to feign astonishment and gasp appropriately when I reveal his choice to command the invasion of Portugal?' asked Murray, one eyebrow raised.

'Bless me,' said Hanley.

'Not the most convincing performance – especially as I haven't told you yet – but since you are so evidently waiting with bated breath to hear what you already know, then I will assuage your nervousness. The Army of Portugal is now under the command of Marshal Masséna, the newly minted Prince of Essling.'

'He's well into his sixties, used to be a smuggler

and is probably more than half pirate by instinct,' said Baynes. 'Half blind these days, after he was shot in the eye.'

'In battle?' asked Hanley.

'No, out hunting with the Emperor. It seems our friend Bonaparte is as dangerous to his friends as to his enemies. Boney got excited and peppered him with buckshot.'

'Typical gunner,' muttered Colonel Murray.

'Yes, well, the sequel tells us a good deal about the gallant duke,' said Baynes. 'For quick as a flash he rounds on Marshal Berthier and blames him for firing the shot. Can't have emperors making mistakes, after all, so the good marshal pleads guilty and now he and Masséna pretend to be enemies to keep up the charade. Truth is such a malleable thing.' The merchant seemed filled with admiration.

'Masséna is a rogue, and a clever one at that, and though perhaps I should not say it, those are admirable qualifications for the commander of an army.' Colonel Murray did not look at all abashed. 'He's been fighting since the nineties, against half of Europe, and he keeps on winning. Last year he saved the day when Boney was really up against it with the Austrians on the Danube.'

'We are told that he is not fully recovered from taking a tumble off his horse during that campaign,' Baynes added, 'and the suspicion is that he was none too pleased to be chosen by the Emperor.'

'My source writes that he looks very old and

weary,' Hanley said. 'The lady saw him when he arrived at Salamanca on 11th May.' Both Murray and Baynes knew La Doña Margarita and were aware that she was living in Salamanca. There was no need to be so incautious as to mention her name. 'General Junot and his wife were there with Ney waiting to greet him. Madame Junot is heavily with child, and has befriended our source, and so she was able to witness an unfortunate encounter.'

'You have us intrigued,' said Murray.

'Marshal Masséna has an additional member of his staff, who travels in his carriage. Quite often it is simply the two of them.'

'Get on with it, man!' The colonel's tone was jovial. 'Although since you were not polite enough to get the vapours at my revelations, I'll be damned if I'll get too excited about your stories.'

'This special ADC is married to one of his officers and is the sister of another of his aides. She dresses as a dragoon officer.'

'High boots and tight breeches,' said Murray to Baynes.

'The "officer" was presented to Madame Junot at Valladolid, and ushered into rooms in the same wing of the palace. General Junot shook her hand happily, but his wife was embarrassed and angry.'

Baynes was amused. 'From all I've heard the lady in question is no blushing virgin herself, but I suppose since Boney gave them all titles they must act the part.'

'Fascinating in its way, I am sure,' said Murray,

'and no doubt all soldiers will admire the marshal for providing himself with such a complete set of campaigning kit, but it makes little difference for our purposes.'

'Save that there is little love lost between Masséna and his commanders. Ney resents being placed under the command of another marshal, and the strong feelings of Madame Junot will probably persuade her husband in time.'

'None of that is new. Most of these fellows will take orders from Boney, but resent it from anyone else,' said Murray.

'It is no bad way to prevent the emergence of a rival,' Baynes added.

'But not really the best way to fight a war,' Murray concluded. 'Soult has bombarded Ney with order after order to attack Ciudad Rodrigo since the start of the year, and he has done almost nothing. If you ask me he has probably been right, but that's neither here nor there.

'Up until now they have not had the strength, but it looks as if they will soon be ready, and it is hard to believe that they will not move now that Masséna is here. It's harder to ignore a direct order than a letter. Since Astorga fell, Junot is free with his Eighth Corps. Ney's Sixth Corps has been reinforced by a third division. Reynier with the Second Corps is still down south for the moment. Reinforcements for most of the regiments within these corps have arrived or are on their way, and fresh units are coming as well. Your reports and all the others speak of the gathering of supplies.'

Hanley gave a summary of his latest information. 'They seem to be preparing for a good deal of construction, gathering timber, nails and tools – oh, and they have sewn hundreds of sacks and been making big wicker containers.'

'Sandbags, gabions and fascines for the engineers,' said Murray. 'Everything speaks of siege works.'

'Are we sure they will not bypass Ciudad Rodrigo and Almeida,' Baynes asked, 'and just leave some soldiers to watch their garrisons? By the sound of it they will have enough men.'

'Lord Wellington thinks not,' said Murray. 'It would certainly be a risk to leave them in their rear. Apart from that, every stronghold taken is a blow to people's confidence. Especially if they surrender. Cox will fight, but . . .' Murray left the thought unfinished.

'The French outposts are now almost within sight of Ciudad Rodrigo,' he continued. It looks like they are not much more than brigade strength at the moment, but Herrasti is getting hysterical and begging us to come and drive them away. Frankly he's got the numbers to do that himself if it were so critical.'

'His soldiers are mainly raw,' said Hanley, 'and I believe he is cautious about risking them in the open field. At our last meeting he did ask me to emphasise that he would be greatly aided by the sending of the guns left behind last year. They are Spanish after all, and bigger than anything he has at the moment.'

'Which is precisely why he cannot have them.' Baynes' irony was once again heavy, and it was clear that he and Murray had discussed the matter already. 'It is a question of trust.'

The colonel grunted. 'Or lack of trust, as you damned well know. Look, Hanley, if we let him have those pieces and Ciudad Rodrigo falls, then we have just given the French a bigger siege train with which to batter Almeida.'

'Herrasti rejected another summons to surrender earlier this month.' Hanley's support was cautious.

Murray was dismissive. 'By a small force without the slightest chance of actually taking the place. Can we be sure what he will do when the real army arrives?'

'He wants to fight,' said Hanley. 'I am fully convinced of that, but he fears that we will not support him and the refusal to give him the guns will weaken his support. There are elements within the city less stubborn in their will to resist. Some despair, and I suspect that generous offers are being presented by agents of King Joseph.'

Baynes immediately became intent. 'Are you sure?'

'It's just a feeling. The way some of them are starting to speak.'

Hanley had expected Murray to be sceptical of such a vague impression, and was surprised that he took him so seriously. 'Lord Wellington will not give him those guns. Another powder convoy is being prepared. General Craufurd says that there should be no difficulty in getting it through as the French encirclement is far from complete.'

'That should help.'

'Lord Wellington has also written to assure the governor that he will come to his aid and is willing to fight an action outside Ciudad Rodrigo if the chance offers.' Murray looked doubtful. 'Whether the man will realise that we cannot risk going up against such great numbers if the French concentrate all their forces is another matter.'

'Once again, trust and mistrust.' Hanley was privately toying with an idea.

'If the French concentrate against Ciudad Rodrigo then nothing in the world will stop them from taking it in the end,' said Murray flatly. 'The only question is how long it will take. Personally I suspect that Almeida will delay them longer, but that city will also fall in the end. We need as much time as they can give us, and so we want Herrasti to fight.'

'And he will only do that if he believes he can trust us to save him, which we cannot actually do,' Hanley finished the thought. 'The presence of British soldiers would help.'

Murray frowned. 'Wellington won't waste any of his battalions inside a doomed fortress. Even Cox has only Portuguese.'

'It does not need to be a battalion.' Hanley was

slightly disturbed by what he was about to suggest. Although less by the idea itself than his own willingness to do it.

'A token gesture.' Baynes watched the lieutenant closely; the merchant's face betrayed excitement and Hanley suspected he had guessed what he had in mind.

'No more than that, but a few redcoats walking the walls would make it easier for Herrasti to believe, and for him to convince the rest of the city.'

'Some of Colonel MacAndrews' men, perhaps?' suggested Baynes with a passable impersonation of innocence. The merchant continued to stare at Hanley. 'There is a lot to be said in favour of such an idea.'

Murray looked dubious, but clearly saw the potential of the plan. 'That would need the peer's permission,' he said, using the name commonly employed by Wellington's staff following his elevation. 'Once the French close the circle around the city, there is a strong chance that they will not get out again.'

'They could not leave once they are there. That would give the wrong sort of gesture altogether and spoil any good it had done.' Baynes still watched Hanley, and there was a trace of admiration in his voice. 'We must be prepared to pay a price for this. The only chance would be if the city fell, and by then they might be dead or trapped without any hope of escape.'

'Yes,' said Hanley, 'they might indeed, and Herrasti will know that, and so be more inclined to feel that we will save him.'

Murray remained sceptical. 'I shall ask. If Lord Wellington says yes, then in the circumstances we would also need to speak to the Spanish.'

'I cannot see them refusing.' Baynes was confident and his gaze fell on the lieutenant. 'An individual may be able to sneak out of the city more easily, especially if he is clever.'

'That is reasonable to suppose,' Hanley said, returning the stare.

'If Joseph's agents are at work in Ciudad Rodrigo, then I believe you should go and look for them before they do serious harm. You will be able to call on your friends for assistance, should it prove necessary.'

'You have already chosen the ones to go?'

'And you have not?' Baynes gave a half-smile, ignoring the slightly puzzled expression of Colonel Murray. 'My dear William, do not think I am sending you to Ciudad Rodrigo as some form of penance. If someone, perhaps Velarde, is there, then he must be found and prevented from doing us harm.'

Hanley rubbed his chin, and realised that he must have forgotten to shave, for his normally thick stubble felt very rough indeed. 'Before that I believe I should go to Salamanca.'

For the first time Baynes registered the slightest trace of surprise, before the mask returned an instant later.

'Velarde is more likely to be there, at least at the moment.' Hanley tried to sound more confident than he felt. 'If he is there, then our sources may be in danger and should be warned.'

'Sentiment?' said Baynes.

'Simple practicality. They are little use to us dead. I also suspect that it will be easier to find Velarde's trail from there.'

'If he is there.'

'Yes, if he is.' Hanley tried and failed to read Baynes' secret thoughts.

'Hmm, I think we shall be wise to let you follow your instincts, wherever they lead. You had better not go alone, though. I have someone suitable to accompany you.'

'As protection?'

'Let us say to preserve what you know.'

Hanley was shrewd enough not to find that a great comfort.

'Of course.'

'I do like a willing volunteer,' said Colonel Murray, 'and now I should leave you to plan your sinister schemes and try to get the peer's attention.'

CHAPTER 14

Compared to Fort La Concepción, Ciudad Rodrigo looked very old.

'Moorish work, do you think?' Williams asked Pringle as they looked out from the north-western corner of the roughly square city walls. Behind them was the high domed tower of the cathedral.

'Looks like it, although someone must have made them thicker at some point.' The high medieval walls were now wide enough to take a cannon and let it slam back in recoil without tumbling off. There were a few old towers, but no bastions and only simple embrasures cut out of the parapet. It would be hard to fire many guns at the same target, and when the enemy got closer there were most likely blind spots safe from the blasts of the defenders' cannons. Height was no longer the advantage it had once been. There was a ditch in front of the wall, and this was divided into two by an earth wall and given modern bastions, but these did not mount cannon at present and it was hard to imagine the defenders being able to hold these once the besiegers worked their way closer. The spoil of the ditch was used to make a glacis, but the walls were too high for this to offer much protection.

'That's the way they'll come,' said Williams, and rested his telescope on the battlement. It was a heavy glass, intended to be mounted on a tripod, and had been a gift from his mother when he joined the army. The magnification was excellent, but it was really too cumbersome for a soldier. Williams refused to accept this, and carried the bulky thing with stubborn determination.

Billy Pringle did not need to draw his own glass to know that his lieutenant was right. To the south of the town was the River Agueda, filled to the brim with spring rain and making even these old city walls very difficult to attack. East of the town sprawled a suburb, with dozens of stone houses and walled gardens. In the last year the governor had fortified three stoutly built convents and thrown up earthworks around the whole area. It was not impossible to come that way, but it was difficult. To the west beside the river yet another convent had been turned into a miniature fortress, and walled orchards and gardens offered more good defensive positions.

It did not matter. Williams looked to the north, where a few hundred yards from the north-western corner of the town a hill rose up sharply. Beyond it was another, even bigger hill.

'They are called the Little and Great Tesons,' said Pringle. From the Great Teson French gunners could look down over the glacis and see the base of the old medieval wall. The hill was well within range of siege guns, and if the artillerymen could see a target then they could also pound it steadily, and the Moorish architects had not built their wall to withstand the weapons of the future. Sieges were slow affairs, as the attackers dug their way gradually closer and closer. By the time the French reached the Little Teson, the walls would most surely be breached if their gunners were any good at all – and the artillery was the Emperor's own arm and many said that French gunners were the best in the world. Once they had batteries on the nearer hill they could pound the city and its defences to dust.

'It seems that we have some distinguished guests.' Williams drew back from his glass and pointed. Pringle gratefully pushed his spectacles back to the top of his head and leaned down to take a look. The lens needed some adjustment for his eye, but as the blurs became sharp he saw a group of horsemen atop the Great Teson. Some were gaudily dressed – no doubt the ADCs – but the important men were in dark blue coats and from this distance he could not really make out the heavy gold lace and the thick plumes on their cocked hats. The men were generals, perhaps even one of the marshals who had made all Europe tremble.

'Captain Pringle, sir.' The interruption came from Lieutenant Leyne, an eager young Irishman whose voice was still apt to break at moments of excitement like this. 'The governor wants us.' Leyne was short and a good deal bigger around the middle than Pringle himself. The dash up to the ramparts to find his commander had left him with a face nearly as scarlet as his jacket. 'All of us, sir!' added Leyne, almost bursting with enthusiasm.

'Bills, you had better form the company. Now, young Philip, you had better show me the way.' Pringle was twenty-six, and that seemed so ancient compared to the seventeen-year-old lieutenant beside him. Perhaps, he thought ruefully, the real difference was that Leyne had yet to see any action. That tended to age a man quickly.

An hour later and it seemed as if Leyne would very soon get his long-desired first whiff of powder. A major from General Herrasti's staff had led them to the lee of the Convent of Santa Cruz, the outpost beyond the western walls of the fortress.

Pringle had his entire command of almost fifty officers and men with him. Apart from Williams and Leyne, he had Lieutenant Dolosa, and while Billy continued to have doubts about the man, so far he had more than played his part, helping them to settle in since their arrival five days ago. If any of the officers looked nervous, it was Leyne, who could not keep still and continually hopped from foot to foot.

His NCOs were all good. Dobson and Murphy were old comrades, and Corporal Rose of the 51st was a quietly competent young man from Warwickshire. That all three shared a mutual respect for the Spanish sergeant and two corporals was an extremely high recommendation; they seemed part of some instinctive brotherhood of non-commissioned officers. His thirty-nine men were a different matter, part of the second batch of raw recruits to come to Fort La Concepción. Although Spanish and British instructors had done their best, the men had simply not yet had the time to be ready.

Nevertheless, the orders had come to send a company to Ciudad Rodrigo. Pringle could see that MacAndrews was none too pleased, especially since the orders had specified that Billy was to command and Williams to go with him. The instructions claimed that they would help to train the garrison of the city, but there was no hint of that once they arrived. They were a reinforcement pure and simple, and Pringle found it worrying to think that they might be one of the better-trained companies in the garrison. Of even greater concern was his suspicion that Hanley had played a part in their new orders. His friend was a worthy chap in many ways, but he was also a gambler who got a thrill from the scale of the stakes. A year before he had helped engineer an attack on a detachment under Pringle's command, so that the enemy would in turn be surprised by Allied cavalry. It had worked – just barely – but men had died and Billy doubted that Hanley thought of such things and instead focused solely on winning.

The Spanish major looked at his watch and then led them behind the high convent walls and threaded his way through the gardens and orchards. Eventually he halted them, and gestured for Pringle to come with him to an arched gateway and told him in French to be careful. The man spoke the language well, and it seemed their best chance of avoiding confusion.

They walked to a bank topped by a hedge and the major took off his hat before he peered over the top. Pringle copied him, and saw that there was an outpost of French infantry on a low knoll ahead of them. He counted twenty men, a couple of them on guard looking towards the city and the rest sitting on their packs, most smoking short clay pipes. It was a warmer day, and, although it was cloudy, the rain stayed away, yet the Frenchmen wore their dark blue coats. Their collars were yellow, their epaulettes green and yellow and they had tall plumes on their shakos. The men were voltigeurs, the skirmishers of a French battalion.

'At eleven o'clock the general will send a thousand men out of the main gate against the French,' said the major. 'Ten minutes later, take your company and attack this picket. Another company from the Majorca Regiment has worked round through the gardens and will come up behind them. With luck, they will be trapped between you and you can take or kill them all.'

Pringle's experience made him deeply suspicious of any plan relying on luck. He would have liked to meet the commander of the other company. It seemed strange that he had not seen them pass as they waited, but it was possible that the Majorca men had been in position for hours.

'I must go,' the major announced, and that was also worrying, and then Pringle wondered whether he was simply innately suspicious of commanders he did not know – especially ones who were not British.

Pringle called his officers forward and explained the plan. Dolosa's English was now much improved, and his only questions were ones of detail, not understanding.

'Is there a signal that will tell us the Majorca Regiment is in position?'

Pringle shook his head, his own doubts reinforced by the expressions of Williams and the Spanish lieutenant. Leyne's nervous excitement clearly did not permit him similar thoughts.

At eleven o'clock cannon opened fire from all along the city walls. The sound was encouraging, and no doubt that was the intention, but good targets were few as the French outposts were scattered and at some distance. Between the shots they heard cheering, and Pringle guessed that this was the main column launching its attack.

Ten minutes seemed more like hours as they

waited. Pringle told Williams to keep the French picket under observation.

'They've formed up,' he whispered as soon as the main attack began.

Pringle was counting in his head, and only when he thought it was getting close did he fish out his watch and flick open the cover. There was almost a minute to go. The Spanish sergeant had just finished checking the men's flints. Pringle had not given the order, but the man had gone ahead, knowing that having something to do helped soldiers to deal with their nerves. In time, and with such NCOs, Billy was sure that this could become a good company.

It was ten past eleven.

'Bills, take your party through and watch our left.'

Williams and the three redcoats would act as skirmishers. It was little more than a token, for four men could scarcely form a serious skirmish line, but Billy Pringle reckoned that the lieutenant and the three NCOs might do more good than if they simply reinforced the line.

The four men jogged through the gap in the hedge. Pringle gave them a moment and then gestured to the company. Sergeant Rodriguez bellowed the command and the recruits followed the British captain. They went in a little column two abreast, and once they were through into the field beyond, the sergeant shouted again and they wheeled to the right to form a line two deep. That was the British way and the method MacAndrews had taught. The Spanish, like the French and all the rest of Europe, usually deployed in three ranks, giving their line greater solidity. For a moment Pringle wished he had thought of doing this, but in truth he had too few men.

Williams was kneeling, ahead and over to the left, and then he pulled the trigger. Rose fired a moment later, and then both were reloading as Dobson and Murphy respectively covered them. Sergeants of a grenadier company were supposed to carry a solid half-pike, but Dobson disliked so basic a weapon and Murphy was newly promoted, and both had stuck to their old muskets.

A Frenchman was down, clutching at his knee, but the rest of the picket had shaken out into a chain of skirmishers facing them. It was this movement that had prompted Williams to open fire. Surprise had gone.

Pringle took the company forward, standing a few paces ahead of its right flank. Leyne was behind him and Dolosa watched the left. Billy felt his boots sinking an inch or so into the mud and was surprised at just how waterlogged the field was. Already the ranks were uneven, the rudimentary drill his soldiers had failing to cope with the slippery ground. Flecks of mud were already peppered over Pringle's boots and his white breeches.

The French were still more than a hundred yards away. That was quite a long range for accurate musketry, but the enemy were already firing. Pringle heard a ball fly close by his cheek. He made himself march on without showing any emotion. His Talavera wound began to itch. There was no sign of the Majorca Regiment, but perhaps they were behind the French outpost and were creeping steadily closer, unnoticed because all of the voltigeurs' attention was fixed on his men.

Dobson and Murphy fired, now that Williams and Rose had reloaded and were ready to cover them. Half a dozen voltigeurs were aiming at the redcoats, but all the rest shot at the better target of the formed company. There was a terrible, high-pitched scream as one of the recruits was hit in the groin, blood gushing out on to his grey trousers.

'Keep going!' called Pringle.

The company stopped, men staring in horror as the man cried out and tried in vain to staunch the flow.

Dolosa was yelling and so were the NCOs, all of them trying to get the company moving again. Sergeant Rodriguez took one man by the shoulders and bodily pushed him forward, and then did the same to the man beside him, but the first one had already frozen again.

Someone fired, not aiming the musket, but simply swinging it down from the shoulder and sending a ball high above the voltigeurs. The sergeant bawled at the man, telling him he would be punished, but it was simply too much for the young soldiers to stand by and not do something against the enemy firing at them. Three more men fired and then the rest copied them. It was no volley, instead more like the spattering of raindrops on a window at the start of a heavy shower. No Frenchmen fell, and Pringle doubted that any shot came anywhere near its target.

The recruits were happier now, the enemy more than half hidden behind a cloud of dirty grey powder smoke. They began reloading, but they were painfully slow. Men fumbled as they fished for cartridges in their pouches, then spilled half the powder when they bit through the paper. More than one dropped the ball without noticing, and went on regardless. Sergeant Rodriguez cuffed a man who tipped ball and cartridge down the barrel without first taking a pinch of powder for the pan. The young soldier stared blankly at the angry NCO, and then a ball struck him in the chest and he dropped, a look of utter astonishment on his face.

None of the men managed to reload in less than a minute, and they ignored the orders to wait and fired as soon as they were ready. Pringle was better placed to see past the smoke and once again did not see any Frenchman fall. Nor was there the slightest sign of the company from the Majorca Regiment. If they stayed where they were they would lose men and probably do little damage to the enemy. That was fine if the other company arrived behind the French, but would be sheer waste if they did not. Billy Pringle made a decision.

'Bayonets!' he shouted. 'Bayonets!'

Dolosa, Sergeant Rodriguez and the corporals began jostling the men to stop them from loading. With much cursing and a good few blows, one by one they got the recruits to draw bayonets. Once again it was clumsy. Bayonets slipped from nervous hands, and one man dropped the butt of his musket so hard that the hammer slammed down and it fired, driving the ball through his own left wrist. Rodriguez pulled the man out of the line and sent him to the rear, telling him not to make a fuss. The boy – like the rest of them he was really no more than a boy – looked surprised to be rebuked, and then silently walked away, looking like a child worried at being scolded by a parent.

Lieutenant Dolosa was yelling, speaking so fast that Pringle could only just understand the words, telling the men that this was their chance to punish the French for invading their land.

'Forward march!' called Pringle. He strode ahead, keeping his gaze fixed on the enemy, not wanting to let the men see that he doubted whether or not they would follow him. Sergeant Rodriguez was haranguing them. A shot snapped past not too far above his head, and there was a thud and a moan as someone was hit.

Then the French were going back. Pringle was surprised, but the French were skirmishers and did not want to let formed troops get too close.

They did it well, and under control, working in pairs like Williams and his men. One man helped another to the rear, and a third voltigeur was stretched in the grass, unmoving, and Billy suspected that one of the redcoats must have hit him because he doubted any of the shots fired by the company had struck home.

Someone fired from behind him, and Pringle turned and swore as he saw that the company had halted again. Men skinned their knuckles as they went through the loading drill with bayonets fixed. Rodriguez was trying to drag men forward, and Dolosa was screaming at them to move, but they would not.

'Come on, my brave lads!' The voice was shrill as Leyne ran past Pringle waving his sword. 'Come on to glory!'

'*Viva el rey Fernando!*' Dolosa set off after him. The rough company line rippled as some men shuffled a few paces forward.

'French on our left!' That was Williams, shouting a warning, and when Pringle looked he saw a formed company appearing from a fold in the ground. The men had tall red plumes and red epaulettes and that marked them as grenadiers.

'Back!' Billy shouted. Going forward now would only help the grenadiers to get behind them.

'On, my lads, follow me!' Leyne was still yelling, and then he staggered as a ball broke his right arm above the elbow. He dropped his slim sword, but kept running at the voltigeurs and urging the men on. A few of the recruits were charging now, but in the back rank others responded to Pringle's command and turned and ran.

Leyne was shot again, this time in the stomach, and his shouts turned into a long-drawn-out shriek as he slumped to his knees, his one good hand pressed over this second wound. Dolosa was beside him, and then he too stumbled and fell, blood bright just above the top of his left boot.

The company collapsed. All the recruits were now running, streaming back towards the gap in the hedge.

'*En avant!*' a man on horseback sent the grenadiers into a sudden screaming charge. The man had a white cloak and a silver helmet shaped like the ones dragoons wore, and that seemed strange for the commander of infantry.

'Back, Bills! Get back!' screamed Billy. Williams fired, as did Rose, and then all four redcoats were running.

One of the Spanish corporals ran forward to rescue Dolosa and somehow he inspired a recruit to go with him. Pringle called to Rodriguez, pointing at the gap. 'We need to hold there!' Whether or not he understood all the words, the man was experienced enough to guess the sense. 'Bills, stop at the hedge!' Pringle added.

The horseman had spurred forward, and now hacked down once, the heavy blade wielded with practised strength so that it cut through the corporal's bicorne hat and skull. The recruit stopped, frozen in horror, and was still staring blankly when the Frenchman freed his blade, and turned his horse back. The recruit died from a thrust through the collar of his jacket. Grenadiers were running around them now. Dolosa staggered to his feet, screaming insults at the enemy, and sliced with his sword to nick the arm of the first grenadier to reach him. For a moment the French soldiers fell back a couple of steps. Then one brought his musket up and shot the Spanish lieutenant in the head.

One of the recruits lost a boot in the mud. He ran on awkwardly for a few paces and then slipped and fell. By the time he had pushed himself up a grenadier with the single gold stripe of a sergeant on the sleeve of his jacket was on him. The young soldier raised his hands. The sergeant ignored him and jabbed precisely with his bayonet, the point sliding between the man's ribs to pierce his heart.

Two more recruits tried to surrender, and Pringle watched as one was shot and the other bayoneted. He had not seen warfare quite as brutal as this, for the French and British generally treated each other with great respect. The grenadiers did not look wild, in a state when even mild men might kill without hesitation. Instead they seemed to slaughter the helpless men almost casually. Billy felt that he was no longer in a war he knew, and that thought was chilling. Leyne was stretched on the ground, not moving, but Pringle had not seen anyone deliver a death blow so hoped that they would allow the poor young Irishman the chance to surrender.

210

Williams and Rose stood behind the kneeling Dobson and Murphy as Billy jogged through the gap in the hedge. Once he was past, the two kneeling men fired.

'Back to the garden!' Billy pointed to show Williams where he meant, and then turned to see Rodriguez and the remaining corporal standing just behind the hedge. He gestured and they came forward to cover the gap. The French were forming up again, the helmeted horseman urging them into the attack.

Pringle glanced back and saw that Williams and his men were in the arched gateway of the walled garden. He gave them enough time to reload before giving the order.

'Fire!'

The two Spaniards took careful aim and then fired.

'Now, get back!' yelled Pringle, and he waited for the two men to go before following. The smoke from their shots thinned enough for him to see that a grenadier was down. Shots came back in reply, shaking the hedge as they struck.

The French did not follow, and that was just as well because with only Williams and the five NCOs Pringle doubted that they could have held them off long enough to escape.

That evening Pringle remained angry with himself for the failure, and even more bitter at the confused and ill-thought-out orders behind the attack. The main sally had failed, and now he had discovered that the company from the Majorca Regiment had been ordered to a different task at the last minute, but that no one had informed the major who gave him his orders.

His men – and they were his even if they still seemed strangers and he could not claim to know them and their moods in the same way that he knew his own grenadiers – had broken and fled. Most had run as far back as the convent and then waited there, and once again they had looked like schoolboys, this time caught out in some misdemeanour. One source of relief was that none of them had dropped his musket, and that suggested that the panic was not total.

Yet when they had marched back into the town, people they passed had cheered them and shouted out '*Viva los ingleses!*' They seemed happy that the garrison was striking at the enemy, and happier still that the British were here.

Pringle wondered how long the mood would last. Josepha dozed beside him, and as he shifted to get more comfortable he tried his best not to wake her. Personally he doubted that the British army would be willing to take too great a risk to save Ciudad Rodrigo. He had never before experienced a siege, and was none too enthusiastic about the prospect. It was hard to lose men, and he suspected that the day's casualties would not be the last.

Even more he worried about Josepha. Pringle had not known that she had gone to Ciudad

Rodrigo to stay with the widowed cousin of her mother, a lady who appeared to have generous views on the freedom allowed to young people. Civilians were not safe in a siege. Indeed, they were probably not safe from the French almost anywhere in Spain, but when a city fell it was worse. Soldiers forced to fight their way over or through the walls of a fortress were apt to run wild. Pringle already wondered whether he would be able to protect her when the time came.

Yet worse than that was the realisation of Josepha's desperation. They had met when he led a training march through Fuentes de Oñoro and he had accepted her family's hospitality. He had returned at every opportunity, for the girl's mother was dead, her father almost always absent and her enthusiasm was so great. She had spoken of her betrothal, but so dismissively that he had not felt worried. Now the fellow was here, and a bloodthirsty leader of partisans no doubt unlikely to take too kindly to a rival.

That mattered less than the words she had spoken before she had drifted off. Josepha had talked of marriage and going to England, and there had been such desperation in her voice. Pringle had not realised that she was looking for such a thing, and then wondered whether that was because at first his Spanish had been limited. Had he given her some hope of that without meaning to do so? That would be unfortunate, because she was a sweet-natured girl of immense kindness. The truth was that in the last months he had once or twice thought of marriage, but not with this pretty child. Instead he found himself thinking of Miss Anne Williams more and more often. His life seemed to be becoming much more serious.

Billy Pringle was worried, and for the first time since returning to Spain he really wanted to be so drunk that the world and his cares faded away for a few hours. He wished MacAndrews or someone else was here, for then he would not be senior and could indulge himself. Instead, he stared up through the high window at the silhouette of the castle's tower and simply worried.

CHAPTER 15

The ball hit the old stone battlements and flicked up a little puff of dust as it flattened. A moment later a second bullet punched yet another hole in the hat held on a stick above the parapet by one of the recruits. Corporal Rose grinned at him, and the lad was by now confident enough to smile back. Pringle was pleased, for he felt the men were beginning to get used to being under fire.

Shots had so far come in groups of four, and so Rose waited for two more to strike the wall and then bobbed up in the embrasure. He took a moment to aim and steady himself and then fired down into the field beyond the glacis. As he ducked back behind the battlements he exchanged his musket for one freshly loaded. Pringle had six of the company up on the wall assisting Rose. Five loaded and the other raised the hat on a stick to give the French sharpshooters a target. Rose was probably the best shot in the company and so he was given this job, while the others drilled the remainder of the recruits. Pringle wanted to avoid another shambles like the last sortie.

Day by day, the French were drawing an ever tighter ring around the town. Before dawn, pairs of their voltigeurs crept forward to within musket range of the wall. Some had scraped pits for cover, while others used garden walls or fallen trees. Throughout the day they sniped at the defenders, shooting especially at the embrasures they knew contained guns. Not many gunners had been hit so far. Inevitably almost all were struck in the head or shoulders since the rest of them was protected by the parapet, and so the wounds were bad or fatal.

The chances of Rose hitting any of the concealed Frenchmen was slight, and Pringle kept wishing that they had one of the 95th with them to use his more accurate, rifled musket. He was more concerned with making his men feel valuable, and giving obvious purpose to practising loading.

His men had not been ordered to take part in any of the sallies launched after the first day. None had gone well, for the French regiments closest to the town were obviously veterans. Sometimes they gave way a little when surprised, but it was never long before they struck back, usually from an unexpected direction and always with ferocious confidence. A day ago Pringle and Williams had watched helplessly from the walls as they saw voltigeurs working their way around both flanks of a strong column from one of the volunteer battalions. Suddenly shot at from the sides and rear, the citizens turned so recently to soldiers had panicked and fled. So had many of the townsfolk

216

lining the battlements, for while the sallies were launched the French skirmishers were too busy to fire at the walls and so it was safe to stand there. Women had screamed and then the two British officers found themselves clinging on to the battlements to stop themselves from being swept away by the stampede. Fighting outside played to all the strengths of the French.

That afternoon Pringle heard the senior engineer officer Brigadier Don Juan de Beletá say as much at a meeting held by the governor. He had found himself summoned to these daily sessions, and was by far the most junior in rank to attend. Sometimes it was just the soldiers who were brought together, but on other days the bishop who held civilian authority and other town worthies were also present. Pringle struggled to follow the rapid Spanish, but noticed that the soldiers usually did their best to speak slowly, or sometimes employed French.

'It is better than sitting and doing nothing,' said Herrasti after patiently listening to his subordinate's observations. 'Soldiers and civilians alike feel better because we are doing something. They are inspired, too, by your raids, Don Julián.' The governor gave a slight bow.

El Charro responded with equal courtesy. 'I'll ride out again tonight with all my men. Half will strike at their bridges.'

'What progress have they made?' asked the senior engineer, particularly interested in his French counterparts. Marshal Ney had set his men to building two bridges across the Agueda. The town's guns controlled the stone bridge under its walls, and there were no other crossings for a great distance with the water so high.

'The first is finished,' Don Julián Sánchez said tonelessly. 'The second will soon be complete. They are still throwing up redoubts to protect each one.' That was chilling, because it would give the French much greater access to the far bank and help them to surround Ciudad Rodrigo completely.

'Everything we have sent down the river at them has not made much difference,' Beletá explained. His men had floated heavy logs, and even tried a barge set on fire, but the current had not worked well and the French intercepted almost everything. 'How much damage can you do?'

Don Julián shrugged. 'Well, we'll rob them of sleep, and maybe kill one or two we find wandering about, but there is no point flinging my men against ramparts.' He looked around the table, glancing at each face in turn and lingering. Pringle was not sure whether or not El Charro paused just a little longer when looking at him. It was very strange to be in the same room as Josepha's betrothed. Pringle was surprised at his small size, but that impression swiftly faded in the face of the guerrilla leader's controlled force. The others were older men, of higher rank in the regular army, and yet all clearly respected the former sergeant. El

Charro knew how to fight, and governor and townsfolk alike felt happier that he was here.

'While half my men go for the bridges,' Don Julián continued, 'I shall take the rest and slip through the French outposts. We shall head for the Salamanca road and see if there are any supply convoys to snap up.' There were still wide gaps in the French outpost line. Messengers and even large parties could pass through with care.

'Then may God go with you, for we could dearly do with a victory,' said the governor. 'Still, I have received a letter from Lord Wellington assuring me of his support.' He beamed at Pringle. 'Gentlemen, we must be careful, but we will continue to raid and harry the enemy as much as possible. The trick will be never to go so far that we cannot readily escape.

'I cannot say how much we will hurt them, but even the least thing will help. And we can slow them down. Every hour spent standing to arms and facing one of our attacks is an hour they cannot be labouring on the siege works, so let them spend more time floundering in the mud.' Pringle's orders to Rose and his party followed the same reasoning, perhaps creating a nuisance, and at least helping to instil some experience into his raw soldiers.

'The artillery will only fire in support of our sallies or if some magnificent target appears.' This was the Commandant General in charge of the artillery. 'We must save powder and shot to smash

219

their batteries when those are built and cannon mounted in them. A little practice now will help our gunners to learn, but we do not want to wear out the guns or their crews so early on.'

Herrasti dealt with a few more minor matters, before asking the bishop to close in prayer. At the end he smiled encouragingly. 'Well, that is all for today. Thank you, gentlemen.'

As they left, Captain Pringle thought it best to let all the senior men go first, and so was almost the last to leave the room. Don Julián Sánchez was waiting in the corridor, and the little man fell into step beside him, holding his helmet under one arm.

'I believe we have a mutual friend.' El Charro was smiling, but Pringle could not help thinking that the same was true of many a predator before it pounced. He hoped that his face betrayed no emotion. The man should not know of his affair with Josepha, but then guerrillas were surely very good at finding out about their enemies. Billy Pringle dearly hoped this small and cheerful man was not his enemy.

'Guillermo Hanley,' the guerrilla explained.

Pringle hoped his own broad smile would pass for simple pleasure and not relief. 'Oh, Hanley. Yes, he is an excellent fellow.'

'He said the company coming from La Concepción would be led by two of his comrades and that you were both men to be trusted.'

Was there an edge in El Charro's voice? 'Decent

of him, although to tell you the truth, I cannot see what good we are doing here.'

'You are here as a symbol,' said Don Julián Sánchez. 'People feel that if redcoats are here with us, then your general will be all the more ready to come and save them when the crisis comes.'

'Then why keep us out of the way rather than parade us marching out to new attacks?'

'Herrasti has done that once, and it cost him one of your number. You are no use to him if you all get killed.'

They came out of the castle into the market square.

'*Viva El Charro!*' The shout went up almost instantly, soldiers joining in with the women and the elderly civilians going about their business. '*Viva El Charro y viva los ingleses!*'

The guerrilla leader waved to the crowd. A few women ran forward and knelt to kiss his hand. 'You see what I mean,' he said to Pringle as they at last got through the crowd. 'I do know all about being a symbol. We give them hope, and that is a rare and precious thing in a doomed town.'

Pringle was shocked at the words, and this time he obviously betrayed his feelings.

'Do you really think Wellington will let his army be destroyed outside these walls?' El Charro looked up at him, his head leaning slightly to the left. 'What would that achieve?'

'If the French give him a chance, he will take it.'

'If. Well, they sometimes do make mistakes, but

221

not too often. They're good, and there are a lot more of them than there are redcoats.'

'There are now the Portuguese as well.'

As a Spaniard El Charro instinctively winced, but as a skilled leader and a practical man who had lived on the borders, he let himself consider the point. 'Still not enough of them to even the odds.'

'So the war is lost.' Pringle thought of Reynolds drunkenly holding forth. He had heard plenty of other British officers express similar thoughts, but had not expected them from so feared a guerrilla.

'It is not over.' El Charro's voice rasped the words and he grabbed Pringle firmly by each arm. 'As God is my witness it is not over. The fight must go on because there are Frenchmen in Spain and it will not stop until they are dead or gone.' He let go, and forced a smile, but the steel in his expression remained. Pringle did not doubt he meant every word he said.

'We fight the little war. Ciudad Rodrigo is not Spain. What is one more town fallen as long as men survive to kill more Frenchmen? The little war continues, and if the French keep winning that does not matter if we do not lose. We live and we keep killing – one by one or two by two. It is better than nothing. The little war is not about fighting, it is about killing without being killed. We can wait.

'I think your Lord Wellington understands this,

and that is why I like him and why I know he will not come to save Ciudad Rodrigo. You should know that I understand because I do not think the governor or the others will let themselves admit the truth. If I were Lord Wellington then I would not come to this place. He will watch and wait, and let the French waste time and blood and food outside this town.'

'And what will he do with that time?'

'Just the same as me. He will still be alive at the end and so will his army and that means he can kill Frenchmen.'

'You do not plan to stay here?'

'For what purpose? In the little war there is no shame in running, only good sense. I will stay while I can be of use, but I do not intend to die or be captured here. As I say, there are Frenchmen to kill, and until the last of those whoresons has been buried or fled Spain it would be a terrible waste to die.' He patted Pringle on the arms, gently this time. 'Besides, a symbol should not be killed.

'And speaking of whores, when I come back from this raid you must come and dine. My betrothed has foolishly come to stay with a relative here and is now trapped. Their hospitality will be generous.'

Pringle wondered whether this was how the French felt when facing the guerrillas, always surprised and wrong-footed by opponents who struck unexpectedly when you felt safe. 'I should be delighted,' he managed, 'at least when my duties permit.'

'Excellent. Well then, I suppose I had better pay my respects to her before I leave. Not that she cares. In the autumn she ran off with a commissary in your army. Some pale-faced German, if you would believe! Then it was a captain in the dragoons, so I suppose you can say she likes your army!'

'You do not seem upset?' Pringle felt no menace, and wondered whether he was being deliberately disillusioned rather than threatened.

El Charro spread his arms wide. 'Why should I? There are French to kill, and that is more important. Let her father worry. All I care about is that he supports me, helps to pay and feed my men, and through him many villagers are as friendly. If he wants the promise of a stronger alliance then that is fine.

'Go with God, Captain Pringle. I promised Hanley that I would look after you, and I shall do my best.'

'Obliged to you,' said Pringle as manners automatically took over, and then he made himself turn and walk away as naturally as could be. Billy Pringle's mind was swimming, but most of all he pitied the French officers tasked with hunting El Charro.

CHAPTER 16

Jenny Dobson smiled, and only someone who knew her well would have caught traces of nervousness.

At their last encounter Hanley had been half drunk and heavily drugged, and his swimming senses had not realised who it was until afterwards. That was well over a year ago, and this time he could see how much the girl had changed into a young woman. Jenny was more than eighteen now, somewhat taller, and carried herself far straighter. She looked even older, but then growing up with the regiment tended to age the young quickly, and since she had fled from that life, who knew what she had been through. From the reports and information she gathered, it was clear that she now spoke French and Spanish well. While she was with the army Hanley had not even known that she could read and write in English.

Yet the biggest difference was the nervousness.

'You're a damned fool, Mr Hanley. Do you want both our necks stretched?'

That was the old Jenny, never hesitating to speak her mind.

'My apologies, but I needed to meet with "Molly", and find out if it was you.'

She let the hood of her cape fall back completely, and now Hanley could see more than just her face. That too was the old Jenny, aware that men would look and wanting to make it worth their while. He remembered her two years ago, always ready to pose, her expression – and often her words and actions – at once flirting and challenging. Now her hair was piled high and tied with ribbon like a fashionable lady's. It was so blonde that it was almost white. Jenny's skin was fair and she carried the look well enough in a country where fair hair was uncommon and desirable, but Hanley felt her own rich brown suited her better.

'You finished gawping?'

'Once again, I apologise, but it is remarkable to see you. You look well, and seem to be thriving.' Hanley could see the edge of her dress and it was silk, as were the white gloves she wore.

'And you look better in red.'

Hanley had on a dark priest's robe and hat. The French blamed monks and priests for leading the bitterest opposition to them and often this would not be a good disguise. Salamanca was different. With several seminaries still managing to operate, there were plenty of young men in orders – too many for one more to be noticed, especially now that the city was crowded with troops from the French headquarters of the entire army as well as the staff and supporting units of 6th Corps.

'I doubt my regimental jacket would make me too popular here.'

'Nor me for being with you, so you had better get on with it. Where's the money?'

'Here,' he said, patting under his robe. 'There is twice as much as you asked for.'

'Bloody right, too,' Jenny replied, and there was a part of her still very much the daughter of the regiment. 'I'm sure these shoes are ruined.' They were in an alley far from the main streets or plazas. Until a week ago the French had used the pens at the end of the alley to house cattle, which had since been slaughtered and their meat salted to feed the army. There were plenty of signs on the old paving stones of animals' recent presence.

'Once again, I am sorry.'

'You say that a lot, and still you don't get on with it. Maybe you're one of those men more excited before than during?'

Hanley laughed. 'Would that there were time to prove you wrong!' He pulled out a small purse. 'The letters?'

Jenny had a wicker basket on her arm, and fished among pieces of material and some fruit to produce a heavy sealed envelope.

'The Spaniard you mentioned,' he asked. 'This man Espinosa who usually dresses as a civilian, but is close to the marshal, have you seen him again?'

'There's a mention in there. He visits Emile sometimes. Likes the food and the wine and drools over me when he thinks Emile isn't looking.'

'I need to know everything you can tell me about him.' From the description Hanley was sure that it was Velarde. It no doubt pleased his humour to adopt the name of the man he had betrayed. 'Be careful, though, he is very dangerous.'

'Doesn't look it,' said Jenny, but Hanley thought she understood. 'Not like that one.' She nodded at the shadowy figure watching them from across the street. It was Langer, the escort provided by Baynes, and Hanley fully agreed with the girl's judgement.

'Don't mind him,' he said, and wished that he had got used to the man's almost continuous lurking presence. Langer was a deserter from one of Napoleon's Swiss regiments, but from what Hanley could gather he had served in half the armies – and probably half the jails – of Europe. 'Now, is there anything else to tell me which is not in the papers?'

Jenny thought for a moment. 'No,' she said. 'It's all there. Lists mostly this time. Convoys of mules, powder and guns leaving Salamanca.' Then for a moment the little girl appeared again, and she bit her lip softly before speaking. 'Have you seen my da lately?'

'He's well. In fact, he's inside Ciudad Rodrigo with Pringle and Williams.'

'Didn't know the regiment was there.'

Hanley felt a moment of absurd surprise. It was so easy to forget that his well-informed sources knew only what they saw and often had no idea at all of the wider world. 'It isn't. In fact it's still

228

back in England, although there is talk of going abroad again. No, a few of them are there to help train the Spanish. He's married again. Did you know?'

'Not surprised. Doesn't like being on his own.'

'It's the former Mrs Rawson.'

Jenny made a face. 'Bit sour, but kind in her way. Might do the old sod a lot of good.'

'Your son is well and in England, looked after by Mrs MacAndrews.' Hanley felt he ought to say something, even though there was no sign of the mother asking.

'Good. He'll probably never know me and have no cause to love me if he does, but I am glad he is being looked after.'

Hanley had never really met his own mother, and he knew that part of him still yearned for her approval, and so he wondered whether her son would grow to be as indifferent to his mother as Jenny expected. He changed the subject, for they really had been together too long. 'Is Major Bertrand here?' The girl shook her head at the mention of her lover. 'At Ciudad Rodrigo?'

She nodded. 'There's more detail in that lot. He went there with Masséna, but is due back in a few days. Misses his comforts.' Jenny had always been inclined to speak of men far older than her as if they were no more than infants.

'I bet he does.' Bertrand had been given one floor of a grand house as a billet, and had installed a groom and two cooks as well as his mistress.

'He takes his servants with him to camp, but I said no. I've done enough sleeping in tents – or without 'em, for that matter.'

'What have you told him about yourself?' Hanley asked. It was partly curiosity, but he also wondered how far Jenny might be useful now and in the future.

'That I was a companion to an English lady who was travelling in Spain for her health before the war started. Only she died and left me stranded without the money to get home.'

'And he believes it?'

'He met me in a whorehouse. Don't think he's got too many illusions, but it's what he tells his friends. He likes the idea of keeping an Englishwoman. Makes him feel like a victor. They're very confident. You know that, don't you?'

'Then it will be all the more of a surprise when they find out that they are wrong.'

Jenny brushed her free hand through her hair. 'You really believe that, don't you?'

'Yes, I do,' Hanley said, and he knew that he genuinely did, although he could still see no good reason why the French should not win by the end of the year.

'Good, I want to be sure I'm on the right side.'

'Any message for your father?'

'Don't think he will want to hear from me,' Jenny said doubtfully. 'But you can tell him I wish him good luck.'

'I will.'

'Then I'm leaving. Don't try to follow me.' She

turned and walked away, trying to thread a path between the filth spread over the stones, her nose now wrinkled up at the smell which had been there all the time.

'Already know where you live,' he said.

'Oh yes?' Jenny turned and gave an impish grin. 'Been peeking, have you?'

Hanley smiled back. 'Reckon it's worth it.'

'I'll have to charge you for that as well, then, won't I!'

Late in the afternoon, Hanley had a second meeting, this time with Ramón, La Doña Margarita's groom – and as Hanley knew, also her real father. They met in a quiet cloister near the cathedral, where there would be no mystery about a servant giving something to a priest.

Ramón was never a man for much speech. He was small, with the slightly bowed legs of a cavalryman, and the faraway gaze of a man who had spent years in Mexico, fighting Indians and the desert itself.

'She says you are a fool to be here,' he said. 'Do not come anywhere near the house because the French have started watching.'

'When?'

'A week ago. Just before the man Velarde who now calls himself "Espinosa" arrived.'

'Are you in danger?'

'Her name will protect her. And if not, I will.' Hanley had seen Ramón kill and knew this was

231

no idle boast, but one man could only do so much.

'Be careful,' he said.

Ramón spat to express his opinion of that advice.

'You are sure that you were not followed here?' Hanley asked, although he was confident since Langer had waited outside the entrance to watch for any signs.

'Sure.'

'How do you know?'

'I've fought the Comanches and I'm still alive.'

From the tone, Hanley guessed this was a clinching argument.

'I am most grateful for the reports.'

'There will be more by the usual means. Do not come to the house. Don't stay in Salamanca, either. You are too much of a risk to us all.' Such a flow of speech was unusual.

The information he brought tied in neatly with that from Jenny and the other sources, helped by the ease with which La Doña Margarita heard gossip from the staff and families of the marshals and generals. The real siege was about to begin, and men and material were setting out every day to reinforce the troops already outside Ciudad Rodrigo. General Junot's 8th Corps was on the march to screen Marshal Ney's 6th Corps as it prepared to assault the town. Ney was worried, feeling that he was vulnerable to a sudden attack by Wellington, and was unwilling to prosecute the siege until Junot's men were in place. Within a day or two they would be protecting him, and the heavy guns were already beginning their laborious progress so that they would reach Ciudad Rodrigo by the time emplacements had been built for them. Letters spoke of the frustrations of the officers in charge dealing with terrible roads and weak horses and bullocks, so that teams had to be double or even treble the normal size.

Things were moving, and Hanley suspected that Ramón was right and he should leave Salamanca soon. Yet a rumour that Marshal Masséna had just received detailed instructions from the Emperor made him wonder whether it was worth delaying. La Doña Margarita seemed confident that she might be able to obtain some idea of what was in them, although she did not say how this might be possible.

Tomorrow night, he decided. They would go tomorrow night and allow one more day to gather reports.

It took an hour for Hanley to get back to his own room. He walked on his own, with Langer shadowing him in the hope of spotting any undue interest. If the Swiss hurried past then it was a sign that Hanley was to stop where he was and pretend to pay attention to something or someone. That meant the deserter was not sure, and needed time to loop around and see whether the officer really was being followed. Hanley was to give him ten minutes and then proceed, trusting that the problem had gone. Then it was simply a matter of trust, relying on Langer to have reassured himself that there was no problem, to have dealt with it in some way, or to warn him. The Swiss had never explained just what the warning would be.

'You'll know, if things have gone wrong,' was all that the man offered, and Hanley was left to trust him. He did, at least up to a point, for the man was good at what he did. On the few occasions he glanced behind him he would never be able to spot Langer, and yet somehow he felt he was there. Baynes had chosen well, as usual, although since Hanley could only guess at his guide's full instructions, that might not be entirely comforting.

The plazas were better, because as the evening approached people were coming out again and mingling with the hordes of foreign soldiers. Hanley loved Spanish cities in the evenings, with their colour and life, so very different from drab English towns – even London, which he loved in a different way.

He walked comfortably, for he had lived so long in Spain that he never felt a stranger. His skin was darker than that of many locals, and if he was tall, there were other big men in the crowds and not all of them in army uniform. He exchanged greetings with a rangy, fair-haired fellow of at least six foot three and suspected the young priest was Irish, for there was a college dedicated to training such men in Salamanca.

Langer passed him. Hanley did not see his face,

but the hunched posture of the man with his lank and rather greasy hair was unmistakable.

Hanley stopped at a market stall and bought a couple of pastries. French soldiers began to shout, and for a moment he was worried until he realised that they were simply clearing a path through the crowd for a party of horsemen. Half a dozen chasseurs in green, but with the fur caps and red epaulettes of the elite company, preceded twice that number of generals in blue coats and ADCs wearing every colour in the rainbow, before the rest of the chasseur company followed. Hanley looked at the faces, curiosity piqued at the thought of seeing Marshal Masséna himself, but he recognised none of the riders.

Cheering started, no doubt encouraged by the infantry officer in charge of clearing the path. Hanley amused himself by joining in. A good twenty minutes had gone by the time the generals had passed. He had seen no more sign of Langer so he went on his way.

A few hours earlier, Jenny was surprised by someone else from her past. Loud banging on the door interrupted her as she prepared a simple meal for herself. With the cooks gone, she rather enjoyed less sauce and garlic than was the colonel's taste, and she still felt a simple joy in having plenty of good food to eat. Earlier today she had bought a cut of ham and now began to boil it with some potatoes.

Bertrand was a kind and generous man, but even so she hoped that he was not back early for she was enjoying the days of freedom. Seeing Hanley had helped her to realise that she was free of the drudgery of marching with a regiment and sleeping out in the mud.

The banging redoubled in force. Halfway to the door she froze, thinking of Hanley's warning about the Spaniard.

'Who is there?' she asked in French.

'A friend,' came a voice that was too faint to recognise.

Jenny wished that there was a window to open in the door. There was no other way to leave the rooms apart from through one of the windows, and it was a long drop. She realised that she was still holding a kitchen knife, and squeezed the handle tightly. The bolt was always stiff, and she was afraid for a moment that she would have to put down the knife and use both hands to slide it back, until a little jerk to the side shifted it. Only the catch remained, and Jenny lifted that slowly, keeping the knife down low and ready in her right hand.

The door slammed back, knocking her into the room, and a big man barged through. One gloved hand grabbed her wrist so tightly that it hurt, while the other grabbed her throat and lifted so that she had to stand on her toes.

'What's this as a welcome, Jenny?' said Dalmas, twisting her wrist so that she cried out and dropped the knife. He forced her a few more steps into the room, then kicked back with his heel to slam the door shut.

'Surprised to see me?' he said, and then let her go so that she staggered for balance.

'No. Men always come back.' She spoke as defiantly as she was able.

'Same old Jenny, ready to defy the world.' The cuirassier captain smiled. At the start of last year his men had found this English girl, being looked after by an old peasant woman as she barely recovered from fever and recent childbirth. By the time Dalmas saw her she was just well enough to speak, her skin still yellow and waxy, and yet she had hidden her fear, joking with and snapping at him as if she were his equal. He liked her from the beginning.

Dalmas had just been beaten for the first time in his career and he did not like that. It made him angry, and also eager to learn about the British so that he would win next time. One way to do that was to understand them, and that meant first learning the language. He had taken Jenny with him, feeding her, getting her clean clothes. Slowly and with difficulty, she taught him English while he taught her French. When Jenny was well enough recovered, Dalmas also took her into his bed, and had to admit that even then he was not the only one doing the teaching. For over a month he was posted to Madrid and kept her there. Then they had gone their separate ways when he returned to the army and she went to work in one of the city's better brothels.

'Bertrand is boasting all the time of his mistress, and something sounded so familiar that I thought it must be you.'

'He looks happy, does he?'

'In truth, he looks exhausted.' Dalmas smiled. He had taken off his helmet, and now unfastened his cloak to show his blue tunic underneath. 'However, that may not be entirely the result of your skills, my dear. Like all the other engineers, he now has to deal with the mud as well as the Spanish.'

'Do you think he'd like the thought of you coming visiting?' Jenny asked.

'I can be very discreet. But first, tell me what you are going to give me to eat.' When he heard the answer, Dalmas winced at such Anglo-Saxon savagery. 'I should have taught you more than simply how to speak a civilised tongue.'

In answer to that Jenny stuck hers out at him.

'Oh, Jenny, I have missed you a good deal. But now I think you can help me.'

'Lonely, are we?'

'Busy actually. I am sent here to aid a Spanish spy in finding an English spy. And I think that you can help me.' The hardness had returned to his voice. 'It would be better if you do.'

CHAPTER 17

Sergeant Rodriguez patted the man on the shoulder. Their company was providing sentries for the night down in the earthworks forming the glacis and this man had been the first one to hear. Pringle strained to listen. At first there was nothing, and then he caught the rhythmic scraping drifting down from the high ground ahead of them.

'They're digging,' Williams whispered beside him. 'Up there on the Great Teson.'

Pringle knew he was right. 'And they would not be doing it in the dark unless it was something we wouldn't like.'

He went straight to Colonel Camarga of the Avila Regiment, who had charge of the outposts this night. The colonel came and listened, and more reports were coming in so that there could be no doubt. The governor was roused. At 3.30, still almost an hour and a half before dawn on 16th June, every gun that could be brought to bear at the top of the bigger hill opened fire.

Down behind the glacis it was like the rolling thunder and flame of a dreadful storm.

'Well done, lad,' Pringle shouted at the sentry who had first spotted the noise and then done his duty and reported it.

The Spanish guns pounded the top of the hill. They could not see their target, but they knew where the hill was and gun captains guessed at the elevation and charge. The Great Teson had always been there and most of them had stood so many hours watching from the walls that they could picture it well in their minds. The crews were still slow at loading, but this was not a job for rapid fire and so that mattered less than in a battle. They fired, and each time the cannon roared and slammed back on its trails, the gunners hauled it back halfway to make it easier to work, sponged, rammed down powder and shot, and then pulled on the ropes again to bring the muzzle fully out of the embrasure.

Each shot produced a great tongue of flame stabbing into the night and sometimes a shower of sparks from burning wadding that fluttered down. There were some stubby, short-barrelled howitzers, and these lobbed their shells up at the hill, their burning fuses leaving a bright trail as they whizzed through the night sky. Herrasti's men also had mortars, the barrels so massive that they were not fired from a wheeled carriage, but from immensely heavy wooden frames. It took several men using specially shaped carrying staffs to lift one of their shells into the mortar, and their fuses had to be lit separately before the gunner applied his burning linstock to the quill of powder in the touch-hole that set off the main charge and sent the heavy metal sphere hurtling high up to lob down on to the enemy. So much bigger, mortar shells were even noisier and more visible as they arched through the sky, but Pringle wondered whether it would be so easy to see them when they were coming towards you. It must be very hard to guess where they would land and that would make for awful seconds not knowing if you were soon to be smashed to fragments.

The explosions of the mortar shells looked big even from this far away. They lit up the whole top of the ridgeline, and there were smaller objects flying amid the instant splashes of flame, and perhaps these were lumps of earth or the torn remains of people. From here they could not tell, and on the whole he would rather not know. All of the company had come to watch. No one could have slept through the noise, but it was more enthusiasm of the moment. Pringle watched their faces in the flickering and flaring light and sensed the excitement he felt himself. Very slowly he was learning about these men. It was still sometimes hard to know what they were thinking, but tonight it was very simple because he and Williams and Dobson and all the others had just the same thought – we are hitting back.

'Really is quite something to behold,' said Williams.

Pringle chuckled at a memory. 'I seem to

remember you said something like that about Talavera!'

'Well, that was also quite a thing to see.'

'I'm sure His Majesty will be relieved to hear that you don't find the war dull, Bills.'

It was not one-sided. The French had a few guns down on the plain in protected positions and these fired at the Spanish cannon. They too had had time to note the position of the embrasures on the walls, but the flame of each shot was enough to shout out the presence of a field piece and give them an aiming point. The mortars were another matter, for these fired in such a high arc that they could be hidden completely behind an earth bank or stone wall. The French could see the light from their discharge, but none was sited so carelessly that they could be seen and fired at by the enemy. As yet, the French revealed no mortars of their own and so they had to submit without answer to the heavy shells as they thumped into the ground. Ney's gunners had some howitzers, and so they saw the fire-trails of these smaller shells coming back at the city.

'Look out! Heads down!' shouted Dobson in that wonderful sergeant's voice able to carry over the worst chaos. The veteran had spotted a sputtering trail of sparks looping towards them.

Pringle saw that his men pressed themselves down, shoulders hunched against the stone reinforcement that kept the inside of the glacis steep. He saw that Williams was still standing and had simply drawn his head down as if seeking shelter from the rain, and so did the same.

Both were hit by a pattering spray of earth when the six-inch shell smacked into the front of the earth bank and exploded instantly. Pringle took off his glasses, and brushed away the dirt.

'Everyone all right?' he asked. No one was injured, and the men's eyes were shining with excitement, for the near-miss had made them all feel involved in the artillery duel. Pringle was willing to bet that if he gave the order they would happily fire their muskets again and again up at the ridiculously distant hill just to make noise and be involved.

'Mr Pringle, sir, and Mr Williams.' Dobson was just beside them, speaking as softly as he could and yet still be heard over the thundering barrage. 'This is not the open field, sirs, and there is no need to show off.'

'I don't follow, Dob,' Williams said, and a sudden brief pause in the noise caused several of the recruits to turn and stare in puzzlement.

'Next time, when there is a ditch to hide in, you bloody well take cover in it!' Dobson stiffened to attention. 'With every respect, sirs.'

'Thank you, Sergeant Dobson,' Pringle said.

Williams appeared unconvinced. 'What about setting an example?'

'What about having your giblets spread over the side of the wall?' Dobson was respectfully belligerent, but had to wait for a particularly intense concentration of shot and shell to batter their ears and eyes. 'This is going to go on for days. You can be lucky once or twice, but if you don't hide you will die.' Three big mortar shells went off in an almost perfect line on the top of the Greater Teson. 'Think about them poor sods up there. They've been at it for hours, digging harder than they ever have in their lives because they know that if they don't they'll die once they're spotted. It's not about showing pluck or good discipline, it's just you and your fellows with spade and pick trying to hack the deepest ditch you can to save you from the enemy guns.'

'It's called a parallel,' Williams said a few moments later. 'The trench they are digging is called a parallel.' As the name suggested, a parallel was built opposite the enemy fortress and ran parallel to it. Once they had the trench, the besiegers would add battery positions and protected magazines for ammunition. Then they would start forward, digging saps out of the parallel, taking them closer to the enemy walls. These could not go straight, otherwise a single shot would run down them and slaughter everyone inside, and so the diggers or sappers went at an angle to the way they wanted, zigzagging slowly and laboriously nearer. In time there might be more parallels closer and closer to the walls, with more batteries to pound the defences at shorter and shorter distances.

'Thank you, sir.' Dobson kept a straight face.

'Be glad to know that the next time I have to shovel away to make the ruddy thing.'

Williams grinned, half shouting over the noise. 'I remember you showing me how to use a spade.'

'God help us, you needed to be shown, sir!'

The sky was beginning to hint at dawn and for a change it looked as if it would be a dry clear day. The guns kept pounding, and when the sun rose they could see the churned soil on top of the Great Teson. The line of the French parallel was clear, spoil piled into a rampart strengthened with sacks filled with earth and tied shut and big wicker gabions filled with more spoil. Sometimes these were hit and shattered, debris flying high. As yet the trench could not have been more than a few feet deep, and the French must have crouched as they worked, yet some were still maimed and died. Later in the morning Pringle borrowed Williams' telescope and watched for a while from the wall near the cathedral. Once he saw a man clearly, raising a pick over his shoulders as he worked in the ditch, and then a shot puffed up earth a little short of the parallel, skimming up and shattering the French soldier's head.

Herrasti kept the guns firing all day, for this was the time when the workers were most vulnerable. Some balls and shells killed or maimed, and others smashed the rampart and so delayed the time when the parallel would be completed and offer them good protection. The governor sent out a sally, and if it was quickly driven off then it added to the sense of striking back. A proclamation was made announcing that the English would soon be coming to drive the French away. Pringle and the other redcoats were cheered more than usual when they went through the streets.

On the following days the guns thundered on in a slower, steadier pounding of the French siege works. Each morning, as early as their duties permitted, Pringle and Williams went up to the walls on their own, and from one of the little turrets too small to mount a gun they stared at the enemy works and tried to spot the changes. The pace was slow.

'I remember my father talking about battles at sea,' said Pringle once, as he watched a tiny lizard standing stock still on the top of the battlement, obviously convinced that this made it invisible. He lost his train of thought, wondering how all this seemed to animals and why they did not all have the sense to go somewhere less dangerous. The French skirmishers still sniped at the walls, although periodic sallies were keeping them back, and the governor had mounted more guns down in the earthworks protecting the ditch to contest that area. Frequent raids from the gardens and Convent of Santa Cruz had also prompted the enemy to start digging another ditch facing this threat.

'We are quite a long way from the sea.' Williams broke the news as gently as possible.

'Damned good thing too! My apologies, my dear

fellow, I wandered off for a moment. No, it was simply that the thing that most puzzled me as a boy was the time everything took. Father would speak of sighting the French, and so they would beat to quarters and do all sorts of other splendidly nautical things, but then the captain would order a hot breakfast served to everyone while they waited.'

'Very civilised, the Navy.'

'Weevils in the food give the place a certain distinction, I suppose. But it all seemed to happen so slowly. They'd spend hours watching each other, working for wind, and sometimes it was even days before they closed and fought. Didn't ever think I'd be part of something even slower.'

'They've started saps,' said Williams after a few minutes staring through his glass. 'Two of them.'

'May I see?'

'Look for where most of the shot is striking.' The Spanish gunners must have already seen the same thing and were aiming at the heads of the trenches as they were dug. The French would have put gabions there as the men struggled to deepen and improve the ditch behind, but a clear strike would knock these down and plunge into the knot of workmen as they toiled.

The next day, Pringle was unable to join Williams on the walls until after he had attended a meeting summoned by the governor. As they climbed up into the little turret, Billy had still not worked out how to tell his friend the sickening news, and so for a while he delayed and they just scanned the siege works.

'Saps are closer,' Williams noted quickly.

A musket ball chipped the stonework where the lizard had posed the day before and Pringle was relieved that the little chap was not in evidence today. He hoped he was all right.

'They're closer too,' the Welshman added, referring to the French skirmishers.

'The governor found out from a prisoner that they are a special battalion, the *chasseurs de siège*, formed from the pick of the voltigeur companies.' Pringle passed on the information flatly.

'That's good. Be a shame to be shot by someone who isn't a good soldier.'

Pringle sometimes forgot how much time Williams had spent around Dobson. He cleared his throat. 'I've got some bad news, Bills,' he said.

Williams took his eye from the glass and looked at his friend.

'Who?' he asked, and clearly expected to hear that one of their men had fallen.

'Not that. It's just that I'm leaving.'

'That sounds like good news,' Williams said, and obviously meant it.

'Only me,' Billy spoke bitterly. 'Not you, not Dobson, Murphy and Rose, or our boys. Just me.'

'Still good news. I was not intending to say anything, but your snoring lately . . .' Williams was grinning. They had shared a room since they arrived in Ciudad Rodrigo, apart from the nights when Pringle had gone to visit his 'friend', but that had only happened once in the last week.

'The governor has written to Lord Wellington and wants to send a British officer to report on the seriousness of the situation. I said that he should send you, but he insisted that a captain would carry more weight.'

Williams grinned.

'Spare me the joke,' said Pringle, although he broke into a smile for a brief moment. 'I really am very sorry.'

'It is an order. Really, do not concern yourself, and I still think it is excellent news. When you get a chance, write to Anne and say that I am well.'

And inside a doomed fortress, thought Pringle. There was one more thing, and the mention of Williams' sister made him feel more awkward, even though he doubted his friend yet sensed his interest in Anne as anything more than friendly. 'I must ask a favour.'

'Of course.'

'If things turn bad, would you do what you can to protect Josepha?' Pringle had spoken a little to Williams of the girl, and although his puritanical side did not quite approve, the Welshman remained a true friend.

'Won't Don Julián's men do that?'

'I am going out with El Charro and his lancers tonight. The governor has decided that cavalry and their horses are so many useless mouths during a siege and would be of more use on the frontier.'

'Sensible decision,' Williams said, adopting what he clearly felt was a wise expression. 'Of course, I will do whatever I can.'

'Thank you.'

The bell in the cathedral chimed twice. The sound was a little muted near the castle, but tonight there was not much firing from the walls to drown the sound. It was dark, for the sky was cloudy and already a faint drizzle was falling. Pringle's nose was full of the smell of damp horses and leather. He glanced behind him at the column of almost a hundred riders in the weird harlequin combinations of uniform worn by Don Julián's lancers. He could not see the colours in the dark, but men had coats, hats and weapons of every shape and size. A man walked past, checking that rags were properly tied over the hoofs of each little horse to muffle their sound.

The governor stood at the side of the square, the bishop beside him, and Billy caught a muffled 'Go with God' as they conferred with El Charro, and then the guerrilla leader walked his horse over to join him.

'Time to go,' he said.

They began to move. Men were waiting holding torches to guide them through the streets. The Gate of San Jago near the river had stood open each day and night for more than a week, and now they walked their horses through the archway. It was strange how immediately the air felt more open than in the streets of the city.

'If anything happens and you get lost, then it's to the right on the far bank and then south-west.'

'Thanks,' said Pringle.

'I promised Hanley.' Billy caught the glint of El Charro's smile.

Still walking their horses, the column went along the sunken way inside the ditch until this ran out and they came to open ground beside the River Agueda. The river was wide and although full it flowed nearly silently.

The lancers halted for a moment in front of the low Roman bridge while a sentry reported. Early on in the siege, the French had taken the suburb on the far bank. In the daytime, they did not maintain any outposts in the field ahead of the houses and gardens, but there were expected to be pickets at night.

A softly given order and the hundred horsemen set off, still keeping to a walk. The sound changed as the animals' feet came on to the stone surface of the bridge, but the horses either had wrapped feet or were unshod ponies and it was no more than a soft drumming. It still seemed loud enough to Pringle, as did the inevitable creaks of harness and saddle as men shifted their weight and the gentle thumps of equipment shaking with the motion. Yet the discipline of El Charro's men impressed him. They worked well as a team, and if the style was different from a well-run battalion – it was at once less formal and yet blatantly auto-cratic – it clearly served them well.

251

Halfway across the bridge and still silence. The fine rain had stopped, and a slow drift of wind uncovered a thin crescent moon. Pringle could see the shapes of rooftops in the suburb of Santa Marina, and the memory came to him of Williams complaining about the Spanish fondness for religious names, and Billy knew that it was a sign of his nervousness whenever he started remembering such ridiculous things. He had to stifle an urge to laugh. His right thigh began to twitch and he was half tempted to pull the leg free from the stirrup and flex it, but knew that he could not risk anything so stupid when his very life might depend on keeping a good seat.

'*Qui vive?*'

The shout came from ahead, on the far bank; they were almost at the end of the bridge already. Without an order the lancers went into a trot, Pringle's horse copying the others before he had asked it.

'*Qui vive?* ' Pringle pitied the poor sentry and wondered whether the second challenge was a rigorous obedience of orders or a desperate hope that someone would answer '*Amis!*'

A shot split the darkness.

'Go!' yelled El Charro, and the lancers gave their horses their heads. Pringle's borrowed mount lurched as it quickened pace and he bounced uncomfortably for a moment before it fell into a nice rhythm.

There was a scream as the French sentry was

spitted on one of the long lances, the guerrilla expertly using his own momentum to flick the point free and ride on. Beside him another man with lesser skill drove his spear so deeply into a second infantryman that the point came through the man's stomach and stuck fast, so he let it go and rode on.

More shots came, this time in a little volley, and Pringle guessed that this was the supports for the sentries, and again he felt sorry for the sergeant and ten or twenty men who found themselves at night suddenly faced by scores of wild devils on horseback.

'Go!' called El Charro again. It was not a formed charge, but a deluge of galloping horsemen. Pringle saw that one man was already down, his horse shot, but El Charro had ordered his men not to stop for anyone and no one paused to help him. Men who fell were to find their own way out or back to the town – or try to take a Frenchman with them before they died.

They were past now, but shots pursued them, and Pringle heard a scream as a rider was shot through the body and tumbled from the saddle. There were shouts too, and a bell ringing, which must be an alarm. On they went, still galloping, and now they were on a wide earth road.

Pringle was near the head of the pack, and saw the sudden burst of flame stabbing at them as a cannon fired from just beside the road. Almost instantly there was a deep growling tear as a ball punched the air. The rider beside him vanished from the waist up, his chest, arms and head disintegrating and spraying blood, flesh, bone and pieces of clothing all around. Billy was drenched with still-warm blood and something heavier slapped against his cheek.

More flames, from a volley this time, and there were screams of pain from men and horses. Riders were down, and all were slowing. Billy Pringle's mount lurched again, dropping its shoulder, and he almost lost balance, but the speed had gone from the column.

'Go! Kill them all!' El Charro's voice carried over the confusion. As more muskets flared, Billy saw the guerrilla leader gallop straight at the line of French soldiers, his sabre gleaming red as it caught the light of a fire. A French officer rode to meet him, the man much bigger than the guerrilla leader.

'El Charro! El Charro!' His men shouted their leader's name and drove their big spurs deep to bloody their horses' flanks, and the animals surged forward again. Lance points dropped into the attack.

Don Julián dodged the officer's thrust, and cut once, tumbling his opponent with ease. The French infantry wavered, some beginning to run, and the guerrilla leader was now in among them, horse rearing to pummel with his front hoofs, while the rider cut down precisely to left and right.

Then the lancers arrived. Pringle was in the middle of the mass and could see little. There was the clatter of blade on blade, some shots, the discharges almost blindingly bright, and the thud of points driving into flesh and bullets striking home. More horses were down, and Billy's mount was kicked by an animal thrashing out in its agony, but there seemed to be no serious harm done.

'Go!' yelled El Charro once more.

The column was moving on. Pringle had come near the head again. He had never seen a Frenchman up close, and now the enemy was gone. At least, they were gone for the moment.

Don Julián's lancers rode on into the night.

CHAPTER 18

Hanley did his best to appear interested in the stall-owner's boasts.

'It is the finest ivory,' the little man maintained, 'from China itself.' His smile radiating honesty with such fervent intensity that even had Hanley not known that neither statement was true he would still have been reluctant to trust the man.

He was in the market again, waiting and feigning interest because Langer had brushed past him in warning. It was the second time already today and that was worrying. He did not think the Swiss was the type of man to start at shadows.

'No thank you,' Hanley said to the trader, but then asked to look at a poorly painted metal figure of the Madonna simply to keep the fellow talking. The one statue occupied the trader's rapturous enthusiasm for the rest of the ten minutes, encouraged by no more than one or two gestures of continued interest. Hanley bought the piece in the end, paying more than it was worth, and as he walked away he smirked at the thought that if they were being watched the stall-owner might well find himself arrested by the French for passing something to an English spy.

There seemed to be even more soldiers in Salamanca today: the wide square was packed, so that it was difficult to move through the crowd. Being jostled became normal, and then someone punched him heavily in the stomach.

'Sorry, Father,' said a voice, and as Hanley gasped for breath he saw that it was Ramón. A bundle was pressed into his hands as they clutched at his belly. 'So sorry, Father.' The last words were in a whisper. 'Get out!' Then the man was gone.

Hanley slipped the bundle into his robes and walked on, still aching. A couple of men in French-style coats that were red rather than blue grinned at the sight of a priest almost being knocked over and joked with each other in German. Hanley bit back the urge to snarl at them in the same language.

Everything now seemed more sinister, but the officer did his best to walk at a pace that was steady, without being unnaturally slow. He made himself stop and give his approximation of a blessing to an old woman who implored him to pray for her granddaughter. Part of him wondered whether even this was a trap. Ramón had said yesterday that the message would be delivered in the usual manner, and so Hanley had been on his way to pick it up from a little covered niche in a spot they knew in an out-of-the-way cloister. That Ramón had come to him was as big a warning as the man's words.

Hanley walked in no particular direction for twenty minutes, in the vague hope that this might be confusing to anyone following. He trusted that Langer was back in place, but somehow he did not feel the man watching him. Perhaps it was simply his growing nervousness. Then he headed towards their room. If time permitted he would scan the contents of the package before gathering his things for the journey.

The door of his little room above the potter's shop creaked with appalling loudness as Hanley edged it open. It had always done this, but today it seemed unnecessarily sinister. He peered in and saw no one, and then his tension seemed to deflate, for there was no need to fear an immediate threat.

Ramón's package was well worth the risk of the extra day. There were lists of the numbers and the weights of the heavy siege train rolling towards Ciudad Rodrigo – almost fifty pieces in total. Better yet, La Doña Margarita had been as good as her word, and gained some insight into the Emperor's orders. Masséna had been told to move slowly, taking both Ciudad Rodrigo and Almeida. He was not to aim to be in Lisbon before the end of August, the Emperor 'not choosing' to go there any earlier, since it would be difficult to feed the captured town before the local harvest. Hanley marvelled at the complacency, and knew from all Murray and Baynes had said that this would be very pleasing to Lord Wellington.

There was one note, in Jenny Dobson's sprawling letters.

HAVE THE NEWS YOU WANTED. BRING

MONEY. SAME PLACE AT 6. He smiled when he saw there was another message from the girl in with La Doña Margarita's papers.

It was now a quarter to five. Langer had not appeared, and the man had never before taken so long. Hanley took off his priest's robes. He donned plain boots, drab trousers and a thin shirt and then buttoned on his uniform jacket and sash. Over the top went a long brown overcoat like the ones worn by coachmen, and a broad straw hat.

Before five Hanley slipped out of the door, made his way to the busy street where Jenny lived and waited. There were enough loafers as well as passers-by to make it easy to blend in, and he stayed a few hundred yards further along the street, where a tavern spilled out its customers, and so he drank, surrounded by as many soldiers as townsfolk. No one paid him particular attention.

He almost missed Jenny as she left, and if her hood had not fallen for a brief moment and given a flash of movement and bleached hair, he suspected that he would have missed her as he tried not to watch too obviously.

Hanley swallowed the rest of his wine, grimaced because it was not good and then followed the girl through the streets, keeping as far back as he could. Jenny was alone, and he saw no one following her. For five minutes they stayed on the main street, Hanley finding the girl's slow progress frustrating. Then they were into ever smaller and less frequented roads and narrow alleys. There was still no sign of anything wrong.

Jenny turned a corner, and Hanley hurried after the young woman because he knew this place was a maze and did not want to lose her. Just before the turn he stopped and then peered cautiously around.

'Hello.'

Hanley gave a start, yelping in surprise.

Jenny laughed. 'Like following girls, do you?' She turned so that her back was to him again and gave an exaggerated wiggle of her hips.

As usual with Jenny, Hanley felt there was little choice but to laugh with her, even though his heart was still pounding. He came around the corner.

'What do you have for me?'

The girl leered and gave another shake of her hips, before feigning enlightenment. 'Oh, you mean news. Seen that fellow again. He's . . .' Jenny's eyes suddenly widened. 'Look out!'

Hanley spun around. A figure emerged from the mouth of a lane on the opposite side of the alley, a pistol aimed at the British officer.

The shot was sudden, and numbingly loud as it echoed off the high walls, and Hanley threw himself at Jenny, knowing it was too late, but hoping perhaps he could save her. They rolled in the mud, the girl struggling and cursing.

'You English are so romantic,' said a voice.

Hanley was on top of the girl, his face pressed against her chest and feeling the bare skin above her dress because Jenny's cloak had come undone. He knew the voice and the style. He pushed with his hands against the mud of the alleyway to raise himself; there was something in his mouth until he spat out one of the draw-strings of the girl's cloak.

Jenny was silent, and that was unusual for her. She said nothing in response to Hanley's apologies as he got to his feet and helped her up. No more shots had come. Langer lay in the mud and dung, the back of his head missing. Jenny saw the corpse and bit back a scream.

'I have just saved your life, Guillermo,' said Luiz Velarde as he emerged fully into the alley. A still smoking pistol was in his right hand, and one that was surely loaded now held out in his left.

'To kill me yourself?' Hanley asked.

'The pistol? Merely a precaution. I intend to live to enjoy a fine and debauched old age.'

Hanley said nothing. The muzzle of the pistol looked very big, and was pointing straight at him.

'That man had orders to kill you. Do you believe that?'

The British officer did suspect Baynes had told the man not to let the French capture him alive, but saw no point in honesty. 'No,' he said.

'It's true. And since I was the one who ordered him to kill you, I do feel that I should know.' Velarde spotted the flicker of reaction. 'Ah, at last some surprise. This may not be a complete waste of effort after all.' He tossed the empty pistol aside and reached with his free hand for something. 'Langer's desertion last year was at my encouragement. He was to make himself useful to the British, and I believe he did that rather well for so unimaginative a brute.

'However, such stories can wait. At the place you were supposed to meet with your charming companion, a French officer named Dalmas is waiting with several men. They will most certainly kill you. Eventually.'

'I am a British officer, wearing uniform.' Hanley reached up to unbutton his coat, saw Velarde stiffen and so stopped, spreading his hands wide and then keeping his gestures very slow. Pulling back the top of the coat, he revealed his scarlet jacket.

Velarde was unimpressed. 'You would not be wearing that when they hang you, and who would ever know the truth. Dalmas is very capable.' The Spaniard took a pace closer and undid his own long coat. Beneath was a tunic cut in the French pattern, but from brown cloth. 'Do you like it? I am a colonel these days, in the new army of Spain. *Viva tío Pepe!*' he added, using one of the kindlier nicknames given by the Spanish to Joseph Napoleon.

Hanley watched him closely, looking for an opportunity. If Velarde came within reach and relaxed his guard for a moment, Hanley could lunge and . . . and perhaps get a lead bullet driven through his brain or belly, he thought chillingly.

Jenny's father would know what to do. So too would Williams, but Hanley thought back to the duel all those months ago and how Billy had so suddenly said that he had never killed anyone. Nor had Hanley, and there must be better alternatives than trying to find out whether he was capable of such a thing in so unfavourable a situation.

'Thank you, Molly – or should I say Jenny,' Velarde said, without looking away from Hanley. 'You played your part admirably. I hope the French have already paid you, but here is the same amount again, from me.' He produced a jingling purse from his jacket pocket.

'You slut!' Hanley spat the words at the girl, stepping away from her in disgust. 'You treacherous slut!'

For once Jenny Dobson was neither defiant nor mocking. She looked down as she took the purse and avoided Hanley's gaze.

'Perhaps, but she is such a lovely and clever slut that the whole world should be glad. She wants to be rich, and you cannot blame her for that. And you should be thankful that she betrayed you not simply to Dalmas, but to me as well.

'Jenny, you had better go. You still have time to appear at the meeting place.'

'Yes,' she said softly. Jenny glanced at the British officer, but the intended words died on her lips and she walked away.

'What is the point?' Hanley asked. 'You already have me.'

'But Dalmas and the French do not.'

'There is a difference.' Hanley wanted to unsettle Velarde, but past experience suggested that would not be easy.

'All the difference in the world, and for that, too, you should be grateful. Do not worry, friend Dalmas will have his catch. Or are you still worried for the woman you so gallantly protected with your body just a short while ago? No. Well, it does not matter, for Jenny is safe. A messenger will come to meet her, bringing information. I know because I sent one. The French will have someone to interrogate.

'But we should not linger.' Velarde stepped closer and used his free hand to pat Hanley's coat until he found a pistol. The weapon went into the Spaniard's own pocket. 'That was the moment to jump me, if you had a mind to do so,' he said, taking a pace back.

'Would it have worked?'

'No, and I might regretfully have had to kill you when I have no desire to do that. You look sceptical?'

Hanley spat, showing his contempt in the local way.

'Very impressive. I am a loyal Spaniard whatever you think – and loyal to a Spain without the French before you say that. Why do you doubt this? We were on the same side last year, and you helped me pretend to desert to the enemy.'

'Espinosa.'

'He was betrayed, but not by me. Should I have died merely to give him company?' Velarde lowered the pistol. 'Know that I will kill you if you give me no choice,' he said. 'It may take you some time to believe me, and so you must know that I will do this thing. Now you have a choice. You can wait here and after a while the French will come and you will be asked many uncomfortable questions. Or you can come with me and help me.'

'Help you?'

'Yes, and Spain, and your own Lord Wellington. I need to get inside Ciudad Rodrigo.'

'Marshal Masséna feels the same way,' Hanley said.

'That is why I need to go there. King Joseph has agents inside the city, whispering to powerful men that the war is his and they should join him to share in the rewards of victory. Some of them are planning to seize power once the siege is advanced, and then surrender to the French. I do not want this to happen, and so I must go there to stop them.'

'Give me their names. I can get word into the city and have them arrested.'

'On what evidence – the word of a French agent?' Velarde threw back his head and laughed, shaking his head. Then his look was pitying. 'I do not trust you enough to trust me that far. Not yet. So I must go, and since it is important to get there, I need your help.'

'I have a choice?'

'Between this and capture, certainly.'

'Then I shall be delighted,' said Hanley.

They left the city openly, riding past long lines of ox-carts piled with food, unoiled axles screaming piercingly, and the drivers jabbing with their goads to keep the poor beasts plodding on. The mud was dreadful, both from the rain and the churning of so many heavily laden wheels over so many days. Velarde kept his uniform covered, but his pass and orders took them past every sentry and questioning officer.

Not long after they left the main road and cut across country to meet with the guide Hanley promised, Velarde told him more of the agent's purpose.

'It is not just Ciudad Rodrigo that is at stake. When that hands itself over to the French and the leaders are praised and rewarded, it will be a gesture to others. The same man is working in Spain, and even, with some assistance, in Portugal.'

'Almeida?'

'The plan is bigger than that. They are in touch with people near the Regency Council in Lisbon. King Joseph wants to give his brother a victory greater even than he expects. Portugal will fall, but it will happen so quickly that cities will be closed to the British. Lord Wellington may have trouble getting his army away. And if the British lost thirty or forty thousand men, would they ever dare to come back to Europe? So he pours out gold like water, and not far from the top in any country there are always plenty of greedy men. Ciudad Rodrigo is meant to be the start. That is why we must make sure it is really the finish.'

Hanley made no comment on that, but pulled his horse up.

Velarde looked puzzled. 'This would not be a good time to jump me.'

'Not that. Espinosa?'

'That poor fat fool.' Velarde sighed. 'I have already explained. I do not know who betrayed him. I did not.'

'What about his people?' Many of Espinosa's sources and messengers had been arrested, tortured and killed.

'I named no one the French did not already know – presumably from whoever betrayed Espinosa himself. Those were dead already, regardless of what I did, and so I informed on them like a good little *afrancesados* and was rewarded with a commission and a good deal of money by King Joseph. What would you have had me do?'

Hanley shrugged and rode on.

CHAPTER 19

Williams walked down the stairs to the lower cloister and shivered when he came into the cold night air. It was cloudy again, and he was glad of the burning torches that gave some light to the arcaded corridors around the little courtyard that led into the main one. Sergeant Rodriguez was waiting, smoking a cheroot, and the officer gestured for the man to finish when he moved to throw the cigar away. Williams was a few minutes early and there was no sense in wasting tobacco in a city where supplies were bound to grow short. He shook his head at the offer of taking a puff. Then the world exploded.

With savage violence the gate beside the chapel burst into fire, noise and flying debris, the big timber doors themselves shattered into fragments and all the heavy boxes and sacks piled to reinforce them were flung back and high into the air, scattering around the far end of the courtyard. One sentry was caught and his head smashed by a great smoking beam of timber.

Williams and Rodriguez were sheltered at the

far corner of the high-walled compound, but even so felt the wash of the blast.

'Get the men up!' yelled Williams. The French had taken the Convent of Santa Cruz once already in the siege, but the fortress guns had pounded the place and forced them to withdraw. The scars of that barrage were all around them, and had left none of the roofs intact for its new garrison of the Avila Regiment and Williams' company. 'Put half in the windows of the upper cloister and guard the stairs. Then bring the rest to me down here.' Rodriguez threw down his cheroot and dashed off, already shouting out the alarm, not that anyone could have missed the explosion.

It seemed the French were coming back.

Williams ran towards the chapel, drawing his sword. He wished he was carrying his musket, but he had only expected to do the rounds of his sentries and had not come fully armed.

There were shouts, and figures surged through the open gateway, bayonets long and glinting in the torchlight.

'Sir!' He looked back and saw a man in a white shirt without a tunic. It was Corporal Rose, and the NCO had the Spanish corporal and six recruits with him. There were shots and chaos at the far end of the courtyard. A crash, less violent this time, and suggesting axes, brought the other gate down, and more cheering Frenchmen were charging into the convent.

Williams ran to the men, and pointed back inside

the smaller courtyard. They formed a line, sheltered from sight and ready to flank any mass of French coming through the low arched entrance. Williams heard Colonel Camarga shouting to the men of the Avila Regiment. There were more of them near the main courtyard and he would let them deal with that fight for the moment.

'All loaded?'

The Spanish corporal nodded in confirmation. The young recruits looked nervous, but then a man would be a fool if he was not at a time like this.

'Fix bayonets!' No one dropped any of the long triangular blades and they slotted over the muzzles with satisfying clicks.

Williams heard running feet pounding on the flagstones towards them and gestured to the men to raise their muskets. The first through the entrance was an officer in a bicorne hat, his sword raised high and his long-tailed coat flapping behind him. Bunched behind him were half a dozen men carrying muskets and wearing shakos.

'Fire!' yelled Williams, for the Avila Regiment wore cocked hats and not shakos.

Eight muskets slammed back into the firers' shoulders as the men pulled their triggers and fired at the French. There were screams and men were falling, one already writhing on the ground.

'Charge!' Williams dashed forward, his sword held in a lunge, and the little line followed him. More French spilled through the archway into the smaller courtyard. All had epaulettes on their jackets, and most had the big moustaches of veterans. The officer was down, his white breeches now stained dark with spreading blood. A tall slim man came at Williams, blocking his first thrust, and then swinging suddenly with the butt of his musket so that the Welshman had to jump back, yet still he felt the swish of the heavy brass-plated stock as it flicked past his chin. Beside him one of the recruits had stabbed a Frenchman in the throat, and the boy was twisting his bayonet to free it. Another of the recruits was down, crying out to his real mother and the Holy Mother as he tried so desperately to pull the enemy blade from his own belly.

The Frenchman facing Williams stamped forward and lunged skilfully, forcing him back again, and he could tell that the man knew what he was doing. In such a fight the man with the longer reach of bayonet and musket would most likely win. He waited for the next thrust, but instead of going back he threw himself forward, grabbing the Frenchman's bayonet with his left hand and using all his weight to push it down and aside. His right punched at the man's chin with the hilt of his sword, and although the blow lacked real weight, Williams was a big man, and the shock and surprise were enough to unbalance his opponent. Feeling himself falling, he swung his weight to the right and gave a vicious backhanded slash with his sword, the slight curve in the blade rolling as its wicked edge sliced through the man's collar and neck. Coughing, the Frenchman fell and Williams fell with him, vulnerable to any new attack, but for the moment the enemy had vanished.

Williams pushed himself up. The felled recruit was sobbing as he tried to hold in his own entrails. Another's left arm was bloody and useless, but there were two Frenchmen dead on the ground and four groaning from wounds, and for the moment the attackers had pulled back. He looked into the main courtyard; there was still fighting, but there were far more figures wearing shakos. A Spanish voice was yelling orders to fall back to the cloister.

'Come on,' said Williams. The corporal had propped the badly wounded boy up against the wall. They helped the other man to come with them and hurried back. Williams could see men in the windows overlooking him and that showed that Rodriguez had been active. The sergeant himself with Dobson beside him was just coming down the stairs.

'Back!' Williams shouted. 'We'll take everyone to the upper cloister and make sure we can hold that if nothing else.' The building was big, and he doubted their thirty or so could hold both floors.

'Sir!' Murphy shouted from an upstairs window. 'The colonel, sir!' He pointed. There was one other stairway leading to the higher floor and he guessed that Camarga and his men were going there.

'Tell him we have this one!' Williams shouted back.

They hurried upstairs. Williams was last and all the pounding must have been too much for one of the old boards forming the stairs, for it snapped and gave way beneath his foot. He stumbled against Dobson ahead of him, and both men had to put out hands to the wall to stop themselves falling.

'You're putting on weight, Pug!'

'The sauce of the man,' muttered Williams automatically.

'Sir!'

Williams noticed Dobson staring down at the steps.

'You're a genius,' he said as he understood. 'Use your bayonet!' He turned to call behind him. 'Sergeant Rodriguez. Get the men to prise out the boards from the steps between every third one.'

The Spaniard looked puzzled, but only for a moment, as Dobson, grunting, ripped up the old wooden steps. With care, a man would still be able to climb the stairs, but it would be dangerous to run and harder still to rush up them with a group of men.

The sky glowed red.

'The chapel!' shouted someone from further up. 'The chapel is on fire.'

There was another explosion, not so violent this time and somehow duller, but suggestive of greater power. The flash came from the side facing the French, and Williams guessed that they were blowing a big chunk of wall down so that it would be easy to get into the convent in the future.

Shouts echoed across from the far side of the building. One or two of Williams' men in the furthest windows fired. He ran along to see what was happening.

'They've made a rush at the colonel,' Murphy said, and then raised his musket to aim. A shot came back, whipping between them to flatten against the wall behind.

'Our turn next.' Williams dashed back to where the stairs opened out into the wide corridor. Dobson and Rodriguez appeared, carrying piles of the broken steps.

'We can throw 'em if the powder runs out,' said the veteran, dropping the timber and unslinging his musket.

The Spanish corporal shouted out the alarm and then the order to fire. Muskets banged, although one recruit's hammer slammed down and failed to spark.

The corporal cuffed the young soldier and screamed at him to put in a new flint. Williams went over and stared through the window, but did not go too far forward as shots were coming back from the courtyard.

'Ten, maybe twenty have got into the colonnades,' said the Spanish corporal as he reloaded his own musket. Once they were into the pillared corridors around the cloister, it was impossible to see anyone.

Williams returned to the stairs.

'Reckon we made 'em think,' Dobson said. 'They

came in shouting and screaming and then they stopped short! Won't be long, though.' The veteran, like Williams, had a healthy respect for the ingenuity and boldness of the French.

'Ready, lads!' Williams called in Spanish, and grinned at the half-dozen recruits waiting to load for Rodriguez, Dobson and Rose. It was better to let experienced men do the shooting itself.

The men at the windows were still firing, and then one was pitched backwards by a ball that smashed his teeth and lower jaw. The boy moaned and spat out gobs of frothy blood and fragments of tooth.

'*Vive l'empereur!* ' A voice thundered up the staircase and a man athletically bounded forward, leaping from one step to the next with rapid precision. He was a long-limbed, tall officer in the blue coat and breeches of a light infantry regiment, his shako topped with a green and red plume, with a pistol in one hand and a curved sabre in the other. Behind came a file of men, and they came slowly, looking for the next stair, but that was the only sign of hesitation.

'*En avant!*' The officer shouted again, his voice deep, and unlike so many of Napoleon's men he was clean shaven. Jumping forward, he almost missed his footing, but managed to recover and somehow keep going. The men behind were moving more quickly, risking leaps from one stair to the next.

'Present!' shouted Williams.

The officer was more than halfway up, and the man could see the danger and yet kept coming, for he saw too that victory was close. He launched into another stride and levelled his pistol at the same time.

'Fire!' Williams shouted. The sound of the shots merged as the three NCOs fired, sending flame and more smoke rolling down the stairs.

The French officer's body juddered as he was hit three times in the chest, but it was too dark to see his blood clearly against his blue tunic. He seemed to fold, all grace and balance gone, and then the body was tumbled backwards as new muskets were passed forward. Rodriguez was cursing because the Frenchman had fired his pistol and the ball had scratched his head and ripped off the top of his ear. He snarled when Williams gestured for him to go back.

'Present!' Williams shouted once again. There were clicks as the three men drew back their hammers.

The attack had stalled, one man missing his footing as the officer's corpse rolled back down into him.

'Fire!' More smoke and noise echoing in the narrow staircase, and now one of the soldiers was down. He fell beside the officer, both bodies partly hanging through the gaps between the steps.

New muskets came forward. The noise had slackened from the far side of the cloister and there were no noises from inside, which suggested the men of the Avila Regiment were holding their own. The chapel was burning brighter now, with the flickering red light casting strange shadows along the corridors. Another building flared, and Williams guessed it was the one used as a storeroom. Neither were connected to the cloister and so there should not be any danger of the flames spreading, and as long as they controlled the windows it would be hard for the French to bring in combustible material in sufficient quantity to start a dangerous fire in this big stone building.

Williams took a walk along the corridor behind the men firing through the windows, telling them that they were doing well and the French were losing. He was back at the staircase only moments before another French officer, silent this time and giving no warning, sprang up the steps, taking advantage of the footing offered by the bodies left from the earlier attack. In the silence it seemed almost unreal.

This captain was short and barrel-chested, with a thick red-brown moustache and gold earrings. He wore the round fur hat favoured by the elite skirmishers of some light infantry regiments. If less nimble, he was no less heroic than his prede-cessor, and the light infantrymen followed him as willingly. Williams could only marvel at their sheer pluck; as thoughts raced through his head and he imagined the mingled fear and excitement of the Frenchmen as they attacked.

Rodriguez reacted first, aiming and firing a little

quickly, so the ball went low and slammed into the French captain's thigh just above his right knee. The man stopped, and as Williams was about to yell the order, Dobson fired into the smoke of the Spaniard's musket and the officer dropped, obviously hit badly. With Rose aiming his firelock squarely at them, the light infantrymen dragged their officer back, prompting agonising cries as he bumped down over the broken steps and corpses.

There were no more attacks. Shots came at the windows, and one recruit lost an eye not from a musket ball, but from the big shard of stone it flung off the side of the window arch. The chapel and storeroom burned, but as dawn approached the French withdrew to their lines. The Convent of Santa Cruz was still in Spanish hands. The outside wall was irreparably breached, everything apart from the main cloister was now a burned-out shell, and the cloister itself had been left badly scarred by the Spanish guns days before, but the garrison held on.

The governor issued a proclamation and toured the main defences, praising the gallantry of the Avila Regiment and assuring people that the English would come.

As the company was pulled back to take its turn sleeping in a less exposed post, some citizens still had the energy to cheer the handful of redcoats.

'Ninth night, that,' said Dobson, as he marched beside Williams. 'Ninth since they started digging.'

'It's the 23rd June,' the officer replied. 'No, I tell a lie, that was yesterday. It's now the twenty-fourth.'

'Long way to go still,' said the veteran.

'Here's to Christmas at home!' Williams had found himself reviving the old joke.

Dobson puffed on his clay pipe. 'Aye, that'd be good.'

CHAPTER 20

Velarde was struggling to breathe, lying with his head back against the side of the gully, unable for the moment to speak. Hanley felt as exhausted as the Spaniard looked, but was doing his best not to show it.

'Halfway there,' he panted.

His companion still said nothing, but just gave a faint nod. Both men were covered in mud, so that only their eyes reflected the first hints of dawn light.

'We need to go,' Hanley said after ten minutes. They needed the cover of darkness to sneak through the siege lines and into the town, and it would be day soon. It was all taking too long. Velarde's assurance and papers were fine on the road or with wandering patrols, but the Spaniard had no hope that they would convince officers in charge of pickets not to send him to ever more senior commanders. That meant they had to be careful and avoid attention.

They followed the road from Caridad as long as possible, approaching Ciudad Rodrigo from the east, but for the last few miles they cut across country. Between them they knew something of the French dispositions and judged that this was the most open side. A mile out they left Benito and their horses.

'I don't think that man likes me,' Velarde had said once they were away from the one-armed guerrilla.

Hanley ignored him, for he was trying to find his way in the darkness and had no time for wit. They nearly stumbled across the first group of sentries, but fortunately the soldiers seemed just as surprised as they were, and after a vague challenge the Frenchmen made no attempt to search for the retreating figures. More careful, or perhaps simply luckier, they went slowly and were not surprised again, but the cost was in time. At one point the noises of horses, lots of horses, shifting their feet, snorting or relieving themselves noisily, seemed all around them as they moved bent double through a ditch. Hanley's nostrils told him that there was more than simply wet earth in the clinging mud they squelched through. The sounds of their movements seemed deafening, but there were no shouts or other attention.

When Hanley saw the walls of the town outlined against the night sky he knew that they had gone wrong and had drifted westwards, so that in front of them were the walls and houses of the suburbs. They wandered for half an hour, but the need to avoid the enemy pickets and use every wall, ditch or fold for cover confused them and they were not really much further over by the time they felt that they had worked through the main positions. Ahead would be the outposts closest to the town, men who knew that their own survival depended on stealth, and that would make them very hard to see. From then on they crawled, aware that the darkness contained French skirmishers sitting or lying in holes, not moving, and waiting with loaded muskets for any raiders from the city. The only hope was that all would be looking that way, and not searching for figures slipping through their own lines.

At first they crawled quickly. After ten yards both men were sweating so that their backs were as damp as their mud-smeared fronts, and they soon slowed. By fifty yards they were tired, and yet a glance up revealed that the town walls did not seem to be so much as an inch nearer. At twice that distance the muscles in their arms screamed angrily at the effort required of them. Hanley was in front, and they stopped when over the pounding of his heart he thought he heard something from over to their right. They waited for several minutes, but the pause gave no real rest and as soon as they started again the agony returned. When they tumbled suddenly into the drainage ditch, each man had simply slumped back against the side and stared unseeing up at the sky.

'We need to go,' Hanley said, his voice at least returning.

'Can't we just let Napoleon have Spain,' Velarde gasped, and the humour suggested that he was coming back to life. Neither man moved to get up. The light was changing moment by moment.

Then the guns fired.

Hanley and Velarde had both seen and heard the French grand battery at Talavera when something like sixty field guns had hammered at the redcoats. That had been louder and more terrible than anything either man had ever known, the fury of the guns smashing men into ruin. There were fewer pieces emplaced and firing at Ciudad Rodrigo today, but even so the noise and menace were far greater. The biggest guns at Talavera were twelve-pounders, and there were only a handful of those. This morning these biggest of field pieces were the smallest to take part in the barrage. Today there were substantially larger sixteen-pounder cannon, and some of the even more massive twenty-four pounders, and with them were big howitzers and mortars. They were not in a single long line as at Talavera, but entrenched to protect them, and cunningly sited in groups of half a dozen or less, aiming at vulnerable spots in the defences. This was not a barrage to smash men, but to smash the town itself. The bigger, deeper roar of gun after gun was followed by the dull sound of blows as shot pummelled the medieval stone or buried itself deep in earthen banks. Howitzer and mortar shells exploded, raining debris in great fountains.

Later, Hanley would realise that none of the guns was firing over them, and yet still they felt ripples of shock. The two men instinctively shrank, pulling in their limbs protectively as they lay in the ditch. After the first great, rolling onslaught the silence was so oppressive that he wondered whether he had lost his hearing for ever.

'They're early!' Velarde half shouted the words, sounding more puzzled than involved.

'What?'

'Not supposed to start for two days!'

Hanley shrugged. 'Most inconvenient.'

Siege guns were big, and it took a large team to reload and drag them back into position, and that meant the process was slower. Gun captains took great care aiming, to ensure each shot was worth the effort, and so it was a couple of minutes before the guns began to fire again.

Hanley pushed himself up, looking over the lip of the ditch. He grabbed Velarde.

'Run!' He shouted to be heard over the noise, and without bothering to say more he scrambled over the bank and lumbered into a run. He was stiff, and the movement awkward for a few paces, and then he began to get his stride and the weariness of all that crawling seemed like a distant memory. Velarde followed, although the man looked to be fading. The sun was an immense red ball over to Hanley's left and he squinted as he veered a little in that direction.

The rumbling of the second salvo came to its end and now he could hear shouts. Ahead, two white faces appeared from a pit scraped in the ground and both had muskets, although they were not yet aiming them. Still there was no reply from the town.

Hanley ran on, and now his legs were aching with every step. He swung away from the French skirmishers, ignoring their challenge, and kept going.

'Come on!' he called without looking back, and trusted Velarde to follow him.

A musket banged, the noise close, but almost puny after the great guns. Hanley did not see where the shot went and felt nothing come close to him, so perhaps it was a warning. He did not bother to waste breath on any more encouragement. They were near the suburbs now. He could see the earthworks in front of the nearest houses and saw movement at them.

Another shot, and this time he felt the ball pluck the air close by him, and then there was a thump. Velarde shrieked.

Hanley turned and saw that the Spaniard had been hit in the calf and pitched on to the ground. He turned, ran back and was surprised at how close the man was behind him, for he had not heard his footfalls in the soft earth.

'Come on!' he said, lifting him. 'You have to walk.'

Velarde cursed him and the French, and everyone else, but he let himself be lifted and then they went on, the Spaniard wincing with pain at every step. The soldiers manning the earthwork were firing now, not at them, but at the French, and it was enough to keep the voltigeurs in their holes. Shots snapped the air or flicked the grass near them, but somehow they staggered on, Velarde cursing or complaining.

'Trinidad!' Hanley shouted, and hoped they had not changed the password for a friend. 'Trinidad!'

Hands reached out to pull them up over the chest-high emplacement. At that moment the first guns on the town walls began to reply to the French barrage.

'I am Lieutenant Hanley of the English army,' he announced. 'And this is Colonel Velarde. We must see the governor urgently.'

'You'd have to speak to the major,' said a sergeant dubiously.

'Then get him, man,' Hanley snapped.

They waited, gratefully accepting water and using it as much to clean the mud off their faces as to drink.

'Thank you for saving my life,' Velarde said.

'Well, you saved mine.'

'When did you start to trust me?'

Hanley threw more water over his now moderately clean face simply for the joy of feeling the cold liquid against his hot skin.

'What?' Hanley frowned. 'Oh well, it seemed too big a risk not to trust you. Or perhaps I always have.'

The major appeared, an eager young man who had no doubt found that the war made for rapid promotion and short lives.

'We need to see General Herrasti immediately,' Hanley said convincingly. 'I can assure you that he will want to see us. Now where can we find him?'

Cannon fired again from the high medieval walls.

'The governor will be on the walls,' said the young major proudly.

They were escorted by a sergeant and four men, and Hanley's impression of the major's good sense was reinforced by this sign of still qualified belief. It also helped them to find their way through the suburb and be admitted through the gate into the city itself. Two of the men supported Velarde and that gave the officer someone else to curse. The sergeant said little, but whistled tunelessly just under his breath.

Inside the town, they climbed up to the walls, just as one of the Spanish guns fired, leaping back on its trails, and jetting a cloud of dirty smoke through the embrasure. To the right a French howitzer shell sailed down to land neatly on the wide walkway. Men dived to the floor because there was no cover. The shell spun, fuse sparking, and then erupted in flame and dust and jagged fragments. A boy of twelve carrying buckets of water to the gun crews was left as a bloodstained pile of old clothes. Another lad, who looked even younger, knelt down and wept.

'Dear God,' said Hanley.

Beside them a tall house was burning. The French fire no longer came in great salvoes, but as each crew made ready and found a target. There was a crack as a heavy shot struck the wall itself. Others sailed high, smashing lumps off the parapet or the buildings behind the wall. As they went towards it, acting on reports that the governor had gone that way, Hanley saw that the tower of the cathedral seemed to attract particular attention. Already there were a few scars in the stonework.

They pressed on, waiting whenever a gun was about to fire rather than risk being crushed by the recoil. When they found General Herrasti the old man looked as if he was having the time of his life. He urged on the gun crews and the civilians carrying for them, telling them they were punishing the French and that Napoleon would soon shudder when he heard the name of Ciudad Rodrigo. Orders flowed from him in rapid succession, sending officers scurrying away to shift the positions of some guns, or more often to concentrate their aim on particular French pieces.

'We count forty-six guns and howitzers in their batteries,' the old man said to Hanley when at last they were ushered forward and given a moment of his time. 'I have more than a hundred, but sadly not many can see the French works. Still, we have enough to surprise them. It is good to see you, Hanley, and nice to be giving you information for a change!' He laughed. Hanley thought the general looked years younger. 'Now what can I do for you? You realise I am quite busy!'

'There is a conspiracy to betray the city.' Hanley's

words were lost in the thunder of a Spanish twelve-pounder slamming back on its trails as it flung a shot at the embrasure in one of the French batteries up on the Great Teson. Further along the wall and clear of the smoke, an officer with a glass trained on the spot whooped in delight and shouted out that he saw pieces of sandbag and gabion flying into the air. Between shots, the French gunners covered the vulnerable gaps in their earthworks. Men cheered.

'Well done, boys!' Herrasti yelled, patting the sergeant in charge of the gun on the back. 'That's how it's done.'

Inside the city there was a thunderous explosion when a French shell landed in the open door of a magazine with ammunition ready for immediate use on the walls.

The governor winced. 'Don't worry, boys! Plenty more powder where that came from! You were saying, my dear Hanley?'

'There is a conspiracy to betray Ciudad Rodrigo to the French. Joseph Napoleon has agents working to bribe men to seize power.'

The governor looked grave and dropped his voice. 'You know this? Who?'

'This is Colonel Velarde.' Hanley gestured and Velarde straightened, letting go of the two soldiers, but then he hissed in pain and let one of them support him on the side of his wounded leg.

'Your servant, General.' Velarde managed a feeble bow.

Hanley cut in before he could say any more. 'Colonel Velarde has full information about the plot, sir, because he is a traitor and has come to Ciudad Rodrigo to make it happen.'

Herrasti blinked, just once, but showed no other sign of surprise. 'Indeed.'

Luiz Velarde looked stunned and unbalanced for the first time Hanley could remember. It was only for an instant, and the Englishman suspected that the pain in his leg played a part.

'I strongly suggest that you arrest him and throw him into a cell,' Hanley said.

'It is nonsense!' Velarde reacted at last. 'I am loyal to King Ferdinand and . . .'

A French eight-inch shell dropped from the sky just behind the Spanish gun. Its fuse was a little short, but if the gunner who cut it had ever known he would not have quibbled at the result. It exploded ten feet above the walkway. Twisted pieces of casing killed the gun captain, ripped open the ribcage of the ventman, and smashed limbs on three more of the crew. The biggest shard struck the top of Luiz Velarde's head and shattered it like an overripe fruit, spraying blood, brains and bone over all the others. The soldier supporting him died a few seconds later, killed by part of Velarde's lower jaw which had driven into his neck and severed the artery.

Hanley and the other survivors were knocked down and stunned. His ears rang, and he had to scrape blood and flesh off his face so that he could see again. Feeling his limbs and finding no sign of injury, he pushed himself up. With the sergeant, he helped the governor to rise, relieved that he was unscathed.

'Well, that was all very dramatic,' said the old man. He glanced down and saw what was left of Velarde. 'Oh well, one less traitor. And one less problem.' He turned to the gunners. 'Get those men to the hospital. Captain, I want replacements here immediately. Can't let this one fall silent. We've got them worried, boys, we've got them worried!

'Hanley?'

'Sir.'

'I have a meeting at noon, so you can tell me more then.'

'Yes, sir.' The matter appeared to be closed for the moment. 'Damn,' said William Hanley.

CHAPTER 21

'Unfortunate,' Williams said, 'but surely a good deal better than if you had been struck.' The two sat in the little room he had shared with Pringle. Hanley preferred this to going back to the chamber he had been given in the past. There was something reassuringly simple about his friend, and after the last week he craved simplicity.

'Oh, if ever a man deserved to be killed I suspect it was Luiz Velarde. I just wish I could have got at some of the stuff in his head before it was spread all over the ramparts.' Hanley had looked through the papers the French agent had with him. Some were of minor interest, and although a little stained with mud and gore there were also the letters and passes which had got them past the French patrols, but there was nothing of use concerning the plots here or elsewhere. Hanley had not really expected to find anything, but had still hoped that he was wrong. The only probably important sheet was in a code that he could not fathom.

'He seems a contrary man, even to the last,' Williams said. 'Perhaps it was unwise to take him up on to the wall in the middle of a bombardment?' The irony was heavy.

'My fault – my theatrical nature!' Hanley laughed. 'It seemed a reasonable idea. The man was dangerous, and I wanted to confront him in a place where he could not get away or do mischief. I also wanted to rattle him. Thought he might blurt something out or at least be so sure that he was doomed that he might be willing to talk later. It still seems reasonable,' he finished somewhat defensively.

'And you are sure he was working for the French?'

'Oh yes, since soon after Talavera, and he had not changed his mind.'

'So tell me how you fell in with the fellow, and came up with this imaginative plan – that is if you can explain such things to a simple soldier!' Williams sensed his friend wanted to talk. He was tired, but he liked Hanley a good deal and also sensed that the whole tale might be as extraordinary as the finale. There was little entertainment to pass the evenings in Ciudad Rodrigo.

Hanley did not disappoint. He began with Baynes.

'A wily old fox,' Williams said in a tone where distaste matched admiration.

Then Hanley spoke of his visits to Ciudad Rodrigo, the contacts in Salamanca, and of Jenny Dobson. 'It was Jenny who made it possible,' he said.

'Odd, isn't it, how we still think of her as Jenny Dobson,' Williams interjected. 'Suppose she is still really Mrs Hanks.'

'I reckon she's a Dobson. Too much of her father's steel in her to be anything else.' Hanley smiled. 'She is a cool hand. Easy to forget she is still so young.'

'Sadly, in some ways I doubt she was ever that young.' Williams disapproved of Jenny's morals – she had gone with officers even while with the regiment and he could not understand anyone abandoning a child – and yet he had always liked her.

'For my sake I am glad. She was already providing us with information. At a price, of course, but the same is true of many a source, and consorting with an engineer officer gave her access to some excellent and most specific details.' Hanley spoke of them at some length, and then told Williams of meeting Jenny, and asking her about Velarde. 'Or Espinosa, as he was calling himself. And then fate and Jenny Dobson took charge. An old "acquaintance" of hers, a Captain Dalmas, appears.'

'Dalmas?'

Hanley was intrigued. 'You know him?'

'I fought an officer of that name last January, and saw him again recently. He was tough.'

'Clever?'

'He's a cavalryman.' Williams grinned out of sheer habit. 'But yes, he thought about what he did.'

'Well, this Dalmas was given the task of helping Velarde and looking for me, and wanted to kill two birds with one stone. He wanted Jenny to amuse him and send a message to me, offering Velarde as bait. Dalmas reckoned Jenny must be reporting to us somehow. You have to admire the man.'

'And yet I am guessing he misjudged.'

'Both of them, in fact. Velarde wanted to do things without Dalmas breathing down his neck and asked for her help. She told me about the whole thing by a separate message to La Doña Margarita, and then sent the one they wanted, trusting that I would do something about it.' He explained the rest of the story, surprising himself at how long it took.

At the end Williams whistled through his teeth. 'All too complicated for me. Is Jenny in danger now?'

Surprised, Hanley took a moment to answer. 'I cannot see why she should be. She did everything they asked. Their aim was to get Velarde inside Ciudad Rodrigo. Now it rather looks as if he will never leave. No, she should be fine. I did say that I would give her greetings to her father. Am not sure how he will take it.'

'Well, I suspect. You'll never shock old Dob. And besides, in her way, she is fighting the French.'

'For money.'

'Haven't noticed you turning the King's shillings down of late. When we get them, that is.' Williams looked intently at his friend. 'And what happens now? Will the plotters still strike?'

Hanley rubbed his chin, shaved just a few hours ago and yet already starting to roughen again. 'No, I do not think so. They will be waiting to be contacted with King Joseph's promises. I doubt the French have another agent as senior as Velarde, certainly not here. Perhaps one will be able to let them know that he is dead. I doubt it, though. All that was easier before the siege lines closed around the town.'

'The governor still gets messages through to Wellington, but it is more difficult.' Now that Pringle had gone, Williams was sometimes included in the general's councils. 'He has lost some of the messengers,' he said sadly.

'I did suggest that your company should be sent back to Portugal.' Hanley sighed. 'Afraid the general is determined to keep you.'

'Be hard to leave.' Williams sounded wistful. 'Not too keen on becoming a prisoner, though, if the worst comes to the worst.'

'There will be a way out,' said Hanley, but his friend did not look confident.

Every day the guns pounded. You could hear them at Fort La Concepción as a low rumble, a little like thunder save that it never moved nearer or further away and went on almost all day. Billy Pringle found himself waking each morning at four o'clock when the French artillerymen fired their first salvo as regularly as clockwork. It was not so much the noise as the predictability that jerked him awake from even the very deepest and most dreamless sleep. He remembered during the years at Magdalen how he had woken each day when the chapel clock chimed seven. This time there was even less choice. His eyes sprang open at the first rolling pops and he could never get back to sleep.

On the first day Lord Wellington was one of the many who came to watch. The general visited Almeida for some time to consult with the governor, but then came to the fort and later went a mile to two more to see the bombardment from a convenient rise. With a decent glass, it was possible even to see individual guns go off in the French batteries or on the walls. Pringle remembered staff officers cheering on the plucky Spanish defenders. At night you could see the glow from the fires burning in Ciudad Rodrigo and it was hard to feel so enthusiastic. Pringle worried about his men left behind in the city.

He could tell that MacAndrews worried too, and there was a growing air of depression as the British mission at the fort was dismantled.

'I was becoming accustomed to being called colonel,' the Scotsman said with a grin as they rode out to watch the siege and consult with Brigadier General Craufurd and his staff. The French kept pressing forward, probing the British outpost line and the Spanish supporting them on the flank. While Ciudad Rodrigo was pounded, each day the outlying parties of the field armies fenced with each other.

'Can't say I'm becoming accustomed to having a powder keg as a pillow,' Pringle replied.

'Think of it this way,' Colonel MacAndrews suggested. 'If there ever is a mistake, we shall not know anything about it!'

Fort La Concepción had been repaired a month ago. The Portuguese regulars were called back to Almeida, but in their place had come several companies of redcoats from the 1/45th Foot. Their officers were old friends, for Pringle, along with Williams, Hanley and the others, had served in the same brigade at Talavera. The 45th, with their green facings and Regimental Colour, were a fine, well-drilled battalion, as steady as a rock. MacAndrews had heartily approved, and even cajoled the major in charge into drilling his men a few times so that the Spanish recruits would see that it could all become very easy.

The Spanish recruits were gone now, called back to their army with almost full equipment and rudimentary training. The order recalling them had specified all of the recruits, failing to note that the remainder were in Ciudad Rodrigo. MacAndrews had briefly lost his temper, demanding permission to go and fetch his men out.

There was nothing to be done. All the recruits in the fort had marched away, and a few days later Morillo took his staff and the party of NCOs off as well. Pringle had watched MacAndrews and the Spanish captain say goodbye, seeing the mutual regard and respect in their handshake. Neither man had bemoaned his lot, but he could see faint hints of despondency. Grand plans – always over-ambitious and unrealistic, but worthy enough to make a man want to believe that it was all possible – had come to nothing.

Somehow it all seemed summed up by the change in the fort itself. Captain Burgoyne of the Royal Engineers had spent weeks toiling to repair the damage to the bastion and rampart inflicted by the French back in '08. Then orders came that Fort La Concepción was not to be defended, since in spite of its strength it was too exposed to be supported and must inevitably fall to starvation. Strings of mules had come delivering barrel after barrel of powder, and now Burgoyne was working to undo all that he had achieved so far, setting mines to reduce the fort to rubble. There was no point handing a viable fortification to the French.

Burgoyne assured them repeatedly that his mines were perfectly safe. 'Harmless as lambs,' he was fond of saying. 'Until I stick in the fuses and apply the match, and then we shall have as fine a display as ever graced Vauxhall Gardens on a summer's night. Without perhaps the murmurs of passion from the shrubbery, that is.' The engineer was a cheerful fellow, and like many of his colleagues, Pringle felt he rather courted a reputation for eccentricity.

'Mad as a March hare,' MacAndrews muttered.

'They're all the same. Minds rattled by too many explosions. I dare say no engineer can look at a church or a pretty cottage without wondering how big a charge they would need to turn it all into matchwood.' He shook his head ruefully. 'The name is unlucky, though.'

'Burgoyne?'

'Makes me think of Gentleman Johnny.'

Pringle found it easy to forget that this was not the first big war for the Scotsman. As a young ensign he had fought in America, ending that unhappy war as an escaped prisoner and acting captain – married as well to an American bride.

'Were you at Saratoga?' Pringle asked. MacAndrews rarely talked of the war, and Pringle's knowledge came from some sketchy reading, but he had heard of that first great defeat, when a British army invading from the north had been forced to surrender by the rebels.

'No, thank God. I was with Billy Howe at Philadelphia watching his staff stage pageants and hope the rebellion just went away.' MacAndrews said nothing for a moment, and then surprised Pringle by quoting verse –

'Sir William he, sung as a flea,
lay all the while a-snoring,
Nor dreamed of harm,
As he lay warm,
In bed with Mrs Loring.'

MacAndrews laughed without any trace of amusement. 'Didn't know that that bit of doggerel was still lodged in my mind, although I dare say it would impress my family to hear me quoting any sort of poetry!'

'Who was Mrs Loring?'

'Yes, thought that you'd seize on that bit, young Pringle. Still seeing that girl from Fuentes?'

Pringle was surprised MacAndrews knew about Josepha.

'Got a letter of complaint from her father yesterday,' the colonel explained.

'She's inside Ciudad Rodrigo.'

'Good,' MacAndrews said. 'Probably better to keep it that way. I'll reply that you have cut your connection with the girl. It would be wise,' he added. 'Instead dream of Lizzie Loring, who was a pretty little vixen. She was married to a Tory officer, but he didn't seem to mind and contented himself with fiddling the books so that the prisoners under his charge starved and he got rich. Hell of a way to fight a war.' The colonel sighed, and then grinned. 'If ever you want to learn how not to do something, then read about how we lost the colonies!'

'I'll bear it in mind.'

They rode the next half-mile in silence. 'The battalion is posted abroad,' MacAndrews said suddenly. 'The last batch of letters confirmed it. Gibraltar first, and then perhaps Cadiz or even back here, if Lord Wellington can cling on in Portugal.'

301

'Do you think we can, sir?' Pringle asked.

MacAndrews was a true Highlander, and never answered any question quickly. 'Maybe,' he said with similar Caledonian reluctance to commit. 'The French are obviously so convinced they are going to win that they are dragging their feet. Maybe something can be pulled out of the hat to surprise them.'

'Are we to rejoin the battalion?'

'Nothing certain as yet, although the colonel writes to say that he earnestly hopes to arrange this.'

Pringle thought back to Williams telling him of Dobson's comments all those months ago, and that led him to the fears for his comrades, and the guilt that he was no longer inside the besieged fortress. He had carried the letter from the governor to Celorico, even seen the general read it immediately. Billy Pringle had never for a moment thought that the British commander would march to the town's relief, and all that El Charro had said had only added to that conviction. It seemed a wasted journey, but now it meant that he was safe and his friends were not.

MacAndrews grunted when they saw a cluster of horsemen on the ridge ahead of them and the two men urged their mounts up the slope to join them. Earlier that morning the companies from the 1/45th had also marched away from Fort La Concepción, going back to the irascible General Picton's Third Division. Burgoyne was still there, tinkering with his 'infernal devices', as MacAndrews called them, and there was usually a corporal's picket of the KGL Hussars, but otherwise there was simply the Scotsman and his small party of officers and NCOs.

'Ah, Colonel MacAndrews,' said Brigadier General Craufurd as they arrived. 'I understand that you are to be placed under my command for the moment. What is your establishment?'

'Six officers present, with thirty-six sergeants, corporals and other ranks. One officer and three NCOs are in Ciudad Rodrigo.' They could see the town clearly from the ridge, and watch the flashes of guns, even though the noise of the shots came only later as an indistinct rumble.

'Aye, well, I dare say they're playing their part most gallantly. I have no doubt that we can make use of those of you present.' The general's tone was gruff, but practical. His brigade had now become the Light Division, but as yet its regiments were not divided into two or more brigades, and so Black Bob had no subordinate generals and their staffs to help him run things. Pringle suspected that he and the rest of MacAndrews' little force would soon find themselves running errands and performing all the other little tasks than no one else cared to do. He edged his horse to the fringes of the group of staff officers.

'Well, Pringle, my dear fellow, what a joy to see you!' Billy turned, the voice vaguely familiar, but was still surprised to see Lieutenant Garland beaming delightedly and holding out his hand. It was odd to receive such an enthusiastic greeting from a man whom he had shot at their last meeting.

Pringle smiled broadly, took the hand, and made the appropriate noises. 'I did not know the Fourteenth were up?'

'Oh, can't keep the Hawks out of the thick of things,' said the light dragoon officer with the bounding enthusiasm of a puppy. The 14th Light Dragoons wore the Prussian eagle on the side of their crested Tarleton helmets, an honour bestowed by the Prussian wife of the Duke of York, and had picked up the nickname as a result. 'I've ridden on in advance. Tilney is coming, of course. You really must dine with us when you have a mind.'

The priorities of cavalry officers always baffled Pringle, but after several years in the army he was used to the way they spoke of campaigning as little more than an excursion with friends, and a brief diversion from the serious business of hunting and gaming.

'Is Mr Williams well, may I ask?'

'When last I saw him, but he and a small party are inside Ciudad Rodrigo.'

Garland looked shocked for the briefest moment. 'Ah, can't keep him out of the thick of things! Doesn't surprise me.' He looked more serious, although obviously bursting to speak. 'I wonder whether he has heard from home lately?'

Pringle smiled. 'Sadly, the letters had not arrived

before he left, but may I take this opportunity of offering you the heartiest congratulations on the birth of your daughter.' Anne Williams now wrote regularly to him, but the vagaries of the army's postal deliveries meant that he had recently received three in one batch, the second telling of the birth. 'Mrs Garland is doing very well, I hear.'

'Oh, she's strong stock,' the lieutenant said, almost as warmly as he would speak of a pure-bred hunter. 'And women dearly love having babies,' he added, confiding all the wisdom of his nineteen years. 'We have named her Esmerelda Harriet. After my mother and my grandmother respectively.'

'Very pretty,' Pringle lied. 'You must be eager to see her?'

'Well, duty first. Would not want to miss all this excitement.'

Pringle fought the urge to pat the puppy-like Garland on the head or rub his stomach. The guns rumbled and suddenly there was a great flash. Pringle had not been looking in the right direction, and by the time he turned there was simply a big plume of black smoke coming up from the side of what he guessed was the Great Teson. The general looked amused and his staff were whooping like schoolboys.

'Must have hit a French magazine,' he said.

'Damned good shooting,' Garland said.

'Probably luck, but none the worse for that.'

'I wonder if General Craufurd will attack soon?'

Garland mused. 'He seems quite a firebrand, although they say he knows his business.' The outpost line had held for months and not suffered a serious surprise or reverse, so Pringle would not challenge the statement. 'Did you hear the story about General Craufurd and the commissary, my dear fellow?'

Pringle had heard several, but could see that young Garland was bursting to repeat his tale and so pleaded ignorance. 'Don't believe so.' The commissaries were civilians tasked with arranging supplies for the army, buying where possible, and having them brought as needed and wanted by the troops. The job was difficult, its incumbents a mixture of rogues, fools and the genuinely capable, and they were rarely popular as a breed.

'Well, this commissary goes to Lord Wellington to complain. "My lord, General Craufurd threatens to shoot me unless I deliver his division full supplies by sunset tonight!" "Does he, by God," says Lord Wellington, "well, if I were you I should get him everything he wants in time, for if General Craufurd says he plans to shoot you then he is sure to do it!"'

Pringle laughed along with Garland, even though he had heard the story several times before. Indeed, he had more often heard it told of Picton than Craufurd and doubted that there was any truth in it.

MacAndrews edged his horse through the cluster of riders and gestured to Pringle.

'Time to go,' he said.

Billy nodded to Garland and followed the Scotsman back towards the almost empty Fort La Concepción. Behind them, the guns rumbled on at Ciudad Rodrigo.

CHAPTER 22

Sometimes the French howitzers kept firing through the night. Shells exploded, the wickedly sharp fragments of the casing ripping through the air. Sometimes it was the blast alone that killed, and that could leave no trace at all or scorch and burn terribly.

On the second night Williams returned to their room paler than Hanley had ever seen him before. He was staring unfocused into the far distance, and when he sat down he began to shake, beginning with his hands, until the tremors spread to his entire body. He sputtered and coughed when Hanley gave him some brandy, spitting most of it out, but whether it was the ardent spirit or his revulsion it calmed him a little.

'I was looking at one of the pumps they use to fight the fires,' he said in a quiet, hollow voice. Hanley suspected 'looking' meant that he and Murphy had helped drive the handle of the machine to pump water through the hose, but did not interrupt. He could tell the man needed to talk, and it was better to let him build up to it in his own time. Although he was no longer shaking, there was no colour in the Welshman's face.

'They come from Lisbon, did you know that?'

Hanley nodded. 'They were sent from Lisbon at the governor's request some months ago,' he explained.

'Oh, I did not know. Gave me a shock.' Williams held the empty glass tightly and stared at the bare wall. 'You know my sister is expecting a child?'

Again Hanley nodded. 'It must be hard to be cut off from news.'

Williams stared at the wall for five minutes, and then suddenly looked at his friend. 'Do you remember Josephus? The *Bellum Judaicum*?'

'Yes, been a while since I read it, though.'

'One passage always haunted me. He fought against the Romans, you will remember, before joining them.'

Williams lapsed into silence again, struggling to speak. Hanley tried to remember as much as he could of the story of a first-century war.

'He spoke of catapults, firing great stones whizzing through the air. There was one story so dreadful I wished afterwards that I had never read it so that I could blot the horror from my mind.' He dropped the glass and pressed his hands against his eyes and forehead. 'Dear God, now I have seen it.'

The memory snapped into place with stark horror. 'A woman with child?' Hanley asked, hoping to be wrong. Josephus spoke of standing beside a pregnant woman when she was struck in the belly by a stone from a catapult. The mother died instantly, her whole stomach ripped open, and her unborn child was flung a hundred yards away. Hanley closed his own eyes, as if that could somehow shut off his imagination.

Williams was shaking again. 'I wish I could weep,' he said softly.

Hanley gave his friend water this time, and then helped him to bed and covered him with blankets so that he was warm. The cot shook for a long time before Williams drifted at last into sleep.

At first light the next morning the French guns opened up to join the howitzers, so that the noise redoubled. Two batteries on top of the Great Teson focused all their hate on a short section of the medieval wall in front of the cathedral. Sixteen- and twenty-four-pound shot struck again and again at the centuries-old stone and mortar. The aim was good, and chips became ever widening scars beneath the thick clouds of dust. Then whole stones and larger pieces tumbled down from the wall and into the ditch. The outer face broken, rubble from the inside crumbled quickly.

The next day the French guns returned to their work, the heavy shot slamming again and again into the same stretch of wall. It was quickly clear that the wounds were mortal, as more and more of the wall collapsed into the ditch. By 2 p.m. on the second day of precise fire at this spot some forty yards of wall were down, and the rubble had slumped into the ditch so that it would be no hard thing for a man to walk up from the bottom of the ditch and into the town. He still had to reach the ditch and survive the fire of the defenders, though.

The French artillery kept pounding the town, and all the while the saps zigzagged ever closer to the walls. Each day Williams and Hanley went to study their progress, just as the former had once done with Pringle. After a night's sleep the Welshman seemed his usual self again, but his friend wondered what the cost of such things was in the longer run. He had always felt himself to be a cynical man, and one never swept away by rhetoric of glory and even beauty in sacrifice and warfare. Yet nothing he had imagined had come close to some of the horrors he had seen since the war began. Nor had he dreamed of the closeness he now felt to men like Williams and Pringle. There was an incongruous, almost guilty joy in such friendship, and he had to admit that he had been happier in these last years than ever before. Sometimes Hanley wondered what price his own mind and soul would pay for the things he had seen and done.

That same day he and Williams stood at the back of a meeting of the governor's staff and the city's Junta, listening as a new summons from the French was read out, delivered by an officer under a flag of truce. That man waited under guard near the walls while it was decided what answer to make. The letter began with the usual pleasantries, praising the garrison's resistance.

'. . . but these efforts, always recognised by the French army, will destroy you if you continue your defence much longer. Although with regret, the Prince of Essling will be forced to treat you with all the rigour that the laws of war authorise. If you hoped to be aided by the English' – more than a few heads glanced back at the two redcoats when this was read – 'you are deceived. How could you fail to realise that if this had been their intention, under no condition would they have permitted Ciudad Rodrigo to be reduced to such a deplorable condition? Your situation can only grow worse. You have to choose between honourable capitulation and the terrible vengeance of a victorious army.'

Some of the Junta, and a few of the officers, wanted to give in. Hanley could see it in their eyes, as much as what they said. Several were bitter at the failure of Lord Wellington to appear and drive away the French. Yet most were grimly determined to persist. The bishop gave a speech fuming against the crimes committed by the French in Spain.

'His Excellency is right,' said General Herrasti after listening to all the opinions. 'These people have come to our land as invaders. They kill and they plunder at will.

'Much of what the French prince says is true. They are breaking our defences and when they do assault it will be terrible. Soldiers who fight their way through a breach are little more than animals by the time they get into the city. I will hide none of these things from you.' He looked around the table, staring at each face in turn, holding their gaze.

'Yet we are not beaten. They have made a breach, but will not find it easy to attack. The glacis, ditch and earthworks are almost untouched. After forty-nine years in the service I know the laws of war and my military duty. The fortress of Ciudad Rodrigo is not in a state to capitulate and no breach is formed and sufficiently complete that makes it necessary. There may come a time when surrender will be necessary to save the people of this city. It is not yet. The English may still come, and I will send a new message to Lord Wellington today. If they do not come, it will not be our fault, and I will have no man say that the garrison and citizens of Ciudad Rodrigo did not do all that honour and love of their country demanded.

'If you follow my advice then we shall reject this summons.'

They did not cheer. Instead the mood was one of cold determination, but all voted to support the general. Hanley wondered whether this was the moment when Velarde's conspirators would have struck if he had been there to confirm their resolution. He tried to study the faces, but in truth was not even sure that the cautious men were disloyal. Perhaps the French would now realise that their agent was dead, or at least unable to fulfil his promises. Hanley had spent hours with the coded sheet and remained utterly baffled.

The next day, General Herrasti ordered every gun that could bear to concentrate on the French saps. Williams and Hanley watched through their glasses. Experience is a ready tutor, and the Spanish gunners were now more skilled in serving their pieces. They were more accurate, if not yet able to fire with the precise aim that came only from years of training and practice. The areas around the heads of the saps were deluged with shot, and enough struck squarely, flinging down the gabions and sandbags protecting them. Williams could only imagine the carnage at the head of those trenches.

Yet still the enemy edged closer, with trenches and batteries near the abandoned Convent of Santa Cruz, and a long sap crossing the Lesser Teson and creeping towards the ditch and glacis of the city. Their artillery switched its attention more to the suburb of San Francisco. Soon houses were burning, and the earth ramparts protecting the area were thrown down in many places. The biggest guns fired less often.

'Perhaps they are running out of shot?' suggested Hanley when Williams drew his attention to it. It surprised him that the Welshman could tell so much from the noise.

'Or saving it for particular targets?'

That night the sound of digging was closer. The

314

French slaved each night because darkness protected them from accurate shooting by the garrison. The next morning they could see the line of the Second Parallel, almost touching the slope of the glacis.

'That's the last obstacle!' Williams said, pointing. 'Damn it!' he yelled, and jerked back from the edge of the embrasure as a voltigeur's bullet smacked into the stonework inches from his head. More carefully he moved so that they could look down from the walls into the ditch. 'Do you see the counter-scarp?'

'Possibly, if I knew what it was.'

Williams chuckled. 'You really will have to learn more about your profession one of these days. It is the outside face of the ditch. Here it is faced in stone and a steep, sheer drop. At the moment it would be difficult to jump down without risking broken legs and ankles. It would slow them down, if nothing else, and an attack that slows can readily falter. The French will want to tumble that wall into the ditch so that they can run down and be ready to climb the breach.'

That night the company was on duty, providing pickets and a reserve in the covered way behind the suburb. As senior officer Hanley was naturally in charge, and went forward at nine o'clock to report to the commander of the garrison in the San Francisco convent. The French howitzers and mortars fired for two hours after darkness fell, but then the bombardment slackened. It was not wholly silent, but the break from the explosions and flashes was almost more oppressive than the noise.

Hanley got lost in the maze of walled gardens between the suburb and the town, and now realised that he should have listened to Williams' advice and taken a look in daylight. He walked for five minutes and then almost stumbled into a picket, prompting a flurry of raised weapons and surprised cries. Fortunately the sergeant and his five men were not nervous or over-vigilant and no one fired. Several bayonets were levelled at his chest, but the password and a ready explanation quickly confirmed that he was a friend.

'Dark night, Lieutenant,' said the sergeant, a short, cheerful fellow, whose tone hinted that officers were not safe let out on their own. 'You have come too far to the left. Much further and it might have turned nasty. Listen for a moment.'

Hanley let his breathing steady, did as he was told, and then gasped nervously. The French sounded as if they were just a few yards away. He could hear the spades thunking into the earth, the pickaxes striking stone, the tipping of spoil, and over it all the murmur of voices and softly spoken orders.

'If you'd gone much further you would have changed armies,' said the sergeant.

'How close are they?' Hanley found himself whispering.

The sergeant grinned, teeth white in the soft

light of the waxing moon. 'Sounds closer than it is at night. It's at least a long musket shot, and perhaps a bit more. They're up on the Lesser Teson.'

He gave Hanley directions, and almost to his own surprise the officer made no more mistakes and reached the convent, where he spoke to the commander and listened to the reports from the sentries and patrols. The French were close, but had been for days. There seemed to be nothing untoward.

Hanley decided to retrace his steps, rather than risk getting lost again. When he came towards the picket, he called out the password and waited for the response. Nothing happened. He walked forward slowly, and again gave the watchword. Then his foot struck something. It was one of the recruits, and the whole front of the white waistcoat he wore as uniform was dark with blood. Hanley dropped to a crouch, staring around him. The smell of fresh blood was strong and rank in his nostrils.

The sergeant and his men were all dead, the NCO still with a Frenchman's short sword thrust upwards into his stomach and under his ribcage. Several of the others had their throats cut like the first man he had found. From up on the Lesser Teson, the noise of digging and quiet talk still wafted down.

Hanley's heart was pounding again. This was so sudden. After days inside a besieged town, he had become used to the sight of the French near by, but the same complacent spirit had killed the sergeant and his men. The officer looked around him, trying to pierce the darkness. Reaching down, he pulled his pistol from where it was tucked into his sash. Apart from that he had his sword.

There was no sign of the French. Hanley thought back to the hill at Talavera when he had become caught up in a night attack. He wished that Dobson was at his side this time as well, for the veteran always seemed to know what to do.

A Spanish howitzer fired from an emplacement set into the earthworks by the ditch. The noise and flame were startling, but at least they gave his reeling mind a better sense of his bearings. Keeping at a crouch, he half walked, half jogged back towards where he guessed the company were. The Spanish shell prompted the French to return the compliment. A mortar gave its dull boom and a great shell arched high, trailing sparks to land three or four hundred yards away near the cathedral. Even at that distance the explosion of the big shell made him flinch.

He stopped, and as he looked around again he just made out a darker shade to the night over on his left. Hanley dropped to one knee, knowing it was easier to see anything against the sky, and wondered whether all he had seen was one of the garden walls. Then it moved, and there was the sound of shuffling feet. There were men, certainly dozens and perhaps over a hundred. No Spanish should be moving in the dark.

Hanley eased the hammer back on his pistol, and the click as he cocked it like a brass tray dropping on an empty stage. The French – he was sure they must be French – kept going away from him. He did not worry about aiming, but simply levelled it generally in their direction. He needed to make noise and hope to surprise the French into firing and revealing themselves.

Lieutenant Hanley pulled the trigger, snatching at it a little so that the muzzle jerked up as the hammer slammed down and sparked. Nothing happened, and the main charge did not ignite. Hanley cursed silently, and ruefully remembered Pringle's expression after his second pistol misfired during the duel.

The French seemed to be going away from him, heading for the convent, and he guessed that must be the target of the attack. He was about to shout when half a dozen muskets banged.

'*Vive l'empereur!*' the French cheered. More muskets flamed into the night and in the flashes he could see distinct silhouettes as the French soldiers surged away from him towards the looming shape of the convent.

Hanley ran back towards the glacis and ditch. He could hear shouts, and he bawled out the password. A deep voice called the order to hold their fire, and he recognised it as Sergeant Rodriguez's. Without really knowing what he was doing, he had found his way back to the company.

'Get down, sir!' Dobson bellowed, and Hanley found himself responding to the NCO's tone before the words really registered. He dropped into the cold grass.

'Fire!' Williams shouted, and the company sent a volley towards the French, the balls snapping in the air as they passed over Hanley's head. 'Come on, William,' his friend called.

Hanley pushed himself up and sprinted towards them as the recruits reloaded. Beside them another company fired, the muskets squibbing off in dribs and drabs rather than as one roaring discharge.

No shots came back.

'Must be relying on the bayonet,' Williams said with more than a trace of admiration. He turned as a Spanish major ran up behind him. 'Are we going forward, sir?'

'No. Stay in your position. There are too many of them out there.'

Shots came from the convent and the nearby hospice, the sound sometimes echoing from the courtyards and the little walled gardens. There were shouts and screams.

'Look, sir!' That was Corporal Rose, who seemed to see unusually well at night. Hanley saw the gleam of bayonets and shadows coming towards them.

'Present!' Williams shouted. 'Aim low!' he added in Spanish.

'Fire!' The volley punched into the night and for a moment Hanley clearly saw the line of French soldiers in their bright white cross-belts.

'Sorry, William, I seem to be taking over,' Williams said apologetically.

'Keep them at it,' Hanley said.

The French had pulled back some way, so that they could only just be seen as a deeper shadow in the night. Then a building flamed into light over to the right and as the fire blossomed Hanley could see the line of soldiers more clearly.

'A company,' Williams said before Hanley had finished counting. 'Perhaps another behind.' The French still did not fire. 'They're up to something.'

Shouts and a burst of firing came from further down the glacis on their right.

'Sods have broken through on our flank!' shouted Dobson, who was stationed at that end of the company.

'Back to the town!' shouted the Spanish major. 'Or we'll be cut off!'

The recruits looked nervously over their shoulders, shuffling as they reloaded.

'Stand fast!' Rodriguez shouted.

'Give them one volley, and then we go back,' Williams ordered. He glanced at Hanley for a moment, who saw that they were ready.

'*Vive l'empereur!*' The French ahead of them were advancing again, marching forward in order. There was a flicker of red gleams as their bayonets came down to the charge, catching the glow of the burning house.

'Present!' Hanley shouted, but his voice cracked and he had to cough. 'Present!' he repeated. The small line brought their muskets up to their shoulders. Hanley was sure he saw the French hesitate for an instant, stopping in their tracks.

'Fire!' The volley came almost as one, stabbing into the night.

'Now back!' he called. 'Back!' The sergeants added their shouts and the recruits doubled back down into the covered way and along towards the gate. Hanley waited for a moment and as the smoke thinned he saw that the French line had stopped, with two men down, one of them screaming in agony.

Then the enemy came forward again and he fled.

Williams and the sergeants rallied the men in front of the gate. They were held there with another company for an hour, but the French made no effort to come further and eventually they were dismissed to get two hours' sleep before they were needed again.

No one cheered the redcoats as they walked through the dark streets. Soldiers and civilians alike looked too tired to care or hope.

Hanley was struggling to keep his eyes open when they reached their billet. He felt exhausted, his mind and senses unclear, so that it was an effort simply to walk.

The door of their room was open, and suddenly

Hanley was coldly awake. The cots were tipped on their sides, chairs and table knocked over, and papers strewn about the floor. Williams' Bible was lying open on its face, several pages torn from it. That sight seemed to upset him more than the chaos.

'Damn,' he said, fishing among the debris for the pages of a long letter he was writing to Miss MacAndrews in the hope of being able to send it one day. 'You'd think you would be safe from thieves here.'

Hanley searched carefully. The pouch of letters he had taken from Velarde was still there, but empty. Carefully he hunted for the contents and found everything.

'I do not believe this was a chance robbery,' he said, certainty growing. 'Any money gone?'

'Didn't have much to go,' his friend said gloomily, but made a quick investigation. 'No, although this purse was staring them in the face.'

'Thought not. I suspect this is what they wanted.' Hanley reached into his jacket and pulled out the coded page. 'It must be more important than I thought.'

'Still no idea what it is?'

'Not a clue,' he said.

CHAPTER 23

At dawn the French guns opened fire with renewed fury, dashing hopes of shortages. Twenty-four pound shot deluged the breach, quickly smashing the hasty repairs made by the city's engineers. The work on the Second Parallel was much advanced, and only strict orders from Marshal Masséna prevented the commander of 6th Corps from going there to urge the workers on as they made the new batteries that would fire at point-blank range. Instead, Ney sent one of his ADCs.

'Engineers are all very well,' he said, 'but I need a soldier's opinion.'

Dalmas returned two hours later, covered in mud, much to the amusement of his commander.

'Shocking standards on my staff these days,' Marshal Ney said, his cheeks looking even redder than usual. 'You look like you have been shovelling shit. Good job you weren't wearing that ironmongery of yours otherwise you'd go rusty.'

'Your grace,' Dalmas said, used to the marshal's ways. He was in his single-breasted blue tunic and wore a plain soldier's bonnet rather than his helmet.

'Well, man, tell me, how is it coming along?'

'Battery Eleven is close to completion.'

'The ricochet battery?'

Dalmas nodded. The guns were to be placed so that they could fire at a sharp angle along the wall, grazing or bouncing off it to destroy any repairs and slaughter the defenders who tried to work there. 'I am not sure the angle is right.'

'Useless bloody gunners,' the marshal said, noticing the stiff looks from the artillery officers attending him.

'I do assure you, your grace . . .' one of them began.

'Do it later. The proof will be if the thing does its job. The mines?'

'Progressing well although the ground is rocky and hard to work.' Dalmas had gone into the shafts, and watched the bare-chested sappers carving out a deep mine that would eventually allow them to blow in the counter-scarp. It was a hot day above ground. In the mine, the sweat poured off the toiling men and it was hard to breathe.

'Useless bloody place. We're either drowning in mud or hacking at stone. How long to finish them?' Marshal Ney snapped the question at his senior engineer, who in turn glanced at a subordinate.

'Three more days and nights.'

'Dalmas?'

Again Dalmas nodded. 'Should be ready on time. The men are working in relays in spite of the dreadful conditions.' He offered the praise in part because he did not want to be complicit in the marshal's teasing of his senior officers.

'Good. What if the Spanish try to stop us?'

'They should not know of the mines,' the senior engineer said quickly.

'And they may be blind and deaf, but they are probably not.' The marshal made his impatience clear. 'What if the Spanish try to stop us?' he asked again.

'A half-company fully armed is kept behind the mine workings.' The speaker was Chef de Bataillon Pelet, Marshal Masséna's senior ADC. An engineer and surveyor by training, Pelet's manner was formal and more than a little self-satisfied, but Dalmas felt that the man was competent. 'Two more are in the parallel day and night, and three back here ready to go forward if required.'

Marshal Ney merely grunted his approval.

'Well done, Dalmas,' he said, choosing to give the praise to a member of his own staff. 'Three days, gentlemen, and this city is ours.' There was no formal dismissal of the meeting, but now that they were beginning the fourth week of open trenches the officers were all used to the marshal's brusqueness. He simply turned his back, and shaded his eyes to peer at the city.

Dalmas waited.

'Ah, Dalmas. You should go and get some rest.'

'There is the other matter, your grace,' the captain said.

'Hmm, indeed.' Marshal Ney returned to staring at Ciudad Rodrigo and the cuirassier waited.

'Why should I let you waste your time, and give

326

you soldiers to keep you company?' The question was abrupt, but the marshal did not turn and still had his back to his ADC.

'The Emperor wants it,' Dalmas said immediately. The orders had actually come from Marshal Masséna's staff, but ultimately they were from Paris.

'The Emperor, God save his pride, wants a lot of things. And usually he wants them yesterday.'

'Velarde – or Espinosa as he now calls himself – is valuable.'

'If he is alive. What happened to that surrender we were promised? Now I look a fool, summoning the city to surrender so soon. That one-eyed bastard' – Dalmas knew the marshal meant the Prince of Essling – 'wanted me to do it, but you know damned well that we'll hear no more of that. No quick surrender and so we must do it the hard way and I lose men in this mud. What value does Espinosa or whatever he is called have now?'

'Knowledge, sir. The man knows the names of those favourable to our cause here and in many other places in Spain. He even knows people in Portugal.'

'We have the marquis for Portugal,' Ney said without conviction. 'Assuming someone else buttons his breeches for him first and tells him what to say.' The Marquis d'Alorna travelled with the French army. Opinion varied over whether the Portuguese aristocrat was a true supporter of the French or simply an adventurer. No one thought much of his ability or intelligence.

'Espinosa was clever, your grace. More useful for us and more dangerous.'

'Was?'

'It seems reasonable to assume that he is dead, or at the least captured. If he was outside the city then he would have sent word or appeared.'

Ney turned around. 'So he is dead. Forget him.'

'He carried a paper on him, with a list of names and other details.'

'Then he was a bloody fool,' said the marshal, readily convinced that the past tense was appropriate.

'He carried even more knowledge in his head.' Dalmas flicked his gloves to brush some of the dirt from his jacket. 'It would be a shame if the enemy were to obtain the paper or the information.

'I suspect that the English agent from Salamanca is now in Ciudad Rodrigo.'

'The sod you failed to catch,' Ney added sharply.

Dalmas never minded his commander's provocations. 'Espinosa liked being clever. It was not the plan, but I suspect he found this Englishman and convinced him to help him get into Ciudad Rodrigo. He passed several of our patrols with a companion in uniform.'

'So what went wrong for this clever man?'

'The Englishman probably killed him or had him arrested.'

Marshal Ney gave a nod. 'Not that clever, then.'

'If the Englishman has learned what Espinosa knew, or obtained his papers, then he is dangerous and it would be unwise to let him reach Lord Wellington.' Dalmas imagined the Spanish and Portuguese arresting almost all the key French agents, men close to the regency councils in both countries. 'It will make victory slower and more costly, and a true peace harder to achieve.'

'Hmm.' Ney looked his ADC up and down. 'You really do look filthy. Why do I keep you on my staff?'

'Because I know how to win, your grace. Like you.'

Ney snorted with laughter. 'Do I? Well, what I really know is that the way to win is to smash Wellington in battle, and since he has not come to the rescue of this fleapit, we should not be wasting our time, but advancing on him. Let him fight or run, and in six weeks the war would be over. But sadly I am not in charge.' The marshal's tone suggested the obvious imbecility of such a situation. 'So I must take orders and watch as we waste time, effort and men for nothing. I am instructed by the Prince to put my best man in charge of dealing with this problem. My best men are busy, so I will give him you!

'When the city falls you will find this English agent. To assist you, you may take thirty dragoons from the Fifteenth, and Captain Duroc's company from the Légion du Midi. Understood?'

'Your grace.'

'Before that you can do something useful. The Spanish are sending men down in large parties to draw water from the river. That means they must be short of water and so we should stop them from getting it. In three hours I want a plan to set posts to ambush or drive off anyone going near the riverbank.' Marshal Ney smiled. 'Show me how we win this one. Three hours, Dalmas, three hours.'

The plan worked. New pickets and a few small field pieces, placed to cover the Spanish side of the river while remaining safe from the guns on the walls, caused such heavy losses to the water-gathering parties that the garrison stopped sending them. Small groups of women still came to fill kettles and buckets, but when the regimental commander asked what to do, Marshal Ney sent strict orders to leave them alone. They could not carry enough to make a real difference.

At dawn the next day all the batteries opened fire. Dalmas had the thin satisfaction of hearing the report from the artillery commander that the ricochet battery was indeed at a poor angle to do its work. It did not matter. The newly complete batteries in the Second Parallel were so close to the walls that the eight twenty-four pounders heaved up into them were devastating. Dalmas watched from further along the trenches, so that he could better observe their fire.

The gunners had to be careful. When a piece was loaded they hauled it into place. Only then did men tasked with the job pluck aside the gabions closing the mouth of the embrasure. Aim was perfected in a few moments, for the elevation remained the same and they were so close that it did not need to be exact. The crew sprang back, covering their ears with their hands, and then a gunner touched the burning match into the quill of fine powder thrust into the vent. The quill flared instantly, followed a fraction of a second later by the savage explosion of the main charge, which flung the heavy carriage backwards, driving the planks they had set down underneath it further into the soil. Dalmas could see the strike almost instantly, slamming into the wall with terrible violence. Flimsy repairs thrown up in timber and earth overnight were shattered to matchwood in a moment. The breach grew wider, and as the cuirassier captain watched he saw large chunks of stone crumble. Then whole buttresses collapsed and he saw the spoil inside tumbled down.

It was not one sided. The French batteries were close and in spite of the fire of the supporting batteries the Spanish continued to man the guns on the ramparts. Some could do no more than pummel the earthworks of the batteries, gnawing at them piece by tiny piece. Others were able to fire through the embrasures and so they waited, trying to time the shot for those brief few seconds when these were uncovered, and send a ball straight through into the battery. It was difficult work, requiring delicate aim, and meant the crews waited beside their loaded guns. More than once a well-placed howitzer or mortar shell plopped on to the top of the wall and massacred an entire crew. Other

Spanish gunners died in ones and twos. They were replaced, and if the fire from the wall sometimes slackened it never stopped for long.

One ball whirred through an embrasure to shatter the head of the gunner holding the linstock with its burning match. The headless body stood for a moment, blood pumping high, before it seemed to fold down into itself. In a moment the corpse was dragged away, and a lieutenant took up the match and fired the shot. He stayed there for two more shots before passing the smouldering match and the task over to a corporal. Instead he went to help them covering and uncovering the embrasure, and so was there when a twelve-pound shot came from the walls and struck the rampart, flinging earth and a handful of stones that sprang up to drive into the lieutenant's face and eyes. Dalmas watched as they carried the screaming man back on a stretcher. It was a relief when he passed out.

The first French gun fell silent when another ball glanced off the barrel, ripping off one of the great handles used to help lift it from the travelling to the firing position. Dalmas was close enough to hear the Spanish gunners cheering at this strike. A colonel came to look at the scarred bronze and decided that they could not risk putting in a charge until the gun had been tested. A second twenty-four pounder fell silent when the top of its left wheel was smashed by another ball. That was not too serious, but a forward battery was not the place to replace the ruined wheel and so the gun would rest quietly until night fell and the work could be done. The hit to the third cannon was more serious. Time after time two Spanish guns had put shot into the embrasure, battering down the gabions placed in front. It took a good deal of work and savage cursing to repair the damage and so the gun could not fire for several hours. When the task was complete, it managed only two shots before a six-pounder ball clipped the muzzle and ran up along the barrel with a sound weirdly like a bell pealing. Big cracks opened up in the wooden carriage, pulling it apart from the heavy iron reinforcement, and no one wanted to risk charging the gun in case the barrel exploded.

Reduced to five guns, the two main batteries in the Second Parallel fired throughout the day. That night Dalmas heard that the gunners had sent 1,689 balls and 420 shells into the town between dawn and dusk. At the time Dalmas had simply watched the gunners toiling and seen them dousing whole sheepskins in water to throw over the heavy barrels of the guns, throwing up steam but helping to cool the metal. All artillerymen feared an over-heated barrel setting off the charge prematurely and either bursting the gun into pieces or more likely firing out the rammer or sponge to impale the man loading the piece. Sponges soaked in buckets hissed as they were thrust into the hot barrel after each shot, putting out the dangerous embers. The spongemen did the job thoroughly, another crewman equipped with a heavy leather thumbstock pressing down over the vent so there was no flow of oxygen to reignite the remaining gases and cause a new explosion.

At eight and a half feet long, the brass barrels were far taller than a man and several times the thickness and weight of a field gun. The powder bags were big, and even at this range more than one was fed in, before two men staggered to lift the shot up into the barrel. More often than not the rammer also needed two men to force it down tightly, especially as the crews wearied during the long day. Then the ventman pricked the powder bag and stuck the quill into the charge ready for firing. The gun captain checked that the elevation screw had not altered in the recoil from the last shot – usually he had to do nothing – and then gestured to the men to haul on the drag ropes and heave the great cannon forward again. As well as the half-dozen gunners, there were as many more volunteers from the infantry to help them, and even with all these assistants Dalmas could see the veins straining in the men's faces as they pulled. Gunners and infantrymen alike were all long since in shirtsleeves, backs wet with sweat. A row of jackets lay draped on the inside of the rampart. As well as the usual blue of the line infantry, he spotted a couple of the red jackets worn by the Hanoverian Legion, and the brown-faced blue of the Légion du Midi.

That made Dalmas think of his mission. Tomorrow the city should fall. Such things were less certain in Spain, where the normal rules of war did not always apply, but all things being equal it should fall. Then his hunt would begin. He doubted that his man would meekly surrender, but he might slip out among the prisoners and so the infantry company would sweep through the town and ask the obvious questions. Dalmas had a feeling that a British soldier would not be too popular in a city abandoned to its fate by Lord Wellington. More likely the man would try to escape, either immediately or after a lull.

As the cuirassier officer thought about his orders, the sandbags were pulled from the closest embrasure. The Spanish were waiting for the moment and a ball was fired at the gap, but went high. A moment later, the gunner brought down the linstock and the twenty-four pounder leapt back with the force of the discharge.

Part of Dalmas' mind noted the great lump of masonry tumble down into the ditch, but he was far more focused on a sudden inspiration. He had an idea how the Englishman would make his escape and the audacity of the ploy amused him. It was just what he would do in the same situation. Dalmas laughed out loud because he knew exactly how to catch his spy.

The very ground seemed to rock beneath them. Williams had just been reaching down to adjust the uncomfortable top of his right boot, and the jolt pitched him painfully forward on to the cobblestones.

The low, rumbling explosion was unlike anything they had heard before. It was not yet three in the morning and they had just dismissed the company after a long spell of duty carrying ammunition up to the guns on the walls ready for the next day.

Hanley helped his friend up. The rumble had come from the direction of the breach, and before they had gone half the distance the news was spreading.

'Well, that's the end,' Williams said wearily. The French must have dug mines and had now blown in the counter-scarp. It was impossible to see clearly at the moment, but the approaches to the breach were now most likely complete, and the way into the city lay open.

Hanley patted his friend on the shoulder. 'It's time to go, Bills'. He said. 'I know you don't like it, but you would care even less for being a prisoner.'

'Don't like abandoning the lads.'

'I know, but we cannot take them. Rodriguez will do his best for them.' Hanley had already gone through the arguments with his friend several times. 'The governor has given his permission.' Hanley had managed to see the general privately. Herrasti was in a grim mood, knowing that the end was close and bitter that the British had not come. For a moment, Hanley had wondered whether he would order them held so that at least they would share the garrison's fate. It would have

336

been hard to blame him. Instead, the old man had looked him straight in the eyes. 'Tell Lord Wellington that Ciudad Rodrigo fought with all our strength, and that if there is dishonour in these days, then it does not belong to this city. Tell him that! Do you swear it?'

Hanley had given the oath and knew that he would faithfully report the old general's words, assuming he got the chance. Now he reached out and put his hands on Williams' shoulders. 'We have to go now!'

'Doubt there is time,' Williams said, but they hurried off to fetch the others.

'I fear that I shall not care for the answer,' Hanley began as they walked briskly back to their billet, 'but do you still feel obliged to the girl?'

'I promised Pringle,' Williams said. 'She may wish to stay in the end, but I must make the offer of taking her.'

'This is important for the war, Bills,' Hanley said, knowing it would make no difference.

'Then go without us.'

Hanley grinned. 'I'd only get lost again.' A few minutes later he looked at his watch. 'We are not going to make it before dawn, are we?'

'No.'

'Then we had better follow the other course and hope for better luck tomorrow. We are certainly going to need it. When you say your prayers tonight, young Bills, add a few words for the rest of us!'

'I always do,' the Welshman replied in all

seriousness. He thought for a moment. 'Better make sure we have plenty of food and powder as well.' Williams smiled. 'Never does any harm to help a miracle along.'

Hanley was surprised when Sergeant Rodriguez came along with the three British NCOs.

'My war has not finished yet,' he said simply. Hanley was worried for a moment that this might prompt Williams to return to the company, but the Spaniard assured him that the corporal could cope. 'His leg isn't good enough to come with us,' he added. The corporal had been hit by a small fragment of a mortar shell two days ago and now walked with a pronounced limp.

'What do we do now, sir?' Dobson asked. The officers had not shared the details of their plan.

Hanley took a deep breath, and hoped it would sound more feasible than he feared. 'First we hide,' he said. 'And then we wait.'

CHAPTER 24

Pringle could sense the general's impatience, but had to admit that it required no great prescience.

'Damn your eyes, get moving there!' bellowed Black Bob Craufurd at the greenjackets as they doubled through the stream, water splashing around them. 'Go straight through!' he added angrily when he saw a few of the men trying to pick their way carefully from stone to stone.

'The general hates to see men go around a trivial obstacle for the sake of dry feet or an easier passage,' Shaw Kennedy explained quietly. 'He calculates that a few moments' delay for an individual rapidly magnifies into minutes for a company, and half an hour for a brigade as each soldier waits for the man ahead of him. And so it is strictly regulated by standing orders.'

Pringle understood the reasoning, even if he wondered a little about the arithmetic. He knew that many of the officers of the Light Division bitterly resented the general's 'tyrannical' regulations.

'Drop him, sir! Drop him!'

A brown-uniformed Portuguese soldier from the

3rd *Caçadores* was carrying a diminutive British lieutenant on his back. Pringle guessed that the young officer, a round-faced, snub-nosed young fellow, was reluctant to get his boots wet. The man now looked around, curious to see who had provoked the general's rage.

'Drop him, sir!' the general repeated in a voice that shattered the stillness of the pre-dawn light. The Portuguese light infantryman looked baffled, as did the soldiers around him, who paused, looking in confusion at the mounted officers. Lieutenant Colonel Elder, who commanded the battalion, spurred his horse forward and translated the order. For a moment the *caçador* looked surprised, before delight spread across his face and he let go of the officer's legs and jerked backwards. With a great splash the astonished officer dropped down into the cold stream. The *caçadores* doubled on, most of them cackling with laughter.

'You, sir!' shouted the brigadier general to the hapless lieutenant. 'You have two legs, and in future I suggest you use them. You must set an example and show your men that you can march as far and as fast as any of them. I will say no more to you.' The general flicked his whip and set off at a brisk trot, Pringle and the rest of his staff trailing behind. He noticed Elder rounding on the lieutenant, and no doubt reproving him for showing the battalion in a poor light to its new commander.

It was one of the few moments of light relief in an otherwise frustrating night. After weeks of tentative observation and probing between the outpost lines, General Craufurd had decided to pounce on one of the French foraging parties that the enemy were in the habit of sending impertinently close to the British. At eleven o'clock the night before they had moved out, marching through the darkness. Pringle went as an additional ADC and because he knew the ground well, for they were only a couple of miles from Fort La Concepción.

Things went wrong from the start. One of the two six-pounder cannon became stuck fast in the mud and took a good twenty minutes to free. Then the limber of the other gun threw a wheel and it had to be repaired. Guides lost their way in the darkness. Pringle was sent to find two squadrons of the 14th Light Dragoons who had vanished into the night. That took forty minutes, and he was lucky to have guessed that they had taken the wrong fork in a path and so ended up going much further south than intended. Lieutenant Colonel Talbot of the 14th, clad in a gleamingly bright pair of white nankeen trousers that looked most odd against his heavily braded and snug-fitting jacket, was relieved to see Pringle appear and show them the correct route. The regiment had not long arrived from further south and was still learning the lie of the land.

It was not simply the 14th Light Dragoons who got lost. Marching at night always risked confusion, but Pringle had rarely seen so much go wrong in so short a time. Columns broke up and companies found themselves marching and counter-marching to find their way. It was almost as if the general's impatience to be at the enemy overwhelmed everyone's senses, making them so taut that mistakes kept happening. Yet mostly it was bad luck, and Pringle was glad the enemy were not pressing them. After a night of confusion, cursing and shouted orders, before the sun rose they had left the Portuguese in a valley sheltered from gaze where they could act as reserve. The 1/95th, a few companies of light infantry and the detachment of two guns from the Chestnut Troop were concealed in a few buildings and a swathe of scrubby woodland.

The cavalry pressed on, and the general rode with them, looking as fresh and bursting to be at the enemy as if he had had a good night's sleep. Pringle felt stiff, and would dearly have loved the chance to wash his face and shave, but there was an excitement in riding with so many horsemen. Garland waved cheerily as the staff rode past a squadron of the 14th, Brigadier General Craufurd rapidly edging his way to the front of the entire column. Major Tilney gave no more than a curt nod, and Pringle thought that he looked pale. Then he remembered that this was probably the man's first action and no doubt he had much on his mind.

Pringle followed the general and his staff up to one of the many little crests in this gently rolling landscape. Before they reached the top they dismounted and walked up to peer over the low stone wall of a sheep pen. Ahead of them the sun rose.

'Right on time, the saucy fellows,' Shaw Kennedy said, pointing at the little dust cloud moving along the road towards the village just behind them. Whoever was making it lay hidden in another fold in the ground, but as they watched, a group of horsemen walked their horses over the low ridge. They were little more than a dark smear at this distance, their uniforms impossible to make out. 'Twenty or thirty?' In a few minutes the distant Frenchmen vanished into another piece of dead ground.

A great throbbing rumble rolled over the landscape.

'They're on time as well,' Pringle said, and flicked his watch open to see that it was just after four o'clock, and as usual the French gunners had unleashed their first salvo of the day at Ciudad Rodrigo. 'Reliable fellows, the French.'

'Then let us spoil their routine.' The brigadier general had a predatory look in his eye. One squadron of hussars was detached to work around the enemy's flank in a wide loop. Another squadron of Germans and one from the 16th Light Dragoons were to go forward with the general.

'You are the support, Talbot,' the general called as he rode past the men from the 14th. 'Come on at a steady pace and be ready for my orders.'

By this time the two leading squadrons, each of

343

over one hundred men, had formed into lines two deep. The fields of high maize were open, without walls or other boundaries, and the lines encountered little difficulty as they walked forward. A nod from the general and the captains in charge took their men into a trot, and then a canter. The lines became ragged, but the eager horses ate up the ground, running easily over the smooth earth as they emerged from the grain fields into open country.

Pringle felt a thrill from the power of so many horses running together, hoofs drumming on the ground. There was a rattle of bouncing equipment, scabbards tapping against slung carbines and the bag called a sabretache each horseman carried on his belts. The general and his officers were in the middle, on the track that passed for a road. To Pringle's left were the 1st KGL Hussars, all of them moustached veterans with grey overalls, deep blue jackets with rows of gold braid down the front and a second fur-trimmed jacket or pelisse, slung over their left shoulder and billowing in the breeze. They wore tall brown fur caps with short white-over-red plumes. It was an ornate uniform, and yet these men were very obviously practical and capable soldiers. Even after a night march and months of patrols and picket duty, their horses looked sleek and fit.

On his right the 16th Light Dragoons had high-crested black Tarleton helmets, and red collars and cuffs on their dark blue jackets. These were tight-waisted and the rows of white lace on the front widened at the top, giving the impression of broader shoulders. They were an experienced regiment, and yet it was not simply the uniform or the clean-shaven upper lips that made them look different from the hussars. There was still an air of young soldiers about them.

Both squadrons spread out as the horses ran, and the two neat lines were now vaguer. Pringle thought cavalry charges were supposed to accelerate slowly, giving men and horses their head only at the last minute, so that they hurtled towards the enemy like a great wave. It was over a mile to the next rise and the French were still somewhere beyond it. Looking back, he saw great clouds of dust rising behind the two squadrons and thought that the enemy must see this sign betraying their presence. Perhaps that was why the general hurried on. Two hundred horsemen against thirty should not be a contest – with more squadrons to come on if necessary – and so haste was all that mattered, rushing on to fall upon the enemy before they had a chance to retreat.

The horses surged up the little rise and without an order being given they slipped to a halt. A Frenchman shouted in alarm, and Pringle could imagine the shock of looking up and seeing two hundred enemies suddenly crowning the crest. The French were in green jackets with pink fronts, and had baggy brown trousers and helmets covered with brown cloth to hide the reflections. To

Pringle's astonishment they seemed not to have noticed the approaching dust cloud and were no more than three hundred yards away, meandering along the little track without an apparent care in the world. Ugly great sacks of forage were hung from the rear of each saddle.

'Charge them!' General Craufurd snapped immediately.

'*Mein herr!*' the German captain was pointing to the high grain in a field beyond and to the left of the horsemen. 'Infantry!'

Pringle scanned the gently wafting tops of the maize and saw nothing. Then he caught a flash of something metal, and a moment later more gleams betraying the bayonets of infantry.

'No matter,' snapped the brigadier general. 'They cannot be formed. Sweep them aside. Now go!'

'Draw sabres!' The squadron commanders called out in clear – and in one case heavily accented – voices.

Steel hissed and grated on the metal tops of scabbards as the hussars and light dragoons drew their heavy curved sabres. Pringle's own hand went to the hilt of his sword, but then he realised that the general did not intend leading the charge. That was sensible, for it was not his job, but Billy sensed the excitement and part of him wanted to ride with the squadrons. He had never been in a cavalry charge. A different part of him, instinctively sympathetic to the plight of foot soldiers like himself, felt sorry for the French infantrymen in the cornfield.

'Walk march!' The German order sounded slightly different as the two squadrons went forward, lines still loose.

'Trot!' Horsemen accelerated, the men bouncing in the saddles. Sabres still rested comfortably on their shoulders. Pringle coughed as clouds of dust wafted around them, and prompted the general to ride to the side so that he could see better.

The French dragoons shook themselves into a rough line as the blue-coated British and German horsemen went into a canter and almost immediately a gallop. Sabres were now held out and high, points reaching for the enemy. Pringle looked through the thinning dust, but could no longer see the infantrymen in the corn. On the track the dragoons turned their mounts and fled, running back through the field and trampling the high maize.

'Damn me!' Shaw Kennedy gasped in surprise as there was a ripple of movement in the corn and suddenly there was a neatly formed square of French infantry, three ranks deep, with the second and third ranks standing behind the kneeling men in front. Dawn light flickered along the bright points of levelled bayonets.

'Charge on!' the general shouted, although there was little chance that his voice would carry, but the two squadron captains needed no urging. Men drove spurs into the sides of their mounts and the horses seemed to leap towards the square of soldiers wearing the long drab overcoats beloved of the French line infantry. Pringle had stood in a square little bigger than this one and could imagine the earth trembling under the pounding hoofs, and the infantrymen watching nervously as the line of high horsemen rushed up, sabres bright and horses open mouthed and wide eyed.

It looked as if the French commander had left it too late. There were at least as many horsemen as there were infantrymen in the square, but cavalrymen always filled so much space that they looked more numerous. From the hill, it was if a wave was about to wash away a castle in the sand.

The French fired as neat a volley as Pringle had ever seen, and for a moment the square vanished behind a dense cloud of powder smoke. Men and horses fell, some tumbling down only a few feet from the kneeling French front rank, and the squadrons veered, going around the square instead of into it, and so the wave parted and the castle remained.

'Bugger,' Pringle said, with more than a hint of admiration for the coolness of the French.

'Kennedy, go after them and tell them to chase down those dragoons.' The general barked out the order. 'The rest of you with me.' He turned his horse on a sixpence and was off, haring back over the little ridge. As Pringle came over the crest he saw the leading squadron of the 14th Light Dragoons trotting in a column of fours along the track. Another squadron was half a mile in the rear.

'Colonel Talbot,' the general said as he reined in

beside them. 'There are two hundred French infantry in a square a long musket shot beyond that rise. Ride the fellows down for me, if you would be so kind.'

'Sir.' The commander of the 14th had a leopard-skin band around his Tarleton helmet and now he had an eager smile on his face. Like his men he had bright orange facings to his navy-blue jacket.

'Shall I ride to the infantry?' Pringle asked.

For a moment the general's glance was angry, but it quickly softened. 'No need. And no time.' He turned back to the 14th. 'Good hunting, Talbot! Off you go, while they are still shaken.'

Pringle wondered about the urgency and had grave doubts that the French were in any way shaken. Seeing off a cavalry charge usually gave infantrymen a great boost. Garland was in his place behind the second rank as the squadron deployed into line. The young man was flushed, but he flashed a great smile at Pringle.

'A friend?' asked the general, as they rode back up to watch the attack.

'Yes,' Pringle replied, thinking that the truth was far too complicated.

This was how a cavalry charge should be launched. Talbot was in the lead, mounted on a dark bay, and he effortlessly kept his men on as tight a rein as the gelding. The square had vanished again, the men crouching down in the high maize, but the debris of dead and wounded men and horses from the first charge lay around it and marked out the position.

Talbot walked his men over the crest, the two lines of light dragoons neatly spaced, a horse's length between the ranks so that the fall of one in the lead need not bring down the man behind.

'Trot!' The trumpeter on his grey rode beside the colonel and repeated the order.

Pringle heard only the trumpet calls and could not make out the shouted command that sent the squadron into a canter and then a gallop, and finally, no more than fifty yards from the square, into the all-out charge.

The French stood, their fawn coats blending with the standing corn, but their black shakos stark. Billy Pringle was holding his breath and again he felt the French commander was waiting too long, and then he flinched when flames and smoke engulfed the little square. The noise came a moment later, louder this time, and he suspected that the kneeling front rank had added their fire to the volley.

It may have made the difference. Some light dragoons kept going, flowing around the sides of the square, and more muskets fired, emptying even more saddles. Pringle guessed at least a dozen men had dropped to the first volley and as many or more horses were on the ground or collapsed to their knees. The charge was stopped in its tracks. Through the thinning smoke Pringle glimpsed a few light dragoons up against the square itself, chopping down with their heavy sabres, but bayonets had a longer reach, and one of the light dragoons was already wheeling away, his sword-arm by his side and the sabre hanging uselessly by its wrist strap. A single pistol fired, and another of the riders was tumbled from his mount. Colonel Talbot's bay ran back up the slope towards them, blood thick on its empty saddle.

The general rode back to the supporting squadron of the 14th Light Dragoons, who had halted a quarter of a mile behind the low crest. Pringle wondered for a moment whether these men would also be hurled at the little square. It was hard to imagine that they would make any better impression, for the Frenchmen and their commander were admirably cool.

Major Tilney was at the head of this squadron and was peering through his glass off to the right. A cloud of dust was visible just under a mile away, the dark shape of cavalry beneath it.

'French, sir!' the major reported.

'Damn.' The brigadier general used his own glass to study the approaching column. Pringle did the same, but could not make out any detail.

Shaw Kennedy rode up, his horse skidding to a halt.

'The French dragoons are all killed or taken,' he said. 'But the infantry have run.'

'Run?'

'Turned and fled back to the ford beyond the next rise.'

'Is the squadron of hussars there to cut them off?' the general demanded.

Shaw Kennedy shook his head. 'No sign, sir.'

'God damn them all to bloody German hell!' yelled Black Bob. He turned to Pringle. 'Ride to the Ninety-fifth. Tell them French cavalry are advancing around our flank. They are to hold their position and be ready to cover our withdrawal.'

Pringle galloped off. By the time he returned from his round trip all sense of urgency had vanished.

'The "enemy" proved to be our own German hussars,' Shaw Kennedy said ruefully. All in all the Light Division had sent more than two thousand men marching through the night to launch this raid. The result was thirty or so French dragoons taken, and two hundred enemy infantry escaped. British losses matched the French and far more of them were dead or badly wounded.

Billy Pringle rode forward to look at the wreck of battle left around the square. As he arrived, a weeping German hussar killed a wounded horse with his pistol. Colonel Talbot was dead, shot seven or eight times and probably killed instantly. He and several privates had fallen within yards of the French infantrymen.

'They were noble fellows,' Garland declared as Pringle helped his orderly and another dragoon raise him. The lieutenant was shot in the chest. There was not much blood, although some trickled from the corner of his mouth when he spoke. As they sat him up Billy looked in vain for the hole

352

where the ball had come out. It must be still inside and that was never a good sign. 'Noble fellows,' Garland repeated as if speaking of the opposing side in a cricket match. 'I lay there almost at their very feet, and helpless with this leak in me, and yet not one of them made a move to finish me off. Splendid brave fellows.'

Pringle was puzzled by the delight the young officer took in the quality of the men who had shot him. No wonder Garland was always so warm in greeting his former opponent from the duel. 'Noble fellows,' he agreed. The admiration was genuine, for the French had been in a tight corner and yet had fought their way to freedom. Less pleasant was the thought that with so many infantry and the guns near by, it was only British mistakes that had let them escape.

That afternoon a party of light dragoons buried Lieutenant Colonel Talbot on the glacis at Fort La Concepción, firing a volley from their carbines over the grave. Major Tilney read the words of the service flatly, but there were clear signs of emotion from the officers and men who had known the colonel better. Several cheeks were moist by the time the little service was over.

Pringle watched with MacAndrews, and as they walked away the Scotsman surprised him.

'Do you hear that?' he asked.

Pringle listened, wondering whether he meant the cry of a bird perched on the wall of the fort. 'Sounds like a crow to me,' he said, for his interest in such things was even less than his knowledge. 'Otherwise I hear nothing.'

'That is the point.'

Billy Pringle suddenly understood. In all the activity and confusion of the morning's skirmish it had not registered, but the guns had fallen silent at Ciudad Rodrigo.

'Been like that for hours,' MacAndrews said gloomily. 'I do fear that it is all over.'

CHAPTER 25

The night seemed to last for ever. Williams tried to stay awake, concerned that at any moment their hiding place would be discovered and the cellar invaded by French soldiers. He knew it was night, because Hanley's watch told him so, and more than once he lifted the round brass piece and held it to his ear to reassure himself that it was still ticking. During the daylight hours there were tiny cracks of light between the floorboards above their head, but when night fell the darkness in the cellar was almost impenetrable. At need they lit a small candle, but were too cautious to risk a brighter light in case it betrayed them.

It was noon before the French guns ceased to pound the city, and another half-hour before the Spanish guns also fell silent. Then they had waited, not knowing what was going on. Josepha's mother's cousin and her servants stayed in the house, and once or twice she sent one of the men down to tell them what was happening. Ciudad Rodrigo had surrendered, just as the enemy were preparing for their final assault. The governor himself had gone to the top of the breach with a white flag.

At first things were ordered. The garrison laid down its arms and returned to its billets to await captivity. Some companies of French climbed through the breach and marched to secure key points in the town. As night fell the order vanished. More soldiers slipped inside the city, with or without permission. They heard heavy footsteps in the house above them, and shouts demanding wine and food. Before they blew out the candle Williams saw Dobson running a sharpening stone over his bayonet. Josepha was suddenly next to him, clinging tightly, and Williams wished that they had been able to persuade the lady of the house to join them as well. Then he heard her raised voice, calmly telling the Frenchmen to eat their fill from the table already laid out before them. The tone was as commanding as it was welcoming.

More soldiers came during the night, and not all were French as some of the garrison were eager to befriend their captors and show them good places to find food. A few were angry, and he worried that things were getting out of hand. If the men began to search then it would not take them long to shift the empty barrels that lay on top of the trapdoor leading to the cellar. Josepha held him so close that he could feel her heart beating, as well as her wiry hair against his cheek.

The girl had a habit of stroking his thigh that was pleasant, but scarcely calming.

Angry shouts came from above, the lady screaming insults, and Williams prepared to free himself and take his sword up into the house. Josepha pulled him even tighter, the scent of onions on her breath strong.

More shouts, from a new voice now, and Hanley whispered to him that it was a French officer damning the men and telling them to get out and go back to their regiments. A sergeant yelled orders, so the officer was clearly wise enough to confront the looters with disciplined men to back him up. It grew quieter, footsteps and softer conversation lasting for a while before there was silence. An hour later the footman came to explain that a senior French officer had commandeered the house and was now sound asleep, leaving guards on the door. For the moment they were safe, but they were also trapped.

Night passed eventually, and at some point Williams must have dropped off to sleep because he awoke with the girl snoring softly, her head on his chest and his left arm uncomfortably beneath her. There were slivers of daylight from the floor above them, but the house was silent. He could dimly see Murphy sitting awake and on guard, his firelock over his lap. The Irishman winked at him, although whether his amusement came from their predicament or the officer's good luck in waking with such a pretty companion was hard to say.

With a struggle, Williams managed to reach Hanley's watch. It was just a few minutes after five in the morning.

The day crept by even more slowly than the night. The French officer remained in residence, and even when he left to go about his duties his servant and several soldiers stayed in or just outside the house.

'Could we take them?' Hanley whispered to Dobson when the room above seemed to be empty and the cellar was full of dim light. 'Quietly, so that no one would know.'

The veteran thought for a while. 'Aye, probably. What then?'

'Slip away as we planned,' Hanley said quietly. 'Although best to wait for darkness.'

Williams watched as Dobson continued to stare at the officer.

'I do not think Dob is talking about us,' Williams explained. 'How can we leave the ladies with a house full of dead Frenchmen?'

'We could take them somewhere,' Hanley suggested without any conviction.

'Aye, carry bodies or lead prisoners through a captured town.' The veteran's irony was heavy. 'For the moment we're stuck,' he added.

'Wasn't thinking,' Hanley muttered and they fell back into silence.

Another night and day crawled by. Josepha wanted to go out, and said that her appearance could easily be explained. 'We want the Frog to leave, don't we,' Dobson said. 'Can't see the lady's presence helping that.' The girl could not follow the sergeant's heavy accent, but when Hanley translated she was delighted at the compliment and soon persuaded to stay. Williams had to admit he was glad, for she continued to find comfort sleeping with her arms around him.

The lady of the house once came down in person to see Josepha and ask whether they needed anything. A servant came with her to take away their night soil, and in truth the air in the cellar was becoming less and less wholesome by the hour. Fortunately the smell of burned buildings and hastily buried corpses pervaded the streets of the city so strongly that this was unlikely to be noticed outside.

'Colonel Pelet tells me that he must regretfully leave my house tomorrow. Yesterday he was out for three hours with this French prince, touring the ramparts. He tells me that we were very brave, but badly led and betrayed by the English.'

'Did he tell you to expect other officers when he departs?' Hanley asked.

'He has said nothing about that.'

They waited for the rest of the day and through the long, long night. With a good deal of stamping and loud farewells, the French staff officer left early the next morning, and a servant came to say that his soldiers had gone with him. Two hours later an officious NCO arrived, demanding that the widow hand over any surplus loaves of bread she had in her possession.

'Bribe him, bribe him,' Hanley said under his breath as if the idea would somehow reach the lady in the house. Footsteps came alarmingly close to the hidden trapdoor as the man continued to rant about his orders and the needs of the Emperor's brave soldiers. Williams gestured for the girl to go to the corner of the room, but she clung determinedly to his side as the NCOs readied their weapons.

Then the lady's voice came, too faint to catch the words, but it calmed the man. A few minutes later he and his party left, no doubt a little richer even if the brave Emperor's soldiers were poorer by a few loaves. Williams felt himself breathe again.

Minutes dripped slowly into hours and they waited nervously, fearing the appearance of more French soldiers. Darkness fell, and still they waited. Then Hanley showed Williams his watch. It was half past eleven and as good a time as any to take the risk. He led them up the stairs, treading warily although that was absurd, and tapped on the trap-door as they had arranged. They heard the barrels shifting and the alarmingly loud creak of the door. Hanley spoke quietly to the lady.

'All clear,' he said, and climbed up into the house, his long cloak trailing behind him. Dobson followed, then Rodriguez, Rose and Murphy, each of them wearing their long greatcoats and forage caps, their shakos stowed away in their packs.

'Goodbye, Josepha,' Williams said softly to the girl. 'I wish you every happiness.' For a while she had wanted to come with them, and it had taken a long time and the older lady's stern refusal to dissuade the girl.

Josepha wrapped her arms around him. The embrace came naturally, as did the long kiss, and after so many days close together Williams revelled in the sensation of holding her. He understood Pringle's interest, but hoped fate had some more permanent lover in store for the sweet child.

Murphy put his head back down through the trapdoor and gave another theatrical wink.

'Ready, sir?'

Williams left the cellar with more reluctance than he would have expected.

Outside in the street it felt cold and dangerously exposed.

'This way,' Hanley said, and set off with Williams at his side and the men marching two by two. He nodded amicably and acknowledged the salute of a corporal passing with a file of artillerymen in blue coats and trousers and carrying heavy sacks. With their cocked hats and cloaks he and Williams were obviously officers, and there was no particular reason for anyone they passed to assume they belonged to any army other than their own.

'Fine night,' Hanley said to a captain and lieutenant walking arm in arm in that amicable French way. One offered them a puff on his cheroot, and they took it happily, prompting a fit of coughing from Williams.

'Germans, eh?' Hanley had decided to act as if Williams and his men were from the redcoated Hanoverian Legion. It would explain both their uniform and their poor French should the need arise.

The two French officers grinned, and one patted Williams on the back cheerfully.

'More used to powder smoke, I'll be bound,' the man said.

Bidding them good evening, Hanley took his little band on past the castle, returning the sentries' salutes, and went towards the Gate of San Jago. This would be the first serious test. The soldiers forming the guard looked different, and as they came closer Williams noticed that their jackets were a deep brown with blue fronts and cuffs.

'I am Colonel Espinosa of King Joseph's staff,' Hanley said in response to the challenge, 'and my business is urgent. This is Lieutenant Langer of the Hanoverian Legion, who is my escort.'

The sentry called for the sergeant.

'You had better send for an officer, but damned well do it quickly.' Hanley exuded arrogant certainty, and Williams could not help being impressed, but it was hard to stop his hand from reaching for the hilt of his sword.

A sous-lieutenant appeared, his jacket unbuttoned.

'Stand to attention, man, when you talk to me!' Hanley hissed at him.

Williams wondered whether he was overdoing the act, but the officer paled and fumbled with his buttons.

'I am not permitted to let anyone through the gate without checking their papers,' the man said, almost as if expecting reproof.

Instead Hanley smiled. 'Of course, Lieutenant.' He reached inside his jacket and handed over a letter bearing the royal seal and commanding obedience and cooperation with the bearer, Colonel Espinosa. 'And here is a pass from the Prince of Essling,' he added casually, producing a second letter.

'Your men?' the sous-lieutenant asked almost apologetically, handing back the letters.

'I dare say they have a pass from their regiment, if you would care to see it. But they are simply here to escort me and the dispatches I carry.'

Williams felt a pang of fear that this was a mistake, for surely dispatches would be taken on horseback or by coach and they were on foot. The French officer did not seem to notice. Instead he saluted.

'Thank you, Colonel. May I bid you a good evening.'

'You may, Lieutenant, you may indeed.' Hanley nudged his hat with his hand, somewhere between a wave and a salute. Their boots echoed on the cobblestones as they marched out under the arched gate. The sentries outside merely brought their muskets up to the salute as the officers passed. For a while they processed along the road, until Williams paused, ostensibly inspecting his little command as it passed. A glance back towards the city showed that they were out of sight.

'Now,' he said, and they left the road and plunged into the deeper darkness of the fir trees that ran down to the river. It took a few minutes, but then they found a path and followed it to a little stone hut beside the water.

'This is the spot,' Hanley said. So far everything had gone as planned. Weeks ago, before the siege started, there had been talk of sneaking him upriver to meet with a guerrilla band. After the heavy rain, the idea proved impractical and they had failed to make any headway, but the governor had assured him that the little boat was still kept in the same spot.

'I don't see anything.' Williams tried not to sound worried. Rose and Dobson passed him their fire-locks to hold and splashed into the water, reaching down to feel with their hands.

'Here,' said the sergeant after a moment. He began to lift some heavy stones out of the water. 'Give me a hand!' Murphy and Rodriguez rested their own muskets on the ground and waded in to join the other two. More stones came out, and Williams saw something rise to the surface.

'Is it in one piece?' Hanley asked, less cool now than he had been at the gate.

A few more of the weights were tossed to thud dully on the bank. 'Looks fine, sir,' the sergeant replied after a moment. He gestured to the others and with a struggle they lifted the flat punt on its side to tip out the bulk of the remaining water, before righting it again. It would be a squeeze, but the six of them could all sit or squat in the damp-smelling wooden boat.

'Quickly, get the packs and muskets on board,' Hanley hissed. Williams went into the water, handing their firelocks to Dobson and Rose. He went back for the other weapons, but first tossed the packs to each man. Murphy and Rodriguez pushed the flat boat out into the water, wading behind it until they felt that they were near the main channel and then scrambling aboard.

It was a clear night and the moon was already beginning to rise. Ahead of them they could see the long low shape of the Roman bridge. That was the first danger, for there were most likely sentries patrolling its length. The current was sluggish, but it took the laden boat and soon they were running quickly, almost out in the centre of the wide river.

Williams could see the shape of a soldier walking beside the wall of the bridge, his musket on his shoulder. It seemed impossible that the man could not see them, but perhaps he was not looking. Long hours on sentry were rarely conducive to alertness; no doubt the man was happier being somewhere where he did not have to worry too much about a guerrilla knifing him in the dark.

The bridge loomed up surprisingly quickly. Dobson was trying to steer, but he hissed at

Murphy to be ready with his firelock to fend them away from the stone pier. In the end he managed to edge them away, but the flat bottom grated for a moment on some boulder beneath the surface, and they stuck fast. Williams could not believe that the sentries had not noticed them. Dobson was cursing under his breath as Rose and Rodriguez leaned over the side and pushed down at the rock underneath them with the butts of their muskets.

'*Qui vive?*' Came the shouted challenge, but it was not for them. Iron-shod hoofs clattered on the stone of the bridge. Williams heard an impatient answer thrown back at the sentry.

The punt came free, and almost immediately they were under the great arch, ducking because it was lower than they had thought with the water so high after all the months of rain. Murphy poled them away from the wall when they veered into it and then they were out again in the open.

Someone shouted. There were cavalry on the bridge, men in helmets with flowing horsehair crests. At their head was a big man on a horse taller than all the rest. His cloak was bright in the growing light of the rising moon, and something gleamed silver where it parted in front. Men turned, their faces pale as they looked down into the water.

A musket flamed, but the sentry had not troubled to aim and Williams neither saw nor felt the ball come close. Already they were fifty yards from the bridge. Men were clambering down from their horses. Most French cavalry were equipped with

366

carbines, but dragoons had once been trained as mounted infantry and they carried muskets only a little shorter and lighter than those of the infantry. Thankfully they rarely kept them loaded when they were mounted, because the motion of a running horse tended to shake powder from the pan and loosen the charge.

They were a hundred yards away before the next shot came, surprisingly accurate for a musket and flicking up a little fountain of water just beside the punt. Murphy raised his own firelock and fired back, the explosion deafeningly loud and dazzlingly bright just inches from Williams' head.

'May worry 'em,' said the Irishman, as he brought the musket back down, and used the butt as an oar.

'Tells 'em where we are, though,' Dobson hissed in reproof.

More shots came from the darkness which sheltered them, but the punt was running too fast for good aim. One ball snapped through the air over their heads, but no more came close enough to notice.

Williams looked back and there was movement on the bridge. He could not see clearly, but it took no great imagination to guess that the dragoons were mounting again, ready to come after them.

'That was Dalmas,' he said to Hanley.

'Are you sure?'

'Can't be many cuirassiers in these parts. Do you think he was hunting for Espinosa?'

Hanley pressed his teeth against his lower lip as he thought. 'Better not try that trick again, then.' He tapped his jacket where it held the coded page he had taken from Velarde. 'Probably wants this.'

'How far can we go on the river?' At the moment they were running at a faster pace than any horse could maintain for long.

'A good few miles, but not far enough for safety.'

'Thought so.'

The chase had begun.

CHAPTER 26

'Shameful, quite shameful.' Captain Burgoyne of the engineers was truly angry. 'How will the Spanish ever trust us, after breaking such a solemn promise?'

Ciudad Rodrigo was taken, and now the British were withdrawing to Almeida and so the engineer officer had just finished checking the fuses to his mines.

'I recall the Spanish breaking a few promises to us last summer,' Pringle said. Nothing had been heard of his friends in Ciudad Rodrigo and they were most likely captured or even dead.

'There were not the numbers to face the French in the open,' MacAndrews added in support.

'But we could at least have tried.' Burgoyne was truly agitated.

'Aye, laddie, we could.' The Scotsman said. 'Not that it would have done them or us any good at all. Now are you ready?'

The engineer came back to the task in hand. 'Yes. Time to move back while I take my sergeant in and light the fuses. Be worth warning those dragoons that they are too close.'

'Captain Pringle, if you would be so kind.' MacAndrews grinned. 'Might as well enjoy the privilege of temporary rank before it and the fort are blown to ruin.'

'Certainly, Colonel,' Billy replied deliberately. 'Although I have already told them once.'

He trotted over to where some of the 14th Light Dragoons had tethered their horses and lit a cooking fire.

'Morning, Pringle.' Major Tilney raised a chipped mug in greeting. 'Care for a spot of tea?'

Billy Pringle concealed his shudder at the prospect. 'Thank you for the offer, but Captain Burgoyne informs me that he is to set off his mines, and suggests that you and your men move back to a safer distance.'

'Man is starting at shadows,' the major replied dismissively. They were a good one hundred yards away from the low ramparts of the fort. 'There is no danger.'

'He was most positive in his opinion.' Pringle could not understand the major's stubbornness. 'By the way, may I ask about the health of young Garland?'

'Fine, I believe. Are you sure about the tea? My corporal makes an excellent brew.'

'Thank you again, but I must decline, and rejoin Colonel MacAndrews.'

'As you wish.' Pringle thought he detected a faint hint of scorn in the light dragoon officer's face, but decided to ignore it.

'Bloody fools,' MacAndrews said when Pringle repeated the exchange. 'Typical cavalrymen.'

Captain Burgoyne was more polite when he trotted up. 'Most unwise,' he said, 'indeed truly unwise. I would suggest that we retreat a little further. The fuse will burn through in about five minutes.'

Pringle was somewhat uncomfortable with the 'about', for he had watched engineers make enough mistakes on that long road to Corunna. He and his grenadiers had also ended up too close to one explosion and felt something of its power.

The first sound was muffled, quieter than the noise of the cannon from Ciudad Rodrigo during the siege, and then a second later the ground shook and the bastions of Fort La Concepción erupted. Pringle glimpsed tongues of flame shooting up before everything was swamped in fountains of thick black dust and smoke, which rolled out across the plain, engulfing the light dragoons and their horses. Some of the mounts broke free of their tethers, for soon the animals ran out of the cloud, obviously terrified.

It took minutes to clear, and when Pringle and the others rode forward they pressed handkerchiefs to their mouths to breathe more easily. One of the 14th was dead, his head crushed by a chunk of masonry, and two more were badly injured. Major Tilney's right arm was broken and there was another bruise on his face. Pringle suspected the man would soon be on his way home, no doubt considered a hero after his few months on campaign. The injured privates would be less fortunate. A chunk of stone had shattered the ribcage of one man. He sobbed, his lips bubbling as he struggled for breath, and it was doubtful that he would live long.

The remains of another light dragoon lay nearer to the fort, for one of the mines had ripped open part of the glacis and with it the new grave of Colonel Talbot, flinging pieces of his corpse over a wide area. The biting stench of decay floated through the air with the dust and Pringle found himself gagging. An appalled sergeant from the RE vomited loudly.

'Unfortunate,' Captain Burgoyne said, choking on the word, but unable to say more.

His party of engineers helped the light dragoons rebury their colonel and the fresh body of the private.

'Most unfortunate,' Burgoyne repeated as he watched them. 'One of the mines did not ignite.' He pursed his lips. 'Perhaps two.'

Pringle was left unsure whether he was concerned by the dead or the failure of his charge. 'The damage appears extensive.'

'Oh yes, the fort is slighted well enough to make it of little use to the French, but it is frustrating to leave a task incomplete.'

Before they left, MacAndrews stopped to stare back at the smoking remains of the fort. Other than Pringle, his remaining men had gone on ahead, escorting wagons carrying the powder and other provisions left in Fort La Concepción and now going to add to the reserves in Almeida. It was scarcely a task suited for such experienced NCOs, but typical of the mundane fatigues falling to any spare men placed at the disposal of the divisional staff. Most of the men had already applied to return to their own corps, and Reynolds of the 51st had gone off to a staff appointment in Lisbon.

'Ah well, it's back to major for me,' MacAndrews said after a while, and turned his horse away. Pringle followed and kept silent.

Williams saw the plume of smoke rise high into the sky. They had heard the dull crump of the explosion and he had felt it worth investigating.

'A few miles away,' he said when he got back into the shelter of the pine grove. 'The direction and distance are right, so my guess would be that it is Fort Conception.'

'The French?' Hanley asked.

'Probably us. There would be no point leaving the place for the enemy.'

'So we are retreating.'

Williams nodded. 'Not far yet. They'll want to slow the French as they go towards Almeida. There must be the best part of a division camped in the villages to the north.' They had seen the glow of the French campfires last night, and almost walked into their picket line. Williams saw his friend look doubtful. 'This is still the best way. The valley to the north is no more than a ravine, and I doubt we could have made it through.'

They had floated along the river at a good pace for three and a half hours, before pushing on to a stony beach where a tributary joined the Agueda. It was the last spot before the banks turned into cliffs. They used some stones to weigh the punt down, and then Williams, Dobson and Murphy had stripped and waded out, pushing the boat into the flow in the hope that it would keep going and confuse any pursuit. The officer had lost his footing in some soft sand and almost been swept away himself, but Murphy grabbed him, and then Dobson took hold and hauled the spluttering Williams from the current.

The six men headed inland, staying off the main paths. The ground was rocky, with low hills and little valleys that made it hard to keep in a straight line heading westwards. Within twenty minutes they saw the first French sentries, helped because the bored soldiers were chatting in low voices that carried a long way in the night air. They doubled back and went on a wide loop around, but soon came up against another outpost. Dawn was less than an hour away, and then Williams recognised a distinctive silhouette against the lightening sky.

'Signal Mount,' he said, and after a whispered conference it seemed wisest to head south and try to hide up somewhere there during the hours of daylight. It was hard walking, with another pause of ten minutes to let a patrol of a dozen French infantry pass by before they could cross a track. They stumbled on the loose stony slopes, but slowly began to climb. There was a good chance that the French would have an outpost on top of the hill, but Williams doubted that there would be more men away from the main villages and tracks. Even so there was a nervous half-hour of dawn light before they found the grove a good three-quarters of the way up the side of the big hill. Exhausted, they posted a sentry and soon fell asleep.

'It will be hard to slip past them, even at night,' Williams said after he had explained the French disposition to Hanley in more detail.

'We must try.'

'Yes.' The Welshman lay back on the grass with a sigh. 'Do you think Dalmas is after us?' he asked.

'After me,' Hanley said. 'And after this,' he added, touching the papers in his pocket. 'Perhaps we should split up?'

'Would not do any good. If he is looking for a British officer he will be after any redcoats trying to slip through the lines. Like it or not, we are all at equal risk whatever we do.'

Hanley put his palm to his chest and gave a little bow. 'Thank you anyway.'

'Delighted, of course!' Williams pondered the problem. 'I do not believe he will find it easy to track us.'

Corporal Rose came through the trees and slid to a crouch beside the officers.

'French cavalry, sir!' he reported.

Williams shrugged. 'I suspect my belief is about to be tested.' He followed Rose back out of the trees to a little knoll where Rodriguez lay, searching ahead of him with Hanley's glass. Williams got down beside him.

There were French dragoons down on the track where they had seen the French patrol the night before. It was more than a mile away, and even with the magnification of his own glass Williams could barely make out the individual men and horses, but the gleam of brass helmets was clear.

After a few minutes he half jogged, half slid back down the little slope into the trees.

'Dragoons. A dozen at least, and probably more.'

'Dalmas?'

'Didn't see him, but it's too far to see anything with certainty. It may just be a patrol or foraging party.' Williams did not sound convinced. 'I doubt it, though. Don't think we can afford to assume that they are not searching for us. We may have left more of a trail than I hoped. Perhaps they have even followed us from the river. He knew we left that way, after all, and there are not too many places where you can land safely.'

'Should we move?'

Williams rubbed his chin. 'They are still a long way away, and it will be hard for dragoons to follow us quickly up these slopes.'

'There may be infantry as well.'

'Yes. And this may be one patrol of many. If we move now then they have more chance of spotting us. Hard to walk up here without kicking stones and throwing up dust. Best to keep a close watch, of course, but we will be better off moving at night.'

They waited. Three weeks into July the days were just a little shorter, but it was still a long wait until the sun began to sink beneath the horizon and the six men set out. For a while they made as good progress as the rocky slopes of the hills allowed. Below them they could see lights from the village of Gallegos, and the twinkling cooking fires of the French infantry camping around the straggle of low stone houses. Soon they found their path blocked by a line of pickets at half-company strength.

Williams took them south, helped by the NCOs, who had all led training marches through the area. The French outposts all had fires. Rodriguez said that the enemy liked light as they felt it made it harder for the guerrillas to creep up on them.

It was certainly useful, and made it easier to avoid their pickets, but all the time they were forced to loop back on themselves and go round. After three hours they came to the well-churned mud road leading to Fuentes de Oñoro and wondered about heading in that direction in the hope of finding the British lines. Williams was dubious.

'If they've blown up Conception then I cannot see them staying this far forward.'

They crossed the road and kept going across country, heading into the maze of little hills and valleys near the source of another of the Agueda's tributaries. Williams took them deliberately further south, as he doubted that it would be safe to use any of the bridges lower down. Even so they lost their way, and found themselves faced with the little stream tumbling down a steep valley. The water was fairly shallow, but when they found a spot where the banks dipped down, they still took great care as they crossed. Williams felt the water pushing hard at his boots, and once again was amazed at the force in even so small a stream.

The River de Dos Casas and then the River Turones still lay ahead of them, and both were much bigger affairs than this. There was a bridge on the road to Fort La Concepción, several miles to the north, and another somewhat closer, and they began to march towards them.

It was no good. Fires betrayed the presence of French outposts in their path, and Williams knew from experience that the ravine made the first river impossible to ford above Fuentes de Oñoro. Light was beginning to grow at the edges of the sky and dawn was less than an hour away. There was no way round, and instead they looked for a hiding place. Dobson and Rodriguez went ahead and found a little gully not far from the low cliffs above the river. It was open to the air, but bushes along the edges offered cover for a sentry and there was no good reason why anyone should go there.

Williams reckoned they had covered less than four miles as the crow flies, although they had tramped for three or four times that distance to do it. All were weary. They had a couple of hardening loaves and some thin ham to eat, as well as a few doughboys. Water was less of a problem, for they had filled their canteens when they crossed the stream.

The officers took their turns lying against the side of the slope and acting as sentries. Williams found it difficult to stay awake, for within a few hundred yards the view was blocked by slopes in all directions. If the French did find them, then there would be little time to do anything about it.

As the day went on, cloud built up until the sun was blotted from sight. It grew dull and surprisingly cold. The gully was not big enough for them to remain hidden and move around much and so the chill gradually seeped into them.

The first spots of rain fell late in the afternoon. The sky was dark and brooding, and the promise of more was soon fulfilled. Lightning flashed in the sky, and the great peal of thunder followed only a few seconds later. Big drops of rain slammed down in a torrent.

'Might be our best chance,' Williams shouted to Hanley over the drumming noise. Another great flash, and this time the crack and boom of thunder was almost instant.

Hanley pulled his cloak around him. 'What?'

'The storm. Only a fool would go out on a night like this!'

'How encouraging!' Hanley did his best to smile as the water poured down his face. 'But you are Welsh,' he said. 'This is your natural element.'

'I'm half Scots.'

'A distinction without a difference where rain is concerned, I should have thought.'

'Very poetic,' Williams said. They waited an hour, hunched like animals in their coats or cloaks, the locks of their muskets wrapped in cloth in the hope of keeping the powder dry. The slamming rain drenched them, soaking through their clothes.

'Time to go,' Williams said, before it was fully dark. The storm raged and surely no sentry would be vigilant at so miserable a time. The six men forced the pace, glad to get their limbs moving. None of them felt warm for half an hour, and then the sweat added to the dampness wrapping their bodies. Williams' face was sore from the stinging strikes of the rain.

Finding their way was difficult, the rain so heavy that it was hard to see very far at all. Darkness made it even harder, and the slopes were treacherously slippery. All of them fell, and there were plenty of bruises, but luckily no broken bones.

Williams insisted on leading, with Dobson off to the left, and they groped through the hills until they reached a track leading down towards a village not far from the bridge. They moved cautiously, but saw no sign of the French, and it seemed that their pickets had been pulled back, probably because of the weather.

'They could not see much at the moment out here,' Williams suggested when they stopped for a conference.

There seemed no end to the rain. The thunder and lightning slackened for a while, before returning with even greater fury. It was in a flash of forked lightning that Dobson glimpsed the bridge and the shape of two sentries.

'Poor sods,' he whispered to Williams after they stopped.

'Yes, who'd be out in this weather.'

Then the veteran had an idea, and the sheer brazenness of it rapidly convinced Hanley. Williams was more sceptical, but his senses were dulled after so many long hours of fumbling in this storm.

Hanley marched them all down in a little column towards the bridge, the NCOs in twos and Williams at the rear with his own musket over his shoulder.

'*Qui vive!*' The challenge came very late and was barely audible through the pounding of the rain on the water and against the stone of the bridge.

Hanley called out that they were relieved.

Williams barely heard a muttered 'Thank God' as they marched across the bridge. Hanley saluted, and then Dobson leapt forward, slamming into one sentry at waist height, knocking the man down. Murphy's knee jerked up into the other Frenchman's groin, and as the man crumpled, the Irishman hit him hard on the head with the butt of his musket. Dobson was struggling with his man, but Rodriguez rushed to his side and with a neat jab knocked the man out.

'Shall I kill them?' he asked Hanley.

'No need. Tip the muskets in the river and drag this pair away to the far side. Tie their hands, gag them and leave them.'

The Spanish sergeant looked as if he felt this was a lot of work, but helped the others drag the unconscious Frenchmen away. There was no sign of the stronger picket that must surely be near by.

'No sense in looking for trouble,' Williams said, and then pressed on, keeping parallel with the road so that they would not get lost.

Again it was Dobson who spotted the horsemen coming from the west along the road. He stopped dead, raising his hand, and they threw themselves down into the mud. Williams watched as the dozen or so horsemen splashed through the deep puddles on a road now little better than a quagmire. There was a flash of lightning, but so distant that it gave barely any light and he could not see the men in more detail. He could rarely remember being so cold and miserable and it took real effort to push himself up again when the horsemen had gone.

They kept going, forcing themselves on although their limbs were numbed and heavy. Williams had lost all track of time and the night remained so solidly dark that it gave no real clue. On they trudged, clothes heavy with water.

The rain stopped suddenly, and for a while it was strange not to hear it constantly or to feel the sharp jabs of windblown drops hitting skin. Soon afterwards the sky began to grow lighter and Williams guessed that it was nearly three. There was no sign of a French picket when they came to the little bridge over the second river. They were back on the road now, for that was the only way across.

'Dob?' Williams asked softly. Any talk sounded appallingly loud now that the storm was over.

'Looks quiet,' the veteran hissed, down on one knee.

'I'll take a look. Wait here.' Williams pushed himself up and walked forward. He sensed that the fatigue was making him careless, but it was better for just one of them to take the risk.

The officer strolled on to the bridge, looking warily around him. He had unslung his musket and held it down low. Williams doubted any cartridge could have survived the deluge of the night, but it gave him comfort to feel the firelock's weight.

No one shouted a challenge or fired. There was silence apart from the eager bubbling of a river swollen by the storm.

Williams turned and beckoned to the others. There was no one there, and so they marched along the road, daring to hope that they had got through the French lines. The sun rose, a fiery red that shaded the cloudy sky in lavish pinks and golds.

'Red sky in the morning . . .' Hanley did not finish the quote, but Williams wished he had not spoken.

There were houses up ahead, the familiar dull stone and faded tiles of the region.

'San Pedro,' Williams said.

'São, I believe,' Hanley said automatically.

Then the horsemen burst from the shelter of the little streets. Six went to the right and the same number to the left. They were in dark blue jackets and had round fur caps.

'Muskets!' Williams shouted. The four NCOs already had their weapons ready before he gave the order, for what good it would do them.

Three more horsemen came from the village, and one had the high-crested helmet of the British light dragoons. Williams dared to hope.

'My God, Hanley!' said the man in the helmet.

Williams watched his friend blink a few times, still slow with fatigue and surprise.

'Cocks,' he said after a moment. 'Well, you're a sight for sore eyes.'

'Where the hell have you sprung from?' The light dragoon officer needed a shave, but that only seemed to add to his striking good looks. 'It's only the French that way, or should be at least!'

'Thank God we are through them,' Hanley said. 'We have come from Ciudad Rodrigo.'

'Have ye indeed. Well, I'm damned.' He spoke in rapid and fluent German to the KGL Hussars.

'Best cavalry we have in the army,' he said to Hanley and Williams after quick explanations had been made. 'And I say that as a proud member of the Sixteenth!

'Well, I dare say the generals will want to hear your story. The French are up to something. I need to take some of these fellows over the river and see what we can see, but I'll get half a dozen to take you to Almeida.'

With little fuss the German hussars unstrapped their saddle blankets from the rear and put them in front of them. That allowed the six men to ride behind the cavalrymen. It was a kind gesture, but the position was uncomfortable and after a few minutes Williams wished that they had walked, for without stirrups he felt as if he was always about to fall.

They rode north along the road, and in time passed by the west bank of the river close to Fort La Concepción on the far side, although it was too far for Williams to see the place clearly. He could see a chain of French cavalry videttes already on this eastern bank.

Jean-Baptiste Dalmas did not like failing, but was beginning to wonder whether he had lost until suddenly his luck changed in this bright dawn.

Things had begun to go wrong when that fool of a sous-lieutenant at Ciudad Rodrigo had been slow to obey orders and report the appearance of 'Espinosa'. The man was not from the company assigned to Dalmas, but even so his orders had been clear to all the guard commanders and the idiot had waited for a good twenty minutes before doing what he was told.

The boat had been a surprise, and Dalmas was annoyed that he had not thought of it, but if warned that someone was claiming to be Espinosa his men would have been ready to move and at the very least the sentries on the bridge made vigilant. Dalmas had followed, found the place where the enemy landed and a few miles on spotted the wreckage of their little boat smashed on the rocks.

It was hard to track men in this country, especially since the French were advancing and there were outposts and parties of soldiers everywhere. That must have made it difficult for the enemy to move. Again he had orders sent round to look for some redcoats or for a Spanish officer claiming to be on the King's staff, but the Englishman was not so foolish as to try that ploy a second time. Once or twice his men thought that they had picked up the trail. Nothing came of it, and instead he broke them up into patrols and tried to look at all the places they might cross if trying to get to their own army. That was why he had taken ten dragoons and gone over the bridge past the ruined Spanish fort and so had chanced to be in the right place at the right moment.

Dalmas watched the half-dozen hussars and their passengers. It was a guess, but he was sure these were his men and they did not know that he was there. Dalmas was further forward than any French patrol, and during the night his men had led their horses slowly, sneaking past the thin line of British outposts. That led him to this valley parallel to the road, and as he lay on the grass he could watch the enemy. Before they came forward, the cuirassier officer had seen the preparations for the big attack and guessed that the British would soon be going back a lot faster.

He ordered his men to remove their helmets and don their cloaks. From a distance it should not be obvious that they were French. He hoped to avoid being seen at all, until he was ready to strike, but he did not know this country and could not be sure that they would be able to remain hidden. Then they mounted and rode along behind the hills, trying to match the course of the road.

Dalmas followed his prey, looking for the right moment when his ten men could swoop, take or kill the enemy, and escape. He needed to be careful and so he waited, always calculating his chances.

Then, as they drew near Almeida, Captain Dalmas saw an opportunity so beautiful that it warmed his soldier's heart. For the moment the spy was forgotten, for the cuirassier could see how to hand a victory to Marshal Ney.

'Perfect,' he said.

'Sir?' his corporal asked.

'Nothing.' Dalmas scribbled a note. The corporal seemed to be the ablest man with him at that moment. 'Take this to corps headquarters!' he said and gave a wolfish smile. Jean-Baptiste Dalmas was going to win after all.

CHAPTER 27

The greenjackets of the 95th proved to be generous hosts. Steaming mugs of tea appeared immediately, and were soon followed by bowls of hot stew. Williams wondered whether he had ever tasted anything so delicious. He had taken off his greatcoat and was hoping that the sun would at least begin to dry his sodden woollen jacket.

Captain O'Hare's company – the same men who had held the bridge at Barba del Puerco – were doing their best to dry themselves out and clean their rifles. Some tried putting a fresh pinch of powder in the pan and then squibbing off into the air, but the previous night's deluge had usually turned the barrel's contents into a useless sludge. That took more care to clean. Rodriguez and the redcoated NCOs were soon performing the same laborious task with their muskets. Williams had propped his own piece against a rock, and planned to follow their example once he had eaten, but then an eager young private offered to do it for him. He thought for a moment, and then remembered him as the lad who had shot his ramrod into a Frenchman during that bitter fight back in March. It seemed an age ago to Williams, and the memories were hazy and confused. Somehow that always seemed to be the way with battles.

'Green, isn't it?'

'Yes, sir.'

'It is very kind of you.'

The boy looked delighted to help; it seemed that news of their escape from Ciudad Rodrigo had lent the new arrivals a measure of glamour. Second Lieutenant Simmons was evidently eager to press him for details, since O'Hare had taken Hanley away and kept him to himself.

Williams spooned down the last of the stew, wondered for a moment where the chicken had come from and thought it probably better not to ask. He did have one burning question, though.

'Why are you all here, Mr Simmons?' The rolling ground made it hard to see more than a section of the line, but they had learned that all five battalions of the Light Division, as well as the Chesnut Troop and several squadrons of cavalry, were spread in a long line over these hills. Behind him, some of the redcoats of the 43rd Light Infantry held a ruined stone tower that had once been a windmill. It stood almost on the glacis of Almeida itself.

Simmons was not sure. 'The captain says that the general wants to encourage the garrison of the city by showing a bold face to the French.' The young officer was clearly doubtful of this logic, but unaccustomed to criticising his superiors.

Williams knew this patch of country well from the months spent at the fort. Behind them was the deep ravine of the River Côa, crossed by a single bridge, itself reached by a narrow road that wound and twisted sharply as it came down the side of the valley.

The sound of firing drifted towards them on the breeze. These were not sporadic shots of men trying to clear barrels. They had a purpose and intent, even if the sound was not of concentrated volleys. A cannon boomed dully, and that left no doubt that the outposts were facing a real enemy. Bugles sounded all along the line.

'Stand to!' Captain O'Hare shouted, chivvying his men to get moving. 'Stand to!' Men stamped out campfires, pouring unfinished tea on the ground as they stowed cups and camp kettles in their packs. The men moved with practised speed, and Williams could not help being impressed. He thanked Private Green as the boy passed him his musket.

'Loaded and ready, sir,' he said with a smile.

In just a couple of minutes the company was formed up in two ranks and prepared to move. A staff officer with the buff facings of the 52nd rode up.

'Captain Stewart's picket is under attack. Go forward with your company and support him, Captain O'Hare. Cover his withdrawal if necessary.'

Williams looked at Hanley. The four NCOs were less formal, Murphy with his musket held in the crook of his arm like a gentleman ready for a day's game shooting, but they had also formed up expectantly.

Hanley sighed. 'If we must.'

'Probably more dangerous to go wandering without purpose.'

The greenjackets were doubling forward over the brow of the low ridge. Behind them Williams noticed redcoats from the 43rd forming fifty yards back behind a drystone wall. The two officers, three sergeants and a corporal followed the riflemen.

'Damn the rain,' Brigadier General Craufurd said bitterly. This morning there was no dust to betray the movement of troops, or give an indication of their numbers.

Major MacAndrews waited while the general scanned the horizon with his glass, but doubted that he could see much in the rolling land ahead of them. The French were coming on, but in what strength and with what purpose was unclear.

'I'll do nothing precipitate, MacAndrews.' The Scotsman had come to ask permission to move the column of supply wagons and artillery vehicles waiting on the road. He wanted plenty of time to get them across the river and out of the way in case the Light Division had to retreat. 'This is probably another feint.' In the last days the French had made demonstrations in some strength, but had always stopped short of launching an attack. They nibbled at the outpost line with enough force to edge the British back a little, but they did not press the issue.

'It would do no harm to start taking the baggage back across the river, sir,' MacAndrews' tone was respectful. 'Just in case this is not a feint.'

'No,' the general said firmly. 'There is plenty of time should the need arise and I do not want it to look to the Portuguese as if we are running.' Rumours abounded that, after seeing Ciudad Rodrigo abandoned, the defenders of Almeida would open their gates to the enemy. 'You stay here, and if the matter becomes pressing I shall give you the order directly.

'Come, gentlemen, we had better see what is happening.' The general sped away, followed by his staff. MacAndrews fell in alongside Pringle, who was again serving as an additional ADC. He remembered the captain's account of the mishandled raid on the French foragers. Black Bob was most certainly a skilful commander of outposts. The sheer fact that he had held the frontier with a small force for so many months was proof of that. Yet it was less clear how sure a hand he was as a commander in battle. The surrender of his brigade in South America surely nagged at the man, and his obvious impatience of character was not reassuring. In truth MacAndrews wondered why the Light Division was still on this side of the Côa at all. All his instincts told him that the French were likely to attack in force, and the battalions were spread over far too wide a front to resist any serious assault. Alastair MacAndrews was worried, and tried to tell himself that he was simply getting old and nervous.

They met an ADC as they neared the top of the hill.

'Stewart is driven in, sir,' he reported. 'The French have cavalry in the lead. Several regiments at least, with infantry and guns behind.'

They could see little more from the brow, for another ridge hid the advance post, but further in the distance were the dark masses of French columns.

MacAndrews looked at the general expectantly.

'Bring them in,' the general said. 'But the rest of the division is to maintain its position. Their main body is not yet close and this is scarcely good cavalry country.'

'The French have paraded brigades in front of us more than once in the last week,' Pringle whispered to MacAndrews, prompting a grunt of acknowledgement.

The Scotsman waited in vain for the order to set his convoy moving.

Skidding in the mud and sending up fountains of dirty water, the heavy limber and gun turned the tight corner and sped up the hill, the drivers flogging the team of six chestnut horses. Gunners wearing Tarleton helmets like the light dragoons clung desperately to the seats on the limber, while others followed riding horses of their own. Then the second team came past with as much noise and spray as the first.

Williams, Hanley and their small band knelt on the slope beside the track, watching O'Hare and half his company jog back past them. Another group of greenjackets was retreating beyond the Royal Horse Artillery, presumably men of the picket. They went quickly, and soon a line of French voltigeurs appeared behind them.

O'Hare waved as he passed them, taking his twenty or so men further back to the false crest above them where they stopped and waited. Simmons and the rest of the company appeared, working in pairs as they withdrew.

'We go with them,' Williams said. Hanley had told him to give the orders for the moment and he did so without embarrassment. He glanced back over his left shoulder and thought how odd it was to see the ramparts of a fortress rising up beyond the old mill.

Some of the greenjackets stopped to fire their rifles at a target Williams and the others could not see. A roundshot skipped through the grass and somehow missed all of the riflemen, but the presence of light guns suggested a serious attack.

'Cavalry, sir!' Dobson called.

A squadron was approaching on their left. It had appeared suddenly, its approach masked by a fold in the ground. There were about a hundred of them in two ranks, coming on in silence at a steady pace.

'Ware cavalry!' Williams shouted, although one of Simmons' sergeants had already spotted them and called a warning to his officer.

The young second lieutenant looked at the horsemen and then turned to call up to the little knot of redcoats. 'They're ours! The Germans!' His men continued to skirmish with the enemy in front of him, and only slowly withdrew.

The cavalry trotted up the gentle slope. Williams saw their round fur hats, slung pelisses and braided jackets. The uniforms looked drab, more grey than dark blue, but then cloth faded, and the men in the rear were liberally spattered with mud from the hoofs of the front rank's horses. Behind the first squadron another appeared over the fold in the ground, their jackets so dark they were almost black with bright pink fronts. These men wore helmets covered with drab cloth, but their leader boldly wore a steel-coloured high helmet with a black horsehair crest.

'Damn,' Williams said as it sank in. 'They're French,' he yelled.

Simmons looked back, confused. The hussars wheeled a little and with a fluid motion drew their curved sabres. Then they surged forward in a canter. They were already behind the riflemen.

'Back!' Simmons shouted, making a snap decision.

'Back, lads! Back!' His sergeant took up the call and the half-company dashed up the slope. There was a smattering of shots and one man dropped, his leg bleeding, and Williams could now see the first of the voltigeurs coming over the brow.

'Back, but keep together,' Williams said.

Captain O'Hare had formed his men with the front rank kneeling, but the unevenness of the ground meant that he could not yet see the French cavalry so he held his fire. Simmons and his men pelted back up the slope, Williams and the redcoats jogging ahead of them. Then the first of the grey-uniformed hussars appeared, the tall red plumes nodding in their fur caps as the horses rushed forward.

'Present!' shouted O'Hare, and the first rifle banged a moment later, flinging an hussar from his saddle.

There was a much deeper boom, followed by another and another, so much louder than the French guns that they drowned the lighter cracks of the rifles altogether. Williams instinctively looked up and saw clouds of smoke drifting from the rampart of Almeida. A shot bounced just behind O'Hare's line, skidding along and ripping the lower leg off the man at the end of the rear rank. He fell, screaming in agony and clutching at his shattered knee. The line broke up, the men startled and confused by this sudden onslaught, and the greenjackets fired wildly or did not fire at all. No more hussars fell, but a second shot threw up enough mud to panic a few of the horses before it decapitated a running private of the 95th. The man's body stood for a long moment, blood gushing up from his neck like a fountain, before it slumped down.

Williams wondered why the guns were firing. Were they aiming at the French and simply firing wildly or had they mistaken the dark green uniforms of the 95th for French blue?

The leading hussars were among Simmons' men, sabres glinting as they hissed down to hack at heads and shoulders. One greenjacket stopped and, firing from the hip, put a ball under the chin of one of the hussars, punching through the brass chinstrap of his fur hat and driving up into his brain. The man rolled out of the saddle, but his foot did not come free of the stirrup and he was dragged along by his frightened horse. Two more hussars converged on the rifleman. He parried a slash from the first, a big splinter of wood flying from the stock of his rifle when the sabre cut into it, but the other man cut down across his body and neatly severed the infantryman's right arm just below the shoulder. The other hussar pulled at his reins, making his horse rear, and hacked down on the man's head, cutting through the felt shako and into the bone. The greenjacket was reeling, mouth open, but no cry coming, until two more slices pitched him down into the mud.

Rodriguez and Rose fired almost at the same moment, and the horse of one of the leading hussars sank down, its front legs giving way and flinging the surprised rider over its head. Not bothering to reload, the two NCOs turned and started running again, reaching for their bayonets as they went. Another heavy shot came from the fortress, tearing a ghastly lump from the neck of a horse.

'Bugger!' Murphy spat out the word, and was clutching at his leg, blood spreading over his thigh. Dobson ran to help him and Hanley grabbed his other side. Williams tried to cover them, musket ready, and that meant he saw the hussars as they chopped down again and again at the fleeing riflemen. The French troopers gasped with the effort of cutting through bone and flesh, and most of the wounds were to the head and shoulders because it was hard for a horseman to reach lower than that. One hussar with a drooping moustache that flapped as he rode through the mass headed for young Simmons, beating the officer's light sabre aside. The Frenchman sliced down twice, and the boy was knocked to his knees. Then Williams saw the rolled greatcoat, which he wore wrapped around his body and over his shoulder, part and fall away. A cannonball drove into the ground at the horse's feet, making the animal shy, and that gave the young officer the chance to spring up and flee.

Williams was walking backwards, but knew that he must soon run because the French were mingling now with O'Hare's men. He saw the rough-faced officer pistol one hussar from his saddle. The French dragoons were nearly upon them as well, Dalmas at their head, and he saw the big cuirassier give a cry and start to force his way through the press of horses, chopping down to kill a rifleman as he passed. Some men were surrendering, many of them horribly cut about the face, but most still tried to escape and a few had the energy and presence of mind to dodge.

A quick glance behind and Williams could see that Hanley and Dobson had got Murphy a long way back. The officer turned and ran after them. Rose was a little ahead of him and then a shot from Almeida hit the corporal at the waist, slicing him in two and spraying blood and entrails over the Spanish sergeant and a French hussar who was catching him up. The stunned cavalryman reined in, aghast at the sight, and Rodriguez spun around and in the same motion drove his long bayonet into the hussar's stomach. The Frenchman gave a high-pitched scream, his sabre hanging loose on its wrist strap, and the scream turned into a gasp as the Spaniard wrenched the blade free and ran on.

Ahead of them was the low wall lined by redcoats of the 43rd. Williams could see the men levelling their muskets and sped on towards them. Several hussars were ahead of him, slicing down at will at the running men. The pounding of hoofs mingled with grunts of effort and pain, and the sound of steel striking flesh and bone. Some of the riflemen still tried to fight and a few were loaded and fired at the pursuers, but scattered men on foot had little chance against cavalrymen and only one or two of the French fell. The greenjackets died or fell from wounds and were captured.

Williams saw Rodriguez reach his other men, and turn protectively. The Spaniard shouted something, and he tried to glance over his shoulder, but then his boot slipped on the wet ground and Williams fell hard, the wind knocked out of him. Hoofs drummed just behind him, and then he cringed as an immense horse's foot landed inches from his face. He felt rather than saw the heavy animal above him, the smell of horse sweat, mud and wet leather all around him, and then the first rider was past him, but more followed and Williams flinched as he lay there, seized by terror of being crushed.

There was the familiar sound of an ordered volley, like the heaviest-weight cloth being ripped savagely apart, and he heard balls whizzing over him. A rifleman tumbled down just a few yards away, blood oozing from the hole in his forehead. Horses were screaming in pain as they fell, and beyond the dead rifleman a dragoon in a dark green coat cried out as his dying horse rolled over him.

Williams scrambled up, grabbing his fallen musket. Dalmas and a dragoon were closing on the little group of redcoats. The cuirassier barged Rodriguez aside with his big horse, and as he passed sliced down. The Spaniard dodged, so that the tip of the blade merely sliced a line across the skin just above his eyebrows. Ahead of them,

Dobson let go of Murphy, leaving Hanley to take him on. The veteran brought his musket up to his shoulder. Williams knelt, steadying his aim. A second platoon volley came from the 43rd, but Dalmas and his dragoon rode through it untouched. Williams guessed that the redcoats were aiming high to hit the main body of hussars.

He pulled the trigger, felt the butt of his musket slam reassuringly against his shoulder, and then pushed himself up to run through the smoke. Dalmas' big horse was reeling away, head twisted at an unnatural angle, and then the animal folded down, and the cuirassier jumped free to roll on the grass. Dobson fired a moment later, putting a ball through the body of the French dragoon and the man wheeled away, the pink front of his jacket dark with blood.

Shots came from behind them, flicking through the rough grass. Rodriguez was on his knees, hands clutched to a face that was a sheet of blood, and Williams ran for him, grabbing the man by the arm to lift him. The 43rd fired another well-controlled platoon volley, a drill that was intended to provide a constant succession of fire rippling up and down the line. Dalmas was on his knees, struggling to get up, and Williams felt a great temptation to finish the man off, but knew that there was not time unless he abandoned Rodriguez.

'Come on, old fellow,' he said, and lurched into a run, the Spaniard easily keeping pace. Rodriguez managed to clear the muck from one eye and whooped with sheer joy because he could see again.

The volleys had driven back the cavalry, and some of the light infantrymen jeered as they watched the cuirassier officer limp away, but most were busy reloading or helping the survivors clamber over the wall. Simmons and O'Hare were there, along with a dozen of their men, but more than thirty lay stretched out in the muddy field or were bleeding and being led away as prisoners. For the moment the French voltigeurs pulled back a little way. Dobson washed the wound on Sergeant Rodriguez's scalp and Williams was relieved to see that it was little more than a scratch. Head wounds always bled abominably, but all men feared to lose their eyes, almost as much as losing their manhood, and they were apt to panic when the flow of blood plunged them into darkness. The cut bound up, the Spaniard helped Murphy off to the rear.

A horseman appeared, reining in behind the line of the 43rd to give orders. Hanley smiled broadly.

'Well, will you look at that,' he said. 'Billy Pringle no less.'

There were smiles, shaking of hands and slapping of backs. Explanations had to be brief.

'I need to get back to the general,' Pringle explained. 'Reckon you ought to come along. He may have some questions.'

'Happy to oblige,' Hanley replied. 'What is going on?'

'Not much at the moment. The French have

403

pulled back. For a while at least. We're staying here and waiting to see what happens. Are you coming as well, Bills?'

Williams looked at Dobson before shaking his head. 'Reckon we can help here.'

Pringle chuckled. 'Bloodthirsty young hound,' he said before turning to Hanley. 'Probably won't be able to find you a horse until we get there. Don't worry, I'll keep this fellow at a walk.' He reached to pat his horse's neck. 'And I shall feel terribly guilty all the way!'

Major MacAndrews still waited for the order. It was half an hour since the first French thrust, led by their cavalry.

'Four regiments at least, sir. Hussars, dragoons and probably chasseurs,' a staff major reported. 'Only a few skirmishers behind the cavalry, but at least a brigade of infantry and some guns are following, so most likely a division in total.'

This was more than had appeared before, and they were certainly more aggressive. One company of the 95th had been cut to ribbons, and another roughly handled. Other battalions reported a few losses from outlying pickets cut off by the sudden attack of the enemy cavalry.

'Everyone has pulled back on to the heights.' MacAndrews felt the word meant little in such rolling country. 'The First Forty-third are on the left near Almeida, with the Ninety-fifth beside them and ready to form a skirmish line to their front. The cavalry are behind the flank. In the centre the two regiments of Portuguese chasseurs, with the Third on the right, next to the Fifty-second.'

'Good,' the general said curtly. 'If they come on we shall give them a warm reception.' They could see the dark French columns half a mile or more ahead of them.

Pringle arrived, reporting from the left of the line, and the Scotsman was delighted to see Hanley, and even more pleased to hear that Williams and the others were largely unscathed. It was good news, but it did not ease his fears that the general was hesitating too long.

It took time for Hanley to report, and then an ADC came in with more news and another half-hour had passed before MacAndrews had his chance.

'Sir,' he asked. 'May I have you permission to start moving?'

Black Bob's dark eyes flashed angrily. He flexed his gloved hand and seemed to calm a little, but for a few moments he stared at the major.

'Yes,' he said.

MacAndrews saluted and turned his horse. He just caught the general muttering something about getting some peace at last.

CHAPTER 28

'Well done, Dalmas! First blood to us, eh!' Marshal Ney was excited, his eyes gleaming and a glass of wine in his hand as he took a hasty breakfast. The cuirassier's note had reported that the English were spread out along a wide front, and reported a defile that would allow a quick-moving column of horsemen to get around the enemy flank. In reply, the marshal had sent him a few squadrons of the 3ième Hussars. 'Chopped up some of their grasshoppers, I hear!' he added, using the soldiers' nickname for the British greenjackets.

'Caught them in the open,' Dalmas said.

'No damned good having their slow-loading rifles there!' Dalmas doubted that the armament of the infantry made much difference. He had hit them from the flank and if not in square infantrymen were at the mercy of cavalry. 'Lost your horse, I see,' the marshal continued delightedly. 'Lucky bastard. Nothing like having a horse shot from under you to bring on a good appetite. Have some of this. It's good!' The commander of 6th Corps held up a leg of roast chicken. All around them, the infantry were forming into four big columns, each of them two or three battalions strong. Drivers whipped their weary and half-starved horses to drag forward some light guns. On the flanks the cavalry squadrons rested. Soon the main attack would be ready, and for the moment there was nothing for the marshal to do except eat.

'I'm fine, thank you, your grace.'

'As you wish. Got yourself another horse?'

'Owner doesn't need her any more.'

Marshal Ney laughed. 'All about luck in the end, isn't it. Thankfully I was born lucky. We have them, my boy. I'll follow this chicken with a dessert of rosbifs!'

A staff officer rode up. 'The English have not moved.'

'Truly?'

'Standing like stones. About five battalions spread over two miles or more, and with a river behind them.'

'Bloody fools. Well, we'll soon carve them up.'

The staff officer looked at him. 'The reconnaissance, your grace?'

'Will consist of counting dead Englishmen,' Ney said happily. 'That should give the Prince all the information he needs.'

'Yes, sir.'

'They tell me to press the English gently and learn about them.' The marshal snorted derisively. 'Makes me sound like some virgin. Tell me, Dalmas, am I that?'

'No, your grace.'

Marshal Ney puffed out his chest and stretched, his thick brown hair more than usually shaggy. He roared with laughter. 'No, your grace! I am like a sailor on shore after a year and seeing his first woman!'

'The poor English,' Dalmas said.

'Then they shouldn't have been waiting on the dockside.' Ney beckoned to another of his staff officers. 'Send the voltigeurs forward. Main columns to follow in twenty minutes with cavalry in support. How are the men?'

'Almost dried out, but still angry.'

'Excellent. Tell the regimental commanders to keep going forward. Never give them a chance to recover and we shall have their dresses and petticoats off in no time!'

'Your grace?' The ADC was puzzled.

'Just tell them to keep going forward.

'Now, Dalmas, your company has come up?'

'Nearly here. Should arrive in ten minutes, your grace.'

'Good. Keep them ready. I want you to stay on the right. Make sure the attack keeps going. Outflank any position if you can't roll them over from the front. Use whatever cavalry you need, but always keep going. Get another couple of horses killed under you and the day will surely be ours!'

'Yes, your grace!' Dalmas saluted. 'And the spy, your grace. I almost had him.'

'Sod him. This is more important. If I can chop

up one of their best divisions it will be the finest start to the invasion of Portugal we could have. Lisbon in a few months and then who will give a damn about spies and codes.

'Hound them, Dalmas, hound them!'

The French skirmish line was thick, and the men forming it knew their job. All along the front muskets and rifles banged. The voltigeurs moved well, using cover like the veterans they were, and gradually the British and Portuguese gave ground. A scattering of green- and brown-jacketed bodies were left behind, and there were a few dead and wounded men in blue stranded by the tide of the French advance, but mostly the pressure was enough. The British gave way before the fighting became more serious.

O'Hare's remaining men lined the wall beside the 43rd and added their fire to the redcoats' muskets. Voltigeurs with tall yellow and green plumes darted from rock to rock in the field ahead of them. Williams was still not used to the 95th's practice of firing without specific orders, but he and Dobson joined in, loading and firing in their own rhythm. The stink of powder was all around them, for the breeze had dropped and it was hard to see the French through the fog of smoke blossoming all along the wall. Balls snapped through the air past them, or smacked into the stones to show that the largely invisible enemy was still there.

Then they heard the drums.

'Here they come, lads.' Captain O'Hare's voice carried along the little line.

Two beats, drummers pounding their sticks on tight drumskins, then two more, and then a flourishing roll, the rhythm repeated again and again in the sound that had carried the French to victory throughout Europe.

A ball hit the top of the wall and flicked up, grazing Williams on the cheek. He touched the spot, winced because it was sore, but there was only a little blood on his fingers and he knew that it was no more than a scratch.

'Pull back! Pull back!' A tall captain of the 43rd with a pelisse hung fashionably from his shoulder shouted to O'Hare. 'The French are coming around the flank! Retire by alternate companies. Take your lads back first!'

The rifle captain waved in acknowledgement.

'Right, you rogues, we are going back. Rally at that next wall.' He pointed up the slope.

The drums beat on, but the main column or columns were still out of sight. Williams and Dobson jogged back with the greenjackets. Behind them the 43rd fired a platoon volley, while another of their companies doubled up the slope and vanished through the gate of a walled orchard. O'Hare reformed his men and then blew a whistle to extend them as a chain of skirmishers in a line beside the low wall.

'Just like old times, Pug,' Dobson said as he knelt down in front of the officer, musket ready. They were at the end of the line, down in a little gully so steep that they could not see whether or not there was someone beyond it protecting their flank, and only a few of the riflemen were visible.

The nearest company of the 43rd retreated in turn, running back with their muskets held low at the trail. Quite a few of the men had their other hand pressed to their tall shako to hold the hats on as they ran.

Williams could hear a muffled shout now as the drummers paused before plunging again into that aggressive beat. Ahead, French voltigeurs were at the wall so recently occupied by the British. Dobson fired, and so did several riflemen. Williams moved to the side and knelt down, bringing his own musket to his shoulder to cover the veteran as he loaded. A few enemy skirmishers scrambled over the wall. Williams fired as several rifles cracked and one of the voltigeurs was flung back and lay draped over the top of the wall until comrades pulled him down.

'*Vive l'empereur!*' He caught the words this time and then the drummers added their noise again.

A volley thundered out, and that was presumably the 43rd although he could not see them. Shots came from the other direction too, which was reassuring because it suggested that someone was there.

Another voltigeur was hit, and lay unmoving in the grass, while the rest scampered back behind the wall.

'*Vive l'empereur! En avant!*' The main body was getting close now, shouts and drumming carrying over the gunfire. Ranks of men appeared behind the wall, muskets with fixed bayonets still held nonchalantly at their shoulders as if all they needed to do was march over the enemy. Williams could not see well, but he guessed that there were two companies of blue-coated infantry and that meant this was the front of a column at least a battalion in strength. A mounted officer screamed at them to go on as the drummers pounded away.

'*Vive l'empereur! Vive l'empereur!*' He could see the mouths of the men opening wide to chant, but still they waited at the wall. Men never liked to cross an obstacle. The closest company were grenadiers, wearing the high bearskin caps that were supposed to have been replaced by shakos several years ago. A lot of colonels liked the expensive, old-fashioned headgear and had ignored the new regulation. Grenadiers were chosen from the biggest men, and the extra foot or so of height from their tall caps made them seem like giants looming out of the smoke.

Dobson fired, the noise loud in Williams' ears, and all around them riflemen were shooting. The white front of a grenadier's jacket was suddenly bright red, his musket dropping as he slumped down. The mounted colonel was unscathed, still pointing with his sword and calling for his men to go on. A young officer vaulted the wall and turned to beckon his men to follow. Another sprang on to the wall itself, hat balanced on the tip of the sword he was waving in the air as he showed the men that they had nothing to fear.

Another volley crashed out from the 43rd, and some of the French grenadiers brought their muskets down and levelled them. The colonel was bawling at them to keep going, but a few pulled triggers. At the top of the slope a rifleman took a ball in his left hand, smashing two fingers.

Williams fired at the same moment as several of the 95th and at first could see little through the smoke, and so he did not see the French officer capering on the wall getting struck in the groin. All he heard was a terrible shriek of agony, and by the time the smoke cleared the man had gone, but French grenadiers were climbing over the drystone wall. The colonel spun his horse around and went back before taking a run and jumping the wall neatly. He was calling to his men to form up and still he remained untouched by all the balls flying through the air.

'Back, sir!' Dobson tapped Williams on the shoulder and pointed at the greenjackets doubling away. For the moment the closest drums were silent, as the drummers clambered over the wall.

'*Vive l'empereur!*' The drums began again, and then the cry turned into a wild yell as the grenadiers charged up the slope.

Williams and the riflemen kept running, and as he came to the mouth of the gully he could see a loose mass of the 43rd going back as well. The ground dipped down again, before rising steeply for a few yards to a little crest crowned by yet another wall, although this was little more than a loose pile of stones. It was enough to halt the men, and officers and sergeants shouted for them to form up. The French paused before the dip, as they too reformed. Then the drums began again.

'The Fifty-second report French cavalry trying to work around their flank. A regiment of lights, they think, probably chasseurs.'

Brigadier General Craufurd's face looked taut as he stared ahead at the swarming columns of the enemy. After months of skirmishing and posturing, suddenly the enemy were flinging themselves at his command and he knew that he was not ready.

'Tell them to hold on as long as possible. I shall send word when I want them to pull back.' The 1/52nd were to his right, and if they gave way the French could strike at the river and cut off most of the division. Memories of Buenos Aires flooded chillingly back. 'Not again,' the general said so faintly that Hanley barely heard the words and did not understand them.

'Ride to the First Chasseurs!' the general told another ADC. 'Tell them to begin to withdraw to the far side of the river. After that ride on to the Third Regiment, and tell Elder he is to follow once the First have gone. Go!'

The French were pressing hardest at the flanks,

and so the general would withdraw his centre first, and hope that the enemy would not see what was happening in time to do anything about it. His cavalry were already retiring across the river with the guns and supply wagons. That meant the three British infantry battalions would have to hold out alone on his flanks against two or three times their numbers of French supported by horse and guns. The battle teetered on the brink of chaos, with the nightmare of the enemy sweeping down on a road blocked by crowds of men retreating in confusion. The general needed to seize back control.

'You! Lieutenant Hanley.'

'Sir!'

'Ride to Colonel Elder of the Third Regiment and tell him that he is to wait on this side of the bridge until everyone else is across. He is not to cross the bridge until ordered.'

Hanley rode off, knowing that the Portuguese were not far behind them.

Another order went to Colonel Beckwith of the 95th, telling him only to give ground when sorely pressed. Then it was Pringle's turn.

'Find the left wing of the Forty-third. They are to hold fast as long as possible. Tell them we must hold for an hour before starting to retire. On your way!'

'*Vive l'empereur! En avant, mes amis!*' The French pressed on. A few men dropped at the heads of their columns to the little volleys fired by companies of the 43rd or were singled out by the riflemen, but the blue-coated infantry never stopped for more than a few minutes. Even when they did, voltigeurs ran out again from the flanks of the formed battalion and were soon firing. One rifleman was helping along another hit in the thigh, when he too was struck by a ball that shattered the long bone in his right arm.

Williams and Dobson were in a sunken lane, bordered on both sides by walls and crowded with men with the white facings of the 43rd. More of the light infantrymen spilled down into the path from a gap in the one of the field boundaries.

'That way!' a mounted officer shouted in a clear voice, gesturing at a gateway on the far side of the lane, opening into another field, this one higher-walled. The network of lane and fields was a maze, and Williams was struggling to maintain his sense of direction and so readily led Dobson after the officer. Another horseman forced his way through the crowd, and this one was having difficulty controlling his mount.

'Come on, you bitch!' he shouted. The beast wheeled on the spot, frightened by something, and then lashed out with his hind legs, narrowly missing a corporal from the 43rd and instead kicking a hole in the wall behind him.

'Billy!' Williams shouted to his friend.

Dobson turned and fired back up at a figure looking down into the lane. More voltigeurs appeared. Muskets flamed and the light infantry corporal gasped as a ball slammed into his chest and knocked the breath from him. Pringle's horse was hit in the head. Its eyes rolled and its long tongue drooped from its mouth and then it fell.

Williams raised his own musket and pulled the trigger. There was a satisfying yelp from one of the Frenchmen at the wall.

'In here! This way,' the mounted officer was still calling. Williams and Dobson grabbed Pringle and half dragged him with the men of the 43rd through the gateway. The enclosed field was big, and more than two hundred redcoats and a few riflemen were there. The mounted officer was the last one through the gate, pursued by a smattering of shots, and he shouted at the men to form up and cover the entrance.

'Bugger!' Dobson spat the word. The walls were a good eight or nine feet high, and he had just seen that there was no way out apart from the way they had come.

Pringle had recovered and pointed to the far end of the field. 'Make sure there isn't a hidden gate in the corner,' he said without much hope, and headed towards the mounted officer. 'Orders from the general!' he shouted. 'You are to hold as long as possible and only withdraw on specific orders.'

The mounted major stared at him.

'I know,' Pringle said with a shrug.

The major realised that they were trapped. 'Looks as if we can't damned well go anywhere.'

417

Two ranks of light infantry formed up in the gate fired a volley out into the lane.

Pringle went to join his friends.

'Nothing,' Williams said, and slammed the butt of his musket against the wall in frustration. Then he remembered Pringle's horse kicking down the wall outside. 'Dob, give me a hand.' He hit the wall again, and a stone came loose. 'You, Sergeant!' he called to an NCO from the 43rd. The man looked surprised and then smiled.

'Rudden.' The name came to Williams almost immediately and he grinned back. 'Good to see you.' The sergeant had served in his company of the Battalion of Detachments last summer. 'Get some men, we need to weaken this wall and make a way out.'

Sergeant Rudden shouted orders and men attacked the wall with their bayonets or the butts of the muskets. Triangular blades were thrust into the gaps between stones and then levered to work them loose.

'Well, we've got it worried,' Pringle said, looking at the stonework after five minutes of grunting effort. 'All of you, push!' He and Williams leaned with the others, using all their weight and strength. 'Come on, heave!' he shouted as they strained against the wall. 'Push for your lives!'

Williams felt the stone shifting slightly, and then almost fell forward as it gave way and a cloud of dust choked them as several yards of wall collapsed outwards.

'This way!' Pringle shouted back towards the major at the other end of the field.

Williams and Dobson went through. There was a walled orchard off to the left, and a small sheep pen on the right, but otherwise the ground was open and strewn with boulders as it dipped and then rose to another low ridge where there was a small barn and another drystone wall.

Behind them a volley was fired through the open gate.

'Come on, Rudden!' Williams called, and began jogging towards the barn. Dobson and several dozen men from the 43rd followed him. Officers and NCOs were shouting as they tried to reform their men, but no one was in a mood to stop. Little clusters of men grouped together as they hurried across the open field.

'French!' yelled Pringle in warning.

Williams heard the sound of hoofs and looked back. Dragoons in brass helmets and green coats with pink fronts and collars were walking their horses around the corner of the high-walled field. Then he saw Dalmas, polished cuirass glinting in the sunlight. The cuirassier shouted and his men spurred their mounts into a run, long swords stretched out, wrist turned so that the point was aimed down.

'Loaded, Dob?'

The veteran shook his head.

'Keep going!' He sprinted ahead to the wall beside the barn. 'Come on!' he yelled back.

Williams leapt, banged his knee painfully on the top of the wall, but pressed down with his hand and was over.

'Form here! Form on me!' Dobson was beside him, as was Rudden, who was calling out to the men by name. 'Reload!' Williams shouted.

Williams watched as a dozen French dragoons rode in among the mob of redcoats. He saw one chop down and slice into a light infantryman's pack, knocking the man off his feet, but leaving him unscathed. Others were more skilled. One man with the red stripe of a sergeant on his sleeve jabbed down and punched through a man's forehead with the point of his long sword, letting the momentum of his horse free the blade as he rode on. Dalmas took another man in the neck, before slicing down through an officer's shoulder, almost severing his arm.

A dragoon was down, thrown from his horse after a redcoat smashed the butt of his musket into its mouth, and the cavalryman screamed as he lay on his back and was stabbed by two bayonets. More dragoons appeared, urging their mounts on as soon as they saw the enemy.

'Present!' Williams called out as loud as he could, hoping that the threat of a volley might deter the French. There were thirty men lining the wall, and more pressed through the opening or clambered back to join him.

'Aim high, lads!' The field was full of redcoats. Firing high risked wasting the balls, but stood a chance of missing the infantrymen and emptying some saddles.

Dalmas was heading towards a cluster of men retiring around the battalion's Colours, the heavy standards still in their leather cases, and Williams wondered whether that was why he had not noticed them until now.

Men were falling to the dragoons' swords, but fortunately there were too few Frenchmen to turn the retreat into a massacre and many of the men simply barged through. The major galloped through the gap made by Pringle and his men, and behind him came a mass of redcoats, bayonets fixed. A dragoon's horse reared as it was stabbed in the flank, and the rider was pulled down into the grass to be clubbed and stabbed. Other cavalrymen were wheeling away.

'Aim high,' Williams shouted. 'Fire!'

One dragoon was hit in the teeth, and one of them took a ball in the left arm and another in the belly so that he slumped in the saddle, barely keeping his seat. The charge of the major's men and the volley took the heart from the cavalrymen. Momentum was their best weapon, and there was little to be said for standing and fighting in the middle of so many enemy infantrymen. Dalmas went back with them.

'Well done,' the major said to Pringle as he rode into the new field, and then he said the same to Williams before getting to the matter in hand. 'Form up, lads, form up. We can hold them here!'

421

Williams wondered for how long, and then he heard the drums beating again and the sound of thousands of men chanting together.

'*Vive l'empereur!*'

Voltigeurs appeared in the gap they had made in the other enclosure and a moment later a musket ball pecked the top of the wall they lined.

Lieutenant Williams reached into his pocket for a cartridge and realised that it was his last one. Unlike a soldier, an officer did not carry a pouch on his belt, and he usually took only a couple of dozen paper cartridges in his pockets. Grimly, he bit off the bullet and began to reload.

CHAPTER 29

Major Alastair MacAndrews saw the powder wagon lurch as it tried to round the bend in the track. As it had come down the steep road it had picked up speed, the weight of the heavy barrels making the horses skid and sparks fly from the brake as the driver frantically pulled it against the wheel. It was a sharp turn, the road still dropping as it approached the bridge itself. The major's heart sank as the front left-hand wheel went off the road and into a ditch, slamming hard against the wall. The team of horses whinnied in panic and the lead pair reared up as they came to such an abrupt halt. A half-empty barrel came loose and fell, rolling down the short slope to drop down the steep bank into the flooded river. Good barrels were hard to find up on the frontier, and although there was little powder in it, its loss was still unfortunate.

At the moment the Scotsman did not have time to worry about that. The wagon and its team were jammed up at the very entrance to the bridge. In the circumstances there was only one thing to do. Major MacAndrews began to shout.

423

'Sergeant Hargreaves! Get that cart shifted.' Hargreaves was one of his men, a stocky Cumbrian from the 34th Foot.

'Right, lads! You heard the major, get moving!' The sergeant had a dozen men with him, all of them NCOs and so used to commanding, but they were all good practical men and knew the seriousness of the situation. They ran to the trapped cart and began to push as the driver flogged his team.

'Hold up there!' MacAndrews had galloped around the corner of the road. Thankfully the drivers were keeping to the distances he had ordered and there was time for the next cart to rein in in spite of the slope. 'Wait. There's a cart blocking the bridge. Stay here until I give the order.'

The cavalry were already across, and that was a blessing. The halted cart and the one behind it were the last of MacAndrews' convoy, but behind them were two guns of the Chestnut Troop and half of the artillery's additional limbers and wagons.

A gun fired, the noise clear over the smattering shots and occasional volleys of muskets and rifles. The sounds were coming closer, and the cannon must be French because it was too light a boom to be from the fortress, and all the British guns were either across the river or waiting on the road winding up the side of the valley above him. MacAndrews had not heard any French guns firing for a good ten minutes. Some of that was due to the strange way sound carried amid these hills, and some to the noise of animals and screeching wheels and the shouts needed to chivvy men over the river. He suspected that the French were struggling to get their cannon into action and only the lightest horse artillery pieces were managing to deploy. That was good for the men trying to hold the enemy back. It also suggested that the French were advancing so quickly that their gunners could not keep up. The Light Division was being tumbled back towards the river and that meant the bridge had to be kept open.

The rest of his men were picketing the sandy hilltop above them. It commanded both the road to the bridge and another running south along the river. MacAndrews knew that his small force could not hold it for long, but if the French got up there before the whole division was across the river then there would be the devil to pay. He hoped that someone with more troops would see the same danger, but until they did he would keep as many men up there as he could spare.

MacAndrews wrenched his horse round and kicked it into a canter back around the corner. Hargreaves and his men were straining as some pushed at the cart and others tried to lift the wheel and axle out of the little ditch. There was no point yelling encouragement. MacAndrews flicked his boots free of the stirrups and jumped down to lend a hand. His hat dropped on to the ground and his white hair waved in its usual wild manner.

'Come on, lads,' he said, and began to heave. Corporal Raynor was beside him, and the clerk looked back over his shoulder in wonder to see his commander staining his scarlet coat with grease and pushing just like the rest of them. MacAndrews grinned at him.

There was the sound of running feet. Hundreds of Portuguese soldiers in the brown of the *caçadores* were scrambling down the slope towards the bridge, avoiding the clogged road. The men had black collars and light blue cuffs and that made them the 1st Regiment.

'Stop! Lend a hand here!' MacAndrews shouted, glad to see help arriving. The small, dark-skinned soldiers in their drab uniforms ignored him.

'Sorry, sir, orders!' shouted a British officer whose brown tunic was heavily laced in black. 'We have to get across the river.'

The man did not stop, but kept running, the same strained expression on his face as on those of the rest of the men. They barged past the redcoats clustered around the wagon, and past the team of horses, sprinting across the long bridge.

'Stop, you damned fool,' MacAndrews yelled.

'Stop!' Hargreaves had one of those booming sergeant's voices no officer could ever match, and yet the call made no difference. Another of the NCOs grabbed one of the brown-coated soldiers. The man stared at him, complaining in rapid Portuguese.

Another company of *caçadores* followed the first, running with the same intensity, pushing past anyone in their way. The battalion had broken up into groups as they retired, and their orders were to retreat to the far bank and so that is what they did, officers and young soldiers alike.

Hargreaves spat his disgust and other redcoats expressed their opinion in words. The driver went into a new frenzy of whipping his horse, and perhaps it was this or the flood of soldiers pushing their way past and running over the bridge that made the animals panic and suddenly pull with a new strength, making the sunken wheel climb a little.

'Heave, lads, heave!' MacAndrews called out.

The redcoats flung themselves back against the vehicle and pushed. Raynor was heaving on the right-side rear wheel itself, his left arm looped through the spokes so that he could bring his weight to bear.

'Look out!' the major shouted in warning, but then the wagon came back on to the road and shot forward. Corporal Raynor screamed as his arm was shattered by the wheel as it spun into sudden motion. MacAndrews flung himself forward, grabbing the corporal and plunging them both down on to the road, knocking over several *caçadores* as they fell. The corporal was sobbing with pain and there were pieces of bone sticking out through the sleeve of his red coat, now stained darker with blood.

'Get him off the road.' MacAndrews felt his own eyes ready to moisten at the waste of a good man, who had done his best in the past months after being forced into the army by desperation. He wondered what future there was for a one-armed clerk, but thankfully there was too much to do here and now and so his mind took refuge in activity. 'Look after him,' he said to one of the drummers. Not bothering with his horse, the Scotsman ran back up the road and beckoned the next wagon on. The bridge was still filled with Portuguese soldiers, but the men were sensible enough to move to the sides or wait when the big vehicles crossed. This was not panic, thought the major, although it could readily degenerate into it.

A mounted officer in brown uniform led the last of the regiment down the slope and on to the bridge. The man was obviously angry at losing control of his battalion and concerned at the light this cast on his men.

'My fault,' he called to MacAndrews in strongly accented English. 'I just assumed they would rally and wait before they crossed. We were told to retreat quickly by the general and so that is what we did, but I should have kept them in better order.'

'Easily happens.'

'Should not in my regiment,' the Portuguese colonel said bitterly, and then touched his shako with his crop before pushing on. The last company of the regiment to go over the bridge marched in order. MacAndrews could understand the display, but it was frustrating when there was still a gun team and a line of limbers and wagons waiting to go over.

More and more soldiers were spilling over the ridge above them, and the sound of firing was very close now. MacAndrews had not heard another cannon firing for some minutes and guessed that once again the French columns were outrunning their artillery teams. He stood aside as the last of the Chestnut Troop's six-pounders passed in a jingle of harness and rumbling of wheels. As the whirling spokes of the grey-painted limber and gun went by he thought again of the injured corporal. After more than thirty years as a soldier MacAndrews was used to seeing his men killed or maimed. Even after all that time it had not become easy.

He turned back to look up the slope and saw the groups of men in green, red and brown jackets coming down towards the river and the safety of the far bank. The battalions were all jumbled up, but the British and Portuguese soldiers alike were not flooding to the rear and moved slowly and with deliberation. The Scotsman walked by the side of the road back down towards the bridge as a mobile forge followed the gun team downhill. It was hard not to smile as the driver of the lead pair passed, a look of intense concentration on his face and his tongue sticking out from pursed lips as he carefully negotiated the bend.

A party of redcoats filed down on to the road beside him and he recognised his own men.

'Colonel Elder's compliments, sir,' Sergeant Coombs reported after delivering the most formal of salutes. 'He thanks you for holding the position, but has now taken over.' Coombs was a slim, very active man of less than medium height, and his pale grey eyes shone with an intelligence that MacAndrews had seen demonstrated more than once in the last few months. The Scotsman had deliberately chosen a party where everyone else was junior to the twenty-four-year-old with his slow Devon accent and quick wit. 'The colonel has companies from the Ninety-fifth and Forty-third with him as well as his own fellows,' Coombs added, obviously implying that the presence of the British soldiers was what really mattered.

'Very good, Sergeant. Come with me.'

MacAndrews took them down to the open area just before the bridge proper began and turned sharply to the right. Hargreaves and his men were waiting there, and one held the reins of his horse in one hand and his cocked hat in the other.

'Got trampled a bit, I'm afraid, sir,' the redcoat said, clearly amused.

'I've worn worse,' he replied cheerfully, and put the thing firmly on his head. 'Thank you, Foster.'

There were shots from the top of the valley above them. At the moment it was still the sporadic fire of skirmishers. Parties of retiring soldiers were on the road, having been let in between the last few vehicles of the artillery, and MacAndrews silently cursed the courtesy of the drivers for letting them in or the obstinacy of infantry officers for forcing their way.

'The wheel wagon and three more tumbrels still

to come, sir,' a Royal Horse Artillery lieutenant called out, using the old name for the ammunition cars. 'But the rearmost two are a long way back in all this mess.' The man's face was lined, and MacAndrews guessed that he was thirty at least. Promotion in the engineers and artillery was purely by seniority, untainted by purchase or patronage. The system was fair, but painfully slow, and on balance the Scotsman did not envy them. He raised a hand in thanks.

'Keep moving!' he called to a company of green-jackets heading over the bridge.

Behind them came the general and his staff. Hanley was there, but there was no sign of Pringle and no opportunity to ask.

'Ah, MacAndrews.' Brigadier General Craufurd looked calm, save that his eyes darted quickly from side to side. 'I have ordered one wing of the Forty-third over the river. The train is almost across, I observe.'

'Four left, sir.'

'Good. Well done, Major. Get the rest over as fast as you can.' There was the sound of a volley from not far away, and just for an instant the general's composure cracked and he looked nervously behind him. MacAndrews, a prisoner once himself, could guess something of the waking nightmare faced by a man who had once surrendered a brigade and now stood again on the brink of disaster. 'We must get everyone across quickly. Five minutes and I shall recall the rearguard.'

MacAndrews doubted that that was enough time, but knew there was little point in arguing.

'Keep moving,' the general called out as several hundred *caçadores* doubled along behind the cart carrying the gunners' spare wheels. These men had yellow cuffs on their dark brown jackets and so came from Colonel Elder's 3rd Regiment. Behind them were riflemen in green and then the first of the ammunition cars. 'Keep going! Keep going!' MacAndrews' voice was hoarse from urging the column on.

Several hundred men of the 43rd came down the road, and all the time smaller groups from the different regiments retreated down the slopes and pressed into the crowd. A strong body of men in the buff facings of the 52nd followed behind.

'I must arrange the defence of the eastern bank,' Craufurd said abruptly, no doubt frustrated at his inability to do more than urge men on where he stood at the moment. 'I have recalled the rear-guard.' With that the general and his staff forced their horses into the press and made their way over the bridge. Hanley gave an apologetic shrug as he followed.

The last two ammunition cars followed the 52nd. By the time the first one managed the tight bend before the bridge and then the sharp right turn of the crossing itself, MacAndrews could see the mixture of different uniforms coming down from the hilltop overlooking the road.

'Right, lads,' MacAndrews said to his own men.

'We'll be going across in a moment.' The second car reached the bridge, its wheels flinging up a lot of muddy water as it turned, and then the noise changed as the horseshoes struck the stone of the bridge. The major felt relief washing over him.

Then the right-hand wheel of the leading car broke with a loud crack, followed quickly by an echoing crash as the heavily loaded cart fell against the side wall and flagstones of the bridge. One man at a time could squeeze through the gap between the crippled ammunition wagon and the far wall of the bridge, as long as he went slowly, but there was no room for the second car to get by.

The rearguard halted, some on the slopes and others in the roadway. Men already on the bridge began filing past the cart. Beyond them the lieutenant appeared again, face red with anger under his Tarleton helmet.

'Be twenty minutes or more to fix this, sir!' he called.

'How many men do you need?' MacAndrews shouted back.

'I'll take a dozen of these and that will be plenty,' the artilleryman called, pointing at some of the greenjackets on the bridge.

There were shouts from the far side, and now the gunner was looking down the valley, pointing at something. MacAndrews turned in the saddle, but it was hard to see much beyond the spur jutting out behind him. Then, a good half a mile away, he saw movement as a column of redcoats followed the winding road leading from downriver towards the bridge.

'It's the Fifty-second,' said a voice beside him, and MacAndrews remembered that the light infantry battalion had held the southern flank. Now it seemed several companies were still some distance away and must have been forgotten in the chaos of the retreat.

'God damn it, they'll be trapped,' the voice continued, and the major saw that it came from a captain with the buff collar and cuffs of the 52nd.

There was a sound like a heavy slap, and the officer's cheek burst open as a musket ball smashed through his teeth. He gaped, but when he tried to speak no words came and he spat out blood and gobbets of flesh.

The French were on top of the hill.

Dalmas was almost beginning to believe in luck, but perhaps it was simply the strange nature of the English. They made so many mistakes, deploying badly and falling into confusion, and yet the redcoats and greenjackets still fought like devils when they had already lost the battle. Perhaps he should have learned this from Jenny Dobson, who was uncouth and childlike while at the same time cunning and stubborn. The cuirassier officer smiled at the thought, although it reminded him of his failure to catch the English spy. At least the last few hours had gone some way to balancing that mistake. Yet somehow he doubted the marshal would dismiss the matter so easily once the battle was over. So far Dalmas had helped to turf the English out of four positions, slipping with his dragoons around their flank. He reckoned his men had accounted for a good hundred of the enemy already, killed or captured, but he needed something more spectacular.

Then he saw his chance, and wondered that the enemy would serve it up to him so easily. For a moment he feared a trap, but that made no sense, and then he realised that the redcoats had simply made another mistake, abandoning the hill that overlooked the river valley and the only bridge across it.

'Come on,' he called to the company of infantrymen following him, and sent his horse down the gully and up the slope on the other side. The soldiers were panting after their forced march to catch up, tanned faces reddening with effort as the soldiers in their brown coats with blue fronts skidded down the stony hillside and then struggled up the other side. Tall yellow and green plumes nodded on their shakos, for these were the voltigeurs of the Légion du Midi, the men attached to him in his hunt for the spy and now following him to a better victory that would smash an enemy division.

Dalmas' horse rushed up the slope, and he was impressed with the animal's surefootedness. It did not stumble once.

435

Just before the crest the horse began to struggle, and the French captain felt his chest tighten beneath his steel cuirass as he imagined a line of redcoats waiting on the far side of the ridge, muskets at their shoulders ready to fire. At that range his armour would do no more than distort the balls as they punched through the breastplate, making the wounds they caused far more terrible.

The horse wanted to go a little to the left and he trusted it enough to let the animal have its head. Three more strides brought him to the very top of the hill and presented him with the truly beautiful sight of the enemy at his mercy. No line of redcoats waited to end his life. The nearest were a hundred yards away, down at the bottom of the slope, milling in a crowd on the approach to the bridge – a bridge blocked by wagons.

Some men might have given a shout of victory or invoked the precious name of the Emperor, as if he could witness their triumph from afar. Jean-Baptiste Dalmas was a soldier and knew that his emperor valued a winner over a flamboyant fool.

'Skirmish line,' he shouted to the voltigeurs struggling up in his wake. 'Here, along the hilltop!'

Further along to his left more French soldiers, also voltigeurs, but in the normal blue jackets of the line regiments, were dashing to the top of the high ground. He walked his horse towards them, and although he could not remember the man's name, the officer leading them waved in recognition.

'We have them, Dalmas!' he shouted.

'Extend your men to my left,' he called back. Looking behind, he saw a team of horses appear over the ridgeline to the rear, drivers whipping the animals to pull a four-pounder cannon and its limber. His men were already firing, the shots plunging down into the crowded road beneath them. Even one small field gun like that would turn the bridge into a slaughterhouse. Dalmas beckoned to the gunners to come to him.

'Dalmas!' It was the officer from the company beside him. The cuirassier turned and could not help smiling when he saw half a battalion of English infantry struggling along the road as they headed towards the bridge.

'Too late, my friends,' he said out loud. Jean-Baptiste Dalmas decided that he believed in luck after all, and now he would give his marshal and his emperor a victory to delight their cold hearts.

CHAPTER 30

'What the hell is going on?' Young Simmons was unable to see past the press of men on the road.

'The bridge is blocked,' said the taller Williams, able to see over the crowd. He and Dobson had found themselves once again with the second lieutenant and a few men from his company. Pringle was behind them, among the 43rd.

Then the balls began to rain down on them. A redcoat clutched his shoulder, blood pulsing between his fingers. Williams looked up and saw the puffs of smoke from the hilltop above them, where he and the rest of the rearguard had so recently been stationed.

Some men pushed on, heading for the crossing and hoping to squeeze through. Most forced their way to the side of the road, seeking cover in the refuge of the boulders at the foot of the slope. Bullets struck shards off the big stones, or sometimes ricocheted up, screaming like fiends.

A rifle officer was down in the road, a ball in his leg. Another subaltern ran to help him, leading a party of greenjackets, and then he too was hit, this time in the thigh, and so the soldiers helped both back across the bridge, balls flicking up dust around them. The hilltop was a long musket shot away, but the French simply fired at the road and bridge and knew that some bullets would find a mark and so the English would die one by one.

Men fired back up the slope, and perhaps some of the voltigeurs were hit. It did not make the fire slacken. Pringle and Dobson were behind one big boulder with several of the 43rd. Williams crouched behind another with Simmons and then another officer from the 95th ran up to join them.

'Damned saucy fellows,' the newcomer said, and peered up over the stone in an effort to spot the enemy. The ball must have arrived the instant he raised his head, for he sprang back, blood jetting out of a wound in his throat. Williams and Simmons pulled him under cover, and the Welshman tried to stem the flow by pressing his fingers tightly over the man's neck. His hands were drenched, and he could feel the force pumping the blood out just as he watched the life drain from the poor man's eyes. In less than a minute he was unconscious, and although the flow of blood was held by a rough bandage the man's face was as pale as a sheet. Dobson looked for a moment and then shook his head.

'Poor Pratt,' Simmons said. Williams tried to wipe the already congealing liquid from his hands. He was not wearing gloves any more, for they made it too difficult to load a musket. Not that he had a single cartridge to his name. His last few, robbed from the pouch of a dead redcoat, had been fired off on top of the hill.

'We need to get up there.'

As if in answer to the thought, a voice began shouting over the confusion.

'Lads, we need to drive those *crapauds* away!' Major MacAndrews walked his horse along the road, somehow unscathed by the bullets that smacked into the surface or snapped through the air around him. The Scotsman was waving his hat, and his white hair was ruffling in the wind. 'Form up! Our boys will be trapped if we let the Frogs stay there, so we're going up that hill.'

Williams did not want to stand up. Behind the rock it was safe, and apart from the danger he felt so utterly weary that more than anything else he wanted to lie down and rest. He glanced over to the next boulder and saw Pringle and Dobson there.

'Oh, sod it,' the veteran said, and got to his feet, reaching for his bayonet as he did so. Pringle shuffled up beside the sergeant and from nowhere there was Sergeant Rodriguez behind him. Williams found himself standing and did not remember getting up. Simmons was beside him, and so were the men from his company. Next to them was Sergeant Rudden with a file of men in the white facings of the 43rd and once again the NCO nodded amicably to Williams.

'Bayonets, lads!' MacAndrews' voice echoed up

the road. 'Let's give these blackguards a taste of British steel!' The Scotsman flung away his hat and reached down to draw his sword. Blades scraped on the tops of scabbards as men drew their slim bayonets, or heavy swords if they were riflemen, and then clicked them into place. Next to Williams young Simmons had a light, highly curved blade. The youth's teeth were bared, clenched tight with that mix of fear and determination Williams knew so well. His musket was slung on his shoulder, and now he drew his sword.

A rifleman sank down groaning, hands pressed to the wound in his belly. Then a Portuguese *caçador* was shot through the head, a gaping hole where his right eye had been a moment before and the man made no sound as he fell. One of the 95th went to help the wounded greenjacket, but the man pushed him away, saying that he would be all right on his own.

'Come on, lads!' MacAndrews half screamed the words as he set his horse at the steep slope. The animal jumped the low bank edging the road, and then scrabbled for a grip in the soft sandy soil, but then it was racing ahead. Men cheered, pouring all their fear into a great shout of rage, and Williams yelled with them.

This was no ordered charge, a formed line splitting into individuals only when they were at last released from discipline and sent forward. This was a rush of redcoats, riflemen and *caçadores*, all intermingled, officers and sergeants alongside

441

privates, and none of them giving orders, simply running up the soft slope, following the white-haired Scotsman because they all knew that it had to be done.

The French had the high ground and they were all veterans who had already chased the enemy back several miles. If they were surprised by the sudden onslaught they did not flinch. Muskets banged all along the ridge, puffs of smoke appearing from behind the boulders that sheltered them.

One of the 43rd took a ball on the shin and pitched forward into the sandy soil, dropping his musket. A moment later a rifleman gasped as he was hit in the chest. He dropped, tripping another greenjacket who fell with him, cursing foully.

Williams ran on, slipping on the soft earth, and then was almost tipped over when his boot caught in a loop of the long straggly grass that covered the slope. His musket banged uncomfortably against his back as he ran. The slope became steeper and he wondered about swinging to the side, but there were men all around him and he did not want to fall behind, so he pushed on, his left hand pressing the ground as he struggled for balance. A ball slashed a path through the long grass just inches from his bloodstained fingers and then struck with a deep thump. Someone cried out behind him, but he did not look. MacAndrews was still riding at their head, his sword gleaming in the sunlight, and although his horse was slowing the Scotsman was still a good length in front of the leading men. The French skirmishers must have been singling out the mounted officer, but somehow he rode on unscathed. There was less cheering now, men gulping in lungfuls of air as they forced their aching limbs to clamber up the steep slope.

The top was close now. Williams could see the tall plumed shakos of the voltigeurs, and then the heads and shoulders of men crouching among the rocks, and even a few kneeling out in the open, and behind was an officer on horseback calling them on. It was Dalmas, in armour and helmet as usual, and Williams wondered why the wretched man kept plaguing them, but had no time to think.

'Come on!' he called, to himself as much as to anyone else. The slope was gentler now, so that he was able to crouch without using his hand to stay up and run forward.

'Follow me, boys!' Simmons shouted beside him and the youngster spurted ahead.

Williams saw the spark of the musket, then the bold flame of the main charge before the voltigeur vanished behind the gout of smoke. The second lieutenant yelped as he was flung backwards, tumbling down the slope until he struck hard against a rock. Simmons looked confused, but already his hands were feeling for the wound and came away from his thigh red with fresh blood. Rudden dropped to one knee, pulling free his sash, crimson silk striped with the white of his regiment, but now dyed a dark red as he tied it to use as a tourniquet.

'You'll be fine, sir,' he said softly to the officer, bending over him, and then a French bullet struck the side of his head and the back of his skull exploded, flinging its contents in a red smear behind him. The lifeless sergeant dropped forward, making the officer yell as he landed on his wounded leg, but then Simmons was rising gently to shift the corpse.

Williams ran up the last few yards. He could not believe he was unscathed, but there were Pringle, Dobson and the Spanish sergeant alongside him, and more men swarming up the slope with them, and MacAndrews was still at their head, urging his horse between the boulders and then cutting down with his sabre.

A Frenchman stood, swinging his musket round so that he could jab with the butt at the officer as he bounded up between two big stones. Williams dodged the blow and grabbed the man's epaulette, jerking hard forward so that the voltigeur was flung back over the crest. Dobson and Rodriguez thrust with their bayonets at almost the same instant. Another French skirmisher came at Williams, this one with a bayonet fixed, and he only just recovered his balance in time to parry the attack, and then he swept his blade back in a wild slash, carving the air at eye level and making the voltigeur jump back. Williams kept going, and behind him more men spilled through the gap between the boulders.

The skirmisher lunged again, making him dodge to the side, and the movement worked the sling of his musket loose so that it rolled off his shoulder and the heavy weight hung off his left elbow. He slashed again, spinning into the backhanded cut, and the voltigeur had put too much weight into the thrust so that Williams' sword gouged a deep furrow across the side of his face. The skirmisher screamed, dropping his musket, and left himself open as Rodriguez stabbed him in the belly. Another voltigeur appeared, wearing a brown jacket like the others, and Dobson's musket flamed just beside Williams' head, the noise hammering at his ears, as the Frenchman was flung back.

Over to their left a cannon fired, but to Williams the noise seemed less terrible than the musket let off just beside him. The canister burst soon after it left the barrel of the four-pounder, spreading a hail of musket-sized balls. Two redcoats and a greenjacket were knocked down, each struck by half a dozen bullets which made little mushrooms of blood fountain on their faces, chests and limbs. The slope was too steep for the gun to fire down at the British as they charged, and the men were hit before the cone from the canister had spread that widely.

The French were giving way. Rodriguez dropped to one knee, steadied himself and then fired, but Williams could not see whether he hit any of the retiring voltigeurs. A man in brown loomed out from behind the boulder on his right and the officer raised his sword to strike and only just managed to hold back the blow when he realised that it was one of the Portuguese light infantrymen. The man looked at him with a puzzled expression on his face, and then his high-fronted shako was knocked from his head by a bullet. He grinned, patting his head in relief, and then turned to fire down into the valley in front of them.

Men ran towards the French cannon, the green paint on its carriage faded by wind, sun and rain. The crew were already hooking the trails of the four-pounder back on to the low limber, not bothering to lift the barrel to its travelling position. One dropped, hit in the leg by the ball from an officer's pistol, and another was clubbed to the ground by a corporal from the 52nd. The other gunners scrambled on to their horses – there were no seats on a French limber – and followed the four-pounder and its team as they fled, the wheels flinging up the soft sandy soil, half slipping their way down the slope.

'Pour it into them, lads!' MacAndrews rode along the top of the hill, his horse carefully picking its way through the rocks, and urged the men to fire down at the retreating enemy. The major was still in one piece and to Williams that seemed like a miracle, and yet it was surely a miracle that they had driven the French back with their wild charge and lost so few men.

A ball pinged noisily off the rock beside him and he ducked down. Dobson looked at him and shook his head in amusement, then bit the ball from another cartridge. Williams looked for Dalmas, but could not see him among the French who had re-formed their skirmish line on the slope facing them. There was no sign of an armoured corpse either, so he guessed the Frenchman must have escaped. As he looked, he saw the body of a sergeant, sprawled in that ungainly sack-of-old-clothes fashion only ever made by the dead or the very deepest of sleeps. The man's ginger hair was dark with blood and no one would sleep in such a place, so there could be no doubt that the man was dead. There were yellow facings on his red jacket.

'Hargreaves,' Dobson said, seeing the direction in which the officer was looking. The veteran pulled back the hammer to full cock and brought his firelock up to his shoulder, searching for a target.

Williams had not realised that MacAndrews' men had formed part of the charge. Rodriguez said something to Dobson and the two men fired together, the Spaniard grunting in satisfaction. Faintly, Williams caught the sound of drums, which meant that the main columns of French infantry were catching up with their skirmishers. He doubted that the ragged bunch of men on top of the hill could resist a full attack. Then he looked behind and saw that the companies of the 52nd were already crossing the bridge, squeezing past the two tumbrels blocking the middle span.

A big man in the green of the 95th was talking to MacAndrews. The pair shook hands in satisfaction, and Williams recognised Lieutenant Colonel Beckwith and guessed that he had probably led his own charge up the hill at the same time as the major.

'The Ninety-fifth will form the rearguard!' MacAndrews shouted, walking his horse towards them. In the distance, Beckwith's voice boomed out the same instruction. 'Everyone else will come with me back across the bridge. Keep it slow, lads, there is no need to rush. We've shown these blackguards that they need to keep their distance!'

Men obeyed. They all felt the tiredness that so often followed a charge or a hard-fought combat and some swayed as they walked back down the slope. MacAndrews' horse stumbled for the first time, and he lurched forward and almost lost his balance before the animal recovered. Men slipped on the soft sandy slope more than they had during the charge.

'Hot work,' Pringle said as he walked beside Williams, and then the stones gave way under his left boot and he lost his balance, falling and rolling for three or four yards.

'Bugger,' he said, sitting up. 'Can anyone see my glasses?'

Williams, Dobson and Rodriguez stopped to look, but told the surprising number of other willing volunteers to keep going. Pringle was on all fours, but his eyesight was poor and he felt rather than looked for the spectacles. Already most of MacAndrews' men were filing on to the road. There were shots from up above them, growing in intensity, and Williams guessed that the French were beginning to press forward again. Something crunched underfoot and with terrible certainty he knew that he had found the missing glasses. One lens was cracked, and the brass arms bent, although that could be remedied. Pringle put them on, shutting the eye behind the broken lens so that he could see.

'Well,' he said, 'that's quite ruined my battle.'

The 95th began to come back down the hill. On the bridge the Royal Horse Artillery lieutenant and his men had almost finished replacing the broken wheel.

'Hold them back for a few minutes!' he called. Williams and the others helped his men keep the horse team calm as Beckwith led most of his men across. A captain stayed with his company, the forty or so riflemen using the parapets for cover and firing back up the hill now reoccupied by the enemy. Bullets pecked the stonework and one hit a private in the foot. His comrades grinned as he hopped and angrily cursed the French, but then two of them took him back.

At last the repair was complete. The drivers urged the team onwards, gently at first to test the new wheel, but when it seemed solid they whipped them and hurried across, followed by the second cart. The little group of redcoats and the company of 95th ran after them. As Williams and the others came to the far bank, he saw a wall above them lined by Portuguese soldiers with their oddly shaped shakos. There were greenjackets crouched among the ruins of a house and several formed companies from the redcoats of the light infantry. More men waited as a chain of skirmishers, using all the boulders and folds in the ground for cover.

MacAndrews waited for them, Beckwith beside him again. 'This way,' he said. 'They want us to get up to the top of the hill.'

'You have more than played your part already,' the colonel of the 95th added in his deep voice.

As they followed the road, Williams saw guns of the Chestnut Troop already deployed for action and waiting to pound the far side of the valley or sweep the bridge.

Twenty minutes later the French sent three companies of grenadiers across the bridge. Williams watched from high up on the slope and so did not see the details. He saw the smoke blossom all along the hillside beneath him, heard the cracks of rifles, the duller bangs of muskets and the deep-throated roar of six-pounders. The French fired as well, and the shape of the valley made the noise echo back and forth, but it was hard to pick out the British and Portuguese in their places of cover.

The grenadiers were in open view, with only the slight protection of the walls on either side of the bridge. They came on boldly, led by a couple of officers, one of them on horseback, and although

450

a few men fell they were still running when they got halfway across the bridge. Then the attack withered. Williams saw the column shudder as if it were a single being, suddenly hit with great force. The mounted officer was down. The one on foot ran on, but only a handful came with him and soon they were pinned down, crawling for safety among the boulders below the western side of the bridge. Behind them blue-coated bodies piled in mounds on the flagstones.

CHAPTER 31

'I want that bridge.' Marshal Ney flicked his gloves impatiently against his hip, startling his horse as he looked down into the valley. He calmed her almost as unthinkingly as he had startled her in the first place. 'Full-strength attack this time, with two battalions of the Sixty-sixth.' The colonel trotted away to prepare his columns. 'I want as many guns as possible to support.'

'Don't think we will hit much, your grace,' the battery commander said doubtfully.

'Doesn't matter. It may keep their heads down and it will perk up our lads.'

'Your grace.' The horse artilleryman rode a mule, and it took him a while to get the stubborn animal moving so that he could give the necessary orders.

Marshal Ney grinned with all the friendliness of a wolf. 'Dalmas.'

The cuirassier officer clicked his heels as he stood to attention.

'Lost another one, have you?'

'Yes, your grace. Broke its legs coming down the slope.'

'Better it than you.'

'Yes, your grace.' Dalmas had shot the beast. He had done this more than a few times before, because horses wore out, but even after all these years a part of him was always sad. The Emperor's armies used up horses at a prodigious rate, and sometimes he wondered whether one day there would be no more remounts to replace them.

'You've done well today. Nearly cut them off.' Dalmas felt there was an emphasis on the 'nearly' and guessed what was going to happen. He did not offer any explanation or excuse. Winning was what counted, and although he had won a succession of little victories earlier on, the final failure was all that would matter.

Marshal Ney pointed across the valley. 'I want to break them, Dalmas. Take their confidence now and they will not stand up to us again. Sixth Corps are the finest regiments at the Emperor's command and with lads like these you can do anything.

'You didn't get their spy.' Dalmas remembered that just a few hours ago the marshal had said he did not give a damn about spies. It did not surprise him. He would have done the same if he were a marshal of France. 'So you need a victory Dalmas.'

The cuirassier felt that he might as well play the game. 'Your grace, I ask permission to lead the attack on the bridge.'

Marshal Ney tried and failed to feign surprise. 'That is good. I need my best man to do this.' After almost two years Dalmas was still a temporary ADC, without the full pay and privileges of the permanent staff. 'Lead the Sixty-sixth. You won't need a horse for that! Take them over the bridge and drive the rosbifs off at the point of the bayonet.

'It is simple, Dalmas.' The marshal reached down to pat him on the shoulder. 'Storm the bridge and you will be a major by the end of the day, and have your own regiment within two years. Who knows?' Ney smiled again, taking his hand away and waving it in the air. 'One day a general or even a marshal!'

Dalmas brought his bloodstained sword up in salute.

'I can see I have chosen the right man. Take that bridge at any price and do it quickly.'

It took half an hour to form the regiment up on the approach road, where they were at least sheltered from the sporadic shots coming from the far bank. The companies were formed six abreast, for no more than that could fit on the bridge.

'The cross of the legion to the first men over!' General Ferey promised the men as he inspected them.

Dalmas hoped that luck was real and that he still had plenty of it. He had dispensed with his cuirass, but kept the helmet and had no choice but to wear his high cavalry boots. They were not designed for running, but there were too many corpses on the bridge to try to ride across. It did not matter. If he could keep his men going, then speed itself was not so important. An attack like this would succeed if the enemy believed that it was unstoppable. The British must crack, or this column would be mown down like grass before the scythe, just as in the first assault. They needed luck, and they needed the British to be so unnerved by being chased from one position to another and hustled over the river that they would break. Dalmas had seen it often enough in cavalry charges, had seen enemy lines slow, and then seem almost to shiver as horses began to turn. Press on then, and the enemy would flee and those who did not go fast enough would easily be chopped from their saddles.

He turned to look beside him. The grenadier companies were too badly mauled to head this fresh attack and so the men behind him were the fusiliers, who formed the bulk of any regiment. Almost all had the moustaches of veterans. They looked tough, confident men, and Dalmas suspected that if anyone could win this fight then it was these soldiers.

Jean-Baptiste Dalmas raised his sword high.

'*Vive l'empereur!*' he shouted. The men took up the cry and the drummers began to beat. Above them on the valley sides, voltigeurs fired at the far bank and a moment later the battery of horse artillery vomited smoke and noise.

Dalmas walked forward, not looking back now and trusting the infantrymen to follow. He went down the curving road, and then turned sharply. Now he could see the bridge ahead of him, its three big arches curving over the steep and rocky ravine. The road turned to the right as it joined the bridge, and there were dozens of corpses stretched out on the stones.

'*En avant!*' he called, and began to jog forward in his clumsy boots. Behind him the drummers hammered their drums and the sound of steady marching turned into a pounding of feet as the men followed him. The cuirassier ran on, jumping one corpse, but then landing on another man's hand, and the grenadier yelled out in pain even as he clutched at the wound in his stomach.

'*Vive l'empereur!*' The noise of the battalion raising the shout bounced up off the valley sides.

Then the enemy opened fire and for a moment the great roar of cannon, volleys of musketry and individual shots drowned out everything else. Pieces of canister and bullets smacked into the walls and surface of the bridge. Men fell in the column, and sometimes they tripped the men behind. Other infantrymen toppled when they slipped on the blood and entrails of those killed in the first attack.

The column kept going. With a reverberating clang, Dalmas' head was jerked back as a ball punched through the brass of his helmet's crest holder. He staggered, reached out to steady himself on the top of the wall, and was narrowly missed by a bullet which flicked the stonework. Some of the infantrymen were passing him, and that was no good, so he made himself run on again, his skin cut where the brass chin-scales had driven into it with the force of the strike. The black horsehair crest was badly torn, and flapped against the back of his helmet as he went.

A six-pound round shot skimmed over the parapet and took the heads off two of his men, smashing them to pieces like overripe pumpkins. He could hear the screams of other men being hit behind him. There was red-hot pain in his side as a bullet grazed him, breaking a rib so that his breathing became painful.

Dalmas ran on. The bridge seemed far longer than it had looked from up above, but he was nearing the end now, where it turned sharply on to the bank. A sergeant running beside him dropped face forward, one moment a vigorous, charging soldier, and the next falling with all the life of a sack of turnips.

There were no more cheers, and he could not hear the drums, but the cuirassier officer staggered on. At the end of the bridge he looked behind him and saw that his men were almost all corpses or had fallen back to the west bank. Only four were still with him, and then it was three as one soldier's head was flung back, his forehead bright with blood. Someone called to him, and he led them down off the road and into the big rocks beside it. The survivors of the first attack were there, not daring even to fire up the slopes.

Dalmas flung himself down and leaned his back against a rock, each breath painful. His right wrist

457

hurt and when he looked at his sword he could see that the blade was bent from the strike of a bullet that must have wrenched the hilt in his hand, but he could not remember it.

'Bridges,' he said softly as balls pinged off the rock behind him. He did not have good luck with bridges.

Williams and the others trudged up the hill. They passed a group of four greenjackets carrying young Simmons. The boy was obviously in great pain, and the soldiers carried him in a blanket, moving as gently as possible to spare him.

Brigadier General Craufurd and his staff rode past, going back down towards the fighting. A third French attack had been repulsed, but the two sides still fired at each other across the valley.

'Leave him!' Black Bob called to the 95th. 'Let him lie here until later. You are needed in the fight.'

One of the greenjackets was a corporal and he looked up. 'This is an officer of ours,' he said, 'and we must see him in safety before we leave him.' The group walked on, ignoring the divisional commander.

Williams expected a burst of outrage, and was surprised when the general simply nudged with his heels and went on his way down the hill with his staff. He nodded to MacAndrews, but said no more.

'I would never have believed it,' Williams said

once the senior officers were out of earshot.

Hanley had stayed behind. 'It is a strange day. Ten minutes ago I watched the general ask General Picton to march his Third Division up to support us here. He refused, and the two of them glared at each other for a few minutes, and then bade farewell as if nothing had happened.'

'Nothing he could do,' Pringle said, all but winking at them as he screwed the eye closed behind his broken lens. 'The French won't get across the river.'

Hanley pursed his lips. 'The general seems less certain.'

'The bridge is piled high with their dead,' Williams said, fighting the urge to wink back at his short-sighted friend. 'No point turning his men out and marching them here for the sake of it. The river will hold the enemy back until the level drops. Almeida is cut off, though.'

'Well, another siege for the French. That should hold them for a while.'

'I don't know what else will,' Pringle said gloomily.

The sky had grown darker and darker as they climbed up out of the valley, MacAndrews' little command united again. As they came to the top, lightning flashed its harsh white light to crack on a hilltop to the north. The rain came in heavy drops before the thunder rolled towards them. In moments it slammed into the ground, as heavy as the storm the night before, drenching them quickly. MacAndrews kept patting his horse to calm the frightened animal.

In the valley behind them, the power of nature quickly blotted out the violence of man, and the guns, muskets and rifles fell silent.

EPILOGUE

'Colonel Murray tells me that Wellington cannot bring himself to blame Craufurd,' Baynes said, his face a mask that made it unclear whether or not he agreed. 'He believes he meant well, and that the error was one of judgement, not intention.'

Hanley said nothing. Instead he looked at the people walking beside the road. They were from the villages all around, and they trudged south towards Lisbon, their heads down and great bundles of possessions on their backs.

'As it turns out it rather looks as if Marshal Ney was not supposed to have attacked either. The French high command do not appear to be the happiest of families.' The merchant looked at the long lines of refugees, all of them weary and dirty from travel.

'This is an ancient defence in this country.' Baynes smiled at a young woman carrying a bird in a cage and wearing a silk dress that was probably her finest and so the one she would save. The hem was several inches above the ankle in the local style, but was still spattered with mud. She must have removed shoes and stockings for her feet were bare and dirty. 'They are to leave nothing for the invader to use. No food, no stores, and not even firewood to burn.

'It is humbling, don't you think? They abandon their homes, and sacrifice everything to save their country.'

'But will they?' Hanley asked.

'Lord Wellington believes they will.' Once again the merchant's tone was hard to read. 'And so he invokes the old laws. Those who do not wish to go are made to leave.'

'Not so willing a sacrifice, then.' Hanley tried to ignore the plaintive looks of the people they passed. The two Englishmen were on horseback, not tramping on with what was left of their lives and homes on their backs. The corpulent Baynes scarcely looked as if he ever did without his comforts.

'A sacrifice none the less. Marshal Masséna is about to learn what it is to see a whole army starve.'

'There is food in Lisbon no doubt,' Hanley said.

'Oh aye, warehouses full to the brim.'

'Then they will not starve for long. So perhaps the sacrifice is too high a price to pay for giving the French a few lean weeks? Is that all that the people of Ciudad Rodrigo achieved?'

Baynes smiled. 'Leaving them to their fate has won us few friends in Spain.'

'Except Don Julián Sánchez.'

'Yes, and he is a friend worth having. He understands the war better than many. Perhaps one day

462

they will all understand.' Baynes winked at a little boy being carried by an old man. The child covered its face in fright, but then peeked through his fingers at the beaming merchant.

'I wish I did.'

'Time, William, time. That is what it has all been about. I told you that months ago. Ciudad Rodrigo bought us five precious weeks, perhaps more.'

'And Almeida?'

'That was unfortunate.' Early in the siege, a lucky French shell had landed and ignited a trail of loose powder left behind by a leaking cask. The gunpowder flared and led straight back into the vaults of the cathedral that served as the garrison's magazine. When that vast store exploded, a great swathe of the city was reduced to rubble in the blink of an eye. Hanley and the others had felt a tremor and shortly after heard the dull rumble of the blast even though they were almost forty miles away.

'Unfortunate!' Hundreds had died instantly, and many more been left scorched and maimed. Without powder for their guns and muskets the fortress was defenceless and had surrendered. 'Are we sure it was an accident?' he added after a moment.

Baynes chuckled with delight. 'It is always a joy talking to you, my friend. Yes, there is no hint of anything else. If Velarde was alive, then perhaps I should wonder . . . You are sure that he is dead?'

'Oh yes,' Hanley said, remembering the shell exploding on the walls of the fortress and the man's head shattering.

'Splendid, splendid. He was a dangerous fellow, and if he were still up to no good I would wonder whether he had been at work. Cox did not want to surrender, but his Portuguese officers decided for him and sent out a white flag. Hard to blame them. They had no hope, and after Ciudad Rodrigo they knew the army would not come to save them. A fair few soldiers volunteered to join Napoleon's Portuguese regiment, but many are already back with us, having deserted at the first opportunity. With commanders and soldiers alike, I believe there was more pragmatism than hatred of their ally.'

'What about Lander?' Hanley had told the merchant of Velarde's claim that the Swiss was in his pay. 'How pragmatic was he?'

'The question is now purely academic,' Baynes said, showing not the slightest trace of discomfort. 'I have no good reason to believe that he planned to disobey my instructions. Apart from that, I had no doubt that you would cope.' The merchant's smile was broad. 'You should never underestimate yourself, William.'

Hanley realised that he would get nothing more on that subject and so asked about something else. 'Have you had any luck deciphering the code? Velarde spoke of French sympathisers in Lisbon as well as Spain.'

'Nothing so far, I am afraid.' Baynes seemed genuinely disappointed. 'I know the trouble you went through to get that to us.' He chuckled again. 'Might have helped if you had not dunked it in water so often, but we have a clever fellow working on it and I am sure he will find the key eventually. In the meantime the Regency Council in Lisbon has been persuaded to give Lord Wellington their full support. They do not have a lot of choice if they are to pay all their bills and keep the army in being.'

'More sacrifice?'

'More prudent politics, and that is a murkier and less noble business all around. Much like ours.' The merchant gave another beaming smile.

'To what end?' Hanley was still unconvinced. 'The French have wasted time, although not very much at Almeida. They still have a larger army and there is nothing to stop them marching all the way to Lisbon.'

Baynes looked at him for a while. 'Maybe,' he said, 'maybe. But they will find it less easy than everyone seems to think. Do you recollect those forts we saw being built in the heights beyond Lisbon?'

Hanley nodded, but was not impressed. 'Small works compared to Ciudad Rodrigo and Almeida, and Masséna's men now hold both of those.'

'They do indeed, but those towns did not have all of Lord Wellington's army to wait behind them and attack any force breaking through. Soldiers like Murray assure me these lines of forts will be the toughest of nuts to crack and nothing like them has ever been seen before. By the time he gets there Masséna will be a long way from home, in a country stripped of resources. He may not find a siege too easy.

'Napoleon may have made a great mistake in not coming himself, and in not insisting on more urgency for the campaign. Every week that passes consumes their food supplies and makes us grow stronger. By the sound of it Wellington may risk a battle to slow them down a little more.

'And now I understand that you will be leaving us, William.' It was a statement rather than a question.

'I am ordered to go with Major MacAndrews and the others to join the regiment in Gibraltar.' Hanley had no doubt that Baynes already knew every detail.

'Call on me in Lisbon before you sail.' Baynes spoke lightly. 'I may have some little tasks for you down south. Indeed, for all of you.' Hanley felt the usual mix of fear and excitement at the prospect of playing a role in another of the merchant's schemes.

'*Adiós* for the moment, William. Your friends are at an inn in the village over yonder and I suggest you join them for the night.' It was getting dark and once again the rain was starting to fall. Hanley doubted many of the refugees would find a dry bed or a warm fire tonight.

'And you?'

'Still have a long way to go. So do we all, Hanley.' Baynes set off briskly on the road that led eventually to Lisbon. 'Come to see me, William,' he called back over his shoulder.

Hanley was not surprised that MacAndrews, Pringle, Williams and the others were at the inn as Baynes had said. The merchant always seemed to know. He decided not to mention to the others any talk of 'little tasks'. He knew that Williams did not trust the merchant and suspected that all of them were bitter for being brought here. Their mission had proved a failure, and if MacAndrews' charge at the Côa had won him a name in the army, that was unlikely to bring more tangible reward.

The mood had been gloomy before Hanley left them to meet Baynes and report at headquarters to Murray. They were all proud men and they worried that the war was lost. Williams doggedly claimed that they would win in the end, but even he did not seem to base this on anything other than blind faith. Hanley was not sure that he was yet sufficiently convinced by Baynes to sway them. Perhaps he would say something when they approached the city and saw the lines of forts.

Something had changed, for the gloom now seemed worse than when he had left. Two arrivals had probably done little to help. From nowhere Ensign Hatch had appeared, his face horribly scarred from the wound he had taken in the face at Talavera. He hated Williams, although none of the others understood quite why. With him was Major Wickham, whose well-cultivated good looks only made the ensign seem all the uglier. The major had served in staff postings for some time, but now it seemed both were to return to the 106th. Wickham showed no great enthusiasm for this, and dinner had obviously been an uncomfortable affair for everyone. Williams was sunk more deeply into gloom than Hanley had seen him since the previous year when they had feared half the regiment – and Jane MacAndrews – lost at sea.

Pringle, happy now that he had his spare glasses from his valise, tried to explain when he and Hanley shared a cigar and a glass of brandy together after the others had gone to sleep.

'Garland is dead,' he said flatly. 'The wound turned bad and he just died.'

'I am sorry.'

Pringle gave a humourless laugh. 'Might just as well have shot him last year.' He drank deeply and then refilled his glass.

'Then you would probably have hanged, and perhaps others of us as well.' Hanley stared at his friend until Pringle sensed the scrutiny and looked up from his drink. 'And it would still be Miss Williams, mother of a bastard child, and not the poor widow Mrs Garland and her son. Believe me, I know something of this and would not wish it on anyone.'

Billy Pringle sighed, and then he put down the glass firmly and reached for another cheroot. 'Better for me,' he muttered, and lifted the lighted taper to its tip.

'So is that the cause of Bills' melancholy?'

Pringle blew on the cheroot until it glowed properly. 'No. In fact for all that he says I suspect it is a small part of it. He has had other news, in a joyous letter from Miss MacAndrews telling of her good fortune. A relative has died in America.'

'An ill wind,' Hanley said tartly.

'In this case it has made her a more than moderately wealthy young lady.' He blew out a thin cloud of tobacco smoke with obvious relish.

'Is that not good news?'

'You know Bills,' Pringle explained. 'He says she is now far above him, and that he would seem a fortune hunter if he pursued her.'

'It is scarcely a new affection.'

'Indeed, indeed, but he talks of honour and how he must do the decent thing, and then walks around with a face like sour milk, spreading sunshine all around.'

'Ah, a matter of honour,' said Hanley, shaking his head.

They did not speak for a while. Pringle drank no more and they both took pleasure in the cheroots. Then suddenly Hanley raised his glass.

'Here's to Christmas at home,' he said.

Pringle was jerked from his thoughts, but then smiled at the old toast. 'I suspect "with the regiment" is more likely.'

Hanley thought for a moment. 'I am beginning to wonder if that is the same thing,' he said. 'I certainly do not have another one.'

HISTORICAL NOTE

Like its predecessors, *All in Scarlet Uniform* is a work of fiction, but the setting is based on the real events of 1809–10 and I have tried to make the background as accurate as possible. The 106th Regiment of Foot is an invention, unconnected with the real unit bearing that number which briefly existed in the 1790s. I have done my best to make the fictional characters of this fictional regiment behave in a way true to life for the era. All the major engagements in the story – the night attack at Barba del Puerco, the siege and skirmishes around Ciudad Rodrigo, the botched cavalry raid at Barquilla, and the desperate rearguard action at the Côa – occurred very much as described, many of the small details coming from eyewitness accounts.

Alongside the fictional characters are many real people, and perhaps the most remarkable of these are Marshal Ney and Brigadier General Craufurd. Ney, who had a ruddy complexion and not the red hair often claimed, was later dubbed the 'bravest of the brave' by an emperor fond of such tags. This was after the retreat from Moscow, when the marshal had held together the rearguard, carrying and using a musket just like an ordinary soldier. Later, the Emperor blamed Ney for the failure of the Waterloo campaign, in part to cover up his own mistakes. Ney's repeated – and ultimately fruitless – cavalry charges against the squares of Wellington's infantry have contributed to the image of a man braver than he was prudent, a common enough failing for the hussar he had once been.

This is not quite the whole story. In his earlier campaigns Ney showed considerable skill and subtlety, and he would do so again when his corps formed the rearguard to Masséna's army in 1811. Yet there is no doubting his hot temper, and this made the marshal unpredictable, and an extremely difficult subordinate. At one point in 1810 he tried to incite Junot to join him in rejecting Masséna's orders and effectively leading a mutiny. Fortunately for both of them, Junot had enough sense to refuse. On a smaller scale of disobedience, Ney began the bombardment of Ciudad Rodrigo two days early in spite of an explicit instruction to wait. As in the story, he turned his reconnaissance towards Almeida into a full attack on the Light Division. If he had not, then no doubt critics would accuse him of missing an opportunity, for he came close to inflicting crippling losses on the British and Portuguese regiments.

Craufurd should not have fought the battle. Wellington had sent repeated orders over the preceding week for him to withdraw the Light

Division to the western bank of the River Côa. Instead he lingered, and then seems to have procrastinated on the day itself, leaving his withdrawal until it was almost too late. The words quoted by Baynes in the Epilogue were written by Wellington and reflected his opinion. He had asked specifically for Craufurd and given him the plum command of the Light Division over the heads of more senior generals. Throughout he kept faith with his difficult subordinate and was surely vindicated by the results. Craufurd had managed the outpost line with tremendous skill – it was used as a model for training the army in such work well into the nineteenth century. For all his hot temper, 'Black Bob' was a serious soldier, well versed in theory. He was able to speak to the hussars of the KGL in their own language, was willing to spend hours in the saddle visiting and placing pickets, and created a system whereby the depths of rivers were monitored on a daily basis to know when fords were usable.

Much of the business of maintaining an army's outpost was a question of guessing the enemy's next move, and each side sought to bluff and confuse. On more than one occasion Craufurd deployed the entire division in a single line to make it seem that they were merely the front of a much larger force. The French were experienced and dangerous opponents and we should not forget the skill with which they observed the Light Division and concealed their own intentions. Yet in the end, the Allies were on the defensive, and Craufurd's men kept the enemy at a distance for months on end, maintaining communications with Ciudad Rodrigo for a long time even as the French began the siege. The French were never able to surprise and take any of the Light Division's outposts. Much of the credit must go to the skill of the 1st KGL Hussars, and the regiments of the Light Division, but the control and regulations imposed on them by Craufurd played a big part.

Respected by the ordinary soldiers, the general was not popular with his officers, who were inclined to speak of his tyranny and were rapid to blame him for the near disaster at the Côa. Probably his mistakes were a natural consequence of meeting the enemy's bluffs and feints over so many long weeks. It was a bad misjudgement, and the memory of his surrender in South America may well have gnawed at him and further sapped his judgement on the day. The quality of his regiments got him out of the fix and he was never again to place himself in so bad a situation. Craufurd's ability as a battlefield commander is debatable. That he was clearly the best available commander for leading the army's outposts, rearguard and vanguard is hard to doubt.

In 1810 the chief burden of resisting the French fell for the first time on Wellington's army. Spanish fortunes were at a very low ebb, especially after Soult overran much of the south. Their armies were the shattered remnants of too many defeats, and the greater part of the country, including almost all important cities, was under French control. It took immense optimism – and often a good deal of pride and sheer stubbornness – to keep fighting when the war seemed lost. Yet this is precisely what so many Spaniards did. Herrasti represents one side of this. Old by the time the war began, he was a career soldier who found himself in charge of an outdated fortress with an inadequate garrison and at times a turbulent population. The British were inclined to doubt his resolution, but they were proved wrong. Ciudad Rodrigo resisted stubbornly, and although the French were sometimes dismissive of the skill of the defenders, the fortress held them up for precious weeks. It required a great expenditure of ammunition and material as well as considerable suffering and loss for their soldiers working to dig the parallels and saps. Herrasti and most other Spaniards felt bitter when their efforts were not rewarded by Wellington marching to save the city. He was not strong enough to do this, and wisely did not attempt it, but that was much easier to see with hindsight.

Today 'El Charro' is probably more famous than the elderly governor. The guerrillas then and now had a glamour lacking in the regular army so often beaten in the field. On the other hand, his career highlights the fact that almost all successful partisan leaders eventually turned their bands into something almost indistinguishable from regular units.

Named a brigadier in the army, Don Julián Sánchez García led his regiment of lancers for years, more often than not operating with Wellington's army. On their own the guerrillas made life very difficult for the French, but could never drive them from a region through their efforts alone.

Josepha was also real, although I have brought her story forward by a year and introduced Pringle as an added complication. Betrothed to Don Julián Sánchez, she ran off and lived with the German commissary officer Augustus Schaumann and also Edward Cocks of the 16th Light Dragoons, who appears briefly in the story. In each case she hoped for marriage, since the prospect of wedding the guerrilla leader was clearly unattractive. Her father protested to Wellington, who ordered Schaumann to return her to her family. The German claimed that she went back with her virtue intact, but this seems unlikely. Cocks' diary makes it clear that their relationship was most certainly physical, and although he does not seem to have planned marriage, he was deeply upset when she left him. Her ultimate fate is unknown, but she did not marry El Charro. I could not resist including something of the story on the basis that truth is so often far more unlikely than fiction.

Almost as unlikely – at least to many people on all sides – was the possibility that the French would not reoccupy all of Portugal by the end of 1810. After the Talavera campaign ended in disappointment and retreat, the situation in the

Iberian peninsula looked distinctly bleak for the Allies. The position in central Europe was even worse. Austria had broken the peace with France in 1809, and after some early successes had suffered defeat at Wagram and surrendered. Britain's government had dithered over providing direct support to Austria, and finally launched the expedition to Holland and landed a large army on Walcheren Island. It was too late to help the Austrians. The army captured Flushing, but suffered appalling losses to 'Walcheren fever', which killed or crippled many men who had survived the harsh retreat to Corunna. It is possible that more than one disease was to blame, but malaria played a part and many victims would suffer repeated attacks long after they thought that they had recovered. After a while, Wellington asked that no more regiments that had served on the expedition be sent to him in Spain because the soldiers' health was so poor. This was at a time when he was desperate for reinforcements.

With Austria crushed, there was no prospect of Prussia or Russia risking another war with France, and every reason to believe that Napoleon would go to Spain and complete his victory there. His marriage alliance with Marie Louise of Austria – made possible by the divorce of Josephine – suggested that the French Emperor might well crown his dramatic rise with permanent success. Sir John Moore's opinion that Portugal could not be defended was widely held, and there was talk of abandoning the country and sending the remaining British troops to Cadiz in the hope that this could become the base for an eventual reconquest of Spain. Letters and diaries of many of Wellington's officers from late 1809 and 1810 confidently predicted the forced evacuation of the country. Similar views were expressed in Parliament, and this was a sensitive subject for a newly formed administration – the last having collapsed in the acrimony following the Walcheren fiasco.

Wellington disagreed, and although he made preparations to evacuate the army if it proved necessary, he also began work on the now famous fortified Lines of Torres Vedras protecting the Lisbon peninsula. His strategy accepted that the French would occupy much of Portugal, but that they would be unable to force the lines as long as these were supported by his army. It also required immense sacrifice from the people of Portugal, who were ordered to leave their homes and take or destroy food and anything else likely to be useful to the invaders. The French were to be presented with a land stripped bare, and compulsion was employed to enforce the strict regulations. It is well known that Marshal Masséna and his officers were surprised to be confronted by the Lines of Torres Vedras, for none of their spies had told them of the fortifications. They were far more surprised – and usually impressed or outraged or both – at the ruthlessness of Wellington's plan and the rigour with which he followed it.

It took time and a huge amount of money to construct the lines, mount artillery in the forts and garrison them with militia, and also to stockpile the food, ammunition and other supplies needed to support them. It also took more time and money to prepare an army strong enough to back up the fortifications. Roughly half of this force was Portuguese. Marshal Beresford presided over the reform of a Portuguese army so badly disrupted by the French invasion in 1807 that it was almost a question of starting from scratch. Better supplied, fed and equipped, the new regiments were trained in the British army's drills and the officer corps supplemented by British volunteers. By the end of 1810 the Portuguese had begun to prove themselves very effective soldiers.

Time was the key, as stressed by Murray and Baynes and others throughout the novel. Wellington believed that he could defend Lisbon, and that if the French failed to take the city they would ultimately be driven from Portugal itself, but he needed time to prepare. If Napoleon had returned to Spain himself – or even sent Masséna earlier and injected a greater sense of urgency into him – then it was perfectly possible that the British commander would have been denied the months he needed to prepare.

It was fortunate that the French were so complacent. They faced many difficulties in conducting the war and these help to explain some of the delay. The rapid expansion of Napoleon's empire placed its military and economic systems under great strain. Money was short, and without it, paying soldiers and buying equipment, transport and food for them was difficult. Masséna struggled to deal with these problems, and also with the divided command structure of the armies in Spain. When present, Napoleon was able to enforce his will on his subordinates. No one else ever managed to achieve this. In 1811 Masséna finally dismissed Ney from his command after many disputes.

Ciudad Rodrigo and Almeida forced the French to spend a long time gathering a siege train and supplies for the campaign. Taking Ciudad Rodrigo cost them over a month more. The explosion of the magazine at Almeida cut short the defence of that fortress in the most dramatic way, but by that time the summer was well advanced and Wellington could feel confident that he was ready. He fought a defensive battle on the ridge at Busaco on 27th September, imposing another brief check on the French advance and improving the morale of his army. Several Portuguese regiments had the opportunity to face and defeat French attacks and the newly reformed army began to come of age.

Masséna's men pushed on as far as the Lines of Torres Vedras and then stopped and half starved through the coming months. There were no major actions and such stand-offs do not lend themselves readily to the writers of fiction, and Hanley, Williams, Pringle and the others will instead find more active employment elsewhere. (However, for those wanting a fictional treatment of these months, C. S. Forester's marvellous novel *Death to the French* (1932) is both a good read and a vivid evocation of the problems the French faced.) Masséna surprised Wellington by how long he was able to keep his army so far inside Portugal, but the end result was never in doubt. The invasion failed and the French were never able to try again. Their losses were heavy, but in contrast Wellington's casualties were low and his army grew more healthy as the months passed.

This was not true of the Portuguese civilians who had fled to take shelter behind the lines. Food supplies proved inadequate for them and disease rapidly spread. Many thousands – perhaps tens of thousands – died during these months. When Baynes and Hanley speak of sacrifice at the end of the book they could scarcely have guessed how dreadful that sacrifice would be. The cost of not losing the war, and of having a base from which to begin the slow recovery, was very high, and the price paid by civilians is all too easily forgotten as it lacks the drama of battles and sieges. There was a measure of compulsion in this, just as there was a measure of compulsion in the eventual decision of the Regency Council in Lisbon to accept Wellington's plan and implement it. They were desperate, and could have no hope of defending themselves against Napoleon without the British. The majority of politicians and people alike decided that it was better to resist, and at this heavy cost they were able to preserve the freedom and independence of their country. In the short term, that meant giving up some of that independence to maintain the alliance with Britain.

The Light Division was formed in 1810 and by the end of the war had fought more actions with more success than any other formation in Wellington's army. It also produced the highest proportion of men whose accounts were later published, and this publicity, combined with its genuine achievements, brought it immense fame. The 95th were especially productive of memoirs, diaries and collections of letters, so that its officers and men provided some of the most famous accounts of the war. They were still a new corps and a new concept at the time of this story, and I wanted to show something of their war without getting too caught up in that bigger tale.

Both the British and French considered the Côa a victory. The latter surely had a better claim, for they had driven the Light Division from its position. Losses were disproportionately in favour of the French until their bold but unsuccessful attacks across the bridge. The numbers of infantry actually engaged were roughly equal, although the French did have a marked advantage in cavalry and made good use of this as far as the terrain allowed. However, the rest of Ney's 6th Corps followed behind the leading division, and so if the British had lingered the odds would steadily have swung more and more in the favour of the French.

Craufurd's men were spread over too wide a frontage and lacked proper reserves, and the simple fact was that he had nothing to gain and much to lose by fighting there in the first place. Their success convinced Ney's veterans and the wider army that they could attack and drive the British from any position, and this makes the costly charges over the bridge more reasonable. The British and Portuguese might have panicked and fled, but they did not, and probably the failure of the first assault ought to have shown this. The second attack was led by one of Ney's ADCs, although not the fictional Dalmas. The lesson of these failed attacks was not learned, perhaps because of the ease of the earlier phase of the battle. At Busaco the French would assault a strong position and be punished – one of the attacks being routed by Craufurd and his men.

The Light Division saw the whole engagement differently. They had been attacked by a much stronger enemy in a relatively weak position and although they suffered losses the bulk of them retired in order to the western bank and then dismissively repulsed three enemy assaults. Most realised that they had had come close to disaster. O'Hare's company was caught in the open by French hussars and fired at by their own side and lost three-quarters of its men. Part of the 43rd were trapped in a high-walled enclosure and escaped by breaking down the wall. Several companies of the 52nd were in danger of being cut off when the sandy hill overlooking the bridge was abandoned. Seeing the danger, three officers gathered whatever men they could and charged up to retake the hill. MacAndrews' action is based on the real heroism of Major McLeod of the 43rd, and I hope one Scot will not begrudge the licence of giving another of his countrymen credit for his actions.

MacAndrews' training mission is an invention, but there was serious talk of retraining the Spanish army after the model of the Portuguese. Richard Wellesley proposed the idea during his time as government envoy to the Spanish, as did his successor and younger brother, Sir Henry Wellesley. It was never politically possible, and although there were a few units of Spanish soldiers formed under British control they were never more than a tiny minority.

The story begins with a duel, and so perhaps I should not have left this until the end. Duelling was illegal, and specifically banned by the Army Act regulating the behaviour of officers and soldiers alike. In spite of this it continued, and most regiments would have frowned on an officer who rejected a challenge resulting from serious provocation. Many disputes were settled beforehand. Convention dictated that at least a day elapse between the challenge and the fight itself so this helped to reconcile arguments fuelled by alcohol. Fatalities were rare, wounds more common, but plenty of duels ended without injury to either party

483

and it was considered bad form to appear too keen to hurt your opponent.

On 21st September 1809 two former ministers fought a duel over an argument stemming from the ill-tempered break-up of the government. Lord Castlereagh and George Canning missed each other with their first shot. The former demanded a second opportunity and the seconds reluctantly agreed. This time he shot Canning in the thigh – 'an inch to the right and it would have killed him', according to his friend. Although it was a public scandal, no prosecution resulted. This was usually true of non-fatal encounters, and even some where death resulted. Witnesses might well choose to forget what they had seen even if things came to trial. Yet none of this was certain and there was a risk to all involved. In spite of this duelling continued, and Wellington found it necessary to ban officers from calling each other out when they were serving in his army.

Napoleon probably could have won the Peninsular War in 1810. French mistakes and Allied resistance narrowly thwarted him and he was never again to get a better chance. The war in Spain and Portugal would continue, and in time would lead to other conflicts in wider Europe. There is still much for the 106th Foot to do.

CAST OF CHARACTERS

Names underlined are fictional characters.

The 106th Regiment of Foot

<u>Captain Billy PRINGLE</u> – Born into a family with a long tradition of service in the Royal Navy, Pringle's short-sightedness and severe seasickness led his father to send him to Oxford with a view to him becoming a parson. Instead Pringle persuaded his parents to secure him a commission in the army. Plump, easy-going and overfond of both drink and women, Pringle has found active service easier to deal with than the quiet routine and temptations of garrison duty in Britain. Through the battles in Portugal, and the arduous campaign in Spain, Billy Pringle has won promotion and found himself easing into his role as a leader. Part of a detachment whose ship was driven back to Portugal after being evacuated from Corunna, Pringle served in the 3rd Battalion of Detachments at Talavera and was wounded in the last moments of the battle.

Lieutenant William HANLEY – Illegitimate son of an actress and a banker, Hanley was raised by his grandmother and spent years in Madrid as an aspiring artist. His father's death ended his allowance, and reluctantly Hanley took up a commission in the 106th purchased for him many years before. He served in Portugal in 1808, suffering a wound at Roliça. Since then his fluency in Spanish has led to periodic staff duties. Even so, he was with Pringle and the Grenadier Company throughout the retreat to Corunna. Captured by the French, he escaped and has found himself involved in intelligence work. He was wounded at Talavera.

Lieutenant Hamish WILLIAMS – Williams joined the 106th as a Gentleman Volunteer, serving in the ranks and soon proving himself to be a natural soldier. He was commissioned as ensign following the Battle of Vimeiro. During the retreat to Corunna, he became cut off from the main army. Rallying a band of stragglers, he not only led them back to the main force, but thwarted a French column attempting to outflank the British army. He was praised by Sir John Moore for his actions, and was beside the general when the latter was mortally wounded at Corunna. In 1809 he was promoted to lieutenant and commanded a company in the 3rd Battalion of Detachments and fought with distinction at Talavera. Fervently in love with Jane MacAndrews, Williams' cause seems to be continually thwarted by her unpredictability and his clumsiness.

Captain TRUSCOTT – A close friend of Pringle, Hanley and Williams, the slightly stiff-mannered Truscott was wounded at Vimeiro and suffered the loss of his left arm. A slow recovery kept him from participating in the Corunna campaign. He served in the 3rd Battalion of Detachments and by the end of the Battle of Talavera was its commander.

Major Alastair MacANDREWS – Well into his forties, MacAndrews first saw service as a young ensign in the American War of Independence. A gifted and experienced soldier, his lack of connections or wealth have hindered his career. Raised to major after decades spent as a captain, he took charge of the 106th at Roliça, and led the battalion throughout the retreat to Corunna. Given the local rank of lieutenant colonel, he has been chosen to lead the training mission sent to Spain.

Lieutenant Colonel FITZWILLIAM – The new commander of the 106th, fresh from the Guards. He has some connection with Wickham, although the two do not seem close.

Lance Sergeant DOBSON – Veteran soldier who was Williams' 'front rank man' and took the volunteer under his wing. The relationship between Dobson and the young officers remains quietly paternal. However, at Roliça he displayed a ruthless streak when he killed an ensign who was having an affair with his daughter Jenny. Repeatedly promoted and broken for drunken misbehaviour, he has reformed following the accidental death of his first wife and his remarriage to the prim Mrs Rawson. He was wounded at Talavera.

Corporal MURPHY – A capable soldier, Murphy and his wife suffered a dreadful blow when their child died during the retreat to Corunna.

Ensign HATCH – Former lover of Jenny Dobson, the frequently drunk Hatch was a close friend of Ensign Redman, the officer Dobson murdered at Roliça. Hatch falsely believes that Williams was the killer and has done everything he can to blacken Williams' reputation. Wounded in the face at Talavera, he remained in Spain when the other members of the 106th returned to England.

Brevet Major WICKHAM – Handsome, plausible and well connected, Wickham continues to rise in rank and spends as little time with the 106th as possible, preferring staff appointments. Williams and many others have come to doubt his honour, honesty and courage.

Jenny DOBSON – Elder daughter from Dobson's first marriage, Jenny has ambitions beyond following the drum and flirted with and let herself be seduced by several of the young officers. During the winter she abandoned her newborn son to the care of Williams and Miss MacAndrews and left in search of a better life. She is currently the mistress of a French officer.

Mrs DOBSON – Herself the widow of a sergeant in the Grenadier Company, the very proper Annie Rawson carried her lapdog in a basket throughout the retreat to Corunna. The marriage to Dobson has done much to reform his conduct.

Mrs Esther MacANDREWS – American wife of Major MacAndrews, Esther MacAndrews is a bold, unconventional character who has followed him to garrisons around the world. More recently, she managed to sneak out to Portugal, bringing her daughter with her, and the pair endured the horrors of the retreat to Corunna.

Miss Jane MacANDREWS – Their daughter and sole surviving child, the beautiful Jane has a complicated relationship with Williams. During the retreat to Corunna, she was cut off from the main army and rescued by him, becoming involved in the desperate fight he and a band of stragglers fought to defend a vital bridge against the French under Dalmas.

Miss Ann WILLIAMS – Eldest of Williams' three sisters, Anne is an intelligent and prudent young woman.

Miss Kitty WILLIAMS – The middle sister, Kitty is bright but impulsive, and has become entangled with Garland and Tilney during a visit to Bath.

Miss Charlotte WILLIAMS – The youngest of the three girls, Charlotte is not yet sixteen.

The British

Brigadier General Robert CRAUFURD – Born in 1764, Craufurd was a serious soldier who studied his profession and spent several years with the Austrian and Russian armies on the Continent. In spite of this, he found little opportunity to distinguish himself and his rise was slow. In 1807 he was given charge of a brigade in the disastrous expedition against Buenos Aires where, through no fault of his own, he was forced to surrender. Even so, in 1809 Wellington asked for him and gave him the plum command of the Light Brigade – later the famous Light Division – over the heads of officers who were senior to Craufurd in the army list. Although he was at first unpopular with his officers, the ordinary soldiers respected and liked their tough commander from the start.

Lieutenant Colonel Frederick Shaw KENNEDY – Kennedy was one of Craufurd's ADCs and left a journal describing the months of outpost duty on the Spanish–Portuguese frontier.

Major Frederick TILNEY, 14th Light Dragoons – Son of a general, Tilney has recently purchased a majority in the 14th, transferring from the 12th Light Dragoons. (For more on him, and even more on his family, see *Northanger Abbey*.)

Lieutenant Robert GARLAND, 14th Light Dragoons – The son of a mine owner who purchased his son a commission in a fashionable regiment of light cavalry, the young Garland idolised Major Tilney.

Lieutenant Colonel Neil TALBOT, 14th Light Dragoons – Talbot commanded the regiment and was killed in the charge near Barquilla on 11th July 1810.

Captain John BURGOYNE, Royal Engineers – Burgoyne was sent to Fort La Concepción to rebuild its defences and later tasked with their destruction.

Lieutenant Colonel Sidney BECKWITH, 1/95th – The commander of the 1st Battalion of the 95th was tall, powerful, extremely capable and popular with officers and soldiers alike. He encouraged a system of discipline relying more on appeals to pride and encouraging initiative than trusting to fear of punishment and enforcing blind obedience.

2nd Lieutenant George SIMMONS, 1/95th – An eager young officer serving in his first campaign. Simmons' letters and diaries were later published.

Private William GREEN, 1/95th – Although a young soldier, Green has already survived the hard retreat to Corunna. His account of his time with the 95th was later published.

2nd Lieutenant James MERCER, 1/95th – A capable young officer, Mercer was killed at Barba del Puerco on 19th March 1810.

Captain Peter O'HARE, 1/95th – An experienced officer who had begun his service as a surgeon's mate. His career was slow and by 1810 he had been a captain for seven years.

Private PHIPPS, 1/95th – Phipps is a bugler.

Lieutenant Mathias PRATT, 1/95th – A young officer who received a mortal wound at the Côa.

Colonel Benjamin D'URBAN – British staff officer attached to the army in Portugal.

Mr BAYNES – A merchant with long experience of the Peninsula, now serving as an adviser and agent of the government.

Colonel MURRAY – As Quartermaster-General, Murray served Wellesley in 1808, Sir John Moore in 1808–9, and returned with Wellesley in the spring of 1809. He contributed a great deal to making the headquarters of the army function, and in particular developing a far more effective system for the collection and processing of intelligence.

Lieutenant General Viscount WELLESLEY – After several highly successful campaigns in India, Wellesley returned to Britain and several years of frustrated ambition before being given command of the expedition to Portugal. He managed to win the battles of Roliça and Vimeiro before being superseded. Along with his superiors, Wellesley was then recalled to Britain following the public outrage at the Convention of Cintra, which permitted the defeated French to return home in British ships. Cleared of responsibility, Wellesley was given command in Portugal and honoured with a title for his victory at Talavera.

Major General Thomas PICTON – Born in Pembrokeshire in 1758, Picton was rough-mannered, hot-tempered and one of the abler divisional commanders to serve under Wellington.

Sergeant RUDDEN, 43rd Foot – An NCO from the 43rd Light Infantry who served in the company commanded by Williams at Talavera.

LANGER – A Swiss deserter chosen by Baynes to escort Hanley.

Lieutenant LEYNE – An eager young officer serving as part of MacAndrews' mission and subsequently sent with Pringle and Williams to Ciudad Rodrigo.

Colonel William COX – A British officer in the Portuguese service, Cox is the governor of the fortress of Almeida.

Captain REYNOLDS – An officer in the 51st Foot, Reynolds forms part of MacAndrews' mission.

Corporal ROSE – An NCO from the 51st Foot, Rose forms part of MacAndrews' mission.

Private (later Corporal) James RAYNOR – An unemployed clerk, Raynor is recruited into the 106th Foot by Williams' recruiting party.

Sergeant HARGREAVES – An NCO from the 34th Foot serving with MacAndrews' training mission.

Sergeant COOMBS – A British NCO serving with MacAndrews' training mission.

Captain the Honourable Edward Charles COCKS
– An officer in the 16th Light Dragoons, the intelligent and highly capable Cocks was often employed by Wellington to gather intelligence.

The French

KING JOSEPH Bonaparte – As Napoleon's older brother, Joseph has reluctantly been moved from the comfort of his kingdom in Naples to Spain, where he finds himself less welcome. A man of strong literary and philosophical tastes, he has done his best to win popularity. Recently he has lifted a ban imposed on bull-fighting by the chief minister of his Spanish predecessor.

Marshal Andrea MASSÉNA, Prince of Essling, Duc de Rivoli – Born at Nice in 1758 (which was then part of the Kingdom of Sardinia and not in France), Masséna was the son of a shopkeeper and served in ranks of the French army for fourteen years, but did not become an officer until the Revolution. From then on, his rise was rapid, and he was a general by 1793. He served with great distinction, particularly in a succession of campaigns fought in Italy. Napoleon dubbed him the 'spoiled favourite of victory' and was willing to trust him with independent commands. In 1809 he helped to stave off utter defeat at the Battle of Aspern-Essling. The rigours of campaigning and an unhealthy lifestyle made him appear even older than his sixty-one years, and Masséna hoped to retire to the comfort of his estates. Alongside his reputation as a soldier, he had earned another as a rapacious plunderer, and loot had supplemented official rewards to make him an extremely wealthy man. Although he was perhaps past his best by the time he came to Spain, Wellington had immense respect for Marshal Masséna's skill.

Marshal Michel NEY, Duc d'Elchingen – Born in 1769, the red-faced Ney was the son of a cooper in the Saar country on the border with the German states. He enlisted in the ranks of a hussar regiment, and was another gifted leader who was rapidly promoted after the Revolution. In four years he rose from sergeant-major to general. His courage was never in doubt – Napoleon would later dub him 'the bravest of the brave' – but his judgement was less certain. He was certainly experienced and at times showed great skill. Yet he was also readily offended, and inclined to lose his temper or sulk, and proved a difficult subordinate.

Général Andoche JUNOT – Born in 1771, Junot was a law student who volunteered to join the Revolutionary army in 1793. He caught Napoleon's eye at the siege of Toulon, and received successive promotions in the years that followed. Prone to outbursts of temper, he proved less capable when made a general and given charge of the invasion of Portugal in 1807, and was defeated by the British at Vimeiro a year later.

Chef de Bataillon Jean-Jacques PELET – Masséna's senior ADC in 1810 was a thirty-three-year-old trained geographic engineer who had served in the army since in 1800. His judgement was highly valued by the marshal, and his influence sometimes resented by other officers. He later wrote a highly detailed account of the 1810–11 campaign.

Capitaine Jean-Baptiste DALMAS – A former schoolteacher, Dalmas was conscripted into the army and took readily to the life of a soldier, serving in most of the Emperor's great campaigns and winning promotion. Since 1808 he has served as a supernumerary ADC to Marshal Ney and proved himself to be both a brave and an intelligent officer. The only blemish on his career has been his failure to seize a bridge so that the French could outflank Sir John Moore's British army as it retreated towards Corunna. On that occasion he was repulsed by a ragtag band of stragglers led by Hamish Williams.

Général de Brigade Claude-François FEREY – Aged thirty-nine when he led his men against the British outpost at Barba del Puerco, Ferey was a highly experienced and talented commander who had fought in many of the campaigns during the Revolution and under Napoleon.

Capitaine LEGRAND – Legrand is an ADC to General Ferey.

Major Emile BERTRAND – An engineer officer and the current keeper of Jenny Dobson.

The Spanish

Major Luiz VELARDE – One of Hanley's artistic circle from Madrid, he served as a staff officer with the Spanish army in 1809. At some point he seems to have switched allegiances and defected to King Joseph's regime.

José María ESPINOSA – Another of Hanley's artistic circle, who worked for Joseph Napoleon's regime while feeding information to the Allies. He was discovered and executed by the French after Talavera.

La Doña MARGARITA de Madrigal de las Altas Torres – Posing as a widow recently returned from the New World, whose late husband was the heir to one of the great houses of Old Castile, she was in fact the lady's maid. Under her new guise, she won acclaim as a heroine of the siege of Saragossa and now serves as a courier and gatherer of information for the Allies.

RAMÓN – A former hussar in La Doña Margarita's

husband's regiment in the New World, Ramón poses as her servant, but is in fact her father.

Don Julián SÁNCHEZ García /El CHARRO – One of the most famous of the guerrilla leaders, El Charro operated from Ciudad Rodrigo. A former soldier who had served in the ranks of the Spanish army, over time his band has developed into a regiment of irregular lancers.

BENITO – A member of El Charro's band, who serves as Hanley's guide.

Lieutenant General Don Andrés Pérez de HERRASTI – The elderly governor of Ciudad Rodrigo, Don Andrés managed to hold down the often turbulent population of the city, and led a spirited defence.

Colonel CAMARGA – The commander of the Avila Regiment, Camarga was in charge of the Convent of Santa Cruz outside Ciudad Rodrigo.

JOSEPHA Martín – The daughter of a wealthy local landowner, Josepha is betrothed to El Charro, and is looking for a way to avoid the match.

Captain MORILLO – A grenadier officer from the Princesa Regiment of Infantry, Morillo is sent to Fort La Concepción to cooperate with MacAndrews.

Lieutenant <u>DOLOSA</u> – An officer of the Princesa Regiment, Dolosa is capable but suffering the strain of surviving too many costly defeats.

Corporal <u>GOMEZ</u> – A Spanish NCO sent to Fort La Concepción.

Sergeant <u>RODRIGUEZ</u> – A Spanish NCO sent to Fort La Concepción who travels with the company of recruits sent to Ciudad Rodrigo under Pringle and Williams.